Tour de Force

Books by Elizabeth White

Off the Record

Fair Game

Fireworks

Prairie Christmas

Sweet Delights

Controlling Interest

The Texas Gatekeepers

1 | *Under Cover of Darkness*

2 | *Sounds of Silence*

3 | *On Wings of Deliverance*

Tour de Force

a novel

elizabeth white

ZONDERVAN

Tour de Force

This title is also available as a Zondervan ebook.
Visit www.zondervan.com/ebooks.

This title is also available in a Zondervan audio edition.
Visit www.zondervan.fm.

Requests for information should be addressed to:

Zondervan, *Grand Rapids, Michigan 49530*

Library of Congress Cataloging-in-Publication Data

White, Elizabeth, 1957-
Tour de force / Elizabeth White.
p. cm.
ISBN 978-0-310-27390-5 (pbk.)
1. Ballet—Fiction. I. Title.
PS3623.H574T68 2009
813'.6—dc22 2008046706

Published in association with the literary agency of Alive Communications, Inc., 7680 Goddard Street, Suite 200, Colorado Springs, CO 80920. www.alivecommunications.com

Interior design by Christine Orejuela-Winkelman

Printed in the United States of America

09 10 11 12 13 14 15 • 23 22 21 20 19 18 17 16 15 14 13 12 11 10 9 8 7 6 5 4 3 2 1

For Lori Elizabeth
Whose name means "house of God."

Acknowledgments

For a fairly simple love story, this project required an astonishing amount of research. I hardly know where to start. Maybe in the beauty shop. My friend, confidante, and sister in Christ, Jan Johnson, is a balletomane of the first degree because of her daughter's interest in dance. Not only did Jan brainstorm ideas with me as she cut my hair, but she introduced me to some invaluable resources—not the least of whom was her goddaughter, Kathryn Morgan, a dancer with New York City Ballet. Katie is an exquisite and gifted young woman with a heart for God. She and her mom, Sheila, spent a day with me answering lots of questions and remained available for reading manuscripts and correcting dumb mistakes. Any that remain are mine.

Another important resource was Kathy Thibodeaux, founder and artistic director of *Ballet Magnificat!* in Jackson, Mississippi. *Ballet Magnificat!* is a Christian professional dance company with ministries not just in the South, but all over the world. In the fall of 2007, Kathy graciously allowed me to spend a couple of hours observing a rehearsal in the Jackson studio. I found my mouth hanging open at the raw beauty of the dancers—not to mention the sheer amount of hard work involved in the production of a ballet. If I had not already suspected that dance is one form of worship, I came away convinced that God must be honored by the form of creative passion in his children. I would also like to thank *Ballet Magnificat!*'s operations manager, Brenda Holden, who facilitated my visit.

Thirdly, appreciation goes to Winthrop Cory, artistic director of Mobile Ballet, who allowed me to sit in on a rehearsal of *The Nutcracker.* I curled up under a barre for two hours and watched, delighted, as young dancers in leotards and tights brought flowers and snowflakes to life.

Because much of the story involves the physical demands on the bodies of professional dancers, I am greatly indebted to Donna Sularin and Amanda Pennock. Donna, my longtime friend (as far back as second grade), practices as a licensed pediatric physical therapist and gave me some general ideas for what could and couldn't work in the story. Amanda, one of my former piano students who holds a doctorate in physical therapy and practices in the Midwest, read the manuscript and gave me some great suggestions. Thanks, ladies!

Finally, as always, I'm grateful for the input of my husband, Scott, and my friend Tammy, who brainstormed and laughed at me and told me to suck it up and write. And I deeply appreciate the support of my agent, Beth Jusino, my editors, Leslie Peterson and Becky Philpott, and all the fine folks at Zondervan who believe in putting Christian fiction in the marketplace.

A Note from the Author

Dear Reader,

As I wrote *Tour de Force,* I wanted to explore the fact that Christian artists in any field—music, dance, literature, art—often face tough decisions about how and where art infuses Christian lifestyle. Debates have gone on for decades (probably centuries, for all I know). For example, C. S. Lewis and J. R. R. Tolkien, the story goes, discussed whether the world needs more "Christian writers" or "writers who are Christian." The only way I knew how to tackle the subject was to create characters who must face those questions, take a stand, and either live for God—or not.

It's my belief that flawed people are more interesting than perfect ones. They're also more real. Though Gilly and Jacob aren't "real" in the obvious sense, they do struggle to cope with universal issues. How much overt "witnessing" should a Christian performer or teacher do? What's the line of grace between acceptance ("tolerance") of the lifestyle choices of non-believing friends and sticking up for morality and truth? How should we respond when God seems to pull the rug out from under our dreams and desires? Are Christians allowed to feel disappointed?

The only clear answers, of course, are found in God's Word. I hope that this story has whetted your appetite for it. The Father loves you and longs to draw you to himself. If Gilly learned anything, it was that the source of joy in all circumstances is, as demonstrated in the sacrifice of Mary of Bethany, to pour oneself out at the feet of Jesus.

I pray, dear reader, that you'll do that today.

Warmly,
Beth

Glossary of Ballet Terms

**Taken from *Technical Manual and Dictionary of Classical Ballet,* 3rd edition by Gail Grant (New York: Dover Publications, 1982). Printed by special permission.

arabesque—a position of the body, in profile, supported on one leg, which can be straight or *demi-plié,* with the other leg extended behind and at right angles to it, and the arms held in various harmonious positions creating the longest possible line from the fingertips to the toes.

balloné—the dancer bounds up from the floor, pauses a moment in the air and descends lightly and softly, only to rebound in the air like the smooth bouncing of a ball.

barre—the horizontal wooden bar fastened to the walls of the ballet classroom or rehearsal hall which the dancer holds for support.

battement battu—beating action of the extended or bent leg

bourrée—a walking or running ballet step usually executed on the points of the toes

cambré—arched. The body is bent from the waist, backward or sideways.

corps de ballet—the dancers in a ballet who do not appear as soloists.

demi-plié—half-bend of the knees

developé—a movement in which the working leg is drawn up to the knee of the supporting leg and slowly extended to an open position *en l'air* and held there with perfect control.

en pointe—with toes pointed

fouettés—a whipping movement; the movement may be a short whipped movement of the raised foot as it passes rapidly in front of or behind the supporting foot or the sharp whipping around of the body from one direction to another.

glissade—a traveling step executed by gliding the working foot from the fifth position in the required direction, the other foot closing to it.

jeté—a jump from one foot to the other in which the working leg is brushed into the air and appears to have been thrown.

pas de deux—dance for two

passé—auxiliary movement in which the foot of the working leg passes the knee of the supporting leg from one position to another.

pencheé—leaning, inclining

pirouette—whirl or spin; a complete turn of the body on one foot, on point or *demi-pointe.*

port de bras—a movement or series of movements made by passing the arm or arms through various positions; the passage of the arms from one position to another.

promenade—a walk

rond de jambe par terre—one leg is made to describe a series of circular movements on the ground. Both legs must be kept perfectly straight and all movement must come from the hip, along with the arching and relaxing of the instep. The toe of the working foot does not rise off the ground and does not pass beyond the fourth position, front or back.

tour de force—an arresting, vital step; a feat of technical skill such as a series of brilliant *pirouettes* or a combination of outstanding jumps and beats.

Gilly Kincade stood *en pointe* to see over the dancers hovering around Meredith Bernard, crumpled in a heap of white tulle in the backstage shadows. Gilly caught a glimpse of stage manager Paul Arther, kneeling with the principal dancer's purpling ankle in his hands.

"Shut up, Meredith, you're not going back on stage." Paul looked over his shoulder. "Gilly, change your costume. I'll hold the curtain five minutes, but you've got to hurry."

Meredith moaned. "No! My ankle's fine. Look!" She struggled to her feet, whimpering as her left heel came in contact with the floor. Her narrow, strong-boned face was ashen, and she blinked away tears.

Gilly wanted to cry with her. Forced off the stage in the middle of a ballet — and in Saratoga Springs … "Paul, are you sure?"

Paul's eyes frosted. "If you don't want the role, I'll put Victoria in."

"No, I—Of course I want it." She'd understudied Odette's variations and knew them cold.

Please, God, help me not to faint.

"Good." Paul slid a pair of scissors under the satin ribbons wrapped around Meredith's ankle and snipped through them, grounding the swan maiden for the foreseeable future. "You'll need to put ice on that ankle, Mer. We'll have somebody drive you to the ER to get it X-rayed."

Meredith began to sob that it was Dmitri's fault that she came down wrong, and he should be fired. Or shot.

Gilly couldn't look at her. Didn't have time anyway. Somebody would have to take her own place in the *corps de ballet*—probably an apprentice waiting in the wings. But that wasn't her problem. She tore into the dressing room. "Frankie! I need the other Odette costume!"

Frankie Silverman looked up from tacking Jarrica Black's leotard onto her tights. "*Now?*"

"Yes! Curtain goes up in five minutes!"

"Gadzooks!" The costume manager leapt to her feet, leaving needle and thread dangling against the back of Jarrica's thigh. "Stay put," she ordered the young *corps* dancer.

Jarrica put her hands on her hips but obeyed.

Gilly stripped off her corps costume and let Frankie help her with the Odette tutu and headpiece, then charged out of the dressing room to stumble through dark backstage territory. With fifteen seconds to spare she made it to her mark. The curtain opened ...

She became Odette, transformed by the evil von Rothbart into a swan, doomed to eternally float on Swan Lake. She lost herself in the movement, the longing for humanity, the longing for her prince's love ... All dance was either elation or longing, rarely anything in between. She knew there had to be some spiritual implication, but for now she was simply a storyteller. Beautiful that she and Tchaikovsky, long dead, could communicate the love story of a doomed princess.

She danced Act Two in a blur, high on the pure adrenaline of the spotlight. Beyond it breathed the audience, a black wall of energy. The corps surrounded her, white tutus forming beautiful lines of motion like lily pads floating on the lake of the stage.

Dmitri Lanskov danced toward her, smiling. "Up you go," he murmured.

She leapt as Dmitri lifted her high, throwing both arms above her head, exploding with joy. He spun with her over his shoulder, carried her across the stage, carefully set her on her toes. She *bourréed,* floating away from Dmitri, drifting into a series of ecstatic arabesques. Then she bourréed toward him again. With her arm lightly curled around his head, they melted into a simple, elegant bow.

The audience came to its feet, roaring applause. Gilly could hardly breathe. She felt God's smile.

Jacob Ferrar rose with the audience under the soaring canopy of the Saratoga Performing Arts Center amphitheater, smashing his hands together until they hurt. He had just been privileged to watch a star burst into place. If he'd had a flower, he would have thrown it onto the stage, but who expected to be confronted with genius in a substitute corps dancer? It was like finding an orchid in a field of clover.

Suddenly he was glad he'd made the long, frustrating trip to attend Ballet New York's final performance in their summer home. He almost forgot to worry about Graham, left with his indulgent grandparents. He almost forgot the effects of insomnia that had dogged him for the last two months. He almost forgot the last time he'd danced on this blazing stage.

After all, Saratoga Springs on a mild summer night was a magical place, even from the audience. Above the canopy of the stage the open sky shimmered with moonlight and far-flung stars, and from his orchestra-level seat he was close enough to see the red-haired dancer's face flushed with triumph, the false lashes and heavy makeup turning her into a porcelain doll. He could almost feel the throb of her pulse with the deep rise and fall of her bosom. He could see the sweat dripping off her dainty, pointed chin.

That made him smile. He glanced at Wendy Kersey, his company's ballet mistress, who had traveled with him from Birmingham to choose guest dancers for their *Nutcracker.* Even as she enthusiastically applauded, Wendy was watching Jacob rather than the pair onstage folded into a graceful double bow.

"What?" He returned his attention to the dancers.

"You've changed your mind, haven't you?" There was humor in Wendy's voice.

He didn't answer for a moment, continued to applaud and cheer until the curtain closed for a final time. Finally he looked at Wendy. "Maybe. What do you think?"

"I think this is your company and you should do what you want."

Jacob laughed. "You've been ballet mistress for three years and never held back your opinion. Why start now?"

Wendy gathered her black lace shawl around her bony shoulders and edged into the aisle. "Because you came here intending to offer a contract to Meredith Bernard, and now you're considering this ingénue who hasn't even made soloist yet."

Jacob picked up his program and followed Wendy toward the theater exit. She was perhaps fifteen years his senior—though her age was a closely guarded state secret and no one knew for sure—but she liked to play a game of deferring to him.

Amused, he caught up to her. "Clearly you don't think that's a good idea."

Wendy stopped in the grassy park outside the covered seating. Subdued laughter and conversation floated around them as the departing audience eddied past. She sighed. "Jacob, your instincts are as good as any director I've worked with to date. Perhaps better. If you think this girl is ready to handle the Sugar Plum role, then by all means, bring her down. But do take note that she has yet to dance it in New York."

"That's true." Jacob shrugged. "Which I don't understand. Poiroux is generally quick to move young dancers into responsible roles almost before they're ready." He shook his head. "But you saw her. Thirty-two *fouettés* perfectly nailed! I couldn't take my eyes off—And she's from Alabama. If we play that up, she'll be a real draw."

"It would be a gamble." Wendy made a wry face. "But at least she'll cost less than the Bernard girl." She lifted her shoulders. "Go for it, then."

"There are reviewers here. The dance bloggers will be talking about her tomorrow."

"Yes, which will drive up the price. Do you have a favor you could call in?"

"Not exactly. But I do know Maurice Poiroux." Jacob could swallow his pride for this. He folded his arms. "I'll talk to him at the cast party tonight."

Wendy studied him. "It's been five years, Jacob."

"But he won't have forgotten." He looked away. "I wouldn't have forgotten."

Her propriety was such that she rarely touched him unless they were demonstrating a dance, but she gently laid her fingers on his wrist. "It's time to forgive yourself, my friend."

"I know. Yes, I know." He smiled, though some of the joy had gone out of the evening, and pulled her hand through the crook of his elbow. They began to thread their way through the crowd. "Let's see if we can find the car in this madhouse. What do you think about Lanskov as her partner?"

Gilly dropped her dance bag on the floor inside the bedroom she had called home for the last three weeks and walked over to the antique dresser. For forty-two weeks out of the year, it and all the rest of the furnishings in this Victorian behemoth belonged to some rich upstate New Yorker involved with the horseracing industry, but she and four other dancers had been renting it during the month of July for the ballet season.

She flattened her hands on top of the white crocheted runner and leaned in to stare at her face in the mirror. Before leaving the theater she'd removed the mask of heavy makeup. Now, clearly visible were the sprinkle of freckles she'd covered up since she was twelve years old, the tiny diamond stud in her nose that nobody could talk her out of, the quirky red eyebrows that bent slightly upward at the tips.

But she was different now.

"Soloist," she whispered. "You. Gillian Frances Kincade. Soloist for Ballet New York."

She grinned and ran to grab her phone. Flinging herself backward on the bed, she pressed the first speed-dial number. It was hard to choose which of her sisters to call first, but Laurel was eldest and the more forceful of the two personalities. It was midnight here, but only eleven o'clock in Montgomery, Alabama. The McGaughans were night owls. They'd have put the girls to bed and stayed up to watch a late-night talk show or a movie.

Laurel answered on the first ring, her drawl distinct and sleepy. "Gilly! Honey, are you all right?"

Gilly laughed. "I'm very all right."

"Oh, good." There was a relieved sigh. "So how did the ballet go tonight? It was the last one, right?"

"Yes." Gilly paused. "Laurel, are you sitting down?"

"I'm ... well, Cole and I were—"

Gilly laughed. "No details, please. I just had to tell you—drum roll—" She took a giddy breath. "Maurice moved me up to soloist tonight. He announced it during the cast party."

Alabama Supreme Court Chief Justice Laurel McGaughan actually squealed. "Oh, Gilly, that's wonderful! Cole—Gilly made soloist."

Gilly could hear her brother-in-law lean in to share the phone. "Congratulations, squirt. You deserve it."

"Thanks." She could feel her smile taking over her face again. "This is almost as cool as the day they invited me to join the company."

"I can imagine." Laurel had the phone back. "So give me the details. How did it happen? What did everybody say?"

"Um, well, everybody was excited for me except Meredith Bernard. She's kind of in the hospital with her ankle in pins—which is why I got a shot at Odette tonight."

"Wow. Poor girl." Laurel understood the critical nature of a dancer's body. She'd seen Gilly alternately pamper, discipline, and abuse hers for the last sixteen years. "But good for you. You must've brought down the house."

"It was great—Oh, Laurel, I've always wanted to dance Odette in *Swan Lake.* Almost as much as Sugar Plum Fairy in *Nutcracker.*"

"Well, maybe that'll be next."

"Maybe. Maurice is kind of … unpredictable about casting."

"That's what I hear. Now that you're a soloist, will he have any objection to you dancing in our arts festival in October? The entertainment committee is so excited about you coming."

"No, there won't be a problem. We did a formal contract, after all. I talked to Tucker and he's all set to do the music. I got my plane ticket rerouted yesterday. The rest of the company will leave Athens and go straight back to New York. I'm flying into Birmingham instead of Montgomery, though. Can you or Cole come pick me up?"

"Of course." Laurel laughed softly. "Mom's a little miffed that you're planning to stay here during your break and not go on to Mobile, but she'll get over it. She and Daddy and Mary Layne's bunch are all coming up for the festival."

"Yay! My whole million-member family all in one place! I can't wait." Gilly stood up to unzip the dress she'd worn to the cast party and shrugged it off. It fell to the floor, and she kicked it aside. "Well, I need a shower before I hit the sack. Don't tell Mary Layne until I can call her tomorrow, okay?"

"All right, baby, have a good rest. I bet you're worn out."

"Pretty much." Gilly padded barefoot to the tiny bathroom off the bedroom. Her energy, fueled by adrenaline, seemed to seep away with each step. "Tell Cole good night for me."

"Okay. Good night, little sister. I'm proud of you."

"'Night, Lolly."

Gilly laid the phone on the counter and rooted in the cabinet for toothbrush and toothpaste, face cleanser, and moisturizer. Tomorrow she'd have to pack it all up and take the train back to the City with the rest of the company. Her little Tribeca apartment had stood empty for three weeks, and it would take a bit of effort to put her things back in order.

By the time she got that done, it would be time to pack again for the company's Mediterranean tour. Maybe she should make a list before she went to bed.

As she squirted Ultra-Brite on her purple Elmo toothbrush, she caught a glimpse of her feet. Several blisters had popped and looked kind of red and weepy. She grimaced. Feet took precedence over lists, and she wasn't going to be awake much longer.

Being the baby of the family, she wasn't a natural organizer, but she'd had to learn to do more for herself since her mother moved back to Mobile three years ago and left her on her own. Amazing the sacrifices her parents had made to give her this chance at chasing a dream.

And now, finally, it was paying off. Soloist.

Scrubbing her back teeth, mouth full of foam, she yawned. She spit and laughed at herself in the mirror. Even swan princesses had to sleep sometime.

Early October

The tall blonde at the end of the *barre* was giving Gilly the evil eye: *Who's the new girl? Why is she in my spot?*

Trying to ignore her, Gilly assumed fifth position as she absorbed curious stares from behind her back as well. The anonymity of the back row would have been nice, but protocol dictated that principals work at the front barre.

Deliberately she straightened her back. The twelve-hour flight from Athens had been a killer, and her eyes stung as if they floated with ground glass. But if she was going to perform tomorrow without falling on her butt, she needed the exercise.

"Ladies and gentlemen!" The ballet mistress, a striking dark-haired woman of about forty, lifted a hand to bring the dancers to attention. "Let's begin." She nodded at the pianist, who struck the opening chord. Thirty dancers dipped into *demi-plié.*

The familiar, soothing movements took over Gilly's body. Bend, stretch, pose. *Rond de jambe par terre.* Fatigue became concentration, discipline. Joy.

As the music continued its stately progression, she watched the ballet mistress. Wendy Kersey had clearly been around the block a few times. Earlier when Gilly introduced herself and asked to take class, the ballet mistress had raked piercing brown eyes from the crown of Gilly's head down to her duck feet, then responded with little more than a brief nod. Nothing warm about this lady, but at least she knew what she was doing.

Then Gilly caught Barbie's pointed gaze.

"Wendy usually introduces guests," the girl hissed. "I'm Alexandra Manchester-Cooper."

"I'm Gillian Kincade," Gilly whispered, trying not to attract the ballet mistress's attention. "Nice to meet you."

There was no reciprocal pleasantry. Alexandra lifted a skeptical eyebrow. "You look awfully young to be a professional."

Gilly didn't appreciate the familiar remark coming from a total stranger. "I'm twenty-one," she said into a sudden break in the music.

There was a titter of laughter from the corps. At a reproving look from the ballet mistress, Alexandra sniffed and went back to work.

After about thirty minutes, barre exercises completed, the class broke to remove the portable barres. Talking and giggling, the dancers spread out for center exercises.

In the mirror Gilly caught the sparkling blue eyes of a girl to her left.

"You're Gillian Kincade, aren't you? I'm Rebecca. I'm dancing Dew Drop."

A hefty role. "Congratulations, but just call me Gilly."

"Okay." Rebecca gave her a glowing smile. "I heard you're going to be Sugar Plum. Are you rehearsing with us today?"

Gilly shook her head. "I'm just passing through on my way to Montgomery."

Rebecca's freckled nose scrunched. "Montgomery?"

"I have a break before I go back to the City. I'm spending a few days with my sister. The closest flight available was a really early one into Birmingham, here." She smiled. "I hate hanging out in airports, so I decided to use the time taking class with you folks."

"You must be the most disciplined dancer in history." Rebecca shook her head but had the rare good manners not to ask more personal questions. "I've read your reviews, and everybody in the City loves you."

Gilly laughed. "Not everybody. A few people would like to push me off the stage."

Rebecca grinned with understanding. "Well, the critics love you anyway." She pirouetted. "I'd love to dance professionally, but my body type's not quite right."

Gilly noted the young dancer's slightly wide hips but said tactfully, "Your facility's lovely. Are you a college student?"

"Yes, I'm majoring in dance ed at the University of Memphis." A sidelong look accompanied Rebecca's next *balloné*. "Have you met Mr. Ferrar?"

"Not yet." The artistic director had negotiated her contract with her manager over the phone. She knew little about him.

Rebecca made a swooning little movement. "Then you're in for—Ooh, here he comes."

A ripple went through the room. The dancers continued their exercises, but posture straightened, smiles and rolling eyes disappeared, concentration focused. Gilly followed Rebecca's gaze in the mirror. As she listened to the ballet mistress's prompts with half an ear, she assessed the man standing in the doorway to the studio. He was young, less than thirty, though self-possession infused his proud stance. He observed the corps with his arms folded, a faint smile hidden in his eyes.

Immune to perfect bodies, Gilly skimmed the height and physique—six-foot-two or so, around one-ninety—the usual fare. But the bony face was that of a black-eyed dark angel who could dance

Prince Ivan or star in a movie or model underwear and make a chunk of change. In the ballet world, men who looked like that were generally gay, promiscuous, or married.

Curiosity evaporating, she went back to work.

An hour later at the end of class, she was gasping for air, bent over with hands on her knees, her entire leotard soaked with sweat. Usually the jumps and turns energized her like a jolt from a car battery, but lack of sleep and the grinding trip overseas had sapped the last of her strength. And she had a cramp in the arch of her left foot from a faulty landing on the last *jeté.* Scary. So scary she didn't want to think about it. Rest was definitely in order before trying any more jumps.

Pushing herself upright, she walked to her duffel in the corner. She pulled out a towel and mopped her neck, listening to the other girls chatter as they rubbed knotted calves and aching feet.

Rebecca, who seemed to have adopted her, wandered over to offer Gilly a bottle of water. "Can you stay and watch rehearsal? It's really rough, of course, but Miss Wendy's whipping us into shape."

Gilly gratefully accepted the water, though she wanted to lie down on the polished wood floor and sleep until Laurel came to pick her up. She'd seen the "Waltz of the Flowers" a bazillion times. But Rebecca's self-conscious smile reminded her that once upon a time she'd been in awe of professional dancers too.

"Sure. I'll just park over here on this bench." She turned around and found her nose planted in a broad chest. "Oops, sorry." She looked straight up at Jacob Ferrar. "Short girl coming through."

Behind her Rebecca gasped. Apparently one did not tease the director.

But a slight smile warmed the straight lines of his face. "Miss Kincade. Welcome to Birmingham." His deep, cultured British drawl brought to mind Sherwood Forest, which she'd visited on last year's tour of England. She'd thought he was American.

Flustered, Gilly stepped back. Up close, his physical presence was powerful, contained. His clothing was simple—a long-sleeved white

T-shirt and black jeans, Sperrys without socks. Most male dancers favored full, romantic hairstyles, but his dark hair was cut close to his head, revealing tidy ears and a long, strong neck.

He really was beautiful. If he was straight, he was too good to be true.

She swallowed. "You know who I am?"

"Everybody in the Alabama dance world knows you." There was not a bit of flattery in his expression.

His droll, matter-of-fact tone made Gilly laugh. "That would be my mother's fault. The ballet mom from you-know-where."

Jacob's eyes lit. "I'm quite familiar with the breed." He hesitated. "I saw a note in the paper that you're dancing in Montgomery tomorrow. At the arts festival?"

"Yes, my sister's church is sponsoring me."

"Really?" He stared at her for a moment.

Not sure what was going on behind that dark, intent gaze, Gilly waited, aware of noises around her: toe boxes hitting the floor, dancers jabbering about school and boyfriends, someone singing the chorus of a pop song. Generally she was gregarious, wide open to new personalities, thrilled with variety. But there was something clicking in here, setting her adrift.

Finally she decided that was all he was going to say. He was interested in her answer.

"Yes, I'm looking forward to it. It'll be different from the classical stage. I choreographed it myself, to music written by a friend of mine."

His expression opened a bit. "I'd thought of driving down with my little boy. He loves that sort of thing."

Scrambling to hang onto this new jag in the conversation, Gilly blurted, "Is there a wife to go with the little boy?" *Oh, whoa, Gilly, that was way too personal—*

"No, Graham is actually my nephew." He opened his hands. "My sister died ..."

Ingrained southern etiquette saved her. "I'm so sorry to hear that.

Well, if you decide to come, I'll be under the train shed at eleven. You can meet my family." Now she had to wring her hands to keep from clapping them over her mouth. Why would this man want to meet her family—particularly the "ballet mom"?

But he smiled. "That would be terrific. I'll see you then." He looked around, taking in the goggle-eyed stare of Rebecca and a couple of other young dancers. A faint blush climbed his sharp cheekbones as he looked at Gilly. "Well, I just wanted to say hullo before starting rehearsal. We'll expect you and Dmitri—second weekend of December, right?"

"I think so," Gilly said rather at random. Jacob Ferrar with a genuine smile on his face was a sight to behold. "We just got back from Athens, and I'm not real sure which continent I'm on at the moment."

Jacob laughed. "All right, then. I'll see you tomorrow morning." Reverting to director mode, he gestured for Rebecca to take her place in line as he moved toward the front of the studio. "Off we go, ladies," he called, snapping his fingers. "We've quite a bit of ground to cover today."

So much for impressing the artistic director with grace and cosmopolitan conversation. Hooking the towel around her neck, Gilly dropped onto the bench and sipped her water, then propped her elbow on one knee and watched the rehearsal, chin in hand. The familiar music, burned into a special track in her brain, became background to Jacob Ferrar's voice. Gilly found herself leaning forward, comparing him to Maurice. The New York ballet master's perfectionism tended toward loud outbursts in passionate French. Jacob ran his rehearsal with an economy of speech just short of abruptness, but his dancers seemed to be used to it. He expected perfection and, by golly, he got it most of the time.

Real curiosity awoke. This regional company had a solid reputation for artistry and had trained several professionals Gilly knew of. Dancers could be a peculiar and varied breed for sure, but Jacob

Ferrar seemed a little ... off from the usual mold. He belonged, but he didn't.

Gilly started when her cell phone buzzed inside the duffel beside her on the bench. Unzipping the bag, she pawed through her clothes, found the phone, and flipped it open. She hurried into the hallway outside the studio. "Laurel! Where are you?"

"In the parking lot." Her sister sighed. "I've driven around this place three times and can't decide which door is the front. I think I'm looking at a delivery entrance."

"Okay. Let me get my stuff together and I'll find you." Hurrying to the locker room where she'd left her luggage, Gilly put aside useless speculation about a man she probably wouldn't see again except on a professional level. She couldn't imagine him traveling two hours to watch her dance in an outdoor community festival sponsored by a church.

Time to focus on reconnecting with her family and getting some rest before heading back to her real life in New York.

Jacob parked on the street at Rick and Cynthia Hawkins' one-story brick ranch-style home at a little after six o'clock to find his nephew wet from the neck down, covered in dog hair, and smelling like burnt marshmallows.

"Uncle Jacob!" Graham flung his arms around Jacob's waist and grinned up at him. "Sunflower had her puppies last night—can I have one?"

Reid Hawkins poked his carroty head out of the vinyl tent set up on the front lawn. "Yeah, can he have one? Then I would get to see it all the time! Mom says—"

"Mom said not to pester Jacob right when he got here." Cynthia Hawkins came down the driveway, pulling the trash can behind her. "Hi, Jacob. Want to come in for a glass of tea?"

Trying to ignore the mud seeping into his white shirt, Jacob studied Cynthia's red-rimmed blue eyes. Her makeup, usually immaculate, looked like she'd put it on in the dark. "Thanks, but I want to get to Alabaster before dark."

Cynthia shoved the trash container in place at the street. "You're spending the weekend with your grandparents?"

"Just tonight." Releasing Graham, Jacob leaned against his car. "I'm thinking about going down to the Riverfront Arts Festival in Montgomery tomorrow. Alabaster's about halfway between here and there."

"That sounds like fun."

It did sound like fun, and Graham would have a blast. But it never would have occurred to Jacob to ask Wendy to run Saturday rehearsals so he could take the day off—not until a certain red-haired ballerina invited him. Because Cynthia looked so surprised, he hurriedly changed the subject. "What time did the puppies arrive?"

"Three a.m. Five-thirty. Ten after six." She sighed. "I thought they were never going to stop coming. Poor Sunflower was exhausted when it was all over."

"You, too, looks like." She gave him a mock frown, and he lifted his hands, laughing. "I mean ... Never mind."

Reid sidled past his mother. "There's nine puppies, Mr. Jacob. Four boys and five girls. You want to see 'em?"

"Guys, Graham and I can't have a dog that big in an apartment." Jacob brushed his hand across the top of Graham's head. Fine, straight brown hair had grown down into his eyes. Time for a haircut.

"But they're just *this* big." Graham held his hands a couple of inches apart.

Cynthia shook her head. "Sunflower's huge, boys. Her puppies will get as big as she is."

"Come on, Uncle Jacob, you gotta at least come look at 'em." Graham pulled at his hand.

Jacob found himself unable to withstand Graham's large hopeful brown eyes. "Okay, but no more than a minute or two. Your Nonna's making supper for us."

Graham bounced. "Is she making dumplings?"

"I don't know, buddy."

Listening to Graham's excited chatter, Jacob followed Cynthia and the boys into the garage, where snuffling, mewling, and scratching sounds emanated from a plastic kennel on the other side of the family minivan.

"See? They're itty-bitty." Graham dropped to his knees to peer into the wire door of the kennel. A low growl greeted him.

"Be careful, don't scare Sunflower!" Cynthia knelt and put her hands on Graham's shoulders. "She wouldn't normally hurt you, but she has to take care of her babies."

Graham looked up from under those long, silky bangs. "My mommy used to take care of me when I was a baby."

Jacob's throat tightened. It still jolted him when Graham mentioned Lily so casually and innocently.

"Jacob takes good care of you now." Cynthia hugged Graham. "You're very blessed."

"But he won't let me have a puppy."

Jacob had a wild urge to take home a golden Labrador, even if it would eventually weigh close to a hundred pounds. But the counselor's cautionary words rang in his head. *Don't let him manipulate you with the orphan card. When you have to say no, stick to your guns.*

"You can play with Laverne and Shirley when you get to Nonna's house." He crouched beside Graham. Sunflower, lying on her side with nine ratlike little bodies attached to her teats, gave him a grumpy stare and closed her eyes again. His heart clenched. He was rather keen on dogs himself.

"I don't want to play with no sissy cats." Graham let out a hefty sigh. "Oh well, at least I get dumplings for supper."

"Now, she didn't exactly promise—"

"And we can have marshmallows for dessert!" In one of his mercurial changes of temperament, Graham grinned at Reid. "Come on, let's show him our tent!" He jumped to his feet, nearly colliding with Cynthia's chin. "'Scuse me, Miss Cynthia," he said politely, then dashed, whooping, out of the garage with Reid.

Cynthia shook her head as Jacob helped her to her feet. "I don't know how you keep up with him by yourself."

"I couldn't do it without you and Rick and Nonna and Poppa." Jacob touched the smear of mud on his shirt. "I don't suppose you've an old towel I could borrow to cover the passenger seat of the car."

"Sure." Cynthia headed for the kitchen door. "I'm sorry he's such a mess. I let them water my flowers to keep them out of my hair for a while."

Jacob laughed. "Never worry. One reason I like for him to come over here is so he can get in on normal little-kid stuff like this. Cynthia ..."

She paused with her hand on the doorknob.

"I really do appreciate you more than I can say. I know Graham isn't so easy to deal with at the moment."

Her round face softened, becoming beautiful in spite of lines of tiredness and the wonky makeup. "You know Rick and I love you both, Jacob. I didn't know Lily, but she must have been a wise lady, giving Graham to you. Hang in there. You'll be fine."

She disappeared into the house, leaving Jacob to follow the boys back to the front yard.

The Hawkins family lived in a subdivision one street over from his apartment complex. Before Lily died, he'd met them at a meeting for new church members. Having little in common at the time, they'd more or less gone their separate ways. But then he'd showed up at a children's choir party with Graham in tow, looking, in Cynthia's words, "like you'd just moved into the monkey house at the zoo." He knew he must be the most inept parent on the planet, but he had to believe God's grace could cover all his stupid mistakes.

"Uncle Jacob, come on!" The two boys' heads stuck out of the tent opening, one above the other, like a couple of cartoon characters.

Amused, Jacob crawled into the tent. The overpowering stench of mown grass, wet boy, and caramelized sugar stung his nose as he settled cross-legged on the ground. "I missed lunch today. Where's my treat?"

"Here ya go." Graham grabbed a paper lunch sack and took out a couple of Ziploc bags filled with squashed, blackened marshmallow puffs. "I wrote your name so you'd know which one is yours. This other one is for Nonna."

Jacob took the bag. That explained the black tattoo on Graham's neck. The boys had apparently experimented with the permanent markers before Cynthia caught them. "Thanks, Gray. Thoughtful for you to save me some."

"Well ... we ate the ones that didn't get burnt," Reid confessed, indoctrinated in devastating truthfulness. "But Daddy said you wouldn't mind."

Jacob opened the bag, prayed for protection from germs and charcoal, and stuck a marshmallow in his mouth. "Where is your dad?"

"He's inside watching Mississippi State stomp all over Auburn."

"Nuh-uh! War Eagle!"

Graham clearly hadn't a clue what that meant, but the Hawkins clan was a family of divided loyalties, and Graham always copied exactly what Cynthia said.

Cynthia's voice interrupted the incipient squabble. "Boys, where are you? Jacob, here's a towel for the car seat."

Jacob backed out of the tent. "Come on, Gray, it's after six o'clock. We have to go. You'll see Reid on Sunday."

"Okay," Graham sighed. He wadded up the paper sack, reducing its contents to an inedible mass. "Can I come back to see the puppies?"

"We'll see." Jacob had learned the hard way that the judicious use of those two words kept him from making promises he couldn't keep. As he knew only too well, there were no guarantees in this life.

Three

Saturday morning as Jacob allowed Graham to tow him through a crowd of mums and dads and kids and senior citizens hunting Christmas presents, he was thinking a leash might not have been such a bad idea. The problem was his head was a bit muggy from lack of sleep.

For one thing, he'd stayed up until the wee hours studying for an anatomy test coming up Monday evening. Then Poppa's rooster had awakened him at the unconscionable hour of four a.m., and he'd just got back to sleep when Graham pounced on his chest demanding to know when they were going to see the fire truck. Groaning, Jacob had levered himself out of his grandmother's feather bed, dressed in jeans and a long-sleeved rugby, then staggered downstairs for oatmeal and bacon. He managed to defer Graham's enthusiasm until eight or so, when he'd piled the two of them in the Jaguar and headed south on I-65 for the state capitol.

All morning he'd kept an eye out for Gillian Kincade, but the crowds were massive, and Graham kept him busy darting from one kid-friendly activity to the next: giant giraffes made out of PVC pipe and recycled inner tubes, palettes of sidewalk that suddenly erupted with sprays of water, the ever-popular fire truck manned by jolly firemen in full turnout. He'd not seen hide nor hair of the little dancer.

Which was probably just as well, since he wasn't quite sure what he'd say to her. About a hundred years ago he'd been quite the ladies' man. Lately, however, he'd found himself making friends at church with married couples like the Hawkinses—people with young children who wouldn't mind swapping play dates, allowing him to get his school work done and take care of Company business. He simply didn't have time to deal with the complications of dating. Much easier to focus whatever energies he had available on his nephew, his ballet company, and his education.

So he let Graham tug him toward a face-painting booth and contented himself with the anticipation of watching Gillian dance again.

And then he saw her, squatting at the other end of the table, dabbing a plastic paintbrush into a pot of yellow paint and streaking sunrays across the cheeks of a tiny urchin with hair approximately the color and texture of dandelion fluff. Gillian was dressed in a black leotard and tights under a knee-length red ballet skirt, her hair mostly confined in a traditional knot at the back of her head. But long coppery lengths of it had come loose to blow around her face and shoulders. A tiny diamond nose stud glinted in the sun. Her lips were pursed in concentration, her eyes alight with laughter.

When she leaned over and kissed the little girl's button nose, collecting a glob of yellow paint on her chin, Jacob was seized with a longing so fierce his breath nearly left his body. This, he realized, was why he'd come here today. This—this was dangerous.

But she looked up just then and saw him, cutting off his chance to change his mind and run. She jumped to her feet and waved. "Jacob! Mr. Ferrar! You came!"

He waved back.

"Look, Uncle Jacob! How do I look?"

Jacob dragged his gaze to Graham, who, for once in his life, stood stock-still while a young woman in a clown costume painted a soccer ball on his forehead. "Scary, mate."

Graham grinned at the girl who'd decorated him. "Thanks, lady!"

"You're welcome," she said, waving off Jacob's thanks and beckoning the next kid in line.

Graham gave a joyful hop. "Now can we get a snow cone?"

Jacob looked at his watch. "Let's wait a bit. It'll be lunchtime before long. Come here. I want you to meet someone." He took Graham's hand and led him toward Gillian. When he got close enough to be heard, he smiled. "Aren't you about due to perform?"

Her eyes widened. "What time is it?"

"Nearly ten-thirty."

She squeaked in dismay. "Oh, no! Ella, come on, we've got to hurry." She picked up the wild-haired little girl. "I'm sorry—I do need to run. This is my niece, and I have to get her back to her mommy before I dance."

"No problem, we'll catch up to you. What stage are you on?"

"The east end of the shed."

"Go. I'll talk to you afterward." He watched her dart through the crowd and disappear.

He felt a tug on his hand. "Uncle Jacob? Can we get a snow cone now?"

Jacob absently shook his head. "After lunch. But first we're going to watch one of the most amazing dancers I've ever seen."

There was no way he was leaving now.

Gilly was annoyed. She had all but broken her neck to get back here on time, running away from Jacob Ferrar like a crazy woman in order to deposit Ella in Mary Layne's lap. The potter was all set up on her little platform in front of the main stage, the wheel prepped and ready to go, clay soaking in water. And where was Tucker McGaughan? Taking his sweet time about situating the microphone pickup in his guitar, teasing her about being dressed like a circus mime, giving her that lazy silver-eyed smile that generally got him whatever he wanted.

Cole's younger brother had pretended to be her boyfriend since she was sixteen, but they both knew it wasn't going anywhere because he was far more in love with music than any real live girl. And probably, to be honest, it worked both ways. She wouldn't have given up ballet to follow him all over the country like some doe-eyed groupie. Cole and Laurel clearly hoped something would come of the bickering flirtation they'd carried on for five years. Gilly refused to address the subject, because Tucker's phantom presence kept undesirable suitors off her back. And Tucker himself was simply too lazy to ride out the emotional complication of officially ending things.

Today, however—today she wanted to slap the good-natured grin off his handsome face and tell him to grow up. On top of being thirty minutes late, he was dressed like an extra in a suntan lotion commercial in baggy plaid shorts, a pink undershirt, and rubber flip-flops. He'd grown a thin, scruffy beard and covered his long dark hair with a bandana. The fact that he had written some of the happiest, most sunshine-filled songs she'd ever heard for her to dance to today only exacerbated her aggravation.

Finally, instrument and accessories ready, Tucker plopped down on a stool he'd scavenged from a funnel cake booth and smiled at her. "Okay, dudette. You're on."

Gilly took a deep breath. *Give it up. He doesn't get it,* she thought, taking her opening position at the back corner of the stage. By now the audience seated in the grassy area beyond the three covered platforms had grown to throng proportions. Someone had gotten the word out—probably Laurel, seasoned campaign professional that she was—that the hometown ballerina and her pop star boyfriend were back in Dixie, and that they'd engaged an exhibition with one of the top pottery artists in the state. Fortunately her family had arrived early. They were spread out across three blankets right in front of the stage.

She looked for Jacob and found him off to the left-hand side, holding his little nephew in his lap. She returned his encouraging smile. The only thing to do was channel her chafed emotions into creative energy and dance.

So she danced.

Jacob waited with Graham by the hand, as Gillian was mobbed by little girls from the audience who clearly had aspirations of tutus and toe shoes. Sitting on the edge of the stage beside the singer-guitarist who had accompanied her while the potter quietly dismantled her wheel and packed her supplies, Gilly obligingly signed programs, the palms of hands, even the backs of T-shirts for a couple of older girls.

This time he'd seen her dance in daylight on a provincial stage accompanied by nothing but a vocalist with a guitar, and she'd been just as thrilling to watch as she'd been when accompanied by the Ballet New York orchestra and some of the premier dancers in the world. Her body moved like silk, but she was somehow innocent and artless, expressive and as pure in movement as a violin. The dance and the music had somehow illustrated the shaping of clay into a useful vessel, applying it to human life. Jacob didn't even have the words to describe it, but he knew he would read reviews someday that would call Gillian Kincade one of the great principal dancers.

And she was a believer. In articles and interviews posted on the Internet after her promotion to soloist, she was never shy about giving her Savior glory for her opportunities. Jacob knew the criticism she invited by such openness, had experienced something of it himself. It seemed imperative that she know how deeply she'd impacted him today.

When the crowd began to scatter, he knelt in front of Graham. "Okay, mate, time for a little man-to-man."

Graham folded his arms, taking a wide stance remarkably like his Poppa's. "Yes, sir. What is it?" The crown of blue balloons bobbed on his head.

Somehow Jacob managed to keep a straight face. "You see that girl over there? The one who danced for us just now?"

Graham pointed. "The one with yellow paint on her chin?"

"Yes," Jacob sighed. "That one. Put your finger down. Now here's the deal. All day today we've been doing what you wanted to do, and now it's my turn. I want to talk to her for a few minutes, and then I promise we'll get lunch and a snow cone." Jacob kept his voice firm. No pleading. "Think you can handle that?"

Graham tipped his head. "Yes, sir. I can definitely do that."

He sounded about forty years old, and this time Jacob did laugh. "Good man." He stood up. "Then hang onto my hand, Prince Caspian. We're riding into uncharted territory."

The two of them reached the stage just as the last of Gillian's fans wandered off and she hopped down onto the grass. The guitarist walked over to talk to a noisy knot of people standing nearby, but Gillian paused to take her hair down and put it up again. She was bent from the waist, the fiery mass hanging almost to the ground, when Jacob cleared his throat.

"That was a remarkable dance, I must say, Miss Kincade. I'm honored to've been in the audience." He enjoyed watching her throw her hair back as she jerked upright, eyes wide.

"Oh! You startled me." But she smiled and looked down at Graham. "Hey, there—I'm Gilly. What's your name?" She began to artlessly bundle her hair into a messy ponytail.

"I'm Graham Haas. Did you know you got paint on your chin?"

"Do I?" She laughed and scrubbed at her chin with the back of her hand.

"I wouldn't bother. It's dry." Jacob couldn't help smiling at her. "I'm really glad I came. You said you did the choreography?"

"Yes, and Tucker wrote the music," she added hurriedly, as if to draw attention away from herself. "It's a little different from what he usually records, don't you think? Better suited for ballet. I'd love to see him do something with it."

"Records?" It took Jacob a moment to follow her. "Is that ... That isn't Tucker McGaughan, is it?" He looked at the guitarist, who stood with his back turned to them, a rather average-looking fellow with long hair and grungy clothes.

Gilly burst out laughing. "Don't tell him you didn't recognize him. He'd be crushed. After his gig on *American Idol,* he thinks he's a household name."

Jacob shook his head. "I never watch that. Don't much care for pop music usually. But this was really good. Like I said, different."

"Come meet him. Brace yourself—this is my whole family." She took Jacob by the arm and towed him toward the clutch of noisy southerners surrounding Tucker the Semi-Famous Rock Star. "Hey, guys, cool it a minute. I want you to meet somebody." They all turned and stared with varying degrees of curiosity and warmth. "This is Jacob Ferrar, the artistic director of the Birmingham company I'll be dancing with in December, and this is his nephew, Graham. You can thank him for giving me a free trip home near Christmas!"

As he nodded and tried to look inoffensive, Jacob felt politely inspected and weighed. He'd seen the look at church, when people thought he didn't notice. *Oh, one of those dance types.*

Then the eldest female of the group sailed up to him and offered her hand. "I'm so pleased to meet you, Jacob. I'm Gilly's mother, Frances Kincade." She had Gilly's pale green eyes, Jacob noticed, but otherwise bore little resemblance to her daughter. "Here's my husband, Dodge, and my two daughters and their families, but I won't expect you to remember all this bunch at once."

"It's a great pleasure, Mrs. Kincade," Jacob said, determining then and there to learn every name, age, and occupation if it killed him.

"My soul, would you listen to that accent," cooed Frances Kincade. "Where did you grow up, darling?"

"My parents are from Alabaster, about an hour from here, but they're career diplomats." Jacob glanced at Gilly's father, who regarded him with a skeptical frown. "I spent most of my childhood in England."

"Are you the Jacob Ferrar who used to dance for BNY?" A dark-haired giant at the back of the group, carrying a little girl on his shoulders, waded through the mob like a barge through a bunch of canoes. He had been staring at Jacob with disconcerting intensity.

Maybe the guy looked vaguely familiar. Jacob nodded. "I left about five years ago."

The tall man smiled and offered a hand. "I interviewed you for the *Journal* shortly after your conversion. Cole McGaughan."

"Oh, yes." Jacob shook hands. "I do remember now. Good to see you again."

McGaughan had been one of the rare reporters who hadn't skewed his story to emphasize its more salacious details. And apparently he was some relation to the young rocker, who had draped an arm around Gilly's shoulders, clearly staking some kind of claim.

"I wondered what happened to you." Cole exchanged glances with Gilly. "This was when I was still living in the city, working on the religion page. It's a small world."

Gilly looked understandably confused. "Conversion? You mean to Christianity?"

"That's right," Jacob said. Finally a chance to let her know he shared her faith. But now that it was out, he didn't know what to do with it. He looked at Cole. "Shortly after that interview, I went to Spain and danced for a couple of years. Then ... some family issues brought me back here. Birmingham Ballet Theatre invited me on as director. I'd always wanted to choreograph."

"I'm going to London on tour after Christmas," said Tucker McGaughan lazily. "Maybe you can recommend some local eateries."

"It's been several years since I was there," Jacob confessed. "I'm sure it's changed a bit, except for the usual tourist traps."

"Hmph." Tucker looked down at Gilly, ignoring her elbow in his ribs. "Speaking of food, I'm starving. How about we check out the shish kebab down at the other end of the shed? I can smell it from here."

Gilly gave Jacob an apologetic look. "We're having a picnic. Would you and Graham like to join us?"

Jacob found himself shaking his head. Barging in on a family party wasn't his cup of tea. "Thanks, but I've promised Graham a treat. We'll be easing on our way." He forced himself not to stare at Gilly and spoke to the McGaughan kid. "I appreciated your music, mate. I especially liked the perfume song." Then, telling himself not to be ridiculous, he looked at Gilly. "The dance on that one was beautiful. Even without the lyrics I'd have known it was Mary's story."

She flushed with pleasure. "Thank you. That means a lot to me."

Tightening his grip on Graham's hand, Jacob backed away from the web of Gilly's family. "It's been great to meet you all. I hope you'll come back for *Nutcracker.* We do a first-class production, and we only bring in the best dancers." He smiled at Gilly and turned.

But Cole followed, walking with him toward the exit. "Hey, I'd like to catch up with you sometime, since you're just up in Birmingham. Maybe do a follow-up article about ... you, Gilly, *The Nutcracker* ..."

Jacob stopped and gave him a cautious look. "I won't talk about my private life."

Cole's gaze was level, sympathetic. "This would be about faith and the arts. Somebody needs to write about it."

"Does Gilly know ... about New York?"

"Not from me." Cole shrugged. "But you'd have to ask her."

Jacob looked down at Graham, who had taken off his crown and sat down on the ground to play with the balloons. "I'd rather she didn't." Was he being a coward? "Have you a business card? I'll give you a call soon."

Cole took out his wallet, found a card, and handed it to Jacob. "That's my cell. Call me anytime. I'm full-time at the *Advertiser* now, but I still occasionally send pieces to the *Journal* if it's the right subject." He offered his hand again with a smile. "Good to see you again, man. Take care." Cole walked off, whistling, in the direction of his family.

Jacob swung Graham to his feet. As usual, just when he seemed to have gotten his life straightened out, something lunged into the path to create confusion. In this case, the something was a *someone*—a beautiful, unattainable woman whom he instinctively recognized as everything he could ever want in a friend and lover.

"I was good, wasn't I, Uncle Jacob?" Graham was squinting up at him. "You talked to the ballerina."

"You were awesome."

"Then can I have a rainbow? That's my favorite flavor."

Jacob nodded, an idea beginning to form. As long as he was handing out rainbows, he might as well treat himself too. Who was to say he didn't deserve a little happiness?

Four

Late Tuesday afternoon Gilly pulled Laurel's Honda into the McGaughan driveway and parked behind an unfamiliar top-down silver Jaguar convertible. *Ooh, pretty.*

But right now she was in charge of two hungry little people who wanted their mama. No time to satisfy curiosity. She hopped out and opened the back passenger seat, where Kate already had her seat belt unfastened.

"Down!" wailed Rosie, still a prisoner in her car seat. "Mommy!"

"All right, give me half a sec." Gilly started wrestling with the buckle.

"I gotta go, Aunt Gilly." Kate, already on the ground, tugged on her shirttail, dancing.

"Oops, okay. Take the diaper bag on into the house while I get Rosie."

Five minutes later Laurel peered over her shoulder. "What's the matter? Kate came in a while ago."

"Mechanical engineers," Gilly muttered, moving aside to let the expert take over. "When I was in high school, I used to haul Mary Layne's kids around all the time and never had this problem."

"Car seats have come a long way since then."

"If they get any safer, you'll have to leave the kids out here and drop food in through the sun roof."

Laurel extracted her sniffling offspring, who clamped arms and legs around her mother. "According to Kate, you had the bestest time ever. Did you not have fun?"

"Of course I did. It just takes a different kind of energy to keep up with two widgets than it does to perform a three-hour ballet." Gilly stretched her tense neck. "I'm sure you're familiar with Rosie's favorite word."

On cue, Rosie lifted her head off Laurel's shoulder. "Nooooo. I don't want a bath!" Her cotton-candy-ringed mouth formed a pink rosebud.

Laurel laughed and headed for the house, Gilly trailing with a huge stuffed giraffe under her arm and a couple of helium balloons tied to her wrist. As they walked past the Jaguar, she glanced at the black duffel bag in its passenger seat. A pair of mirrored designer sunglasses dangled from the rearview mirror, and a CD wallet was clipped to the visor. Otherwise it was surgically neat and clean. "Looks like you've got company."

Laurel glanced over her shoulder, expression quizzical. "You didn't know Jacob Ferrar was coming down today?"

"Jacob Ferrar?" Gilly sucked in a breath. "You mean he's *here*? What's he doing here? Is there a problem with *The Nutcracker*?"

Laurel blinked. "If there is, he didn't mention it. He and Cole are holding forth about old times in New York. But he said he wanted to talk to you about something."

"I can't imagine what." Gilly shook her head. "Rosie's sound asleep, drooling on your shoulder."

"Rats. Too late for a nap and too early for bedtime." Laurel sighed and moved aside to let Gilly open the door. "Go on in the family room and tell Cole I'll be down as soon as I run the girls through the tub." She headed up the stairs.

Gilly paused in the open doorway to the family room, where she found the two men backlit by patchy late-afternoon sunshine coming through the bank of windows facing the patio. Cole sprawled in the recliner, and Jacob sat at one end of the sofa.

Cole grinned at her. "Hey, squirt. Looks like you brought the zoo home with you."

"It was 'Meet the Giraffe' day. What're you gonna do?" Gilly tossed the giraffe to her brother-in-law, then untied the ribbons holding the balloons to her wrist. They floated happily to the ceiling. She looked at Jacob, who had risen the instant she came into the room. Wow, he had good manners. "Hi, Jacob." The what-are-you-doing-here question hung between them.

If Cole was aware of any awkwardness, he ignored it. In fact, he was looking a bit smug. Had he arranged this odd meeting?

"Where are Laurel and the girls?" he asked as Gilly and Jacob sat down at a safe distance on opposite ends of the sofa.

"Bath time. She'll be down shortly." Gilly wished she hadn't let go of the balloons. She needed something to do with her hands. She clasped her hands in her lap. "So … Jacob. How are you?"

"Good, actually." An endearing tide of red climbed Jacob's cheeks. He lifted his hands. "I know this is all a bit … strange. Showing up without calling first. But I was in town today, and I thought you wouldn't mind my coming round." He paused. "I hoped you'd still be here."

"I don't mind. And obviously I'm here." Mystified, Gilly looked at Cole.

He shrugged. "You'd better tell her, Jacob, before she pops from curiosity."

Jacob opened and closed his mouth. "Okay. You're going to think I'm off my nut." He leaned forward, dark brown eyes burning into hers. "But after I watched you dance Saturday at the festival, I couldn't get the idea out of my head. I want you to be Mary."

"Mary who?" Gilly edged farther to the end of the sofa, away from this young madman.

"Mary of Bethany." At her blink of incomprehension, he added impatiently, "In my ballet." He sat back as if that explained everything.

"Your ballet." Comprehension dawned. "You've written a ballet? How very cool!"

"Not just any ballet." Cole, the professional communicator, intervened. "This is a story with an overtly Christian message. Jacob wants to use Tucker's original music, and he's sketched out the story. He just showed it to me. It's called *The Sweetest Perfume*."

Gilly bounced to the edge of the sofa. "Mary anointing Jesus' feet. Oh, I love that! What a great idea!"

A smile built on Jacob Ferrar's angular face, taking him beyond good looks into something incandescent. "Then you'll do it?"

"Whoa. Not so fast." Gilly laughed. "You know I can't commit myself just like that. I'm under contract to BNY—and you're not even supposed to approach me without talking to our manager."

Jacob's deflated expression was almost comical. "But—we can work all that out. I wanted to see if you'd be at all interested, since you gave me the idea. You're perfect for the part." His gaze flicked over her.

Gilly made no protest because his stare was almost clinical, like a painter choosing materials for a work of art. The crazy thing was she understood that. She was used to being looked at for form, line, proportion, even color. Her hair sometimes gave her an edge over less eye-catching dancers.

"Have you ever seen a red-haired Jewess?" she asked, smiling.

Jacob waved a hand. "Oh, that. You'll have on a headdress. The costumes will be different from what you're used to."

"You've really thought this out, haven't you?"

"I want you to be Mary. Please." Jacob stood up. "Let me show you the *pas de deux* with Jesus." He looked around the comfortably crowded room, moved to the largest open space, which happened to be beside the patio door, and pushed aside a plastic doll house with his foot. "Here. Come, I'll show you. Take my hand ..." She did, and followed as he dictated a series of steps. "Arabesque, *glissade* into a grand jeté. Press lift ... bourrée to fourth, *pirouette* and kneel ..."

They finished with Gilly bent backward across his arm. Of course she wasn't properly dressed for dancing, and her sock feet slipped a bit on the polished wooden floor. But the strength of his arm beneath her back told her he would not let her fall. She lay across his arm, staring up into his dark, intense eyes. His breath came quickly. Hers did too.

Oh, goodness.

Somebody started clapping. "Gilly, Jacob, that was beautiful!"

Tipping her head back, Gilly saw Laurel standing in the doorway, a big grin on her face. Kate, dressed in a long pink cotton nightgown, clung to her mother's leg.

"You're upside down, Aunt Gilly." Kate dropped Laurel's hand and climbed up into Cole's lap with the toy giraffe.

Jacob righted Gilly swiftly. "The music will make the difference," he muttered.

Gilly backed away from him and crashed into the miniblinds on the door. "Why aren't you dancing?"

"I just did."

"No, I mean—in New York or Spain or wherever. You. On the stage in a spotlight." She whirled on Cole, who was sitting there with his mouth open. "Did you know about this? Why didn't you tell me?"

Cole shrugged. "I'm just a religion and politics journalist, not an arts critic. I didn't know it was a big—" He scrunched his rather ferocious eyebrows. "Is it a big deal?"

"You just saw that!" Gilly waved her hands.

"Gilly, as much as you would like to alter the fact, the world does not revolve around ballet." Laurel moved to Gilly's vacated seat on the sofa. "Cole's been busy having a life for the last five years."

Gilly turned to Jacob. He stood watching her, arms folded in a stance she began to suspect was more defensive than aggressive. "Why did you leave New York?" she asked more quietly.

"I can't explain it in a sentence." He looked away, relieving her of that scalding but somehow tender stare. "But I'll tell you this. I couldn't have created that dance if I'd stayed in New York."

So he'd laid it out there for her to kick aside or stomp on or whatever she felt like doing. He should have at least waited until she came back in December instead of driving down here on this spur-of-the-moment whim. He didn't have the music secured. It was a reversion to type that scared the—

Catching his thoughts, he looked at her.

To give her credit, Gillian didn't say no immediately. Straightening her top—a loose, finely knit purple thing that hid slender, steel-strong bands of muscle and clashed with her hair—she glanced at her sister. "I think we need some time to discuss this."

"Of course," he said immediately. "I didn't expect ..." Actually, he *had* expected. *Idiot.* Presumptuous idiot. "I know it's too soon, and you don't know me. I just wanted to tell you about it, so you could be thinking. I'd like to contact Maurice and see if he'll release you to dance the role. If I can get the funding. And get my board to approve the change in schedule."

Gillian suddenly laughed. "I love the way you say that. *Shed-jule.*"

Jacob lifted his hands, charmed by her amusement. "British schools."

"It's cute." Gillian was still grinning. She pointed at the sofa. "Sit." When he obeyed without thinking, she all but shoved him back into place beside Laurel. "I need a drink of water. Would you like something?"

Bemused by her enchanting informality, he shook his head. "I can't stay much longer. Graham is with friends, and I have to get back."

"Okay." She backed toward the kitchen. "Cole, would you help me find the ... um, glasses?"

Cole's gaze bounced between Gilly and his wife, who tipped her head toward the kitchen. If he thought it odd that his sister-in-law suddenly couldn't find a glass after being in the house for four days, he kept it to himself. "Sure." Cole got to his feet and ambled after Gillian into the kitchen.

Laurel gave Jacob a mischievous smile. "She's going to give him the third degree about you."

Jacob stared at his hands. "I should have called first. But I wanted to see her face, show her the dance."

"No, no. She's definitely intrigued. So am I." Laurel nodded. "I bet she'll do whatever it takes to convince Maurice to let her go."

Jacob looked at her hopefully. If he could pull this ballet off, make it pay for itself, his reputation would be set. A seed of a grand idea had been birthed along with the libretto. "You think so? A brand-new ballet will take a lot of rehearsal time."

"I do." Laurel sat down in the recliner, and Kate climbed into her lap. "Gilly's done some solo work in churches and what-have-you. But she's never done a whole ballet with a Christ-centered theme. What made you think of her?"

"She's the most beautiful dancer I've ever—"

And there she was, standing in the doorway with a goblet of water in her hand, cheeks a high pink. He must have sounded like a stalker. Dancers, as he knew from personal experience, attracted the attention of ballet fanatics who thought they knew them, begged for autographs, collected worn-out toe shoes, posted rants and raves on dance blogs. It was flattering, sometimes annoying, but part of celebrity.

Gillian cleared her throat and bounced into a chair, somehow without sloshing the water. "So how's *Nutcracker* going? I was impressed by the work your dancers did on Friday."

"Well, you know we're just pulling it back out of the box for the season. My principals have been spending a good bit of time on the gala coming up in a couple of weeks, and we've several new company members."

"I know how that goes."

Of course she did. Though she'd moved to New York right about the time he left, she'd danced in Mobile's small company until she was sixteen years old. "Has Maurice announced casting for the BNY *Nutcracker*?"

She shook her head. "Soon, I hope."

"You'll have some lead roles."

She wrinkled her nose. "I suppose. I danced Dew Drop last year a couple of performances. I'm hoping for a shot at Sugar Plum this time."

"If you get it, I'll come see you dance." The words were out before he realized how they would sound.

But she smiled. "That would be nice. Let me know when you're there." She tipped her head. "Do you still have friends in the city?"

"No one close." Flashes, images, terrible in their clarity, downloaded into his brain. Going back to New York would be a very bad idea. He stood up, looked at Cole. "Thank you for letting me stay and talk to Gillian. I really have to go. Graham will be waiting for me."

"How old is he?" Gilly rose as well, setting the water goblet on the coffee table.

"He's six." Jacob drew his keys out of his pocket. "Tomorrow's a school day, and I have a board meeting. Thanks for listening to me, Gillian."

"No problem. Laurel, stay put, I'll walk him to the door." Gillian casually hooked an arm through his.

Startled, he looked down at her, padding along beside him in sock feet like a red-haired elf. "There is one person ... Is Harold Cook still caretaker of the shoe room?" He hadn't thought of Harold in years, but the feel of her slender arm tucked in his somehow loosened his tongue.

"Yep." Gillian's face lit. "What a sweetie he is."

"He brought me to Christ."

"No way! Harold's a Christian?" She paused at the door, looking up at him, frank curiosity in the bright greenish eyes. "I wish you could stay a little longer. I'd like to get to know you."

Something arced between them again, something elemental and familiar, and he didn't think it was all on his side. Dangerous, especially since she was clearly such an innocent. "I—"

"I'm sorry. I know you have to go." She let go of his arm and stepped back. "There'll be plenty of time when I come back in December. I'm looking forward to it."

"Me too." He offered his hand.

She took it—her grip firm and warm, but brief—then tucked her hands into the back pockets of her jeans. "Good-bye, Jacob."

"Good-bye, Gillian." He turned to open the door, but a touch on his elbow stopped him.

"My friends call me Gilly."

He hesitated just a moment too long. "All right, then. Gilly it is."

As the door closed behind him, he hurried for the Jag. Graham was going to be wound up and impossible to get to bed, and he still had an inbox full of email correspondence to deal with before his own bedtime. But now that he'd danced with Gilly Kincade, he couldn't regret his decision to pursue this mad impulse. His image of the mercurial Mary of Bethany had shifted into focus, limned on the creative side of his brain in a way he'd never before experienced.

He got into the car, raised the top, and reached for his sunglasses against the glare of the setting sun. As he pulled onto the interstate, he hesitated for only a moment before pressing the Call button of his cell phone. He'd programmed the number in earlier but held off on calling it until he'd talked to Gilly.

The phone rang three times and kicked into voice mail. A lazy voice said, "Hey, this is Tucker. Leave a message."

Short and sweet. Jacob smiled and waited for the beep. "Tucker, this is Jacob Ferrar. I'm … a friend of Gilly's. We met Saturday at the arts festival. I'd like to talk to you about using your music for a rock ballet I'm developing for my company in Birmingham. I can offer you some compensation, though frankly not what it's worth, I'm afraid. But I think you'd find it a challenging and satisfying creative effort. I'd appreciate if you'd give me a ring back so we can discuss the idea."

He left his number and closed the phone. There was no way to predict if Tucker would be interested in pursuing such an off-the-beaten-trail endeavor as a ballet. He supposed he could have asked Gilly to run interference for him, but that felt a bit cowardly somehow.

There had been a time when Jacob Ferrar, focused on himself, knew exactly where he was going and blasted full out to get there. Then he'd spent the first few years of his Christian life simply reacting to events as they happened. Leaving New York. Lily's death. Taking in Graham. Even the pursuit of a degree in physical therapy was more time-filler than anything else.

But finally he'd discovered something that lit a passionate fire in his belly. And he was going after it with spiritual guns blazing. So, if God was in this thing, then *he* would provide the music, the funding, the dancers. If Tucker McGaughan didn't want to write music for him, Jacob would find it somewhere else.

Five

Bloomingdale's was running a sale on coats, a fact that normally wouldn't have crossed Gilly's radar screen on her first day back in New York. But Victoria Farigno, the closest thing she had to a best friend, had appeared at her apartment door this morning, apparently in desperate need of retail therapy. As they crossed East 57th, Gilly decided the timing was fortuitous. The temperature had dropped into the fifties overnight, and her camellia-thin blood was already forming ice in her veins.

"I had quite the adventure while you were gone." Victoria, five-foot-nine and considered one of the "tall girls," bent her swanlike neck to look down at Gilly. "Ian got up the nerve to ask me out."

"No way!" Gilly hesitated at the intersection, watching the red "Don't Walk" hand flash. "What did Nicholas say?"

"I never told him, because I didn't want to get him all upset. Nicholas doesn't like competition."

Since Nicholas had been virtually her second roommate for three months, Gilly was well aware of his flaws. Last year she and Victoria, the two youngest members of the company, had tried sharing an apartment. But Gilly got tired of walking in on passionate make-out sessions in the living room, and when Cole offered to sublet his tiny walk-up over the Tribeca bread store to her, she'd jumped at it. Now she could enjoy Victoria's company when it was available without succumbing to the urge to throttle her.

Most of the time.

"Victoria, he's going to find out, because Ian can't keep his mouth shut." Gilly poked the crossing button again. "Wait. You didn't actually go out with Ian, did you?" She looked both ways. There was no traffic in either direction, so she bolted across the street.

"Gilly! You're going to get us killed!" Victoria's long legs caught up in three strides. "No, I didn't go out with him. Ian is a twenty-year-old nobody from Paducah, Kentucky, and already all he talks about is the relative merits of back braces and pain prescriptions. He'll probably wind up teaching ballet in some Midwestern public school. Besides, Nicholas is going to inherit about four million one of these days. How else do you think he affords living in Manhattan on a junior editor's salary?"

"By mooching off his girlfriend?" Dang, it was cold out here. Gilly pulled up the hood of the Ole Miss sweatshirt Laurel had loaned her. She'd forgotten to return it, but Laurel would never miss it.

"He doesn't mooch! You just don't like him because he smokes."

"That's definitely a drawback," Gilly said mildly and pushed through the double doors at Bloomingdale's. The sleepover thing was the biggest problem, as Gilly saw it, but arguing morality with Victoria rarely accomplished anything. She had no point of reference.

"Besides, Ian's kind of cute, and he's really sweet."

Ooh. The shoe department. It was rather a Kincade fetish. She drifted over to a pair of fleece-lined suede boots and picked one up. These would keep her feet warm on those nasty arctic trips to the grocery around the corner.

"You're not going to buy those, are you?" Victoria frowned. "At your height, you need heels."

"Thanks for the reminder." Gilly set the boot down on its little plastic pedestal and headed for the escalator. "I'm not buying heels when my feet will be in shreds again within a few days." She smiled at a woman on a ladder behind the Esteé Lauder counter. Retail freaks. Mid-October, and they were already decorating for Christmas.

"I know." Victoria sighed but brightened as the escalator spit them out on the second floor. "I hope they have long coats this time. Last year I waited too late and never found one. Nearly froze my—"

"Tutu off," Gilly finished with her, groaning. "Keep your day job, girl. Comedy's not your thing."

"Yeah, yeah. So why don't you go for Ian yourself, since you think he's so sweet?"

"You said it yourself: he's a little immature." Gilly was often partnered with Ian because of her small stature. Their relationship had become that of brother and sister. "Besides, I don't have time for fooling around."

"You ought to. You never relax."

"Says the person who gets about six hours' sleep every night. At least I get real rest instead of popping diet pills that keep me up half the night."

Victoria scowled. "I can't afford to pick up even an ounce. You little people are so lucky."

"Victoria—"

"Gilly, shut up about the pills. I've heard all your sermons." Dodging a little boy with an FAO Schwartz balloon, Victoria hooked a left into the outerwear department. "Back to the subject. Did you get to see rocker-boy while you were home?"

Rocker-boy was Victoria's term for Tucker McGaughan. "For a few hours at the arts festival in Montgomery. But there was family around the whole time." Gilly paused in front of a mannequin modeling a down-filled vest over a turtleneck and jeans. There was no explaining Tucker to a born-and-bred New York diva. She fingered the knitted band at the bottom of the vest and moved on. "I was sort of relieved."

"Why?" Victoria frowned in disapproval at the mannequin and followed. Anything remotely athletic—except for dance, of course—gave her hives.

"Because I don't have time for a relationship, especially a long-distance one. There's plenty of time for that later."

"Nobody said you have to marry the boy. Or any boy. Just find one to hang out with and have some fun." Victoria squinted at her. "You do like men, don't you?"

"Of course I like men. I have lots of guy friends." Gilly saw a circular rack of pea coats. "Come on, let's go look over there." She dodged through the coats.

"Yeah, but isn't there one you like in particular? You know, for a little hoochy-coo?"

Gilly stopped and put her hands on her hips. "Life is more than hoochy-coo, Victoria. Sometimes I think the world is obsessed! Sex isn't recreation for me—you know how I feel about that. I'm going to get married one day, and it'll be a private and special thing between me and my husband, so I'm not going to play around with it beforehand."

"You mean you're actually a virgin?" Victoria stared at her as if Gilly had just announced she'd been born on Pluto. "I thought you were kidding—you know, when you mentioned that last spring."

Gilly looked around. The middle of a department store wouldn't have been her first choice of venues for a discussion about the birds and bees with her former roommate. Fortunately, there were few customers in the store this early on a Saturday morning. *Dear God, couldn't you come up with a less embarrassing way for me to talk about you to Victoria?*

She had always believed in honesty. "I wasn't kidding. I didn't try to tell you and Nicholas what to do, but it frankly worries me that you're so casual about it. God invented sex, and I'm looking forward to it—a lot—because he creates spectacular gifts. But I believe it's a powerful bond between two people that ought to be reserved for marriage." She took a deep breath. Victoria was listening hard. Might as well be hung for a sheep as for a lamb. "And marriage is something else I'm not going to experiment with. I try to live my life by the Bible, and the Bible is very specific about the kind of man I'm supposed to be looking for. I haven't seen anybody who matches the description so far. Not even Tucker. And especially not Ian."

"Not *anybody*? My goodness, you're picky." Victoria never said what was expected.

"Yes, I'm picky." A fleeting image of Jacob Ferrar's broken-angel face blinked through her mind. She brushed it aside and smiled at Victoria. "Guilty as charged."

"You're going to be an old maid." Looking disgruntled, Victoria turned to poke through the coats on the rack. "Don't come whining to me if you wind up like Dianne Woo."

The ability of BNY's ballet mistress—indeterminate of age and volcanic of temperament—to terrorize apprentices and corps dancers was legendary. However, Gilly had a hard time believing it had anything to do with her sex life, or lack of it. "If I have half her command of language when I'm her age, I'll be happy."

Victoria sniffed. "You are so weird. Which is, I guess, why I love you. Look at this coat. You think it's long enough for me?"

Gilly looked at the coat. And prayed for Victoria to find truth in something she'd said, in spite of the "weirdness." "It would drag the ground on me. Ought to fit you just fine."

Victoria laughed and took the coat off the hanger. "I hope we get snow for Christmas."

"Yeah, it would be a shame to spend five hundred dollars on a coat and not get to wear it." Gilly grinned.

It was a beautiful party. The Women's Committee had decorated the Hilton Grand Ballroom with swags of orange, umber, and goldenrod fabric draped across the tables and centerpieces of antique brass clocks. Glossy programs beneath the salad plates were printed with the theme, *Time to Dance*. Dessert was a chocolate mousse cake garnished with swirls of dark raspberry and mint leaves. Celtic flutes and harps played softly in the background, above the music of a stone sundial fountain in the center of the room.

As the committee members, flaunting expensive fall suits, stationed their daughters at the doors to greet dance patrons, Jacob looked at his watch. Only two more hours to go.

He remembered once attending a reception for Baryshnikov in Buckingham Palace with his parents—Charles and Diana had still been together at the time, so he must have been a very small boy. It had been characterized by less formality than this southern fundraising luncheon.

And it had been a heck of a lot more fun.

But he had to concede that the fall fashion show was a critical part of his job: it would go a long way to paying for rental of the theater for *Nutcracker*. Members of the Arts Council would be seated at the head table, expecting to be treated as honored guests—acknowledged for their generosity, feted for their good taste in supporting the arts. Jacob would do it, but he'd rather be at the park playing soccer with Graham.

Jacob frowned. He'd warned the women to make sure the dancers chose to model modest outfits, but Brittney Sulley had, as usual, ignored instruction. Her long-sleeved daffodil-colored top, worn over slinky black wide-legged pants, dipped to reveal an alarming amount of young cleavage as she bent over to set her purse down in a chair near the head table. Avoiding her mother's gaze, Brittney smiled at the president of an investment firm that sponsored the inner-city dance program. With a little shimmy of her shoulders, she lifted her long honey-colored hair off her neck as she slowly walked past the head table—away from her mother.

Jacob set his teeth and headed toward Brittney, but a slender hand on his elbow stopped him as he passed the fountain. He looked down to find Alexandra Manchester-Cooper smiling up at him.

"Jacob! I went to your church last weekend, but I didn't see you." She left her hand on his arm.

"You went to my church?" Alexandra was a very pretty young woman, and her clingy dress, like Brittney's, was cleverly designed to draw attention to certain physical attributes. But the flirtatious glint in her eyes set off alarm bells. He stepped back as far as he could without falling into the fountain. "I decided to stay over at my grandparents' house. Graham likes their Sunday school better than ours. Next time, let me know you're coming, and I'll introduce you to some other women." He congratulated himself for his masterful tactics. He didn't want to offend Alexandra, but he also didn't want to give her any undue encouragement.

Her blonde eyebrows drew together a fraction, but her polished lips turned up. "You're so sweet to little Graham. He's a lucky kid."

Jacob shook his head. "I don't know that I'd call him lucky. Losing both your parents before you're six years old is kind of tough." He looked for Brittney and saw her disappear into the hallway. He'd have to talk to her mother later. It was too late now to do anything about the dress anyway. Distracted, he glanced at Alexandra. "What did you think about our church?"

She wrinkled her nose. "It's different. I'm not a big fan of rock music in church. I felt like I was at a concert instead of a worship service."

"It's not for everybody," Jacob admitted. "But if you've never been to church before and don't have any preconceived ideas about what it should be ... We attract a lot of kids who bring their friends."

"I was just surprised since you love classical music so much."

"I do. But there's all kinds of music, just like there's all kinds of dance. I don't think art forms or genres should be specifically religious or secular."

Alexandra stared up at him for a moment, lips pursed, then smiled. "That's a very mature observation. Will you be there—at your church, I mean—tomorrow?"

Jacob hesitated. Here was a beautiful woman wanting to go to church with him. "I'll be there, unless something completely unforeseen happens. Would you—" He cleared his throat. "Would you like for Graham and me to come pick you up?"

Her thin, elegant face lit. "That would be lovely! Thank you so much! What time should I be ready?"

Jacob feared he might have just made a big mistake, but it was too late to rescind the invitation. "We start at nine, so if you'll be ready by eight thirty, that should be about right. I'll call you tonight to get directions."

To his relief, Stephanie MacDowell, the company's marketing and public relations director, waved from across the room.

"Excuse me, Alexandra. I need to see what Stephanie wants." He gave her a perfunctory smile and dodged around tables, feeling Alexandra's blue eyes branding his back as he went.

"Mr. Ferrar." Stephanie greeted him with a relieved smile. "I was afraid we weren't going to get a chance to talk today. I know you're busy, but I have the layout for next year's school brochure ready. I thought you might like to see it before the next board meeting, so I brought it with me."

Jacob raised his brows. "That was speedy. Okay, then, let's meet after the luncheon and I'll look it over. Do you have updated bios and photos of all the teachers and staff?"

"Yes, sir—"

Jacob's phone vibrated, and he glanced at it without intending to answer. The luncheon was due to start shortly. But when the name "Tucker McGaughan" appeared in the ID window, he muttered a hasty apology to Stephanie and hurried into the hallway.

He flipped open the phone. "Hello, Tucker. Jacob Ferrar here."

"Hey, man. Sorry it took me so long to get back to you. I've been in the recording studio, and the hours are pretty strange."

"That's no problem. Thanks for the call." Jacob leaned against the wall. The cell reception in this hallway wasn't the best, but he'd managed to make out about every third word and piece together the rest. "I'd about decided you weren't interested."

"Oh, yeah, it's just weird enough I'm definitely interested." Tucker laughed. "But I need to know a little more about it. I'm in Nashville, but I'm headed down tonight to spend a few days with my brother, so I could stop off there—do you have time to get together?"

"Yes, of course." Jacob struggled not to sound too eager. "If you like Chinese, I could meet you at P. F. Chang's—say around seven? Can you make it that early?"

"Yeah, cool." There was a brief pause, and Jacob thought he'd completely lost the connection, then Tucker's drawl came back crystal-clear. "You heard anything from Gilly since the gig in Montgomery?"

"We met once," Jacob said cautiously. "I drove to your brother's house to approach her with the idea for the ballet."

"Hmm. What'd she say about it?"

"She … seemed enthusiastic."

"I bet she did," Tucker said cryptically. "Well, I gotta jet. Wrapping things up around here, and I'll be on the road by five. See you at Chang's at seven."

"Good. See you." Jacob replaced his phone. He took a minute to pray and collect his scattered thoughts, then reentered the ballroom. Chang's at seven. After meeting with Stephanie, he'd barely have time to return home for his notes and find emergency supervision for Graham. Maybe Cynthia wouldn't mind covering for him an extra couple of hours.

He saw Frank Ireland, board chairman, waving him up to the head table. The banquet was about to start. Sighing, he straightened his tie. Director hat on, creative hat back in pocket.

P. F. Chang's was always crowded on Saturday nights, but Jacob had called ahead, so he and Tucker had to wait less than thirty minutes before they were shown to a table.

"Yeah, we'll wrap the album next week," Tucker said as the hostess left them with menus and silverware. "Then, except for a couple of regional gigs, we're free until we leave for London after Christmas. I'm thinking I could use my vacation to work on the music for your ballet thing." He grimaced. "I get bored just sitting around doing nothing."

It had been so long since Jacob had time to sit around doing nothing, he could hardly sympathize. He had to go home and study gross anatomy and would probably be up past midnight. "Sounds like that would work out perfectly. I'd like to have a demo to play for my board by the middle of December."

Tucker played with his chopsticks for a moment. "I think I could make that happen. You got any ideas about what you want? Gilly told me the basic story about Mary when we were working on the song for the arts festival."

Jacob shook his head. "Actually, that piece is what gave me the idea. I want to build the whole ballet around it—probably use it somewhere in the middle."

"So I could write songs with lyrics if I want to? I thought ballet was all instrumental."

"Ballet can be whatever the composer and choreographer want it to be. We dance to Broadway, jazz, the classical stuff..." Jacob picked up his water glass and toasted Tucker with a smile. "And now ... Christian rock. The dance is designed to fit the music."

Tucker laughed. "Cool, man. I'm in. What's the total length of the project?"

"Hour and a half to two hours." Jacob reached for his portfolio. "I brought an outline of the story, if you want to see."

"Lay it on me, big guy."

For the next hour, the two of them worked, brainstorming ideas, while the server came and went and steaming piles of brown rice, kung pao chicken, and honey orange shrimp disappeared. The kid had a creative brain and had no problem absorbing and expanding what Jacob had in mind.

Putting down his pen, Jacob thanked the waitress as she removed their dishes. He glanced at Tucker, who was watching the girl's departure appreciatively. "There's one thing I should have asked you before we started this."

Tucker's pale eyes returned to Jacob. "What's that?"

"Well, I'm interested in how this whole thing strikes you on a spiritual level. I don't usually get off on that subject with a collaborator, but this is ... different. You know, very personal to me." In fact, Jacob couldn't remember *ever* broaching the subject with another artist, but he ignored the awkwardness. It was the right thing to do.

Tucker frowned. "Why? Because of Gilly?"

Jacob smiled. For once he hadn't been thinking of Gilly. "I hope she'll dance the lead, but—and I hope you won't be insulted—I can't really tell where you are spiritually. I've spent a good bit of time praying about this ballet, and I'm pretty sure God told me to approach you about the music." He opened his hands. "I'm curious, if you wouldn't mind talking about it."

There was a short silence, and Jacob wondered if he'd made a big mistake. The words *unequally yoked* came to mind. He had no problem working with unbelievers on a professional level. He did it every day. But this project was more than a ballet. He hoped it was a God-given *tour de force.*

Tucker propped his hands on the table, linking his fingers and circling the thumbs. "Did my brother tell you to talk to me?"

"Cole? No. Why?"

"Because he's been after me to come out of the Christian closet, so to speak." The silvery eyes were intent on Jacob's face, measuring, testing. "When I met Gilly, I thought she was one of the coolest, most open people I'd ever met. And she had the Jesus-freak thing going on in a big way." Tucker passed his tongue over his lip. "But I wanted to get with her, you know what I mean? So I sort of played a game for a while."

Jacob controlled the impulse to deck the guy. But Tucker was talking past tense. He waited.

"But you know Gil. She's not so much into games." Tucker grinned with a self-deprecating hunch of the shoulders that made

Jacob understand why he had so many fans. Including Gilly. "I tagged around with her, and she let me—but she kept the hand up, you know, until finally I got it. Or, well, Jesus got me. Whichever way it worked, I gave up and realized I was stalling out big time with nobody but me to blame."

Jacob hoped he was following. "Stalling out? You mean with music or Gilly?"

"With everything." Tucker leaned forward. "I was a big back-pedaling zero with nothing important to live for. No wonder she wouldn't give me the time of day." His eyes narrowed. "Funny thing. About the time I gave my life to the Lord, somebody put a video of one of my gigs on UTube, and it took off like a grass fire in Silicon Valley. About two months later I'm fielding three offers from major labels. I didn't have *time* to keep track of Gilly—even if she hadn't been pursuing her own thing in New York." He laughed. "That is one driven little redheaded Betty."

Jacob smiled. "Most dancers at her level are. Or they wouldn't have gotten there at all."

"Yeah, well, what I was getting at is, this music thing took on a life of its own, and I ... kind of have to do what management tells me. You know, the public image and all." Tucker paused, eying Jacob. "I'm a Christian, but I don't want to get too heavy-handed or I'll lose my core audience. Kids cruising around with their iPod buds in their ears. I keep my lyrics clean, I just don't ... advertise, you know what I mean?"

Jacob understood very well. He'd struggled with the same issue right after his own conversion. How much God-talk was too much? "But your brother thinks you're *too* low-key? He thinks you're compromising?"

Tucker shrugged. "He keeps checking on me. Making sure I'm reading my Bible, going to church. Guess he thinks if I'm not telling David Letterman that I'm a born-again holy roller, I'm backsliding."

"You're fortunate to have somebody to keep you accountable."

Jacob wished he'd had a Christian brother to steer him along the way. Maybe he wouldn't have had that stumble with the girl in Spain.

"You don't know me, though," Tucker said. "And if you had to *ask* if I'm a Christian ..." He looked away. "Something's not right."

"Look, I'm the last guy qualified to throw stones. But it makes me feel better to have had this conversation before we get into a creative collaboration like this."

"Yeah. Well, I'm going to do a little more thinking—and praying—on the subject." Tucker cut his eyes back to Jacob. "I answered your question, so I'm gonna pitch you one of my own: what exactly is your interest in Gilly?"

"Professional, of course," Jacob said without having to think about it. "She's an amazing dancer. But I won't lie to you. She's an intriguing young woman."

Tucker nodded. "She is. But you know she's not leaving New York for the foreseeable future." There was Alpha-dog challenge in his pale eyes. "And when she does I'll be waiting on her."

Jacob had quite a bit of wolf in his own blood. He gave Tucker a slow smile. "I wouldn't wait around too long."

Six

Gilly sat cross-legged on the floor in the shoe room, yanking the bottom out of a new pair of *pointe* shoes. The contents of her sewing kit lay scattered around her on the scarred gray floor—scissors, packets of tapestry needles, waxed floss, and a tape measure. She also had lengths of pink elastic and satin ribbon. The relatively mindless process of modifying a new pair of shoes was relaxing. Gave her time to think.

After a year of apprenticeship and another year in the corps de ballet, she'd earned the right to special order her shoes. Three nails, extra glue, cut down the sides, cord instead of elastic drawstring. Before that, she'd worn Iliana Poiroux's rejects. Not that they were bad. Iliana's foot was the same size as Gilly's; she had the same narrow heel and deep arch, and she preferred Gilly's favorite maker, Maltese Cross. Still, it was a mark of professional pride for a dancer to graduate to custom-made shoes.

Gilly held up the slipper she had just finished, letting its fresh, smooth ribbons dangle to the floor. Grandma Kincade would be proud of her neat stitches. When Gilly was small, she spent spring breaks with Daddy's parents at the Kincade nursery in Wilmer, Alabama, learning the rudiments of the azalea business and making aprons and potholders. Grandma's old Singer foot treadle sewing machine was cool, but Gilly had hated the hand sewing because it meant sitting still. Now she was thankful for her grandmother's exacting instructions.

Anything worth doing is worth doing right.

Oh, yeah, Grandma. It is.

Gilly smiled and unfolded her legs to try on the shoe.

"What you doing down there on the floor? We've got perfectly good tables and chairs for you girls to use."

Gilly looked up to find Harold Cook, shoe-room angel, standing in the doorway with his hands in the pockets of his tailored gray slacks. Harold was seventy if he was a day, but people said he'd retire when they carried his cold, stiff body out of the costume room. He'd never been a dancer himself; probably two hundred years ago he'd been a violinist with the Ballet New York orchestra. Then he'd burned his hand in a kitchen grease fire.

Part of his job was helping the men with their costumes, but most weekdays found him organizing and guarding the shoe room. A big tease, he loved to call the girls pet names like "Terminator" and "Quasimodo." Gilly had been "Tree House" since the day she'd entered the shoe room as a nervous apprentice and asked for a ladder to reach the size fives.

"Harold! I've been back in the city for two weeks now, and this is the first time I've seen you. Where've you been?"

"Home. Not feeling too spiffy." He limped into the room to peer over her shoulder. "I'll be all right. Just a little stomach ailment."

"For two weeks? That's some vicious bug." Gilly gathered up her sewing supplies and searched Harold's wrinkled mocha-skinned face.

The whites of his deep-set brown eyes looked yellowish. "Maybe you should sit down. You don't look so hot."

To her surprise, Harold nodded and dragged a straight-backed wooden chair over from one of the sewing tables against the wall. He lowered himself into it as a couple of dancers entered the room with loud laughter. "You folks let me know if I can help," he called over his shoulder.

"Okay, Harold, thanks." The two girls wandered to the far end of the room, leaving Gilly and Harold to continue their conversation.

"How was your trip overseas?" He adjusted his rimless glasses. Harold sometimes played up his New Orleans heritage, but he looked and dressed like a college professor, favoring turtlenecks, sport jackets, and loafers.

"Wonderful. I got to dance Odette again." Gilly put down the shoe and leaned back on her hands. "Have you been to Europe, Harold?"

He nodded. "Studied in Paris on a Fulbright when I was about your age." Sighing, he looked down at the shiny, wrinkled side of his right hand. "Those were the days."

"How long have you been here at BNY?"

"Since the late sixties. Could've gone back South after I burned my hand, but times being what they were ..." He smiled and shrugged.

"We couldn't do without you." Gilly suddenly sat up. "Oh! I almost forgot! I'm dancing *Nutcracker* down in Birmingham next month. Did you know Jacob Ferrar is director there?"

"Jacob Ferrar?" Harold's grizzled brows drew together. "I thought he went to Spain."

"He did. But he's been in Alabama for a few years, I believe. He asked me to tell you hello."

Harold nodded. "That's nice. How did you meet him?"

"I had a few days in Alabama before I came back to New York, and I took class with the Birmingham company. Jacob seemed to ..." Gilly paused, not sure how to describe the connection she had felt with Jacob Ferrar. That encounter in Laurel's living room had marked her. "Anyway, he remembers you with fondness. He said you introduced him to Christ?" She gingerly stuck the question mark on the end of that sentence. You never knew how introducing religion into a conversation would be greeted.

"I did." Harold's gravelly voice was equally cautious. "What else did he tell you?"

Gilly frowned. "Nothing. But he's creating a new ballet and asked me if I'd be interested in debuting the lead."

"I'm not surprised." Harold sat back. "He was one of the most creative dancers I've seen. Saw him dance a Balanchine piece at Saratoga Springs one time. Literally stop-motion on the leaps."

"He's ..." Gilly looked around, reluctant to offend any of her friends, and whispered, "Masculine. You know, athletic."

Harold's eyes twinkled. "Is he?" he teased. "Give you the warm fuzzies?"

"Oh, well. Not so much." Gilly gave a flustered laugh. She hadn't intended to get into this sort of discussion with Harold. "I just meant that I'm thinking about doing it. The ballet, I mean, if Maurice will let me."

"You'll have to approach him right. Make him think it's his idea." Harold shook his head. "He's already letting you go for *The Nutcracker*."

"I know." Gilly chewed her lip. "But originating a leading role, especially in a Christian ballet, is the chance of a lifetime."

"A *Christian* ballet? You mean like the *Prodigal Son*? We've been doing that here for years."

"No, it's more overt even than that. It's called *The Sweetest Perfume*, and it's about Mary of Bethany."

Harold pinched his lower lip thoughtfully. "Sounds like Jacob followed through with his decision. I'm glad."

"Why wouldn't he?"

A small smile curved Harold's mouth. "The good seed falls on all kinds of ground, Tree House. Some weedy, some stony, some rich with manure. You just never know."

Gilly stared up at him, wanting to ask about the circumstances of Jacob's conversion and Harold's role in it. Cole had told her very little that night in the kitchen. Said she should let Jacob tell his own stories. "That's true. Did you know I was a Christian?"

"I suspected. I watch you with the other boys and girls. You're different."

"You didn't say anything."

"Maurice doesn't like for me to bother his dancers. But I prayed for you."

Gilly smiled. "Did you? I wish I'd known. Sometimes I get lonely for my church and my Christian friends down South."

"I imagine. You can come to church with me and Flora sometime."

"That would be awesome." For some reason Gilly hadn't thought about Harold having a wife. "How about this Sunday? Sometimes I go to a fellowship that meets in the Manhattan Center Grand Ballroom. But that's a long way off to go by myself."

"Where do you live?"

"Above the Tribeca bread store on Church Street."

"Okay. That's not far from me. Flora and I will walk down to get you. We go to St. Barbara's."

"Cool!" Gilly looked at her watch. "Oops! Class starts in ten minutes. I've got to scoot." She jumped to her feet and impulsively bent to kiss Harold's cheek. "I'm so glad we got a chance to talk. You go home if you don't get to feeling better, okay?"

"Can't afford to miss any more work." Harold pushed to his feet and picked up the chair. He scowled as he spotted one of the girls in the corner rearranging shoes without permission. "Hey, there! What do you think you're doing?" Sliding a wink at Gilly, he shuffled toward the incipient scene of disaster. "No telling what kind of mess my stock got into while I was out. See you later, Tree House."

"Bye, Harold." Gilly put her sewing kit into her dance bag and hustled down the hall to the biggest studio. She greeted other dancers as she stuffed the bag into a locker, then sat down on a bench in the hall to tie her ribbons.

Dmitri Lanskov flung himself down beside her, muscular legs stretched out. He had on green nylon shorts, and Gilly noticed he had shaved his legs. She couldn't help smiling.

The Russian dancer grinned at her. "Hey, girl, you're looking good in that leotard. Is that new? Don't let anybody ever tell you not to wear red."

"Thanks, Dmitri." She'd bought the leotard full-price at the dance store on Saturday. The series of diamond-patterned cut-outs in its low back and the modest scooped front had been irresistible. Normally she didn't spend much money on work outfits, but Victoria had gone ballistic over this one—and it was the only one left in her size. She was still getting over the guilty feeling of spending money on herself. Not that her family was in the poorhouse, but Daddy had taught his daughters to be frugal. "Did you hear from Meredith during the break?" As Meredith's former partner, Dmitri was the most likely source of information about the injured dancer.

Dmitri's wide grin faded. "No, because she went home. She saw Dr. Glaasmacher, and he took her into surgery on the spot. She won't dance on that ankle for at least a year—and it may end her career. The ligaments were completely torn in two." He shuddered expressively. "Can you imagine the pain?"

"No, and I saw it happen. She wanted to go back onstage and dance on it!" Gilly tucked in the knots of her ribbons and checked to make sure the ends didn't show. She was persnickety about her knots.

"Everybody is saying it was my fault—but it wasn't! She did not land properly." Dmitri's hands circled wildly. "I'm sorry for Meredith's injury, of course, but …" He put his arm around Gilly and leaned close to her ear. "You are so much lighter, my little butterfly." He squeezed her shoulders. "We make a good pair, huh? Come on, it's time for class." He leapt to his feet.

Letting Dmitri pull her up, she followed him into the studio, her stiff new pointe shoes clopping against the floor.

As she worked the barre exercises, she watched Dianne correct

Victoria's arm position. Victoria wasn't exactly sloppy, but she had to work hard to maintain perfect position. Gilly also suspected the diet pills made her tire easily because she didn't get enough natural sleep.

Don't nag, she reminded herself. Victoria can take care of herself.

The ballet mistress looked distracted too. Things were going to be weird around here for a while. Meredith going home created a pucker in the fabric of the company. Maurice, always unpredictable and upset by the slightest variance in routine, would have to recast roles for *Nutcracker* as well as upcoming productions. He'd be a bear, which meant Dianne would be a she-cat. Oh, well, no whining over personalities. These people were perfectionists, which was part and parcel of a professional company.

Dianne walked by her, nodding to the rippling rhythm of Schumann's *Fantasie in C Major.* Unexpectedly she smiled at Gilly, her large almond-shaped dark eyes softening. "Nice," she murmured as she continued her measured pace down the line of dancers.

Gilly nearly fell off her toes. She sneaked a glance over her shoulder at Dianne's board-straight back, her neatly upswept black hair. The ballet mistress never issued compliments.

The apocalypse was indubitably on its way.

Smiling a little, she did a *battement battu.* Just went to prove you never knew when people were paying attention. Generally she didn't think about outside observation, doing the best she could to live what was in the Bible and leaving it at that. But Harold had watched her enough to know she was a Christian. *You're different.* Evidently that was a good thing. And Jacob Ferrar had gone to the trouble of looking her up, securing her for his *Nutcracker,* and requesting her for his own ballet.

That was, admittedly, very flattering. She *really, really* wanted to dance in his perfume ballet. And not just because it would be another excuse to go home. She loved it here in New York. The City was home. Or would be if she ever found a comfortable church.

No, she wanted to dance in Jacob's ballet because she was intrigued by the creator. Handsome, commanding, and adorably shy.

Lord, I want to dance in that ballet. Is that too much to ask?

"Okay, ladies, let's start that one at the top again." Jacob moved to the CD player and hit the Pause button.

The "Waltz of the Flowers" girls broke formation and glided, chattering and giggling, toward the back of the studio. The younger girls' bright blue leotards were a splash of color among the more sober colors of the older girls. Level Seven was allowed to choose the color of their leotards, as long as it was conservative and neat.

Jacob watched to make sure everyone was in place before he started the music again. Brittney Sulley dimpled at him as she slid into her spot at the last second. Frowning at her, he pressed the Play button just as a small, lumpy shadow appeared in the doorway—Yolanda Needham, costume mistress, with an I'm-not-going-away expression on her face. She held his nephew by the hand, and her bangs—spray-netted upright above her forehead in a nineties plume—fairly quivered with indignation.

Great. What had Graham done now?

All the dancers followed Jacob's progress as he hurried toward the back of the room.

Graham, looking mulish, was trying to yank his hand out of Yolanda's firm grasp. "Uncle Jacob, this lady's mean. Alls I did was practice my rubber-band gun on one of those dummies—"

"Mr. Ferrar, this child cannot stay in the costume room anymore." Yolanda's naturally red cheeks looked like vine-ripe tomatoes. "He knocked the Dew Drop costume off into a puddle of glitter paint, and it's going to take me days to get it out."

"And I finished my homework like you said, and I'm hungry!" Graham looked resentfully up at Yolanda. "When can we go home?"

Jacob laid his hand on Graham's sweaty head and gave Yolanda a placating look. He didn't want to know how the glitter paint spilled.

"Yolanda, I promise this won't happen again. He needs to sit with you just until we finish this rehearsal. Thirty minutes ought to do it." He certainly hoped it wouldn't happen again. Reid had some kind of stomach virus, and Cynthia didn't want to expose Graham. But Jacob would almost rather risk bubonic plague than brave Yolanda's disapproving glare.

"Why don't you let him sit in a corner in here and watch? Or let the girls out in the hall play with him?" Yolanda could be crotchety, but she hardly ever directly flouted Jacob's wishes. Graham must have gotten on her last nerve.

Jacob glanced over his shoulder at the dancers taking in this highly entertaining confrontation. Alexandra had started edging her way around the room toward him. If he lost face here he'd never get it back. Folding his arms, he stared down at Graham. "You owe Mrs. Yolanda an apology, sir. You were a guest in her space, and you didn't obey house rules."

Graham's mouth turned down, and tears formed in his big brown eyes. "I'm sorry, Uncle Jacob. I didn't mean to shoot the dummy's head off."

Jacob managed to keep his expression stern. "Tell Yolanda."

Graham sighed. "I'm sorry, Miss Yolanda," he muttered to his feet. "I'll fix your dummy if you want me to."

"It's not the dummy, son, it's the costume. That thing cost hundreds of dollars and took me months to make." Yolanda let go of Graham's hand and awkwardly patted him on the shoulder. "But it'll be okay." She speared Jacob with Witch of Endor eyes. "But he can't come back in there while I'm working on the principals' costumes. Especially when the performance is in two weeks!"

Alexandra came from behind Jacob and bent down, hands on knees, to Graham's level. "Come with me, buddy. You can hold my car keys while I'm dancing."

Graham returned her bright smile with a skeptical frown. "What do I need car keys for? I can't drive."

Jacob could hardly blame Graham for his lack of enthusiasm.

Bringing Alexandra to church had been a mistake. She always talked to Graham in that annoying blend of baby talk and scolding familiarity. He'd been trying to backtrack to an appropriate director-dancer relationship ever since. He gave Alexandra a back-off glance. "No, you have to concentrate. Graham's going out in the hall to sit with Mrs. Sulley."

"Come on, Mr. Ferrar, let him stay." A chorus of feminine pleading rose from the other girls. "He won't distract us. He's so cute!"

Graham looked around at all the pretty girls, reflected multiple times by the three walls of mirrors. It visibly registered on his face that he was the complete center of attention. "Could I watch the rehearsal, Uncle Jacob? I promise I'll be good."

Jacob hesitated. This was one situation where a graceful retreat might ultimately win the war. "All right. You can stay—if you'll let Yolanda take care of your weapon. No guns allowed in the studio."

Actually Jacob wasn't wild about guns at all, but Poppa had made it for Graham last weekend in his hobby shop. "The boy needs some masculine toys, Jacob." Poppa's significant look said plainer than day that he was worried about his great-grandson turning into some kind of sissy under Jacob's influence.

Jacob had gritted his teeth and let Graham keep the wooden clothespin-loading pistol and the accompanying Wal-Mart bag of rubber bands. Hundreds of rubber bands that stung like wasps when they popped one on the neck.

Fortunately Graham was for the moment more interested in mirrors than mayhem. "Here you go, Miss Yolanda." He handed the gun over, adding seriously, "Poppa says not to shoot your eye out."

Yolanda snorted, holstered the gun in her monogrammed ruffled apron pocket, and disappeared before anybody else could saddle her with unwanted little boys or their toys.

Jacob took Graham firmly by the shoulder, found him a spot under a portable barre against the left studio wall, and threatened him on pain of death not to move a muscle.

And he didn't. For at least fifteen minutes.

Jacob looked up in the middle of the Marzipan dance to find his nephew on his feet copying the steps of Kyle Blankenship, the oldest of the company's male dancers, with astonishing accuracy. Kyle, a gifted high school senior, was dancing the role of the Nutcracker for the first time this year.

Resigned to the inevitable, Jacob let the dance continue. When the music ended, he had to smile as Graham mimicked Kyle's deep bow. "Come here, Graham." He beckoned. "We're finished for the night." He shut down the CD player and motioned the girls toward him for wrap-up and rehearsal reminders. "Fine job, Kyle. You'll steal the show."

The teenager flushed at Jacob's rare praise and performed a little jigging step. "Thanks, Mr. Ferrar. My whole family's coming on opening night."

"Good. Make sure you get tickets early. They'll be hard to come by."

"Yes, sir."

Jacob's comments to the group were brief and to the point. "Be here tomorrow night at five for class, then we'll rehearse until seven thirty. If you miss any rehearsals between now and opening night, you'll give up your spot to your understudy."

There was a murmur of horror at the very idea as the group dispersed.

Alexandra was at his elbow, smiling up at him. "I'm going to stop by Quizno's for a salad on the way home. Why don't you and Graham come too?"

Graham latched onto Jacob's leg. "I'd rather have a Happy Meal. Can we get a Happy Meal, Uncle Jacob?"

Jacob looked down at Graham, trying to ignore the hopeful batting of Alexandra's extravagant lashes. "No, we're going home. I've got soup and salad greens there."

"Oh, pooh." Alexandra pulled the elastic out of her hair, releasing its blonde fullness to float around her bare shoulders. She ran her fingers through it, shoving it out of her face. "My roommate never waits on me, and I hate to eat alone." After an awkward pause, during which Jacob took Graham's hand and tugged him toward the exit, Alexandra puffed out a sigh and followed. "Okay, I can take a hint."

Jacob gave her a worried look out of the corner of his eye but knew better than to say anything. He smiled at Graham. "You can get your gun from Yolanda. But don't shoot anybody or anything on the way back!" he shouted as Graham took off running down the hall, dodging dancers and volunteers along the way.

Alexandra touched his arm. "Jacob, you spend entirely too much time with nobody but that little boy. People will get the wrong idea about you."

He froze. "Is that a threat?"

"No, of course not!" Her pretty mouth fell open. "It's just that ... well, I watched you at church that day I went with you. I thought maybe you wouldn't be so standoffish away from here. But it's almost like you're afraid for people to get to know you. I like you — or at least I think I would." She looked around, apparently to make sure they wouldn't be overheard. "There must be a reason you chose me to teach the older girls' classes this fall."

"I chose you to teach because you're a fine dancer." Jacob made himself be blunt. He couldn't afford to be misunderstood. "There was nothing personal in it."

"Ouch." She blinked. "Well, just remember that I'm a friend if you need one." Alexandra smiled, if a bit shakily, as Graham came running toward them from the costume room. "So when is our prima ballerina coming down from New York to grace us with her presence again?"

Jacob accepted the change of subject, grateful for Alexandra's Teflon self-esteem. He couldn't afford to make her angry enough to quit. "Second week of December. Just in time for opening night." He laughed as Graham tore past them in a beeline for the front door. "Come on, I'll walk you to your car," he said to soften his earlier rejection.

She looked pleased. "Thanks. I have to admit the Kincade girl was good. I'd wondered why the board decided to go to the expense of hiring outside people when we have such great talent right here in Birmingham." She directed a coy look up at him. "Rebecca's going to be super as Dew Drop."

"The professionals bring in crowds," he said as offhandedly as he could. "I've wanted to meet Gilly Kincade for quite a while. She's going to be a major star."

"Oh, well." A little moue drew Alexandra's mouth together. "A crowd in New York is exactly like a crowd in Birmingham. The ones down here may even have better appreciation for the arts. I'm sure I'd never have been happy up there with all that smog and congestion and bad weather."

Jacob held the front door open for her. Maybe she'd convinced herself that her failed audition at BNY two years ago had never happened. But she did have a point. "It wasn't one of my favorite parts of living in the city."

"Oh, I'd forgotten you danced for BNY. You never said why you left." Another coy look as Alexandra fished in her dance bag for her keys.

"I had a yen to dance in Spain." He caught Graham just before he dashed into the parking lot. "Come here, lad. We're ready to go home."

"I'd like to dance in Europe someday." Alexandra laughed. "Shoot, I'd like to *see* Europe someday. Can you believe I've never even been to London?" She unlocked her Lexus. "Sometime you'll have to tell me about it."

The woman never gave up. Suddenly disarmed, Jacob grinned at her. "Sometime. Good night, Alexandra. Enjoy your salad. Let's go, Gray."

She wrinkled her elegant nose and waved as she got into the car. It purred to life, then backed out with a jerk.

Jacob shook his head. He'd spent his entire life working around women — except for a few years at Harrow — but still found them a completely different species.

He buckled Graham into his booster seat, then got into the driver's seat. He looked at his nephew. "If I buy you a Happy Meal, can we put that gun up on the closet shelf until we go back to the farm?"

Seven

"Which part of your family is coming for Thanksgiving next week?" Victoria flung herself backwards onto Gilly's bed, sending the teddy bear Tucker gave her for Valentine's Day tumbling to the carpeted floor. "I can't keep track."

Gilly picked up the bear and poked the red felt heart on his chest. "Hug me and pretend I'm Tucker" it said. She thought about shoving him under the bed, but she liked him for his own fuzzy merits, despite Tucker's deficiencies as a boyfriend.

"Laurel and her husband and Mom and Dad." She hugged the bear and pretended it was her father. "I can't wait to see them. I'm so homesick for my family."

"I don't know why. You talk to one of them nearly every day."

Victoria couldn't help being snide. Everyone in her family was in the medical profession and had no time for anything but work. That was the theory, anyway. "I know, but it's not the same as being there.

The kids are so much fun, especially the three littlest ones. You never know what they're going to say, and we always have music."

"Gilly, please." Victoria laughed. "You dance with the Ballet New York orchestra every night."

Gilly shook her head. "You should hear our family music. Everybody plays an instrument, and it's just crazy when we get together. Cole has a banjo, and Parker plays the bagpipes. Me, I don't play anything but the kazoo, but still ... Can you imagine?"

"Unfortunately, yes, I can." Victoria shuddered. "Nicholas and I are going to hear Joshua Bell next Tuesday on our day off. He'll be at Radio City."

"That's nice."

"What's the matter?"

"Nothing." Gilly shrugged. "Who's paying?"

Victoria sat up, looking fierce. "What difference does it make? I wanted to go, I have the money, so I offered to pay."

Gilly stared at Victoria for a moment. She should just keep her mouth shut. She looked away and said brightly, "Never mind. Bell is an amazing violinist. I hope you enjoy it."

"What? *What*, Gilly? I don't know why I hang out with you. You disapprove of everything I do. You religious southern girls give me a twitch. The guy's supposed to pay for everything, and God forbid he actually show physical affection. Well, hello, this is the twenty-first century—I'm a feminist and proud of it. I own myself, and nobody's buying me, you hear that?"

Stunned, Gilly opened and shut her mouth. "Victoria. I didn't criticize you."

"No, but it's on your face every time I mention Nicholas. I know you don't approve of him, but you're not my mother—not that my mother gives a flip what I do, but that's beside the point."

Maybe that *was* the point. Gilly fumbled for words, praying. "I didn't mean to hurt you. I worry about you because I care for you."

"Well, care about somebody else. I'm sick of it."

Gilly got up on her knees and studied Victoria's vivid, classically oval face. It was tense with anger, the dark brown eyes narrowed. "You don't mean that. What's going on with you?"

To her astonishment, Victoria burst into violent, racking sobs. "I'm p-pregnant!"

All the air went out of Gilly's lungs. Along with all ability to put words into sentences. Finally she got out a strangled, "Huh?"

"You h-heard me." Victoria bent over to grip fistfuls of Gilly's comforter, grinding her face into the fabric. "Oh, God, what am I going to do?"

Pregnant? Beautiful, independent Victoria?

Gilly lunged toward the bed and flung her arms around her friend's heaving body. If ever the words "I told you so" had burned her tongue, it was now. "Oh, Victoria, I'm so sorry."

"I don't want a b-baby! I wanted to be the Sugar Plum Fairy. Then you got it—not one performance but *four.* It's so not fair, Gilly. Why is life not fair?"

Gilly had her own speculations about that, but of course Victoria was in no frame of mind for answers to rhetorical questions. "I don't know," she murmured into the top of Victoria's head. "What are you thinking about … you know, doing about it? Have you been to see a counselor?" She wasn't naïve enough to assume Victoria would either get married or give the baby up for adoption. As she'd said, it was the twenty-first century.

"No! I haven't told anybody but you. I've suspected for nearly a week, but I just peed on the stick this morning. It was bright, flaming flamingo pink, Gilly! No question."

"Have you told Nicholas?" Fine father that jerk would make.

"Nobody but you," Victoria repeated. "I may not tell him at all. He doesn't like fat girls."

"You're not fat! Besides, pregnant isn't fat. It's just …" What did she know about pregnancy, except from watching her sisters go through it? "Anyhow, you've got to tell him. It's his baby too."

Victoria was silent.

"Victoria? It's Nicholas's baby, isn't it?"

"I'm pretty sure it is. There was that one time with Ian."

Gilly thought her eyeballs might pop out of her head. "Ian! You had sex with Ian? I thought you didn't even like him! He's too short for you!"

That was ridiculous, of course, but Victoria took her seriously. She lifted her tear-streaked face and scowled at Gilly. "But he's got a great body, and I know he's a hick, but he treats me like a lady. We got drunk one night at a sponsor party, and one thing led to another." She seemed to realize Gilly was incapable of response. "Oh, I knew you'd be judgmental." She grabbed Tucker's teddy bear and backed toward the headboard of the bed, clasping him to her chest. "There's no use asking what *you'd* do. You'd never get yourself into a spot like this. I wasn't going to tell *anybody*, even you. I was just going to get rid of it. If I don't, my career is over."

Gilly bounced to her feet, horrified. "You can't do that! Lots of dancers have babies and come back. Look at Iliana Poiroux—"

"Who is married to the director-in-chief! Gilly, don't be stupid. This isn't a good time for me. I'm working so hard to get noticed. Maurice would replace me and forget all about me within nine months or a year, or whatever it took. And girls our age can't raise babies and dance the grueling schedule we have, not without a husband or a nanny or something."

"Okay, well, what about—" Gilly swallowed. "You could marry Nicholas."

"Nicholas is a perfectly good boyfriend, but he's not husband material. You've always been right about that." Victoria's mouth hardened. "And don't talk to me about adoption. I'm not getting fat as a whale for nine months and having nothing to show for it."

Gilly shook her head helplessly. "Don't do anything hasty ... please. Just think about it for a week or two. I'll pray for you to know the right thing to do."

"I've been praying," Victoria muttered, looking away. "I already know the right thing to do."

"God would never tell you to kill your own baby." Gilly wanted to howl with outrage.

Victoria scrambled off the bed. "Don't throw your narrow religious beliefs at me, you self-righteous—" She bit off an insulting word and hurled the bear at the headboard. "I knew I shouldn't have said anything. If you tell Nicholas or Maurice or anybody else, you'll be sorry." Her dramatic dark eyebrows pinched together. "Do you hear me?"

Gilly wrapped her arms around herself. "I hear you, but I'm not sure you're listening to me."

Victoria grunted and flung herself out of the room. A few seconds later, Gilly heard the apartment door slam.

She walked into the living room and dead-bolted the door. Then leaned against it feeling as if she'd been beaten up.

But how must Victoria feel? Alone and scared and clearly full of rampant hormones. Not to mention a little alien body growing in her womb. Without God.

The tragedy buckled her knees. She dropped down, face into the carpet, and poured out her worry and grief.

On Thanksgiving Day, Jacob sat in his grandfather's recliner with Graham in his lap, both of them still in pajamas. The Macy's Thanksgiving Day parade was blaring on TV, and Nonna was puttering with sweet potatoes and turkey and giblet gravy in the kitchen. Whatever she was cooking smelled like heaven and made his stomach rumble with anticipation.

Bouncing, Graham pointed at the marching band strutting down Broadway with the Snoopy float in the background. "Look, Uncle Jacob—look at that big instrument! What's that called?"

"That's a sousaphone. Named after John Phillip Sousa, the first conductor of the Marine Band."

"Is that the Marine Band?"

Jacob squinted at the glittery sign held by two leggy flag girls.

"No. It looks like the Satsuma High School Marching Band. They're from Alabama." If he wasn't mistaken, Satsuma was close to Mobile, where Gilly Kincade had grown up.

"We're in Alabama!" Graham leaned back against Jacob's chest. "I want to play one of those things, a sousaphone, when I get big. After I dance in *The Nutcracker* and shoot a ten-point buck."

Jacob rested his chin on top of Graham's head. If only his own life goals were that clear. Yawning, he glanced at his laptop on the TV tray, where he'd been working on notes for the perfume ballet late into the night. He'd done some research into commentaries about the biblical accounts of Mary of Bethany. It was exciting to have a creative project and time to think about it. He'd been looking forward to spending these days off at his grandparents' farm.

He wished he had somebody to bounce some questions and ideas off of. Nonna and Poppa couldn't care less about ballet, and he didn't want to bring Wendy into it. Her father was afflicted with Alzheimer's, and she had to spend all her free time at the nursing home. There was Alexandra, he supposed, but he was still trying to keep her at arm's length.

He had to admit, the person he really wanted to talk to was Gillian Kincade. And wouldn't that be a crazy thing to do on Thanksgiving Day? Call her up and interrupt her family time?

Deliberately he put the idea out of his head. He needed to focus on Graham.

"Look, here comes Santa Claus!" Jacob chuckled at Graham's squeal of excitement.

And then he saw her. The camera zoomed in on the audience and caught her, jumping up and down behind the sleigh float. The flaming hair was stuffed under a Christmas green knit hat, and she had on a bright red coat with a striped scarf. She looked like a pink-nosed elf. Beside her were Laurel and Cole McGaughan and her parents. He looked for the boyfriend and didn't see him.

"Ow! You're hugging too hard!" Graham squirmed.

"Sorry." Relaxing, Jacob picked up his cell phone lying on the lamp table and thumbed through the phone book menu. When he hit the Ks—he filed numbers alphabetically by last name—he scrolled down to *Kincade, Gillian,* and pressed the Call button. He'd gotten her number from Cole a couple of weeks ago.

He watched Poppa's thirty-seven-inch TV screen. By now the camera had moved on to a couple of snowmen waddling along behind Santa's sleigh.

She surprised him by answering on the second ring. "Hello?" She wouldn't have recognized his number.

"You look cold," he said. "You should hop on the sleigh."

"Jacob! Where are you?"

He laughed. He wished he could see her looking around for him. "I just saw you on TV. How did you know it was me?"

"The accent—I'm good with voices. Laurel!" she squealed. "They just put us on TV!" She was laughing. "What are you doing, Jacob?"

"I'm at my grandparents'. Planning to tuck into some turkey and stuffing and sweet potatoes here in a bit."

"Oh! I'm so jealous. Nobody makes good sweet potatoes up here. We're going to Carmine's for dinner."

"Ho. Pricey stuff."

"Mom loves it. First place she wants to go when she comes back to the City."

"Your parents lived there before?"

"Just Mom. Believe it or not, she sang with the Met, back in the day. Daddy's a born-and-raised southern boy, hardly stepped foot outside Alabama. Hold on, Jacob. What?"

Jacob clearly heard someone say, "Who're you talking to in the middle of a Thanksgiving parade? Come on, let's go, or we'll miss our reservations."

"Listen," he said quickly, "I'll call you later. I wanted to talk to you about the ballet. When's a good time?"

"It's Jacob Ferrar," she said to one of her companions, then sighed.

"All right. Jacob, I really have to go. I can't hear you very well anyway. Can I call you tonight? How late is too late?"

"I'm a night owl, up 'til midnight most nights. This is my cell, so anytime's good."

"Okay." There was something breathless in her tone. "Jacob?" She paused, and he briefly heard the blare of a band, then an announcer's voice, before she apparently shielded the receiver with her hand. "You surprised me," she whispered, "but I'm really glad you called."

"Me too." Smiling, he ended the call and laid the phone on the table.

Graham was leaning back looking up into his face. He reached up and patted Jacob's stubbly cheek. "Are you happy, Uncle Jacob?"

"Yes." He kissed Graham's forehead. "I'm thankful because it's Thanksgiving."

"Are you thankful to be my daddy?"

Caught completely off guard, Jacob stared into Graham's warm chocolate eyes. Tears stung the back of his nose and threatened to spill over. "You bet I am," he said hoarsely as he hugged his nephew. If anybody had told him three hundred sixty-five days ago he'd be anybody's daddy, he would've recommended a drug test. But at this moment he could almost forget about green eyes and red hair and an angelic dancer's body in a rush of love for this little human being.

Almost, but not quite. Jacob Ferrar, he thought, must be a very shallow person.

Gilly's tiny apartment was wall-to-wall people, and it was going to be a miracle if she found privacy to talk to Jacob. Because of the Christmas rush, the family's favorite hotels had been full, so she'd given her bedroom over to her parents. Laurel took the sofa and Cole had bedded down on a sleeping bag in front of the TV. It was a good thing Mary Layne had offered to keep Kate and Rosie. At eleven o'clock, dressed in warm-up pants and a long-sleeved black "Grinch" T-shirt, Gilly padded into the kitchen to hunt up a mug of herbal tea.

While the water circled on its plate in the microwave, she sat down at the dinette with her feet tucked up and flipped open her cell phone. There was a ridiculous flutter in her stomach as she found her list of recent calls and dialed the number with the Alabama area code. Cole had teased her mercilessly after Jacob called this afternoon, but she'd kept her cool and made swooning motions to play along—which made him give up faster. In her heart of hearts, the swooning wasn't far from the truth. Jacob Ferrar's deep, British inflection plucked an unfamiliar string on her heart.

He answered after one ring. "Gilly. How are you?"

"Stuffed like a turkey." Lord, she had to get rid of that breathless gush. She took a breath. "Carmine's is amazing."

"I hope you're not ignoring your family. This can wait until they've left."

"No, they're all in bed, even Cole." She laughed. "Guess he's getting old. The parade wore everybody out."

"Everyone but you." He chuckled. "You're a little firecracker, I bet."

"I've always been ... energetic." She paused, trying to picture him. "Are you still at your grandparents' house? Where do they live?"

"Alabaster, about halfway between Birmingham and Montgomery. Yes, we're still here."

"You and your nephew? What's his name again?"

"Graham." There was something funny, bemused in his tone.

"What is it?"

He hesitated. "He called me 'Daddy' for the first time today."

"Wow. That's big."

"Very big. I've had him a little more than a year."

The microwave beeped, and Gilly got up to put a tea bag in the mug of steaming water. She stood at the counter dunking it, sock feet in a comfortable third position. Her dad's snores roared out of the bedroom, making her want to laugh. Poor Mom. "He's a lucky little boy."

"People keep saying that. But I'm not so sure. I'm awfully ignorant."

"Anybody who can run a ballet company can raise a child. Especially since you're a Christian." Gilly wished she could see his face. "The Bible is a great instruction manual."

There was another little space of silence. "Thanks. I needed to hear that." Jacob cleared his throat. "But I didn't call to whine about my personal life."

"I called *you.* Feel free to whine."

"Nevertheless—"

"So tell me about your sister. Graham's mom."

Jacob didn't answer for a moment. He seemed to be a very skittish conversationalist. "Lily was a teacher, a college English teacher."

"That's cool." Gilly tried to be encouraging. "Older or younger than you?"

"Older. She would be thirty-two. I'm twenty-eight," he added before she could ask.

"Oh." Gilly hesitated. "How did she die?"

"Uterine cancer." His voice was heavy with sadness. "Once she was diagnosed, she didn't last long. Three months. And she didn't know the Lord ..."

"Oh, Jacob, I'm sorry. But maybe she changed her mind before she died. We can't know for sure. And she left you Graham. She must have had tremendous respect for you and your faith. I'm assuming her husband is dead too?"

"Yes, he was killed in a plane crash when Graham was only four. I came home for the funeral and wound up staying to help out."

"You'd been in Spain?" Gilly disposed of the tea bag and sat down again with her tea.

"Mmm." Gilly could hear Jacob open a cabinet and rattle dishes. "I was ready to come home by then. Spain was great, but I missed the U.S. Lily needed me, and it was time to reconnect with my grandparents."

"What about your parents? Are they in the picture?"

"They're career diplomats—extraordinary and plenipotentiary." Jacob laughed. "Retired, but living in Paris now."

"Paris, huh." It all sounded very dysfunctional. "But you said you went to school in England?"

"We were posted all over the U.K., but mostly England. My background is sort of strange, which is why I want to make Graham's life as normal as possible." He paused. "How did we get onto this? Didn't you want to talk about the ballet?"

"Of course I do. But I wanted to get to know you a little better too." Sounded like she had another artistic freak on her hands. Like Tucker. *Yumpin' yiminy. Let me outta here.* "So how's the work on the ballet going?"

"I've got all this stuff in my head and no place to put it. It's difficult without dancers capable of pulling off what I want to do."

"Can't you try things out with the principals in your company?"

"There are … complications." Jacob's chuckle had an awkward note. "My best soloist has this … crush on me, and I don't want to encourage it. I know that sounds incredibly egotistical, but—"

"Oh, I can imagine it." Gilly sucked in a breath. She must sound like a stage-door groupie herself. "I mean, you know what I mean. It happens all the time. You're the guy in power, and if you're not married or hooked up or anything, girls are bound to get ideas."

"Yes, that's it," he said, sounding relieved. "It's only the power thing. Nothing personal."

Right, Jacob. Keep telling yourself that. Gilly smiled to herself. He hadn't corrected her assumption about the lack of a girlfriend, but there was no way to ask about it without sounding like she was fishing. So she let it lie. "When I come down for *Nutcracker*, maybe we can squeeze in a little time to work on *Perfume*. Would you like to do that?"

"Absolutely. Here's what I want to talk to you about. I've been thinking about the relationship between Mary and her sister and brother. She seems to have been quite the rebel. And lots of scholars think she was the sinful woman of Luke 7."

"I did a little reading on the subject too." Gilly set down her mug and hugged her knees to her chest. "It makes sense to me. Unlikely there'd be two different women doing exactly the same thing recorded in the Bible."

"So she was the spoiled brat little sister who did her own thing, then came to faith in Christ and changed her ways."

"Very likely. I can so identify with her. Won't this be—" Gilly looked up as the pocket door into the kitchen opened and Laurel stuck her head in. She put her hand over the phone. "Oops. Did I wake you up?"

Laurel pulled her lacy bathrobe together. "I can't believe you're still up after such a long day. You have to dance tomorrow, Gilly."

"All right, Mom," Gilly teased. "Go back to bed. I'll get off the phone in just a minute."

"'Night, Gil." Shaking her head, Laurel backed out and slid the door closed again.

"Are we in trouble?" Jacob sounded amused.

Gilly took her hand off the receiver. "Not exactly," she said, lowering her voice, "but I should probably go soon. This apartment is very small, and everybody's trying to sleep. In fact, I'm surprised you can't hear my dad snoring all the way from Alabama."

"I thought it was construction."

Gilly laughed softly. He did have a sense of humor. "Where did you live when you were in New York?"

"I had a studio on Broadway, right across from Lincoln Center."

"Ah. I was rooming with another girl near there, but when Cole decided to give up his loft in Tribeca, I took the lease. I'm much happier living by myself, even though it's a little distance."

"That surprises me. You seem to be a people person."

"Yes, but I need downtime too. In fact, I can be kind of a hermit."

"Really ..." There was a short, reluctant silence. "I suppose I'd best let you get some sleep. Are you dancing tomorrow?"

"Yes. I'm Lead Marzipan for opening night. And I'll be Sugar

Plum four performances in December." There was no need to add that, but she wanted to impress him. Silly girl.

"Ah. That's great. Congratulations."

His warmth pleased her. "I bet you danced Cavalier?"

"I did," he said, then added hurriedly, "I really have to go. It's been great talking to you. I'll look forward to seeing you next month. Good luck tomorrow."

"Thanks. See you then." She closed the phone and stared at it, perplexed by the abrupt ending of their conversation. What had she said to shut him down so suddenly?

The puzzle of Jacob Ferrar grew more confusing every time she talked to him.

Eight

Jacob had enjoyed his Monday-night anatomy class, but it was a good thing there were only two more meetings before the end of the semester. He was burning his candle at both ends in order to keep up with the reading; memorize neurological, skeletal, and muscular maps; and stay awake during breaks in rehearsals.

Though he usually took advantage of the chance to talk to other students after class, tonight he left the building by a side door. If he hurried, he could spend an hour or so in the studio working on the perfume ballet. Earlier in the day Tucker had emailed him an MP3 file with three new songs. Well, technically, a song had words, and all three of these were instrumental. Jacob couldn't wait to listen to them without distractions and begin to imagine the choreography.

Heading for the Jaguar, which he'd left parked in an out-of-the-way lot, he pulled out his phone. He'd already called Gilly twice since Thanksgiving, compelled to take his creative difficulties to a young woman who took his theological questions seriously but somehow made him laugh at himself before he could get neurotic. Her faith, deep and strong, fused out of a lifelong relationship with Jesus, simply stunned him with its purity and practicality.

The more he got to know her, the more he felt like running to catch up. So he'd bought a copy of *Ragamuffin Gospel* because she recommended it and begun to wade through it during his devotional time. He wasn't much of a reader in general, but this book spoke to him and made him think deeply.

She answered on the first ring, just as he unlocked the Jag. "Jacob!" She was panting.

"Hullo there." He settled behind the wheel and cranked the car. "What are you doing?"

"Running behind my neighbor's dog. Ellen had an emergency trip to the corner for diapers, and her biggest baby needed a—" She broke off to pant some more. "Well, I wouldn't call this walking. Hey, Rocky—slow down, big boy. Heel!"

Jacob laughed and pulled out of the parking lot. "Good day in rehearsal?"

"Yeah, the usual routine—but oh, Jacob, I never get tired of it. Hey, the casting list is up for Christmas week. I've got Sugar Plum on Thursday. You'll be done with your *Nutcracker* by then ..." She paused, a different tension in her voice.

He'd told her he might fly up and watch her dance. No, he'd said he *would.* And then he'd remembered why he'd promised himself to stay away from New York ballet. The Bible said to flee temptation. He didn't know Gilly well enough to explain; besides he wanted her to think well of him.

"Jacob? Are you still there?"

"Yes, I'm ..." Change the subject. "I'm looking forward to the end of the semester. I like my anatomy class, but I'm not getting much sleep. And I'm looking forward to having more time for the perfume ballet."

If she was disappointed, she covered it. "How's it going?"

"Tucker sent me MP3s for some new songs. They're amazing."

"Yep, he's quite the composer." There was a funny note in her voice. "He used to send songs to me."

How many ways was he going to step wrong in this conversation? Besides, he didn't want to talk about Tucker McGaughan. "Anyway," he said as he got on the interstate, "I'm headed to the studio to work out some ideas for the funeral scene. I thought of using lengths of black silk for the girls to work with."

To his relief, she responded enthusiastically, and he kept her talking until he reached the studio. By that time she'd circled back to her neighbor's apartment. "Jacob, I've got to deliver Rocky to his mommy, so I'd better go." She hesitated. "It's always fun to hear from you. You can call anytime."

"Yes, I want to talk to you about the book you told me about. I've really enjoyed it."

"I'm glad." She paused, and he could hear the dog panting in the background. The sound of a car whizzing past her. The blare of a horn. "So … good night, Jacob."

"Good night. I'll call you again." He didn't want to hang up.

"Okay." She was still there. Finally she laughed. "You hang up first."

"No, you." Jacob was generally not a silly person, but she made him giddy.

He could hear the smile in her voice. "What a dictator. You're too used to giving orders."

"Yes, I am. So hang up the phone, tell Rocky good night, and get some rest."

"All right," she sighed. "Bye, Jacob."

Hearing the connection end, he closed the phone and got out of the car in front of the studio. When listening to a woman breathe became the epitome of joy, it was time to get counseling.

During the next week and a half, Jacob hardly had time to breathe himself, much less worry about any real or imagined awkwardness between himself and Gilly. This morning he'd gotten caught in traffic on his way to drop Graham off at school and found himself fifteen minutes later than he'd meant to be for the first school performance of *Nutcracker*.

In the Performing Arts Center parking lot he found a slot and slammed on the brakes, grabbed his duffel out of the backseat, and ran for the backstage door. Relieved to find it unlocked, he hurried down the hall and reached the dressing rooms, where the sound of voices and laughter echoed off the concrete walls and floor. Wendy could run the show without him if she had to, but he still felt responsible.

He tapped on the door of the boys' dressing room and stuck his head in. Kyle Blankenship's mother was helping him fasten the red velvet Nutcracker jacket. "How's it going, mate? Are you ready?"

Kyle grinned at Jacob in the mirror, the circles of rouge on his cheeks glowing like stoplights. "Yes, sir. These little kids always go crazy over *The Nutcracker*. I remember the first time I saw it."

"Me too. I was in London at the time." Jacob smiled at Karen Blankenship. "Thanks for helping with the costumes. Yolanda's been a bear lately."

"Oh, I can deal with Yolanda," Karen said, backing off to critically survey her handiwork. "This costume needs to be retired after this year, though. The frogs are rotten, and it stinks."

"I'll put it on the list." Jacob backed out of the room before anything else could be added to his already stretched budget. He passed the girls' room on the way to the auditorium and only stopped when something crashed against the other side of the door. Frowning, he knocked; Kyle's older sister Rebecca appeared in the opening. He glanced at the plastic Marzipan flute in her hand. "Everyone okay in there?"

Rebecca's blue eyes, highlighted with exaggerated eyeliner and glitter, were wide. "Brittney Sulley just threw this across the room."

Jacob frowned. "What on earth?" He generally let Wendy handle company interpersonal drama, but Brittney Sulley had a reputation for creating far-reaching waves.

Rebecca lowered her voice to a whisper. "Miss Wendy took her out of the performance and replaced her with India Raintree."

Jacob's head began to throb. "Why?"

"Well ..." Rebecca looked around and came into the hallway, closing the door behind her. "She was pitching a fit about the mouse costume. Her face doesn't show."

Jacob had heard that one before. "She knew that when she signed the contract. I'm sure you didn't whine a few years ago when *you* were a mouse."

Rebecca's mischievous smile lit her face. "When I was fourteen, I was happy to have my face covered up."

Jacob sighed. This sort of scene could not be tolerated. "Tell her to come here."

He could hear young feminine voices cooing and squealing on the other side of the door as Rebecca slipped back inside. A few moments later, Brittney jerked open the door and came out. Her hair was scraped up into a knot on top of her head, emphasizing the freckles on her blotchy, tear-streaked face. He almost felt sorry for her. Humility was a tough lesson.

"What is the meaning of this?" he demanded, hardening his heart.

She hunched her shoulders. "I worked hard to learn that stupid dance. It's not fair to take me out now."

"Did you or did you not just throw that prop that Yolanda spent hours making?"

"I did, but—"

"Then remove that costume and give it to India."

"Mr. Ferrar! All I did was tell Wendy what I thought about this hideous thing." With a moue of disgust, Brittney looked down at the pointed plastic face of the mask in her hands. "Mama says I ought to at least be a flower. Their costumes are so pretty." She plucked at the side of her shapeless gray velour shift.

"Brittney, we all have to pay our dues."

She scowled. "Alexandra didn't. She says she went straight to being a snowflake."

Jacob lifted a hand. "Nobody said being a dancer was fair. Being a member of the company is a great privilege, and it's the director's job to assign roles for the best production we can put together. Since you don't want your role, your understudy will take it. If you continue to argue, this will be the last *Nutcracker* you perform in Birmingham."

Brittney gasped. "But you can't do that! My grandma came all the way from Chunchula to watch me dance."

"I can and I will." He looked at her as Nanny Penny had looked at him on many an occasion. "And you will cease these histrionics immediately."

"But I can't help the way I feel," Brittney wailed. "I was only telling Wendy how I—"

"Dancing is acting, telling a story. You must control your facial expressions as well as your body. A true ballerina is able to make others feel joy, even when she is sad on the inside."

Brittney stared up at him, a mulish, calculating expression in her reddened eyes. "If I shut up, can I be a flower next year?"

"There are no guarantees," he said with forced callousness, though he kept his tone kind. "I'll choose the best cast available. Give the costume to India. You may watch the performance from the wings or you may go home. It's your choice."

"Can I dance this weekend?"

"That's up to Miss Wendy."

"It's not fair," Brittney blurted again, but when he turned to go, she said quickly, "Okay. I'll stay and watch, but my parents aren't going to be happy."

Jacob looked over his shoulder. "Tell everyone I want them backstage in fifteen minutes," he said calmly.

Trying to ignore the curl of disaster licking at the lining of his stomach, he spent ten minutes with the sound and lighting manager, then checked in with the music director. Last night's dress rehearsal had proceeded with the usual misplaced props and lighting glitches, but apparently all issues had been resolved overnight. His well-trained and conscientious staff made his job on performance days mostly a matter of encouragement and soothing the ruffled nerves of hormone-laden teenagers.

The auditorium was beginning to fill as he pushed through the backstage door. He could hear the roar of children out of school for their annual field trip, overlaid by adults trying to keep order. Over the next thirty minutes, several thousand excited second graders would pile in. At curtain time, his public relations director, Stephanie MacDowell, would hold a scripted conversation with Mrs. Jimenez, president of the Birmingham Arts Council, about the county-wide student art contest related to the performance. They would call Jacob in to announce the top three winners.

As he ducked through the layers of dark velvet curtains, he patted the breast pocket of his jacket, in which he'd tucked the envelope containing the winners' names. He was almost as excited about awarding the nutcracker prizes as he was about the ballet itself.

He jumped as a soft hand rested on his sleeve. "Jacob? What are you smiling about?"

It was dark in this curtained corner, but he'd know Alexandra's expensive scent anywhere. As his eyes adjusted, the white accents in her Marzipan costume glowed. Alarm bells jangled as her hand slid up to his shoulder.

"Nothing." He stepped back, forcing her hand to fall. "Why aren't you with the little girls? I need you for crowd control."

She linked her fingers together gracefully at her waist. "Wendy and Rebecca have it covered. I thought you might want someone to pray with before the performance."

He looked down at her, wary. She looked like a delectable piece of candy, blonde and fragile as spun sugar. And just about as good for him. "That's sweet of you, Alex. But I need to gather the troops together for the usual pep talk. Come on, let's go."

Before he could move, she snagged his arm. "Wait a minute. There's something wrong with the catch on the back of this halter." She turned her back, bare almost to the waist, silken and tanned. "Would you make sure the hook isn't about to come off?"

He stared at her long, elegant nape, where the silvery blonde hairline formed a graceful, curving W. "The hooks look fine. But if you want to make sure, go check with Yolanda."

"You know how snarly she can be on opening day." She looked over her shoulder. "Come on, please, Jacob?"

"Alexandra. You know this isn't …" He looked around. There wasn't a soul in sight, and probably he was making a big deal out of nothing. Reaching up, he gingerly took the satin straps in his fingers and tugged. They held firm. "See?"

"That's all I needed. Thanks." She turned around to smile up at him. "You do a great job, Jacob. I don't know how you keep all the plates in the air, but you do. I'm honored to be one of your dancers."

"Alexandra," he repeated impatiently, then his phone buzzed against his hip. Relieved, he snatched it off the clip and looked at the ID before answering. "Gilly! How are you?"

"Super-duper," she said cheerfully. "Your first school show's this morning, right? Is this a bad time?"

"This is a great time. Curtain goes up in fifteen."

"Oh, golly. Then I'll get off the phone. I just wanted to tell you I'm praying."

Jacob glanced at Alexandra, who clearly had heard every word. Ignoring her pout, he wandered toward the cast's backstage meeting place. He couldn't help smiling. "I'm *very* glad you called. What are you doing?"

"Icing my feet. Tomorrow's my day off, so I'll spend it washing and packing. Then Dmitri and I fly to Birmingham on Friday. I'm so excited! What time is rehearsal?"

"Two-thirty. We'll just run through it once. I realize you know it cold. But my kids want to see you dance, since they'll be backstage during the performance."

"That'll be fine. Okay, I'll let you go then. Have fun today, Jacob!"

"Bye, Gilly." He returned the phone to his clip, resisting the urge to look over his shoulder. Narrow escape. He'd already lost one career to an ambitious ballerina, and he wasn't about to let it happen again.

"Do you want to get a massage after rehearsal?"

Gilly tucked her phone in her dance bag as Victoria dropped into the armchair beside her. The dancers' lounge was otherwise empty; most of the corps had gone for lunch at the deli across the street. Gilly had stayed behind to call Jacob. He'd sounded so happy to hear from her, she was glad she'd obeyed the strong instict that had built the whole time she was in class. It wasn't often the Lord gave her direct instructions, but she always obeyed.

Now here was another situation, and she wasn't sure how to handle it. After their argument nearly a month ago, Victoria had avoided Gilly as if she had leprosy. Gilly was pretty sure her friend had done something tragic. It was all over her guilty face.

And why would she pick now to make nice?

Gilly moved the ice pack from her left foot to her right one. She should've asked Jacob to pray for her, but she'd hated to unload a prayer request for someone he didn't even know. Especially one of such a private nature.

"Aren't you going to answer me?" Victoria sounded peeved.

Gilly sighed. "You're the one who's been running away from me. I guess I could use a rubdown. But I have a lot to do to get ready for my trip this weekend. I can't stay long."

"Good." Victoria sat there for a minute, staring at her hands resting on her knees like a schoolgirl in the principal's office. Finally she murmured, "I did it, you know. Ended the pregnancy." Her voice was tired. "I thought it would make me feel better. I know it was the right thing to do."

Gilly felt like throwing up. From talking to Jacob to this … "I've been praying for you, Victoria. I'll keep on. You can't make me stop."

"I know. I'm a very messed-up person, Gilly. *Life's* messed up, you know? I just don't believe in right and wrong like you do."

"You know what? You're right. Life *is* messed up sometimes." She stopped, then blurted, "Did you know my older brother died in a car crash when I was eight?"

Victoria shook her head. "You never said anything about it."

"It wasn't a happy time for anybody in my family. But that's when I figured out how much I needed Jesus. He's the only reason any of us survived that." Gilly put both her feet on the floor and crushed the ice pack in her hands. "So when you get to the place where you're tired of fighting it on your own, we'll talk."

Victoria stood up, wobbling on her bunion-warped feet. Her smile was sour. "That's fair enough, but don't hold your breath. Come on, let's call to see if Toni's got an opening this afternoon."

"Okay." Gilly put her slippers back on, then let Victoria pull her to her feet. But before they could exit the lounge, Maurice Poiroux whirled in like the Tasmanian devil he was.

"Gillian!" The director flung his arms wide, smiling. "For you all over I look! You are not at lunch with the others? Maybe you should eat while I talk to you?"

Maurice always talked in either exclamation points or questions marks, and his syntax was so garbled some of the dancers called him Yoda behind his back.

Gilly avoided Victoria's gaze, trying not to giggle. "I'm not hungry today. I was going to read during my break."

"Then I talk and you listen." Maurice made a shooing motion toward Victoria. "Good-bye, Victoria."

"Well, that's a nice brush-off." But Victoria good-naturedly wandered toward the door, looking over her shoulder at Gilly. "I'll call Toni. Meet me at the front door in an hour?"

"Sure." Gilly dropped into the same chair she'd just vacated. Might as well ice her feet some more. "Is there something wrong, Maurice?"

"I think not." He moved to the coffeemaker and poured himself a mugful, then dumped two packets of sugar in it. Stirring with Gallic vigor, he leaned against the counter and stared at Gilly from under eyebrows like scrub brushes. His bald head glistened under the fluorescent light. "You are my favorite baby ballerina, you know." His puckish smile lit his dark eyes.

Gilly shook her head. Every dancer in the company had at one time been the recipient of those words. Maurice had told her the same thing on three different occasions. "I'm flattered, Maurice. Thanks."

"No, no. Mean it—I do. And Dianne tells me you have the—the—" He circled a hand, pretending to search for the right word. Maurice could speak the King's English when he chose. He snapped his fingers. "You have the charisma and technique of a supernova."

Now that was worth paying attention to. Dianne was chary with compliments.

But Gilly sat on her hands. Compliments came, compliments went in this profession, like the north wind. "That's good," she murmured. What on earth was he leading up to?

"That is more than good. Superlative it is." He nodded, proud of his vocabulary. "And we decide between us that you will make a perfect Ione."

"Ione?"

"This is the name I give my Little Mermaid—not the silly Disney cartoon, but the great, tragic tale of Hans Christian Anderson, the greatest storyteller ever born."

"You want me to be the Little Mermaid? *The* Little Mermaid?" Gilly goggled at Maurice. "I thought that was just a rumor."

"Of course it is not a rumor. I am seriously dead."

Gilly couldn't help it. She burst out laughing. "You are dead serious."

"That's what I said." Maurice waved his coffee mug. "There will be other girls in the first cast also, but the choreography I will design on you, and it will be very hard work, but you are a girl with brains and talent and a gut. The audience brought you to their feet when you dance Odette in Saratoga."

Gilly stifled her giggles. "Wow. I'm honored, Maurice. I'd love to be Ione."

"Of course you would. We start work in January. Go home after Christmas, eat lots of figgy pudding, and rest your feet. Then you come back for making the mermaid."

"I don't even know what a figgy pudding is, but whatever. I'll definitely be back after Christmas."

"Good. Now I want to talk to you also about this request for release to do another ballet in the South. Is there something going on with Jacob Ferrar?"

A frisson of apprehension raised the hair on Gilly's arms. "Of course not! Why would you think that?"

"He asked for you specifically. Two times in one season. I want to know why." The dark eyes focused eagle-sharp on her face. She felt like a mouse peeking out of a hole.

"He—He and I met back in October. He told me about his new ballet, and it sounded interesting."

"You know it is bad form to discuss contracts with dancers before talking to management. Besides, I know Jacob quite well. I think you must be careful with him."

"Why?" Though she'd looked up Jacob's career on the Internet, just to see if he'd really been as good a dancer as she imagined, she had no patience for backstage gossip—even with her director-in-chief.

"He is the womanizer."

Not from what she'd seen. Besides, she wanted to make up her own mind. She shrugged. "They all are. I can take care of myself." She ignored his skeptical look. "Are you thinking about letting me go?"

He shrugged. "If you are going to dance Ione, you must be in rehearsals."

"You know I'll do whatever my contract dictates."

"It is not just the contract." Maurice's rubbery face was as serious as she'd ever seen it. "The great ballerinas dance until they bleed, in order to interpret a role. You have a choice to make."

A choice? There was no choice. Jacob would be disappointed, but she could not lose the chance to originate a lead role in a brand-new Poiroux ballet. "I told you, Maurice, I'm honored you think I'm ready for this. Of course I'll be at every rehearsal."

He smiled broadly. "See? Brains and guts. And all that lovely red hair." He slurped down the remains of his coffee and set the cup in the sink. "Now you read your book, and I will find my wife and tell her she will be the most beautiful sea witch in history." Carrying himself as usual like the King of Siam, he strode from the room.

Oh boy. Iliana Poiroux was not going to take kindly to being relegated to evil villainess.

And Gilly didn't look forward to calling Jacob and telling him her part in the ballet was off. Maybe she'd wait until she saw him this weekend. Bad news was better delivered face to face.

Grimacing, she put her ice packs in her dance bag and put on her shoes again. Eventually Maurice would put up the winter rehearsal schedule, and a new round of speculations and jealousies would circulate around the studio. Heigh-ho. The dancer's life.

Nine

The board was in full attendance Thursday night, crowding the studio's small conference room. Jacob had left rehearsal at the Samford PAC early, without stopping for supper, and he was anxious to get this meeting behind him. He still had to pick up Graham and make sure they both got to bed early tonight. Tomorrow was a big day.

But the meeting was critical too, so he must stay focused. He couldn't think about Graham driving Cynthia crazy by asking every five minutes when Uncle Jacob would be there.

"All right, let's come to order." Board chairman Frank Ireland shuffled the papers on the table in front of him. He was a bank examiner whose three daughters had danced with the company in the nineties; one was now an instructor in the ballet school. "We'll start with Mr. Ferrar's report on the *Nutcracker* school performances and preparations for the weekend of dancing with the stars." He grinned. "I hope you've all secured your tickets. They've sold well. Also, Jacob, please inform us of any plans for the upcoming season that need to be discussed."

Jacob took a moment to assess the six women and four men who made up his board. Big difference between dancing for an audience blanked out by lights and facing this wall of eyes. His gaze drifted down the table to his right, where cardio surgeon Eric Sulley sat fiddling with his glasses. An important fixture on the board, as well as an influential member of Jacob's church, Eric funneled large dollar amounts into the program and encouraged his wealthy friends to follow suit. He was also the father of the young lady Wendy had ousted from yesterday's school performance. He and Wendy had decided together to make an example of Brittney and prevent her from dancing in the weekend performances as well. If her parents weren't going to teach the child self-control, it was time someone else did.

Wendy had called Sandra Sulley this morning to give her the news, but Jacob had no idea if the good doctor had been informed. The expression on his square face was perfectly neutral.

Jacob had his notes memorized but lined them up on the glass table top so he could see them just in case. "We're all set for opening night tomorrow. The boys and girls are very excited, of course, and we have several dancers performing *Nutcracker* for the first time. The Ballet New York guests will arrive in the morning around eleven, then there'll be an abbreviated rehearsal and a short rest time before opening night. I'm expecting a full house for all three performances—we're sold out." Jacob smiled at the murmur of appreciation that rippled through the room. "It's going to be great, folks. Gillian Kincade and Dmitri Lanskov are phenomenal."

"I've never heard of either one," put in Eric Sulley, who had missed the meeting in which the BNY dancers' appearance had been approved.

"Stars on the rise," Jacob said. "You'll be hearing more of them, trust me. In fact, I'm hoping to bring Miss Kincade back for a new full-length ballet I'm working on. I wanted to bring it up as a proposed addition to the spring calendar. We'd work it in between

Hansel and Gretel and the end-of-year reports of progress." He paused and met the eyes of each person at the table. With the exception of Eric he saw curiosity and interest.

"What's the story based on?" Frank sat back, arms folded.

Jacob addressed Eric Sulley, hoping to connect. "It's the biblical story of Lazarus and his two sisters. They were close to Christ near the end of his life. Mary, the youngest, was a rebel—in fact, sort of a sinful outcast—but she managed to turn her life around in spite of conflict with the 'perfect' sister Martha. After she watched Jesus bring her brother back from the dead, Mary decided she was going to offer up the most expensive possession she had. She scandalized the disciples and the religious leaders by busting into a dinner party for men—and dumping nearly a pint of pure nard all over Jesus. Then she proceeds to bathe his feet with her tears and wipe them off with her hair." In spite of the tension in the room, he plowed on. "The men—especially Judas, who was the treasurer—were outraged at the waste, not to mention her seemingly promiscuous behavior. But Jesus defended her, saying she was anointing him for his coming death." As usual, the emotion of telling the story roughened Jacob's voice. He cleared his throat. "And that's pretty much it."

"That's a great story. What's the music?"

Jacob broke eye contact with Eric and turned to find Heidi Raintree—a widowed coffee shop owner with a promising couple of young dancers—leaning forward eagerly. Relieved to have an advocate, he smiled. "I've got original music by Tucker McGaughan. His debut album topped the alternative rock charts for over six weeks this summer."

"Alternative rock?" Eric's lip curled. "Whatever happened to dancing to the classics?"

"We do that 90 percent of the time," Jacob said reasonably. "But there's nothing wrong with encouraging fresh talent. Young performers in every discipline grow up to become major stars. And I'd like to build bridges between generations stylistically."

"So our kids will be dancing to pop music?" Heidi's enthusiasm had become a dubious raised eyebrow.

"Not in the sense you're thinking of." Jacob struggled to explain in a way that wouldn't invite a cold shower over the whole project. "More like a biblical rock opera. You know we occasionally do children's stories, and even the big professional companies in New York pull from Broadway."

"It sounds sort of ... weird," said Frank, who was usually one of Jacob's staunchest supporters. "Maybe you could play some of the music for us. Demonstrate a couple of the dances."

Jacob nodded. "That's an excellent idea. If I can persuade Gillian Kincade to stay an extra night, I'll have her show you Mary's solo in the second act."

There was a general murmur of acquiescence, even excitement, and the meeting's agenda proceeded smoothly to other topics. With this initial hurdle behind him, Jacob relaxed.

Frank adjourned the meeting shortly before eight, and Jacob began to pack his briefcase. Heidi stopped to speak to him on the way out.

"Mr. Ferrar, I want you to know I'm excited about our kids presenting a Bible story. I looked at the other companies in the area when I was choosing a school for my girls, and I liked the fact that you're careful about what these young people perform."

Jacob looked around cautiously before speaking. "I hope you don't think I'm pushing an agenda. I'm aware that this is a community arts organization."

"It is." She nodded. "But it's time somebody provided a little alternative to some of the ... junk that our children are expected to accept as the norm." She hesitated. "I've been meaning to ask you where you go to church. The girls and I are having trouble handling our old church since my husband died. Things are just ... weird, you know?"

Jacob was all but speechless, he was so caught off guard. "I'm a member of Faith Community Church." He looked at Heidi carefully to determine if there were any ulterior motives to her question. If there were, she kept them well hidden. "I'd love to introduce you around if you'd like to come. In fact ..." He swallowed. "I'm a member of a small Bible study group that meets on Tuesday nights at my neighbor's house. Her name's Cynthia, and kids are welcome. If you'd like, I'll have her give you a call with more information."

Heidi's smile beamed. "That would be great. The girls would love that, I'm sure." She touched his arm and backed toward the door. "Thanks, Jacob. Good luck with the performances."

"Are you coming both nights?"

"Yes. My parents will be here Friday."

"Good." He nodded and stood, latching his briefcase. "Please, introduce them to me at the cast party."

"I will." She slipped out.

Jacob looked around. Eric Sulley had already left, and the opportunity to talk to him about Brittney was gone. He sighed. Maybe he could phone Eric during the day tomorrow.

He didn't need an angry board member hanging over his head with everything else he had to think about this weekend.

Rich people need love too, Gilly reminded herself as she and Dmitri stepped out of a taxi in front of the Bruckheimer mansion in Carnegie Hill. Inside, they handed over their coats to a dour-faced man Gilly assumed to be the butler and paused to scope out the glittering throng. Judging by the loud laughter and erratic dancing, the hundred or so guests clogging the ballroom were nearly as well lit for the holidays as the twelve-foot tree in the soaring, atrium-style foyer.

She'd managed to skip this particular party in previous years, but Dmitri made a safe date, so she'd gone along with his insistence that they share a cab to the balletomanes' annual Christmas fund-raiser bash. "Is it always this crowded?" she shouted over the music booming from surround-sound speakers hidden in the ceiling.

"The crowd is a bit down this year. Come on." Dmitri towed Gilly toward an open doorway extravagantly swagged with evergreen boughs, holly, and gold mesh ribbon. Glancing up at the mistletoe hanging from its center, he bent down to give her a smacking kiss on the forehead. "You look scrumptious," he said benevolently. "I wouldn't have thought black lace would work on you, but I am occasionally wrong."

Gilly smoothed the knee-length skirt of her cocktail dress. She'd had her doubts as well, but it was modest and Laurel said it made her skin look like milk, so she'd caved in and forked out almost two hundred dollars for it. Dmitri had exquisite taste, so probably she was okay.

Blond and handsome in fitted black slacks, a white turtleneck, and a charcoal sports coat, he smiled at her over his shoulder. The slightly manic look in his blue eyes worried her.

Gilly clung to his hand, trying not to trip over the feet of swaying tuxedo- and evening gown-clad partyers. "Where are we going?"

"You must meet Vince and Abby. They asked me to introduce you."

"Oh. Okay." As they wove their way through the crowd, she kept an eye out for familiar faces. Victoria and Nicholas should be here somewhere too.

At the very back of the ballroom, near the plate-glass terrace window, Dmitri stopped in front of a well-preserved brunette, gorgeously dressed in coral silk. She was in animated conversation with a young woman who looked vaguely familiar to Gilly—maybe a soap opera actress?

The hostess waved away the actress and greeted Dmitri with an exuberant air kiss. "Dmitri! I'm so glad you came. And is this Miss Kincade? May I call you Gillian? Oh, you're just as lovely in person as you are onstage! I'm Abby Bruckheimer."

Gillian suffered herself to be cooed over. Grandma Kincade would be appalled at this nonsense and would tell her to grab a dishtowel and start drying something. "Thank you for the invitation, Mrs. Bruckheimer. I'm honored."

"Please. Call me Abby," she gushed, keeping one of each of Gilly's and Dmitri's hands. "We saw you dance last night as Dew Drop and Candy Cane. Vince will be sorry he missed meeting you two. He had to take a business call." She smiled at Gilly. "Sweetheart, you were just exquisite. I read somewhere there are sixty-five crystal drops on that tutu. Isn't it heavy?"

"Almost every costume has some kind of decoration that weighs a bit." Gilly winked at Dmitri. "Candy Cane has a hundred and forty-four jingle bells to deal with."

Dmitri lifted his hands. "What can I say? Every job has its hazards."

Abby Bruckheimer laughed. "Would you like something to drink? Champagne?" She glanced at a waiter hovering nearby.

Dmitri hesitated, then nodded. "Yes, please."

Gilly shook her head. "Sparkling water for me, if it's available."

"Certainly." Abby sent the waiter off and looked Gilly up and down with humorous envy. "I took ballet when I was a little girl, but I was about as coordinated as a snowman on stilts."

Gilly laughed. "Ouch."

"I find that difficult to believe," Dmitri said gallantly.

"It's true. It was not a pretty sight." Abby made a rueful face. "But the experience was so good for me, gave me a little poise and polish, and it was wonderful exercise. I've loved the fine arts ever since. Now tell me how a little southern girl like you wound up in the big city."

The conversation caromed from Alabama to Dmitri's native Russia and back to the craziness of life in New York. The drinks arrived, and Gilly sipped her water slowly, charmed by Abby Bruckheimer's friendly interest and blithe assumption that everyone should appreciate American opportunism as did she and her husband.

Thirty minutes or so into the conversation, Dmitri executed an elegant, if somewhat tipsy, bow. "You will please excuse me," he said owlishly, "but I must see a dog about a man." Without waiting for a reply, he wheeled and threaded his way through the crowded ballroom.

Gilly frowned. "How many drinks has he had?"

"I'm afraid I lost count," Abby admitted. "But it's not a problem. There's plenty to go round."

That wasn't the issue. She'd never seen Dmitri drink before, and she'd noticed something a little agitated in his behavior all night.

Vince Bruckheimer came back from his phone call, and Gilly managed to keep the conversational ball in the air for another half hour before her concern for Dmitri got the better of her. Ruefully she smiled at Abby's puzzled expression. "I'm sorry. Would you repeat that question?"

Her hostess laughed, apparently not at all offended. "I said I'd love to meet your sister sometime. She sounds like one of those women who's managed to grab the brass ring and run with it."

"I'm sure Laurel would love that." Gilly peered around a cluster of people. Where had Dmitri disappeared to? Hopefully he hadn't left her to make it home by herself.

Vince Bruckheimer seemed to have picked up on her distraction. "I'm sorry we've monopolized your time, Gillian. Why don't you find the buffet and enjoy the party? There's plenty of food and more drinks in the dining room."

"All right. It was lovely to meet you." She smiled at Abby. "Thanks for having us in."

"It was wonderful to meet you as well. We'll be back to see you in *Little Mermaid* this spring. I hear it's going to be spectacular."

Gilly took leave of her hosts and started looking for Dmitri. The problem was he could be anywhere in this huge crowd of mostly drunk dance enthusiasts. Maybe she'd be able to see from the mezzanine above. Struggling through the crowd, she managed to get to the top of the stairs and leaned over the rail, searching for her erstwhile escort. She spotted Maurice and Iliana Poiroux chattering, drinks in hand, with a foursome of well-dressed balletomanes, two men and two women. It was hard to tell who was partnered with whom. She continued to scan the swirling crowd, more and more anxious by the moment. Dmitri was nowhere to be seen.

Then someone clasped her around the waist from behind, lifting her off her feet. She caught the scent of Dmitri's expensive cologne.

"Gilly! I lost you! Where have you been?"

"Right where you left me. Put me down!"

When Dmitri dropped her unceremoniously, she turned to face him, hands on hips. He seemed to have imbibed every flute of champagne that crossed his path between the ballroom and the restroom — if indeed that was where he'd been. His face was flushed, his blue eyes watery. His mobile eyebrows rose. "What is the matter, Gilly-Willy?"

She took him by the arm and hauled him down the stairs, dodging stragglers coming up. "I can't believe you're already sloshed." When he just grinned at her, she sighed. "Never mind. My feet hurt, and I want to go home. I'm calling a cab."

"I'll do it for you." He jerked away from her, ran to the beveled glass front door, and leaned out into the frosty New York night. "Hellllooo! We need a cab!" He plopped down on the step and put his head on his knees. "It feels good out here."

Gilly shook her head. Fat lot of good he was. No cabbie was going to see him sitting on his keister. Shutting the door on him, she sent the butler in search of their coats. As she waited in the empty foyer, she looked up at the angel on top of the Christmas tree and listened to the party noise behind her. Was anybody in this house aware of how the celebration even got started? Sometimes she felt like an alien visiting from another planet.

She looked at the dainty silver wristwatch Daddy had given her for her twenty-first birthday. Almost midnight. At home it would be eleven, and her parents would be working a jigsaw puzzle or addressing Christmas cards while they watched *Matlock* reruns. Her sisters would be snuggled up with their husbands after putting the kids in bed.

Nostalgic at the thought of a balmy Mobile Christmas, she sat down on the bottom stairstep and circled her thumbs. Where was that sour-puss butler with her coat? She was ready to go home and ice her feet.

"Hey, Gilly. What're you doing?"

She looked up to find Victoria's significant other, Nicholas, towering over her. One point in his favor: Victoria could wear her heels when she was out with him. "Waiting on my coat. Where's Victoria?"

"Schmoozing with the money." He pushed away a romantic swoop of dark hair hanging over one eye as he sat down beside her. "Got tired of watching." He gave her a sideways look. "Why aren't you in there with her?"

"I'm tired, period." She yawned.

He reached into the pocket of his jacket for a pack of cigarettes. At Gilly's dirty look, he snorted and stuffed the pack back into his pocket. He sat there quietly for several moments, then heaved a sigh. "I'm losing her, Gil."

"What?" Gilly looked at him, though she'd much rather have gotten up and sat out in the cold with Dmitri. "Losing who?"

"Victoria. She hardly talks to me. All she wants to do is dance or watch dance videos or hang out with people who can advance her career. I can't take it anymore."

Gilly stared into Nicholas's dark blue eyes. She had no idea what to say. If ever two people were intensely bad for one another, it was Nicholas and Victoria. But she still felt sorry for him. She cleared her throat. "What—what are you going to do?"

"I dunno." He propped his chin in his hand and closed his eyes. "Probably leave her."

Gilly gave an involuntary little whimper, on behalf of Nicholas's dead baby, on behalf of the sadness that was Victoria. *I have no right to be so happy.*

"I like you, Gilly. I don't know why you don't like me." Nicholas flicked a glance at her. "Well, besides the smoking."

She put her hand through the crook of his elbow. "I love you,

Nicholas. And Victoria does too." She hoped that was the truth. "She's just going through some … hard stuff right now."

"She was really mad at you for some reason last week. She went through her Facebook site and removed every picture of you and her on it." His handsome mouth curled. "What did you do?"

"I talked to her about the Lord again. She hates that." Gilly ventured a smile. "It's like I have a disease."

"You can talk to me about it. I don't have anything else to do." His eyes were drooped half shut, but she could feel his arm tense under her hand.

She was about to go home, and *now* he wanted her to talk about the Lord? "Why don't you come home with me and Dmitri?" she said before she could think about it. "He's drunk, and I could use some protection."

"Dmitri's drunk?" Nicholas straightened. His hand went to the cigarette pocket, patted it absently, and returned to his thigh. "Hmm. Okay. Might be good for Victoria to get left with one of those ballet stalkers." He grinned at Gilly. "I don't know how much protection I'll be, but at least I can keep fairy boy from throwing up on you."

"Don't call him—"

"Oh, don't worry. I'm very politically correct to his face."

The front door opened, and Dmitri's red, chapped face appeared like the Cheshire cat. "Cab's here."

Nicholas stood and offered a hand to Gilly. "Where's your coat?"

"Here it is, sir." The butler puffed in from the direction of an anteroom off the foyer. He gave Gilly's coat to Nicholas, who held it for her to slide her arms in. "Where's the other gentleman?"

"Getting some fresh air. I'll take it to him." Gilly took Dmitri's tailored tweed coat and waited for the butler to open the front door. She handed him a ten. "You coming, Nicholas?"

"Wouldn't miss the show," he said cheerfully and pushed past Dmitri, following her out to the cab.

"Hey! Wait for me." Dmitri staggered after them.

The three of them crowded into the backseat of the taxi, enveloping Gilly in liquor and tobacco fumes. Dmitri promptly laid his head back and went to sleep.

"Did you know he's an alcoholic?" Nicholas said conversationally.

"He is not! I've never seen him drink." Gilly tried to shift away from Nicholas, who had put his arm behind her across the back of the seat. But Dmitri's sprawled body didn't give her much room. Her impulsive offer to share the cab with Nicholas might have been a big mistake.

"That's because he's an alcoholic. Before you moved up to the company, when he was still a corps dancer, he'd stay up every night getting soaked. Maurice sent him to detox that summer and got him dried out. He's stayed on the wagon for three years."

Gilly listened to Dmitri's gentle snoring. Nicholas could be lying. Sometimes she hated the gossipy, malicious company she mixed herself up with. "Why are you telling me this?"

"Because you're so innocent. Not only is your buddy gay as a Mardi Gras float, he's an addictive personality. And Victoria is a whore. She's just waiting on somebody more influential than me to come along, and she'll leave me behind like dirty socks."

Gilly felt dirty herself. *Lord, Lord, cover me here. I'm out of my depth.* "There are worse things than being innocent, Nicholas." She laced her fingers together across her knees. Daddy always told her to act like a lady and she'd be treated like one.

"No, I'm pretty sure innocence is the ultimate sin. What has Victoria done that you're hiding from me? Is she already sleeping with Maurice?"

"Maurice doesn't sleep with his dancers! Well, except for his wife." Iliana Poiroux was a world-renowned principal ballerina, still dancing the great roles on a regular basis. That she was married to the artistic director was a sidebar in her matchless career.

"Iliana started out in the corps twenty years ago and hooked up with Maurice to make soloist. It worked." He laughed.

"You're making this up." Gilly wished she could open the window and take in some fresh, icy air. "How do you know?"

"Gilly, it's common knowledge. Consider this my contribution to your education. So tell me what Victoria's been up to."

"Nothing. You'll have to ask her."

"I'll have to ask her about nothing? Okay, so let's play guessing games, and you can tell me when I get warm. It doesn't sound like she slept with Maurice, so it must be that pretty idiot Ian Hargrove."

Gilly clenched her fingers and turned her face away as the taxi lurched around a corner, skidding on icy streets. She wouldn't lie, but she didn't have to answer.

Nicholas sighed. "Actually I already knew that one. I just wanted to see if you'd deny it. Since you didn't, let's try another one. She's pregnant."

Involuntarily Gilly jerked.

Nicholas swore. "She's pregnant? Is it mine or Ian's?"

"Nicholas, please." Gilly looked up at him, trying not to cry. "If you want to know what's wrong with Victoria, you've got to talk to her, not me."

"Well, it doesn't matter. I'm going to beat the snot out of Hargrove, anyway."

"Nicholas! There is no baby!"

"But you said—Wait a minute." Nicholas's voice roughened. "Did she abort my baby? She did, didn't she?"

He began to softly and methodically curse Victoria and Ian and New York and life in general.

Gilly tried not to listen. *Heavenly Father, rescue me.*

Dmitri suddenly sat up. "Stop the cab. Pull over."

The startled cab driver obeyed. They were at the intersection of Worth and Church Streets, about two blocks from Tribeca.

"Get out," said Dmitri.

Nicholas's mouth hung open for a moment. "Are you crazy? I'm still half a mile from home, and it's snowing."

"I don't care, you foul-mouth piece of dirt. She is nice to you, and you abuse her. Get out."

To Gilly's astonishment, Nicholas pulled out his wallet, took out a twenty, and threw it across the driver's seat. He opened the door and stepped onto the curb. "Merry Christmas," he snarled and slammed the door.

"Dmitri, you can't make him walk home in the middle of the night." As the taxi pulled into the street, Gilly peered out the window and watched Nicholas turn up the collar of his coat.

"He can call his own cab." Dmitri's voice was callous. "What a jerk."

"He's very unhappy. We shouldn't be mean." She turned to look at Dmitri as she slid into the spot Nicholas had vacated. "I thought you were drunk."

"I was. I am, a bit. But not drunk enough letting him talk that way to you."

"Thanks, I think." She hesitated. Dmitri's English, generally pretty good, slipped when he was excited or upset. "Is something bothering you tonight?"

"I am not bothering. I am drunk."

Boy, was she ever not prepared for this. Maybe she should have gotten a counseling degree before moving to New York. "I mean ... Nicholas said—"

"You do not believe him."

"Normally I wouldn't, but I'd noticed you never drink. We teetotalers are kind of rare."

He gave her an odd smile. "You are. You are rare, Gilly. You are the person who makes others more important than yourself."

"That's not what I—"

"Don't ask me questions." He laid his head back against the seat again and closed his eyes. "Not now. The excitement makes me ill."

Gilly huddled on her side of the car, staring at Dmitri. Maybe the Lord had shown love through her somehow. She thought of Nicholas walking the dark, snowy streets alone.

Tough love.

The next morning she woke with her eyes scratchy from lack of sleep. She'd had to pack for the trip to Birmingham before she went to bed—and Lord knew she wouldn't have been able to sleep right away anyway, remembering Dmitri's eyes like burned holes in his pale face. "I'll get a cab and come by for you," he'd said with studied soberness when he left her at her apartment. "We shall have such a good time in Alabama." Then he'd promptly lain down in the backseat of the taxi and started snoring before she could say good night.

She hoped he wouldn't oversleep. Maybe she'd better call him to make sure.

But first she had one more unpleasant duty before she could leave New York with a clear conscience. The biggest reason she hadn't been able to sleep last night was worrying about how Victoria would react when she found out Gilly had inadvertently spilled the beans to Nicholas about the baby. Victoria could be ruthlessly vindictive.

Gilly squinted at the clock. Seven o'clock. She'd almost hoped there wouldn't be time. But if she dressed in a hurry and had her luggage at the door ready to jump in the taxi when Dmitri arrived, she could make it to Victoria's and back by eight thirty. No way could she have this kind of conversation over the phone.

She crawled out of bed and headed for the shower.

Forty-five minutes later she stood at Victoria's door wishing the timing on this thing didn't stink so much. The situation would have been bad enough, but waking Victoria up before eight o'clock—especially when she'd been out until all hours the previous night—was Kamikaze material. And this was going to be a killer of a day. The two-and-a-half-hour flight would be followed by lunch with Jacob and some of his sponsors, then a two-hour rehearsal at the auditorium. Gilly's family was coming in tonight for the performance, after which they were all getting together for a meal.

Gilly swayed a bit and leaned against the door frame. Good thing she was covered in prayer. Dancing when your body was fried with exhaustion could be dangerous. But she knew she was doing what God had asked her to, so she'd push herself and trust prayer to take care of the rest.

She nearly fell over when Victoria, dressed only in a red lace nightgown, jerked the door open and peered through the chain. "Gilly? Have you lost your mind?" She looked over her shoulder, apparently seeking a clock. "Do you know what time it is?"

"Actually, I do. I have to be at the airport by nine, and I need to talk to you."

"Oh, that's right. You're going down to Dixie for the weekend." Victoria yawned and slid back the chain, which fell with a rattle. "Come on in. Just don't expect me to be coherent."

Gilly walked into the living room but didn't sit down. Her stomach was tied in a knot. "Did Nicholas come home last night?"

Victoria flung herself onto the sofa and pulled a pillow over her face. "No," she mumbled. "And it's a good thing he didn't. I'd probably have thrown him out the window, since he left me at the party." She lowered the pillow to squint at Gilly. "Which reminds me, I never saw you there. You were coming with Dmitri, right?"

"I was there." Gilly twisted her fingers together. "Vic, I don't have much time, so I'm just going to come right out and tell you. I'm sorry—"

"What? You're having an affair with Dmitri?" Victoria laughed.

"This isn't funny."

"I beg to differ. That would be *very* funny." Victoria finally seemed to notice Gilly's agitation. "Well, what is it? Did you see Nicholas with some other girl? I wouldn't be totally surprised. He was really mad at me, but I was only trying to make him—"

"Victoria, shut up and listen." Gilly sat down on the coffee table. "He knows. He knows you aborted the baby."

"What?" Victoria jackknifed off the sofa. She towered over Gilly, fists clenched at her sides.

"We rode home together in a cab, me and him and Dmitri." Gilly clamped her arms around herself. "I didn't mean to tell him—he guessed. He's not stupid. He knew something was wrong with you—"

"And you couldn't cover for me?" Victoria's voice rose to a shriek. "What kind of friend are you?"

"The kind who loves you enough to tell you the truth!" Gilly jumped to her feet. She could feel her heart literally trying to hop out of her chest. "I couldn't go off to Alabama all la-di-da and let you find out from him. I told you you should've told him about the baby to begin with, let him have some say in what to do, but *no*—you had to go and *take care of it* by yourself!"

"Yeah, well, it was *my* decision to make." Victoria's voice sounded like grit. "That's what *Roe v. Wade* was all about. *My* body, *my* b-baby, *my* boyfriend! My career! Now you've ruined everything." She burst into enraged tears and, to Gilly's astonishment, stomped from one end of the room to the other banging her hands together.

Gilly hadn't seen such a full-blown tantrum since Mary Layne's eldest stuffed his sister's favorite doll in the toilet. Nothing she could say was going to cure this brand of rage and despair, which ultimately had little to do with her.

She sighed. "Okay, Victoria. I've told you I'm sorry. Well, maybe I didn't, but I am. I'm sorry and I'm sorry *for* you. But I have to go. Just remember I love you and I'll talk to you about it some more after you calm down."

She let herself out the door and took the elevator down to the lobby. Standing on the sidewalk with her hand in the air for any passing cab, she looked at her watch. Eight thirty.

"Well, that went well," she muttered.

Ten

Gilly pressed her hand against the mild flutter of her stomach as the plane descended toward Birmingham's patchwork metropolitan landscape. There was no reason to be nervous. It was just a dancing gig in a mid-sized southern city. She'd already performed Sugar Plum at Lincoln Center, for heaven's sake.

She glanced at Dmitri, head back and sound asleep, his headphones blocking any attempt to bring him to consciousness. He was a white-knuckle flyer, and he'd taken a Dramamine before they took off from LaGuardia. Which precluded meaningful conversation and gave her all the time in the world to anticipate her reunion with Jacob Ferrar—and her family, of course, who would all be attending the Friday night performance.

But for some reason, it was Jacob's charming British accent that filled her head as the airport appeared under the wing just outside her window. He'd called her cell while they were at the airport to make sure there were no last-minute glitches in her travel plans and to ask her to buzz him as soon as she and Dmitri touched down in Birmingham.

As the plane gently shuddered and the landing gear locked into place, she closed her Bible. The last thing she'd read scraped a sensitive nerve. "From everyone who has been given much, much will be demanded; and from the one who has been entrusted with much, much more will be asked." Almost every day someone reminded her of her talent, her opportunity, her privileges. She *tried* to give back some measure of what she'd received along the way.

She glanced at Dmitri again. He still hadn't told her what bothered him enough to start him drinking again, and she didn't know him well enough to pry. Maybe over the course of the weekend he would open up and share. Friendships in the ballet world were so often an uneasy mix of jealousy, company politics, and artistic admiration—and, in her case, spiritual compassion—it was difficult to sort out her moral values and apply them to a sense of mission. God had indeed entrusted her with huge responsibility, plunking her into this privileged, celebrity-based universe, where she could count on one hand people who believed the entirety of the gospel and let it rule their lives. In fact, sometimes she wondered if the two weren't mutually exclusive. After all, Jesus had commanded the rich young ruler to sell everything he had, give it to the poor, and become a disciple.

And she knew plenty of Christians who would be horrified at the notion of sitting here beside Dmitri, watching him sleep, and failing to express proper disgust with his lifestyle. But Jesus didn't seem to be disgusted with people who didn't know him—just people like the Pharisees, who pretended to be holy while they cheated and lied and blasphemed in secret. Jesus had looked at the RYR, as she often thought of him, and loved him. Which was pretty much how she felt about Dmitri—like a little brother who didn't have a clue about what would really make him happy.

All she could say for sure was that she didn't want to fail the Lord. She wanted to pour it all out like Mary of Bethany, no reservations, no worry about scandal. She wanted to love Jesus by feeding his lambs.

Whatever that meant.

She tucked the book into her satchel, elbowed Dmitri, and lifted the closest earphone. "We're landing."

He rolled his head toward her, and a sliver of blue appeared between his lashes. "Huh?"

"We're in Birmingham, big guy. It's time to get conscious. I can't carry you off the plane."

"Yes, right." Yawning, he removed the headphones, then gave a great cracking stretch. "I think we must upgrade to first class on the way home. This is ridiculous." He looked around at the passengers stirring, gathering belongings, and chattering quietly about connections. "Who's meeting us?"

"The director's coming for us himself—Jacob Ferrar. You'll like him."

Dmitri's sleepy eyes brightened. "Will I?"

Gilly flushed. "Not like that. He's … hetero."

"Ah. Then *you* like him."

"Dmitri—"

Dmitri grinned at her. "You are so easy to tease. All right. I shall be nice. Tell me more what to expect from the—" He clutched the arm rests as the plane bumped through a gust of wind and the brakes kicked in. A flood of sibilant Russian blurted out, and his face went white.

Gilly patted his knee. "Close your eyes. I'll let you know when it's safe to look."

Fortunately, there were no delays in the landing process, and they were on the ground and deplaning before Gilly collected more than an aching wrist from Dmitri's death grip on her arm.

As they passed through the security gate, she spotted Jacob, leaning against a rail with his hands in the pockets of a pair of brown chinos, the collar of a blue-striped oxford showing under the neck of a pale blue sweater. He was obviously looking for her, and his eyes lit as she approached.

He'd decided to come on down to meet her without waiting. Wow.

"Gilly! Welcome back to Birmingham." He took her satchel, leaning down to give her a brief, unaffected kiss on the cheek. "How was your flight?"

Gilly restrained the instinct to touch her cheek. "Uneventful, thank goodness," she said with a smile and looked around to find Dmitri favoring her with an eyebrows-up, what-have-we-here look. She frowned at him. "Dmitri, come meet Jacob Ferrar."

Dmitri played nice and shook hands with no more than a cheerful "Pleased."

"Same here." Jacob led the way toward baggage claim.

Gilly was rather disappointed to find that, instead of the Jaguar, they were to make the trip to the hotel in a big silver SUV borrowed from the mother of one of Jacob's students.

Jacob grinned at her as he unlocked the rear gate to stow her and Dmitri's luggage. "You didn't seriously think we were all going to fit in the convertible, did you?"

She poked out her bottom lip. "Well … I suppose not. But will you take me for a ride sometime this weekend?"

"How would you like to go to a soccer game early Saturday morning?"

"That would be awesome." She beamed at him. "Could I play? I've always wanted to learn."

He laughed, opening the passenger door for her to climb up into the huge automobile. "And risk damaging the star of my ballet? I think not. Besides, it's a league for first- and second-graders. You'll have to be content with cheering the Massey Refrigeration Mavericks on to victory."

Gilly turned to Dmitri in the backseat. "You want to come?"

Dmitri shuddered. "I'll be sleeping in, thanks."

Jacob glanced at her as he headed the car for the parking lot exit. "Will your family be coming to see you dance this weekend?"

"Yes, they're coming tonight." She hesitated. "Would you join us for a meal after the performance? Dmitri's coming too."

Jacob shook his head. "Can't, thanks. I've got Graham to think of. But ..." He swallowed and glanced at her, then caught Dmitri's eyes in the rearview mirror. He suddenly went red. "I'd love to host you all at my apartment. That way I could put Gray to bed and we could still have a proper opening-night celebration."

"This sounds like an excellent solution." Amusement vibrated in Dmitri's voice. "Restaurants we get all the time. Home is much nicer, don't you think so, Gilly?"

What was so funny? "Of course it is." She smiled at Jacob, glad to see the high color in his cheeks relenting, his eyes a warm dark brown. "I'll call Mom and Laurel as soon as we get to the hotel. I know they'll be glad to rearrange our plans."

The conversation turned to rehearsal details, and Gilly relaxed against the seat. Jacob would help her talk to Dmitri. He understood better than anyone the dynamics of ballet relationships. And he was a Christ-follower, a man of maturity and depth.

Oh, yes, too good to be true.

The theater was finally empty, rehearsal having come and gone in a mania of costumes, props, lighting technicians, and high-strung violinists. Jacob sprawled in a seat on the back row feeling like Wellington must have felt after Waterloo. And opening night was still to come.

Well, there was nothing to do about it at this point but pray the good Lord would intervene with mercy.

Thankfully, Gilly and Dmitri Lanskov lived up to their billing, dancing their roles with true artistry and professionalism. They'd both been charming with the younger dancers, answering impertinent questions with grace and humor. His main worry was whether

Alexandra might choose to enact the jilted tragedienne. She was like some Hawaiian volcano set to spill red fire into the Pacific Ocean of his company.

Amused by the melodramatic turn of his thoughts, he closed his eyes and clasped his fingers behind his head. *Loony, Ferrar,* he told himself. *You're losing it, old man.*

"What's so funny?"

He looked up to find Gilly standing next to him in the aisle, eyes twinkling. She had on her tailored red wool coat over pink tights, her small feet encased in a pair of orange plaid sneakers. The green knit cap she'd worn at the Macy's parade was pulled over her fiery hair.

Jacob sat up and squinted at her. "You might warn me to put on my sunglasses if you're going to sneak up on me like this. Where's Dmitri?"

"Ha-ha," she said, hoisting her dance bag strap higher on her shoulder. "He's coming. Something about a missing shoe."

Jacob stood. "I'll help him look. You guys have got to be fried, and I want to make sure you have time to rest before the performance."

"Yeah, it's been a long day." Gilly followed him toward the backstage area. "But I'm so excited I don't know if I could sleep." She smiled up at him. "This is a pretty big deal for me—getting to dance for my folks."

Jacob tried to remember the last time he'd performed in front of his parents. Perhaps in England when he'd been about sixteen. Once he'd gotten to be an adult, a professional dancer, they'd not often been in the same country, let alone the same city. "Lily, my sister, and her husband once flew to Madrid to see me at Ballet Spain. We were doing *Sleeping Beauty.*"

"I bet they loved it. Tchaikovsky always makes me cry."

"Lily did cry." He hadn't thought about that in years. "She told me my gift was a God-send. And she didn't even believe in God."

"Don't you miss it?" Gilly was looking up at him, her expression tender, almost anxious. She didn't seem to realize she was leaning against his arm. "Don't you want to just dance sometimes?"

He paused with a hand on the backstage door. "I do dance, but now it's through my students and through the dances I create for them." He smiled. "And I'll be dancing with you tomorrow afternoon. After the soccer game, I'm going to show you the steps for your Mary solo, and we're going to dance the pas de deux for my board of trustees. They want to see it before approving its addition to the spring schedule."

Her eyes widened, regret flashing just before she looked away.

"What's the matter, Gilly?"

She bit her lip. "Oh, Jacob. I'm sorry."

Sick disappointment punched him in the stomach. "You've changed your mind."

"I didn't want to change my mind. I want to do your ballet more than anything except—" Her eyes lifted, swimming with tears. "Except Maurice is creating a new version of *Little Mermaid*, on me. He told me I couldn't leave rehearsals at all if I want the part."

Jacob stared at her for a full ten seconds before he could make himself smile. "Then of course you can't leave. What an opportunity." He slipped his arm around her slight shoulders and squeezed gently. She was obviously embarrassed and maybe even heartbroken that she couldn't be Mary. But no professional dancer would give up a lead role in a Maurice Poiroux ballet to come to Birmingham, Alabama, to dance in an obscure Christian ballet by a little-known choreographer. "Gilly, don't feel bad. I've still got time to find someone to dance the role." God help him, Alexandra would probably jump at the chance.

She nodded against his shoulder. "I know. But I still hate that I got your hopes up and then backed out." She looked up at him, blinking hard. "Could I still help you out tomorrow? Learn the dance to show your board? I'm a quick study, I promise."

He knew she was, after dancing with her at her sister's house back in October. His heartbeat quickened a little. If she danced for the board tomorrow they were bound to approve the ballet. He'd worry about replacing her later.

"All right," he said recklessly. "I'll take you up on it. You're a sweetheart. Now let's go help Dmitri find his shoe. I've got to go pick up Graham from school."

She sniffed and gave him a wobbly smile. "I hope I'm not forfeiting my soul," she said obscurely as she preceded him through the stage door.

Gilly's family, arriving early for a little family time before the performance, had by invitation crashed her hotel suite. The smaller three children had been left at Laurel's house with babysitters, but since Mary Layne deemed this an educational as well as a familial outing, her eldest four—ranging in age from fifteen-year-old Dane to nine-year-old Madison—had been spit-polished, crammed into dress clothes, and lectured on (a) not spitting in public (boys) and (b) keeping one's knees together (girls). The two girls were thrilled at the prospect of watching Aunt Gilly twirl and leap onstage in a tutu, but Dane and Parker had expressed their disdain by sneaking a football into the room. They were in the bathroom taking turns bouncing it against the shower wall.

Since Gilly was finding it difficult to find a place to sit down, let alone have a meaningful conversation, she decided she might as well work off her nervous energy. She stood in the center of the room and clapped her hands. "Yo! Who wants to swing dance?"

"Me! Me! Teach me, Aunt Gilly!" Cherie and Madison jumped to their feet.

The two girls mastered the basic step-touch steps in about ten minutes. But when Cole demanded a turn, Gilly inspected his six-foot-four frame with dubious optimism. The whole group dissolved in laughter as Gilly, humming "Boogie Woogie Bugle Boy," tried to teach him the Lindy Hop. He towered over her by at least a foot and had trod on her feet three times.

"You walk on the bottoms, I'll walk on the tops," he joked, staggering the wrong way.

"You'd never make it on *Dancing with the Stars*." Hysterical with laughter, she let go of his hand and plopped down on the end of the bed. "Just take Laurel to the movies."

He dropped panting into the desk chair. "Who would've thought ballerinas would spend their off time in a dance club? Talk about a busman's holiday."

"It's kind of the new fad." Gilly leaned over to rub one aching foot. "The guys love to show off, and sometimes you see famous people at the clubs."

"Gilly," Mary Layne said hesitantly, "you don't spend a *lot* of time in those clubs, do you? I worry about you ruining your witness for Christ."

Stung, Gilly sat up. "I'd never get to talk to anybody if I sat home and read my Bible all the time—and what good would that do? I stay away from the alcohol, if that's what you're worried about. And you know I don't—" she lowered her voice—"sleep around." She really *didn't* have anything to be ashamed of. Compared to most people in Manhattan, she could be a saint straight out of a convent.

Cole winked at Mary Layne. "When she was about sixteen, she informed me in no uncertain terms that she doesn't chase boys."

"I still don't." Gilly made a face at him. "But the only people I know are dancers. And dancers love to ... dance."

"Just don't up and decide to marry one of those Yankee homeboys," put in Wade, who had apparently given up trying to read in the middle of a circus. "You need to settle down with a good ole boy who drives a truck and roots for Alabama."

"Ole Miss," put in Cole promptly.

To Gilly's relief, the conversation veered off to the SEC playoffs. She lay back and threw her arm across her face. Her experience with Mississippi boys hadn't been any more promising than that with the hometown heroes in Mobile. Tucker was into making music and not much else, his band on the road fifty weeks out of the year. Once a month or so he'd call to say hello, and it always took her a minute to orient herself to his lingo. He didn't even talk like an adult.

And the guys in the ballet corps who were her peers were no better. More than half were homosexual, and even the straight ones tended to be young, most around eighteen or nineteen, since boys moved up the ballet ladder faster than girls. Realistically there was little to distract her from her own career ambitions.

"Gilly, I'm sorry if I hurt your feelings." Mary Layne touched her elbow.

Gilly lowered her arm to smile at her sister. "Goodness, I'm not that fragile."

"I know, but I'm not your mother. I should mind my own business." Mary Layne glanced at Laurel. "People tell me that all the time."

"I don't know where I'd have been the last four years without your wisdom and experience," Laurel said. "Even if I don't tell you so often enough."

"Aw. Group hug." Gilly pressed her palms together against her cheek and batted her eyelashes.

"Smarty-pants." But Laurel smiled. "Who's going to entertain us old married people with Irish jigs and popcorn necklaces when you go back to NYC?"

"If marriage turns you into an old fogie, you can count me out." Gilly sat up and bounced to her feet. "Boys! Come out here!" she yelled into the open bathroom door. "We're all going to play 'Killer.'"

All the adults groaned, while the girls squealed with excitement and the boys came running. Gilly laughed and made them all sit in a circle. Everybody had their role to play, and hers was Life of the Party. Better make the most of it while she could.

There would be no time for playing once she got back to New York, homeboy or no homeboy.

Eleven

"You mean there's truly no alcohol?" Dmitri whispered in Gilly's ear. They were in Jacob's kitchen, scouting out the food. "At all? I mean, of course I'm sitting in the wagon. But you have to admit it's a bit weird."

Smiling at his patent disbelief, she handed him a blue plastic cup. "There'll be a big cast party tomorrow night with all the trimmings. Rich doctor's wife with requisite mansion, free-flowing food, and adult beverages, like you're used to. This is just a little family get-together."

"But there must be twenty-five people here!" Dmitri peered into Jacob's living room, currently stuffed with children, teenagers, and adults of all ages and sizes, most of whom were related to Gilly.

She wrinkled her nose. "Welcome to the American South."

He accepted a bottle of water from her. "You've started to drawl like them, you know. How does that happen?" He headed for the doorway into the living room. "I'm going to talk to your mother. She seems like a cultured woman."

"We're all cultured," Gilly said, annoyed. "Just because we talk slow doesn't mean our minds are slow."

He just waved his hand and disappeared.

Gilly wandered over to investigate the sandwich buffet spread out on the counter next to the stove. She hadn't eaten all day and was starving. She was putting a spoonful of mustard on a lettuce and turkey wrap when Jacob stuck his head in. He'd removed his tuxedo jacket and tie and looked as relaxed as was possible for a man who had just directed a major community arts event.

"There you are." He smiled at her. "My grandparents just got here. They want to meet you."

"Okay, I'd like that." Grabbing a bottle of water, she followed Jacob. "There's no way Graham's going to sleep with this loud crew here."

His smile was rueful. "Yes, he'll be awake for the foreseeable future. But I just couldn't leave him behind again. He enjoyed the performance so much and wanted to meet you and Dmitri." He glanced at the corner where Graham and Mary Layne's kids were involved in a loud game of Uno. "Besides, he's having a great time with your nephews and nieces."

Gilly looked at them fondly. "They're good kids."

"You're fortunate, Gilly." Jacob halted, touching her arm. "I struggle not to be completely envious of your family."

"You've got your grandparents."

"I do." He sighed and looked away. "But they're both getting on in years. Eventually I'm going to have to think about taking care of them as well as Graham."

"But won't your parents come back to the States and take responsibility?"

He shrugged. "Possibly. But I don't count on it."

Gilly could hardly comprehend such callousness. "That's crazy."

He looked at her, a smile pulling at his mouth. After a moment he reached out and brushed his thumb across her upper lip. "Mustard. Where's your napkin?"

Laughing, she wiped her mouth, then took his hand to do away with the yellow streak on his thumb. "We southern belles have a lot of class. No wonder Dmitri thinks we don't wear shoes down here."

Jacob absently clasped her fingers, balling the napkin into her palm. His hands were warm, large, gentle. "I'm sure you've got all the polish you need at your disposal." He drew Gilly's hand through his arm, and she followed him toward a leather sofa and chair grouping, where her mother sat chatting with Cole, Dmitri, and an elderly couple she assumed to be Jacob's grandparents. "Nonna, Poppa, you haven't met our Sugar Plum Fairy yet. This is Gilly Kincade. Gilly, meet Nelson and Claudia Ferrar."

Jacob's grandfather immediately rose to his feet and offered his seat to Gilly with a courtly little nod. "We're glad to meet you, hon," he said in a deep Alabama drawl as Gilly sat down beside his wife.

"Likewise." He reminded Gilly of her own Grandpa Kincade—tall, broad, and stoic of expression. But there was kindness in a pair of deep-set brown eyes extraordinarily like Jacob's.

"Oh, you're just the prettiest little thing," chirped Claudia Ferrar, clasping Gilly in a squishy side hug. "Up there twirling like a music box ballerina, I declare." She released Gilly to place both hands on her cheeks. "And no bigger than an elf in a cookie commercial."

Gilly laughed, even as her mother raised her eyebrows at this excessive familiarity. "I'm definitely vertically challenged. I'm glad you enjoyed the ballet."

"We did, didn't we, Nelson? You all were real pretty." Claudia elbowed her husband, whose attention had drifted to the evening news on the TV screen across the room. He grunted. "Oh, don't mind him. He's got no more sense of class than one of our milk cows. I've been wanting to meet you since you came in October. Jacob hasn't quit talking about you."

"Nonna—"

"You know you haven't." Claudia leaned toward Gilly's mother and spoke out of the side of her mouth. "And Lord knows I was relieved he decided not to date that stuck-up blonde girl that teaches at the dance academy anymore—the one with a hyphen in her last name? What normal person puts a hyphen in their name anyway?"

Gilly's mother blinked and murmured something polite. Gilly herself wanted to shout with laughter, especially since Jacob clearly had no idea how to dam this embarrassing flood of information.

Cole came to the rescue. "You mentioned milk cows. So you and Nelson run a dairy?"

"Lord, no, not anymore." Claudia's double chin wobbled as she vehemently shook her head. "We sold off the herd except for one old cow. Nelson still gets up at four in the morning, though, and milks Daisy, then goes out to the pasture to whack a bucket of golf balls into the pond. Thinks he's Sergio Garcia or somebody."

"Sergio's Mexican," said Nelson without turning his head. "I like the American players."

"I'm pretty fond of golf myself," Cole said. "Do you play, Dmitri?"

Dmitri looked as if he'd landed among a pod of extraterrestrials. "Unfortunately I do not have the time for golf. But sometime I would like to learn."

Jacob's grandfather tuned in unexpectedly. "Come on up the mountain next time you're down this way, and I'll take you out to the pond. I like to practice my driving out there. And Claudia'll fix you a pot of chicken-and-dumplings that'll make you slap your granny."

Dmitri opened and shut his mouth, then nodded. It was the first time Gilly had ever beheld him speechless.

Jacob, perched beside his grandmother on the arm of the sofa, smiled and tucked his arm around her. "I don't know about slapping her, but she makes great dumplings."

Gilly swallowed the remaining bite of her turkey wrap. "I haven't had a dumpling in so long, I've forgotten what they taste like."

It was a mistake to call attention to her diet. Her mother gave her a disapproving frown. "You girls don't eat enough to keep a bird alive. It's dangerous."

"Gilly takes very good care of herself," Dmitri said warmly. "She does not starve like so many of our friends. The body is an instrument which has to get proper fuel. Otherwise it goes—" he sandwiched his hands together—"splat like this."

The others laughed, and conversation veered to the night's performance and all the little glitches and foibles that made live theater so fascinating.

Gilly caught Jacob's thoughtful gaze. She could tell he wondered about her. Well, she wondered about him too. So many questions. Like why he'd chosen to leave New York and had almost a phobia about going back. His brief explanations didn't satisfy her curiosity. Successful dancers quit for innumerable reasons, but usually it boiled down to one of three things: either they were disappointed with their careers, they got injured, or some drastic event forced them to go elsewhere.

He seemed so together, both as an artist and as a human being, that she could hardly imagine him failing as a dancer. Perhaps he'd just been dissatisfied with the New York rat race. She thought about her conversation with Harold in the shoe room. *"The good seed falls on all kinds of ground ..."*

Jacob's smile grew from a faint curve of the lips to a distinct twinkle in the eye.

Realizing she'd been staring quite rudely, she looked at her watch. "Dmitri, it's nearly eleven, and we have another long day tomorrow. We should go. Would somebody mind shuttling us to the hotel?"

Cole stood up. "You're right. Look, Madison's passed out on the floor over there. Laurel, we'd better get these kids in bed."

"Your dad and I'll take you and Dmitri," offered Mom. "We're headed to our hotel too."

The party broke up, Mary Layne and her family piling into their minivan to follow Cole and Laurel back to Montgomery for the weekend.

When Gilly said good-bye to Jacob's grandparents at the door, she received a smile and an awkward pat on the shoulder from Nelson. "You come see us soon, honey," said Claudia with another lavish hug. "I'll fix you a pot of those dumplings and never mind about getting fat. A man likes a little meat on his woman's bones."

"Not the man who has to lift her onto his shoulder," teased Dmitri as he put on his coat.

Gilly felt a tug on her sleeve and looked down.

Graham stood there crooking a finger. "Miss Gilly, I need to tell you something. Come here."

She squatted down to his level. "What is it?" she whispered.

He yawned, then grinned at her. "I think you're nice."

"Gosh, thanks." She hugged him. "I think you're pretty special too."

He laid his head on her shoulder, and she smelled the slightly salty odor of sweaty little boy. "Uncle Jacob says you're going to come watch me play soccer tomorrow."

"Yep." She cupped her hand against his head, enjoying the feel of his straight, fine hair. "So you'd better get to bed and get some sleep."

"Okay. Will you tuck me in?"

"Sure." She picked him up and found him compact and sturdy, but limp as a dishrag. Heavy.

"Nonna will do that," Jacob protested.

She waved him off. "Mom and Dad will wait on me for a minute." She carried Graham toward the bedrooms and peered into the one on the right—a man's room with a queen-sized cherry four-poster covered by a dark blue and green patterned spread. The artwork was tasteful and simple, a couple of framed oil landscapes on either side of an antique armoire and a bronze abstract sculpture on the mirrored dresser. A closet door stood open, revealing neat rows of clothing and shoes. Jacob's room reflected his personality, no big surprise.

She turned left, past the bathroom, and carried Graham into his small bedroom. Remarkably neat for a six-year-old, it had a plain wooden toy box under the window beside a white-painted bookshelf full of children's storybooks, DVDs, and stuffed animals. Several beautiful gemstones in their natural state were arranged on its top shelf. There was a small dresser on the wall opposite the single bed. Both looked handmade.

She set Graham down and turned down the plaid coverlet. "You want your pajamas?"

"Yeah. I mean, yes, ma'am." He yanked open a bottom dresser drawer. After pulling out a pair of cartoon-patterned red flannel pajamas and handing them to Gilly, he sleepily began to undress. Gilly had helped with her nieces and nephews for so many years, it was no big deal to help Graham into the simple night clothes and slide him into the bed.

"Good night, Graham." She leaned over to kiss his forehead.

"Dear God, thank you for Nonna and Poppa and Uncle Jacob," he mumbled.

Bewitched, she knelt beside the bed to listen to him pray. He mentioned the ballet, the party, tomorrow's soccer game, and Gilly. He mentioned Gilly so many times she finally peeked at him in amusement.

His eyes were open, and he was grinning at her.

"Graham, that's enough, you stinker." She gently pinched his ear. "I've got to go."

"Absolutely," came Jacob's deep voice from the doorway. "You should already be asleep."

Gilly looked around and climbed to her feet. "Don't fuss at him too much. At least he was praying."

"He's stalling. Master tactic number two hundred ninety-eight." Jacob crossed the room and bent to kiss Graham's forehead. "Now give over, young man. Tell Miss Gilly good night."

"'Night, Miss Gilly." Graham sighed, closing his eyes.

"'Night." She walked back to the front door, Jacob right behind her.

"Your folks are warming up the car," he told her, helping her on with her coat.

Something in his tone made her look at him over her shoulder. His expression was bland. "What did my mother say to you?"

"Not a thing."

"My dad, then."

Jacob laughed. "It was your brother-in-law. Wade—the one attached to Mary Layne?"

"Oh, no. He didn't mean it." Gilly covered her face.

Jacob turned her around and took her hands. "Look, you endured my grandparents with great aplomb, I must say. I can handle a random brother-in-law."

Something funny was going on in her stomach. He hadn't let go of her hands. "What did Wade say?"

"He asked me if I'm ready to be the Yankee homeboy."

Gilly didn't know where to look, but Jacob wouldn't let go of her. Then it occurred to her he wouldn't have any idea what Wade's crazy question meant. "He probably meant to ask if you're planning to stay in America, or if you intend to move back to Europe. For a preacher he can be a bit inarticulate."

"Oh, no, I understood exactly what he was asking."

She met his laughing eyes, then looked away. "I'm going to kill him. I'm sorry, Jacob, they're all very protective of the baby. But I promise you I never gave anybody the least idea that you—That you and I—"

"I'm sure you didn't." His tone was rueful. "Gilly … look at me, all right?"

"I'm too embarrassed."

"Please."

The soft, deep, almost Victorian sound of his voice brought her eyes up, and what she found there weakened her knees.

"Oh …"

"Yes." He brought one of her hands to his mouth and kissed her fingers. "I know we barely know each other, and you're very young. Too young, I suppose."

"I'm twenty-one!"

He sighed. "Yes. Just please tell your brothers-in-law and any other interested parties that I'm a very cautious chap. There won't be any hurrying along."

"Jacob, I don't know what to say." Her heart trembled like a blossom in a hurricane.

"It's best you don't say anything. Maybe let's just leave it at … I'll see you in the morning. Graham and I will pick you up at nine, okay?"

"Okay. I'll be ready." She took a deep, happy breath and whispered, "Good night."

Smiling, he let go of her fingers, and she hurried toward the headlights of her father's car, where her parents and Dmitri waited. Probably it would not be seemly for a twenty-one-year-old to start skipping.

Later, as she undressed, Gilly stopped and looked at the tips of her fingers. There was something to be said for a man who'd played the roles of princes, knights, and cavaliers. If Tucker had tried kissing her hand, she would've burst out laughing and asked him where the hidden camera was.

On the other hand—no pun intended—there was something slightly suspicious about the fact that that sort of thing came naturally to Jacob. After all, when it came down to it, he was a trained actor.

She yanked back the bedcovers and jumped in. She liked Jacob, she really did, but it was way too soon in their friendship to be oogling over Romeo-esque hand kisses.

As she set the alarm on her phone to make sure she got up in time for the soccer game, this morning's disastrous conversation with Victoria bounced through her head. She'd told Victoria she'd call later when she'd had a chance to calm down. It was late, almost midnight, but if she didn't do it now, there wouldn't be time for another couple of days. Victoria would think she was cold, hard, and un-Christlike.

Well, probably Victoria wouldn't realize it had anything to do with Jesus. But Gilly knew it did.

She took a deep breath and found Victoria's number. Gritting her teeth she pressed Call.

Victoria picked up just before the phone went to voice mail. "Is waking people up from a sound sleep a source of recreation for you?"

"I'm sorry," Gilly said automatically. "Were you asleep?"

"No." Victoria sighed. "Not really. But I was about to take a Lunesta and go for it. And don't preach at me about sleeping pills. Not everybody has your angelic conscience."

Why did I call her? Am I a total masochist? "Will you stop that for five seconds and listen to me? You seem to think I have this sainthood complex going on, but I assure you I have struggles just like everybody else—" Gilly stopped. Defending herself was a side trail. "Did you talk to Nicholas yet?"

"He apparently came in after I went to the studio and left again—he took his toothbrush and shaving kit. I haven't seen him since." Victoria's voice was icy, but Gilly thought she detected a shiver of some emotion underneath.

Wishing she could see her friend's face, she fumbled for the right words. "Vic, there's something else about that conversation between Nicholas and me. Something I think you should know. He knew there was something bothering you, and the first thing he said was he was afraid he was losing you. That tells me he loves you. Which is why he was so nuts over the idea of you and Ian ..." She wanted so badly to hammer home the idea that playing around with sex, sampling in the deep end of the boyfriend pool, was dangerous and counterproductive. But that would be a little like telling a cancer patient to switch brands of Band-Aids.

Victoria wasn't buying it anyway. "He was nuts because he's used to getting his own way. I'm not going to let him come back if he doesn't straighten up. If he hadn't been so selfish I'd never have looked at Ian. And I wouldn't have gotten distracted and careless on the issue of birth control."

Gilly tried to imagine what one of her older sisters would have said to such a monumentally stupid remark. All she could come up with was "Well, I just wanted to remind you I care about you. No matter what you say, that abortion had to have been a difficult thing to do. If you ever need to talk about it—"

"Gilly, it's not something I'm interested in talking about. Ever." She paused, then added, "Thank you for your concern, but I'm fine. Now I really need to get some sleep."

Gilly sighed and said good-bye. She laid the phone on the lamp table, turned over, and prayed herself to sleep.

Jacob was very much afraid he'd blown himself out of the water. How could a man get so out of practice?

Early Saturday morning he sat in the stands watching Graham turn himself wrong-side-out trying to reach the ball, which had been lined across the field by a kid a foot taller than him and twice as big around. Gilly bounced on the metal seat beside him, her colorful hair, coat, and scarf reminding him of the giddy tiger in Graham's "Pooh" video. Fist pumping the air, she screamed at intervals, "Go Massey! Go Mavericks! Kill 'em, Graham!"

She loved Graham, no doubt, and the feeling was mutual. This morning Graham had wrapped his favorite amethyst in a sock and brought it to her as a present. She'd gasped and said she couldn't take it. But when his eyes glossed, she kissed him on the head, told him thank you, and tucked it in her purse.

Barring a quick moment the day at the festival, she'd really only met his nephew last night, but Graham was going to cry when she went back to New York. Jacob couldn't undo that and wasn't sure he would if he could.

What scared him was the force of his feelings after being in this woman's presence only a handful of times. Tipping his hand last night had clearly made her very uncomfortable. No more friendly, open expression when she looked at him, and not once since he'd picked her up at the hotel had she tucked that confiding little hand in the crook of his elbow.

He wanted to go back and rewind the tape of that scene at his front door, playing it out another way in order to restore the playful sweetness of their conversation, the incipient intimacy of mutual interest in spiritual things. He'd always been in too big a hurry, too much of a rush to gain privileges. He'd thought he'd conquered it, but it appeared he'd done it again.

Graham blocked a shot quite neatly, and Jacob stood up to shout encouragement. Gilly jumped to her feet, whooping and clapping, and when Graham sent the ball whizzing toward a teammate who scored, she flung her arms around Jacob's waist. The second he hugged her back, she looked up at him, cheeks pink. He instantly let her go. But darned if he'd apologize.

When the game ended with the Mavericks on top, Jacob and Gilly walked out to the field to collect an ecstatic Graham.

He flung himself at Jacob. "Uncle Jacob! Did you see me block the shot? Did you see?"

"I saw, mate. Great job." He hoisted Graham onto his shoulders. "You're the man!"

"Yea us! Yea me! Mavericks rule!" Graham looked down at Gilly. "Did you see me, Gilly? Coach said I saved the game."

She high-fived him. "You bet I saw. I think somebody deserves a Happy Meal after that."

"Great," Jacob said, rolling his eyes. "Do you know how many times a week we dine at the Golden Arches?"

"Nobody can have too many Happy Meals."

Jacob shook his head. "And what are you going to eat? I bet you wouldn't recognize a french fry if it bit you in the nose."

"They have salads. I'll be fine."

And she was right. She watched Graham down his burger and fries without a twitch of envy, seemingly relishing her healthy food.

Jacob compromised with a grilled chicken sandwich, snitching a couple of ketchup-soaked fries out of Graham's box.

Graham finished his burger in five minutes flat and hopped down from his chair. "Can I go play, Uncle Jacob?"

"You bet. Let me hold your shoes."

Graham scampered to the indoor playground, where he found a clutch of children near his age to play with. Gilly leaned her cheek against her hand and watched him, smiling.

Jacob quietly studied the faint golden sprinkle of freckles across her nose, the delicate arch of her upper lip. Without the childish cap, her hair fell in uneven coppery waves just past her shoulders and clung to her bronze-colored sweater. She was all metallic shades, but somehow retained the warmth of refining fire. He'd give anything to know what she was thinking.

After a moment she turned her head. "What?"

He hesitated. "Did you sleep well last night? Still feel up to tackling the Mary dance in a bit?"

"Of course. Your welcome committee is taking good care of us. Somebody left a basket full of goodies. Very sweet."

"Did … did someone in your family give you a hard time last night?"

"Not exactly." She took a deep breath and let it out. "I generally talk way more than I should, and I'm trying to learn a bit of discretion. But I've been praying, and I think you'll be able to help me. It's Dmitri."

That wasn't at all what he'd expected. "Dmitri? Is he okay?"

"I'm not sure. I'm not the clichéd New York girl with the gay best friend. In fact, I'm still pretty uncomfortable with the openness of people's sexual behavior in general. You know what I mean?" Her green gaze was direct and a bit anxious.

He made a face. "Do I ever."

"Yeah. But we've naturally spent some time together lately, and he's beginning to open up to me, and I think there's something wrong.

I just don't know if I really want to know what it is." She laughed. "Does that make any sense? I guess I'm a terrible Christian."

"It's honest." He shrugged. "Do you want me to say, 'Well, that's okay. Now that you're aware there's something you're uncomfortable with, you've acknowledged it and maybe it'll go away'?"

She stared at him, then said slowly, "I think that's exactly what I want you to say."

Jacob could feel himself tense, even his skin drawing up. He didn't want to seem to attack or criticize Gilly, not at this early stage of a relationship that already seemed like a miracle. But anything he'd ever held onto had been crushed to powder in his hand.

Somebody bumped against his chair, a teenager absorbed by the music on his iPod. The kid mumbled an apology and shuffled into the next booth. The shrieks of the children in the playground blared through an open door. *McDonald's, Lord?* Jacob prayed desperately. Could there be a more ridiculous place to have a conversation like this?

Gilly had known—or suspected she knew—what Laurel or Mary Layne would say. Which was probably why she hadn't broached the subject of Dmitri with either of them. Big sisters would do that. Get into your business, poke holes in your excuses, make you look at things you didn't want to look at.

Jacob's eyes were filled with frank admiration, and she'd halfway expected him to throw her a softball. What she'd gotten was hard and fast and aimed at the inside corner.

So she instinctively jumped back.

"I'm probably imagining things. Everybody I know drinks—it's not like he did anything truly out of the ordinary." She waved a hand. "Besides, why should he listen to me?"

"The same reason I listen to you. You're beautiful and gifted and seem to have your act together. Your family is fascinating, and joy explodes out of you." He rattled those things off like an elementary teacher reciting the multiplication tables.

She didn't feel particularly flattered. She knew she wasn't perfect—witness her disastrous interactions with Victoria—but the outside trappings looked pretty good. "But ..."

Jacob smiled a little. "Dmitri watches you. He's fascinated and halfway hoping you'll screw up somehow and let him off the hook. All I'm saying is be patient. Allow the Lord to work and watch for opportunities to—" He lifted his hands. "People say it until it becomes banal, but I'm going to say it anyway—an opportunity to 'be Jesus' to him."

Feeling rather skinned and frightened in spite of the cartoonish setting of the restaurant, Gilly gulped down the rest of the water in her cup. She watched a set of young parents, lugging a baby carrier between them, herd a couple of preschoolers toward a nearby table. Jacob had taken her question seriously. Now she had to deal with it.

She sneaked a glance at him. "How do you know this?"

"I had a nanny when I was growing up," he said obliquely, in the tone of a storyteller. "Her name was Penny Babbs. Nanny Penny to me."

She giggled. "Sounds like a hen in a children's story."

"There was nothing remotely childish about Penny." He grinned. "She was a tall, boney, horse-faced woman who was too independent to get married—but she had this sort of Queen Elizabeth confidence. She believed God was in charge of the universe and proceeded to appoint herself second-in-command."

Gilly laughed, relaxing. She had no idea what this story had to do with anything, but at least the spotlight was off her. "She sounds a little like my Grandma Kincade."

He nodded. "If we'd lived near family, we wouldn't have needed her. But as it was, with Mum and Dad dragging Lily and me all over the Continent, we needed supervision when we weren't in school. Lily made it her business to disagree with Nanny on every subject, but I tended to take her rather seriously." Jacob leaned forward. "She loved Lily and me in her own way, though. Once, when I was about five years old, she went with my family on holiday to Scotland. I got left behind in an upstairs room of some Scottish castle—I'd accidentally locked myself in a closet. The next morning Penny found me, shivering and miserable. When she opened the door, the bats came squealing and fluttering out."

"Oh, Jacob ..." Gilly impulsively gripped his hands. "That's awful!"

"Well, I toughed it out—trying to be a man, you know. But I loved Penny with doglike devotion from then on."

"I should think so! How could they go off and leave you?"

He shrugged. "It was kind of like the story of boy Jesus from the New Testament, I suppose. Everybody thought I was with someone else. Besides, in the grand scheme of things, I didn't have such a bad life." He paused, gaze inward. After a moment he blinked and smiled at Gilly. "Are you bored yet?"

"Of course not!"

"All right, then." He didn't seem to notice he'd turned his hands to take hers. "Anyway, when I got older and out from under Nanny's thumb, I was—I think most people would say—hell on wheels. You know what the ballet world is like. Nanny's God of Judgment seemed very far away. I apprenticed at seventeen—I was a big chap for my age—and someone decided I was a rising star." A tinge of pink colored his cheekbones as he glanced at her, a slight grin curling his mouth. "It wasn't my mother."

She smiled. "I was fifteen when it happened to me. How long before you were invited into the corps de ballet?"

"A year later. Which was when Nanny Penny came back into my life. It was my first performance with the company in London. My parents were in Luxemburg for some reason, and Lily had already moved to the States for college. I told myself I didn't care and gave my comp tickets to Penny. I took her backstage to meet everybody, and it was the first time I ever saw her speechless." Jacob laughed. "She kept saying, 'Lor' bless me,' gawking at the girls' sequined headdresses and trying not to stare at the men's tights. She kept her eyes on my face the whole time, and I knew she was embarrassed by my costume. But she was proud of me and loved me, which was ..." He squeezed Gilly's fingers. "Well, you know."

"Yes, I know," Gilly said softly. "Then what happened?"

"When I was twenty or so, I took a trip across the pond to visit Nonna and Poppa and Lily for Christmas. While I was here, Lily and I took the opportunity to fly to New York. BNY had developed a reputation as the premier company in the world—the innovative choreography, buckets of Arts Council money, raw talent." He looked down. "I have to admit I saw the potential for fame and wealth, though I don't know if I'd have had the nerve to audition if Lily hadn't encouraged me to make contact. Through a ... an American woman I'd met in England, who put in a good word for me, I secured a meeting with the artistic director. As it happened, one of their principals had just retired, moving a soloist up and leaving a spot for ..." He shrugged. "Me."

He'd looked away as he mentioned the American woman, but Gilly sensed that was all he was going to say about her. "And the rest is history," she said with a smile. "Did you ever see your nanny again?"

"No, but she had a lot to do with my decision to—"

"Uncle Jacob! Miss Gilly! Come watch me climb the slide backwards!"

Gilly looked around to find Graham panting in the doorway between the playground and the restaurant. His cheeks were red, his hair lay in sweaty spikes on his forehead, and his "Massey Refrigeration" T-shirt hung outside his shorts nearly to his knees.

Jacob gave Gilly a rueful look. "I lost track of the time. If you're going to have time to learn the dance we need to go."

Gilly looked at her watch. "You're right. It's almost noon." She beckoned Graham. "Why don't you come get a drink? You look really thirsty."

"Yes, ma'am, but I really want you and Uncle Jacob to watch me climb." He glanced over his shoulder, where the other children were shrieking and laughing, still playing.

Jacob shook his head firmly, holding out his hands. "Come here, mate, I want to talk to you."

Graham hesitated for a moment before he let go of the playground door and came to Jacob, sock feet dragging on the tile floor. "I was really having fun." He allowed Jacob to fold him into his arms with affectionate roughness.

Gilly smiled. "We had fun watching you. We'll come another time. But I need to practice my dancing."

"Are you gonna dance too?" Graham looked up at Jacob.

"Actually, I am. And you can watch us if you want to."

"Really?" Graham's eyes widened. "Can I dance too?"

"Not today." Jacob shook his head. "Gilly's going to help me choreograph a very special dance. But you and I can dance tomorrow morning. Okay?"

Graham slid a look at Gilly. "I want to dance with Gilly."

Jacob smiled at her too. "Don't we all."

They went to the studio and danced until every inch of clothing was saturated with sweat, muscles warm and vibrating. Jacob wouldn't have worked her this hard, but he knew she'd gotten up early to warm up with some Pilates before the soccer game. Besides, she was in top condition, her beautiful muscles tensile strong, joints pliant as India rubber. After an abbreviated session of class exercises, he taught her the steps for the perfume solo by demonstrating it once.

Once. The next time, an incredibly quick study, she performed it perfectly—listening to his suggestions, shifting the turn of her *passé* to accommodate the light touch of his palm against her knee, following the prompting of his voice, turning his vision of the character into a winsome, exquisitely feminine picture of youth and joy.

The third time through, when he turned on the music, she added her own little twists of interpretation with small elegant arm gestures. A tipping of the head here, a curl of the fingers there. He sat on the studio floor and watched her, a helpless smile taking over his face. Of course he'd been right all along. She was born to dance this role.

The music climaxed, took off in a wailing, soaring bleed of electric guitar, synthesized strings and pounding drums, and Gilly sprang into a gravity-defying series of grand jetés that took her from one corner of the room to the other. Coming down from the last in a grand port de bras, she folded, rolled, and flung herself prostrate, spent, hands curled palm upward. He was close enough to see the shallow heaving of her ribcage, the butterfly tremble of her fingertips, though from the audience she would appear utterly still, as if dead.

Jacob didn't know whether to burst into applause or cast himself to the floor beside her in prayer. He did neither; simply stared at her, waiting to see what she would do. The music clicked over to the next track.

Gilly sat up with a fluid economy of movement and collected herself into a tidy lotus. A sheen of perspiration coated her neck and collarbone; her red leotard was dyed a dark ruby, and her hair curled in damp wisps around her glowing face. She smiled at him. "That was fun. Any suggestions?"

Yes, he wanted to shout. *Stay here and do this for me. No, not for me, for him.*

"I think you've about got it," he said as he got up to turn off the sound system. "Besides, I don't want to wear you out before the real performance tonight. The board will be very impressed."

"What time will they be here?"

"At three." He glanced over his shoulder at the clock. It was two o'clock.

She stretched out one leg and bent over to grab her toe. "Let's go ahead and tackle the pas de deux. I remember most of what you showed me in October, but it'll be different with the music."

"Absolutely, and that's because your Tucker is a genius. Come on,

I'll give you a hand up." They grasped each other's wrists, and he pulled her to her feet.

She dropped his hand and bent to massage her calf. "Ooh. Got a knot back here."

"Let me see." He knelt behind her and found the kinked muscle, rotating his thumbs into it. "That better?"

She gave a soft groan. "You should've been a physical therapist. I'd pay big bucks for that."

"That's the plan," he said without thinking.

"What?" Gilly turned around, pulling her leg out of his hands. "You aren't serious."

"I've been in PT school for nearly a year," he admitted, getting to his feet. He felt a little foolish. Here he was, wishing for the impossible: wishing the two of them lived in the same city so they could get to know one another properly—not this ridiculous talk on the cell phone, meet twice a year thing—wishing at the very least she could be the one to dance in his ballet. And at the same time he was entertaining the idea of leaving the ballet world behind.

She seemed to sense his ambivalence. "But Jacob, look at you. You can do this." Frowning, she spread her hands, indicating the mirrors, the scarred gray floor, the barres against the wall.

He looked away but still managed to see his confused self in the mirrors.

Gilly stepped back. "Why? Why would you give this up?"

"Come here. I'll show you why." He headed for the door and heard the *clock-clock* of her toe shoes as she followed him.

When he, Gilly, and Graham had arrived, they'd taken Graham with them into the studio. But he'd quickly gotten bored with the lack of toys and trotted off to the costume room, where Yolanda was conducting her usual last-minute pre-performance costume inventory.

Now they entered Yolanda's domain and found her perched on a stool, gluing glittery fake cookies onto a platter. She looked up. "Afternoon, boss. Y'all done for the day?"

"Not quite," said Jacob, scanning the room. "You haven't tied Graham to the anchor and dropped him overboard, have you?"

Yolanda's hair wobbled with her laughter. "Nope. Not that that's a bad idea. He's in there." She aimed her glue gun at the open door of the prop closet.

Jacob and Gilly peered inside. Graham sat arranging buttons on the floor under a rack of satin Munchkin jackets. He was splendidly arrayed in a pirate hat, eyepatch, and boots, a Santa coat and belt, and at least a dozen green, purple, and gold Mardi Gras necklaces draped around his neck. His cheeks were painted with bright red circles, and he'd enlarged his eyebrows to Groucho Marx proportions.

"He hasn't been a bit of trouble," Yolanda called.

Graham scrambled to his feet, scattering buttons. "Uncle Jacob! Yolanda says I'm the Dread Pirate Roberts. But I wanted to be Captain Jack Sparrow. And she won't let me have a sword, but she gave me some buttons."

Jacob looked at Gilly. "See?"

"There's nothing wrong with playing pirate," she said, eyes alight. "And I'm pretty fond of buttons myself." She crouched. "Here, I'll help you pick them up." She and Graham went crawling, looking for escaped buttons.

Jacob sighed. "The point is my schedule is so crazy I hardly ever see him, and when he's with me he usually winds up entertaining himself with some crazy something like this. I'm trying to think of ways to fix this situation."

Gilly looked up at him as she dumped a handful of buttons in the plastic box on the floor. "What you need to do is relax. This is one cool kid." Remembering Victoria's comment that raising a child as a single dancer would be impossible, she held out a palm for Graham to slap. "Right, dude?"

"Yeah, dude. I mean, yes, ma'am." After slapping her hand, Graham reached in his pocket and produced a small, hard, white crescent, which he placed in her palm. "Would you make sure the tooth fairy gets this? I'm not sure she knows Uncle Jacob."

Gilly laughed as she caught his chin with her free hand. "Let me see. Is it bleeding?"

"A little." He bared his teeth, sticking his tongue through the raw hole on the bottom row, then looked down at a pink spot on the white fake fur of his jacket. "Don't tell Miss Yolanda."

"Mum's the word, matey," Gilly whispered back. "Run to the restroom and rinse your mouth out, okay?" As Graham darted out of the closet, Gilly got to her feet. "Swishing with some warm salt water would be a good idea when you get him home."

"Will do, Cap'n." Jacob saluted. "Let me have that. What's the going rate for a tooth these days?"

She grinned as she handed it over. "I used to get a quarter for one this small. So with inflation … maybe a dollar?"

Jacob winced as he tucked Graham's tooth in the back pocket of his sweat pants. "How many of these have I got to look forward to? I may have to sell my car."

Gilly laughed. "And we're not even talking braces yet."

In the main room Yolanda was putting away her glue gun. "The Dread Pirate just zoomed through here. He show you that tooth? It was hanging on by a thread, but he wouldn't let me pull it."

"It's out now." Jacob peered over her shoulder. "I'll take him off your hands now. Thanks for letting him hang out with you."

"No biggie. He's really a sweet kid when you keep him busy." She pushed her glasses up on her nose with one knuckle. "I've got to get out of here, though. Got my grands coming in for tonight's performance, and I want to make my white chocolate pumpkin spice cake."

"Ooh. Will you adopt me?" Gilly batted her eyelashes.

Cracking a smile, Yolanda lifted her apron over her head and hung it on a hook on the back of the closet door. "We'll see. You locking up, Mr. Ferrar? I don't want anybody sneaking in here to mess with my stuff."

"I'll be happy to. We'll make sure Graham puts the costumes back where they belong too."

"I'd appreciate that." Yolanda hooked her brown leather purse over her round shoulder and paused in the doorway. She sent a speculative look from Jacob to Gilly and back again. "Mr. Ferrar, you know I don't pay attention to gossip."

There was something unfinished about the way she said that. Jacob instinctively put a bit more space between himself and Gilly. "But I imagine you hear a good bit of it," he said with a smile.

"Yes, sir." Looking away, Yolanda moved the purse to the other shoulder. "This place being what it is, a lot of it has to do with your ... personal life. Which, if you ask me, is nobody's business but yours." She cleared her throat. "But I wouldn't feel right if I didn't warn you about spending too much time alone with some of these girls." She gave Gilly an apologetic glance. "Not you, Miss Kincade—you're out-of-town, and you're, well, different. But, Mr. Ferrar, there's one or two of them got their hooks out for you, if you know what I mean. You might want to be careful." She dragged in a deep breath and released it as if she'd done her duty. "And that's all I got to say. I'll see y'all later at the theater."

Yolanda's lumpy little body whisked out the door before Jacob could conquer his astonishment and unglue his tongue from the roof of his mouth.

Gilly's eyebrows were up. Way up. "That was interesting."

"I was hoping it was my imagination." He sighed. "Come on. Let's find Graham and lock up here so we can finish preparing for the board demonstration."

They found Graham in the men's room. The water was running in every faucet, and he was happily squirting water at the mirror by cupping his hand under the stream. The red Santa jacket was wet to the elbows, dripping scarlet dye on the counter and floor.

"Graham!" Jacob roared. "Stop that immediately!"

Graham turned around, eyes wide. "Uncle Jacob! You scared me."

Laughing, Gilly sopped up the water on the counter with a paper towel while Jacob, grumbling, shucked Graham out of the coat, hat, and boots. After returning the costume pieces to their appropriate closets—the jacket had to be hung up separately to dry—Jacob locked the door of the costume room and tossed his nephew up onto his shoulders for the trip back down the hall to the large studio.

"I'm sorry, Uncle Jacob." Graham hooked his feet under Jacob's armpits and clung to his forehead with soapy-smelling little hands. "I didn't remember you told me to hurry."

"Well, I'm going to try to help you remember." He set Graham down and squatted in front of him. "Look here, Gray, we're going to be here just another little while. Miss Gilly and I have one more piece to work on, then some grown-ups are coming to watch us dance. This is very important to me, so sit here in the corner with your book and be quiet."

Graham's feathery eyebrows drew together. "I already read it two times."

"Fair enough." Jacob sighed. "I have another idea." He stood up and drew an imaginary circle with his toe. "You can listen to the music and move however you want to—as long as you stay inside this circle. If you go outside it, I'll know you're too tired to obey, and I'll have Nonna put you to bed early tonight." He brushed his thumb across Graham's forehead. "Got me?"

"Can I dance like a pirate?"

"If you're in the magic circle."

"Arrr!" Graham grimaced to display his newly gapped dental panorama. "I promise I'm not too tired."

"I'm glad to hear it." Jacob met Gilly's smiling eyes in the mirror. She was bent double, stretching to warm up her limbs after the short break. He moved to the center of the room and held out his hand. "Remember the opening steps?"

"I think so." She laid her hand in his.

"Good. Let's sketch the dance first, then we'll do it with the music. I made a few changes near the end. Added a lift." He smiled at her. "You up for it?"

Her eyes crinkled. "I'm hoping that wasn't a deliberate pun."

"Oh, well." He laughed. "So let's give it a try. And ... seven, eight."

She moved through the dance with him efficiently, flawlessly, concentrating on following his lead. He was astounded by her memory and her ability to anticipate improvements he'd developed since the one and only time they'd danced it. The duet was a serious moment in the center of the ballet, Mary and Jesus mourning the loss of Lazarus, their brother and friend. Even without the music he was aware of the magnitude of her art.

The moment for the lift came. "*Cambré* back," he murmured, grasping her waist from behind. "Up you go." His hands easily spanned her waist; she bent her knees and jumped. With a whoosh of expelled air, she firmed the muscles beneath her ribcage to give his hands purchase. As she folded backward over his shoulder, the clean, curving line of one leg extended over his head. Carrying her, he traced an expanding triple circle. He glanced in the mirror. She was light and still as a photograph. Extraordinary.

When he set her down en pointe and turned her by the waist to face him, she hesitated in his arms for a split second. He was breathing hard from the exertion of carrying her around the room, but his heartbeat roared in his ears for another reason entirely.

Their eyes held. He could feel himself bending and took his hand from her waist to cradle her cheek.

She did not move. "I don't remember what to do," she whispered. "I don't know what to do."

He couldn't have told her. He only knew there was a timpani banging around in his chest and he was no longer a character in a ballet, but a man in love with Gilly Kincade.

"Jacob? Is this how it goes?" She was looking at him uneasily.

He took a sharp breath and stepped back. "We'll finish with the *arabesque, promenade* into the deep cambré back like we did before." He turned away, ran his hand around the back of his neck, and stalked toward the sound system controls.

She must think him as bad as any New York predator. He had no business taking advantage of a dance to touch her face in that familiar way. He had almost kissed her. What if he had done it and she'd been forced to push him away? How embarrassing.

In the corner Graham was happily wiggling each of his remaining teeth between thumb and forefinger. Probably taking inventory of the cash potential, like the king in the nursery rhyme about the four-and-twenty blackbirds. At least he hadn't observed his Uncle Jacob making an idiot out of himself.

Jacob cued the computer to the correct piece and monkeyed with the volume level. Taking a deep breath, he turned to face Gilly. She'd taken her place at the far side of the room. They were to meet in the center when the drums kicked in in the ninth measure. She was regarding him with what he could only describe as anxiety.

No, she wasn't looking at him. Her gaze was directed over his shoulder.

He looked around. Alexandra Cooper stood in the studio doorway, poised a bit like a particularly dour department store mannequin—arms folded, rail-thin body draped in a long, synthetic knit sweater with leggings, and high-heeled pumps in modified third position.

She bared her teeth. "I saw your car and wondered what you were up to. Thought you might need a hand with something." Her eyes cut to Gilly. "But I see you've got everything under control."

Thirteen

Gilly was still getting her head wrapped around that near miss with Jacob when she looked up and saw the Hollywood-blonde axe murderess standing in the doorway. Alexandra Hyphen Girl. She had no idea what she'd done to provoke that steely stare, but things being what they were, she knew she didn't really have to do anything. Her mere existence was often enough to make her the target of advanced forms of jealousy.

Once she'd come into the dressing room for a costume change and found her hairpins and makeup scattered all over the floor. Nobody claimed to have seen the culprit. That was back in junior high days when she'd begun to take over roles usually handled by high school seniors. More recently, she'd found ribbons mysteriously yanked off her pointe shoes, globs of glue in the toe boxes, and costumes actually sewn together wrong-side-out. Childish, yes, and certainly not lethal, but maddening nonetheless.

Then Gilly remembered this was the woman she had edged out of lead position in the first row, the one who had dated Jacob. No wonder poison thought-darts were flying across the room.

With a sigh, Gilly sat down to do some butterfly stretches. She wasn't getting involved in this girl's identity crisis. Jacob would have to handle the situation.

He gave Alexandra an offhanded nod before turning back to the sound system controls. "Yes, we're working," he said without turning around. "I'll see you later tonight at the theater."

A violent flush crept up from the neckline of Alexandra's red sweater and stopped just under her chin. She looked like a blonde thermometer. "What are you working on?" she asked, her voice pitched a bit high, though clearly she was trying for calm.

Jacob's shoulder blades tensed. He looked over his shoulder. Gilly had been watching him teach and direct his company for two days. He was exacting, sometimes even peremptory, but never unkind. Still, this level of presumption would test anybody's patience. She couldn't help wondering how familiar his relationship with Alexandra had become.

There was a snap of temper in his brown eyes, but he kept his voice even. "It's not something I'm quite at liberty to talk about yet, Alexandra."

Gilly sighed at the way he said "Alex-ahn-drah." She wished she had a more exotic name herself.

Alexandra didn't seem to appreciate his pronunciation or his tone, much less the dismissive words, but she reined in an obvious inclination to argue. "Would you like me to take charge of Graham while you work? I don't have anything else to do." She smiled at Graham, who had been listening to the boring grown-up conversation with increasing signs of rebellion.

He ventured outside the magic circle and flipped over the nearest barre. "Look! I lost my tooth!" He stuck his tongue through the gap again.

Alexandra made a face. "Ew. I mean, how cute."

"Thanks, but he's fine. Graham, back in the circle." Jacob looked at his watch and frowned. "Look, we really need to get back to work. Would you shut the door behind you?"

"Of course," Alexandra said through her teeth and backed out of the studio, slamming the heavy door.

Gilly was afraid she had just made an enemy for life.

As if nothing out of the ordinary had occurred, Jacob looked at Gilly, eyebrows up. "Are you ready?"

She shrugged. Hyphen Girl needed a spanking, but if Jacob wanted to be gracious, so be it.

The run-through with the music proceeded without a hitch, but there was little time for discussion and adjustments before three o'clock and the first board members arrived.

Jacob introduced Gilly to chairman of the board, Frank Ireland, who came in first—a middle-aged businessman with a graying mustache and well-tailored clothes. Dr. Eric Sulley shook Gilly's hand and ran his eyes over her in a way that made her want to put on a coat. Next came an attractive young mom named Heidi Raintree.

Heidi seemed about to hyperventilate. "I've admired your work since you went to New York," she gushed. "I wish my girls could be here to meet you. Riley's still too young for *Nutcracker*, but India's a Mouse. She's so excited about the cast party tonight."

Gilly smiled. "I'll make a point of looking her up. And I'll sign something for the younger one too."

"That would be awesome!" Heidi backed away, eyes shining. "I used to dance myself when I was young, but I never ..." She swallowed. "Wow, this is so cool."

Gilly shook her head. If people only knew what a complete goober she was sometimes.

After Heidi, the remaining five board members arrived so quickly she couldn't sort out names and occupations.

Jacob was setting up folding chairs along the back wall, to her amusement lining up the front legs of each one in a perfect, rigidly straight row. "This is going to be a very abbreviated demonstration," he told Dr. Sulley, gesturing for him to take a seat. "I just wanted you all to get a flavor of the ballet with two of my favorite pieces. I'll have Gilly perform Mary's solo near the end, then she and I will dance the pas de deux. It's ..." He straightened and smiled at Gilly. "I think it's quite astounding."

Gilly swallowed. This ballet was more to Jacob than just a professional milestone. It was a spiritual gift on many levels. What if she blew it somehow? Disappointed him and ruined his chance to share this creation? She could hardly bear the responsibility. No paid performance this, nor an audition, but something in the nature of a spiritual battle.

Jacob walked over to kneel in front of Graham, laid a hand on his nephew's shoulder, and murmured something that made Graham giggle and plop down on the floor like a marionette with severed strings. Jacob looked over his shoulder at Gilly and gave her a tight, encouraging smile. His shoulders were back, his chin up, but his eyes were opaque, nearly black.

She stood praying silently as he moved to the sound system. She had removed her green leg warmers, giving them to Graham for safekeeping. He'd pulled one of them over his head like a stocking cap, letting it dangle over his shoulder, and tied the other around his waist. He looked like a small gap-toothed Grinch.

Suddenly relaxed by a completely inappropriate urge to laugh, Gilly reached up and removed the elastic band holding her hair. She shook it free, let it spill down her back, over her shoulders, in her face, and raised her arms to launch herself into Mary's sacrificial dance.

Six minutes and an eternity later she lay panting on the floor, the crashing music dying away. Gradually the Marley floor chilled her hot cheek, brought her back into the twenty-first century, quite literally grounded her in the moment. Reluctantly she gathered herself, kneeling, and pushed back her hair. The small audience was applauding with an enthusiasm all out of proportion to the surroundings. She felt almost as if those ten people intruded on a sort of holy of communion with her Savior.

Then she saw Heidi, who was brushing at her cheeks.

Oh, Father. What is this thing you've brought my way?

She saw Jacob's hand and looked up.

"Are you all right?" He was frowning, concern in his eyes.

"Yes, I'm ..." She took his hand and stood up on wobbly knees. She firmed them. "I'm fine. Was that okay?"

He laughed, and at first she thought she'd messed up so badly he was making fun of her. Then she saw that same look in his eyes she'd seen earlier—only this time he quickly masked it, dropping her hand and turning to the board. "Thank you," he said as the applause dwindled. "Please, take your seats. Now the pas de deux. Heidi, would you mind starting the music for us?"

While Gilly and Jacob stationed themselves across the room from one another, Heidi went to the corner where the sound system sat on a sturdy wooden table. Gilly refocused, immersing herself in the persona of a young Jewish woman who had been radically forgiven of every sin, past, present, and future. A woman who believed the Messiah would raise her brother from the dead.

She danced, thinking of her own brother, Michael, who had not been raised from the dead. No miracles there. His death had left jagged scars on everyone in her family, especially Laurel. But it was possible to recover even from a loss like that, to make the scars a point of strength. She had witnessed it herself. Jesus restored life.

She met Jacob's eyes and found him regarding her with a beautiful, tender appreciation. There was nothing inappropriate in his regard or his touch as he caught her, turned her, clasped her hand, but she felt his absorption in the music, his absolute control over his movements. His intent was to make her shine, to present her faultless. She knew she was in the hands of one of the great *danseurs* of her time. Tucker's music climbed in spirals of grand, sweeping strings, deep with cello, full with bass winds, and the magic she'd experienced in that first dance at Laurel's house tingled along her skin.

As the music climaxed in a wailing, tragic upward slide of electric guitar, the moment for the lift in a cambré back arrived. Gilly felt

Jacob behind her, hands grasping her waist. She bent her knees to jump, giving him leverage to lift her, and dropped backward over his shoulder in perfect balance.

And then everything blew out of control. There was an audible snap in her spine. Pain blazed from the center of her body in such violent waves, she couldn't tell where it began and ended.

"Put me down," she gasped. "Jacob, put me down."

Somehow Jacob lowered Gilly without dropping her, though his arms shook as if he'd turned a hundred years old in an instant. When her toes touched the floor, her legs folded like a paperdoll ballerina caught in a shredder. She crumpled onto her side, snow faced, mouth square with some internal pain she had no breath to articulate. He knelt beside her, a hand at the back of her head—he was afraid to touch her anywhere else—guarding her so that no one would try to move her. Somebody was calling 911; he could hear the anxious murmurs of the board members who had swarmed toward them.

Thank God somebody had turned off the music. He turned around to look for Graham and frowned. When had Alexandra come back into the room? She shouldn't be here, but at least she had Graham by the hand, restraining him from running to Jacob.

He looked down at Gilly, who had begun to pant in the panic-stricken way of a deer hit by a car. He began to pray, a numb, wordless keening.

"Is she all right?" he heard somebody ask.

"Of course she's not all right" was the derisive answer. "Look at her."

"But what's *wrong*? Is it her back?"

"We'd better hope not. You don't come back from a back injury."

Jacob felt like shouting at them to shut up.

"Uncle Jacob! Let me go! I want my daddy!"

Jacob looked over his shoulder and saw Graham yanking at Alexandra's hand, trying to get away. Gilly had begun to whimper softly. Jacob stroked her hair without much thought, even as he met Alexandra's worried eyes. "Let him go," he called, not knowing what else to do. Graham's screaming was only adding to the chaos.

Alexandra shrugged and released him. He darted through the circle of adults and flung his arms around Jacob's neck. "What's the matter? Is she dead?"

Jacob put his free arm around his sobbing nephew. "No, of course not," he said as calmly as he could. "But she's hurt, and we're going to take her to the hospital. She'll be fine." He prayed that was the truth.

Gilly took a shallow, hiccupping breath and opened her eyes. They were glazed with pain, but she reached up to tug on the leg warmer tied around Graham's waist. "Of course I'll be fine." Her voice was a fine thread. "Don't ... worry."

"Lie still," Jacob said more sharply than he meant to. "You shouldn't—" He swallowed his own rising panic. "Just don't move, okay?" He laid his fingers against her cheek. "The paramedics will be here any minute."

He knelt there hugging Graham and praying, listening to Gilly breathe, vaguely aware of the other people in the room. A few minutes later he felt a hand on his shoulder. He looked up.

Alexandra bent over him, her face creased with anxiety, whether real or manufactured he couldn't tell. "Is there anything I can do?"

He closed his eyes, trying to think. "Yes, call Wendy and tell her what's happened. She'll take care of cancelling the performance tonight."

"Cancel the performance?" Alexandra straightened. "Why would you do that?"

He wondered if she'd lost her mind. He glanced down at Gilly. "There's no way we can—"

"Jacob, she's just one dancer," Alexandra said impatiently. "You have hundreds of people expecting to see *The Nutcracker* tonight. I can dance that role."

Jacob had a simultaneous urge to shake her for her presumption and wilt with relief. Yes, she could dance Sugar Plum—though not, of course, like Gilly Kincade.

"All right," he forced himself to say. "Tell Wendy I said you can have the role. But she's in charge, and whatever else she says goes." The triumphant flare in her blue eyes made him sick, but he kept his voice even. "Do you understand me, Alexandra?"

"Sure, I've got it." She dug her cell phone out of her purse even as she pushed through the circle of onlookers. "Everything will be fine, so don't worry."

Don't worry, he thought, watching her go. *Right.*

Before he had time to change his mind and call her back, the EMTs arrived with a stretcher, exploding the surrounding crowd like so many marbles and pushing Jacob himself out of the way. He took Graham's hand and watched them gently examine Gilly where she lay, asking questions, not moving her until she was able to tell them exactly where the pain was. Eventually they slowly straightened her against a brace, Velcroed a cuff around her neck, and lifted her carefully onto the gurney.

Jacob followed, holding Graham by the hand, answering the paramedic's questions about his part in the accident. Was it an accident? Was there anything he could have done to prevent it? A dancer could be a millimeter off balance and sustain permanent damage. Injuries of this nature were often blamed on the male partner who had control of angles of trajectory, of height, of support and speed. Gilly had been, quite literally, in his hands.

He and Graham rode to the hospital in front with the ambulance driver, while the other two members of the team tended to Gilly in back. On the way he called Laurel McGaughan.

It was every bit as nightmarish a conversation as he could have imagined.

"How bad is it?" Laurel demanded.

"We don't know yet. The medics have stabilized her, but they won't give her anything for the pain until they know ... Well, of course she's in pain, but she has to be X-rayed before they'll know what to do."

"What hospital?"

Jacob told her, and Laurel shouted something to Cole and hung up.

The hospital was only minutes from the studio. When the ambulance rolled up to the ER, he got out and picked Graham up to hurry inside behind the team pushing the gurney. The waiting room seemed to be swarming with people. He was afraid Gilly would have to wait, but because she came in on the ambulance they seemed to consider her an emergency and took her straight to triage.

Jacob started to follow, but a nurse stopped him.

"Are you her husband?" She glanced down at Graham, who clung to Jacob.

"No, I—she's a guest dancer this weekend for Birmingham Ballet Theater. I'm the artistic director, and we had an accident in a rehearsal. I'm not sure what happened."

Actually he knew exactly what happened. He'd been careless and Gilly was hurt. His stomach heaved.

The nurse seemed to sense his distress. "I see you have her purse," she said with a kind look in her eye. "Maybe you could sit down and give me some information."

"I'm afraid I don't know much. We aren't—I mean, we haven't had much opportunity to become close. Gilly's sister is on the way here from Montgomery." He looked dubiously at Gilly's pink dance bag, which also contained a small brown leather wrist bag, presumably holding her driver's license and insurance information. "If I could just check with her for a moment and get her permission to pull out her ID ..."

The nurse bit her lip. "I guess you ought to. We can't treat her without insurance, and the doctor will want to take her to X-ray and give her pain meds as soon as possible." She looked at Graham again. "You could come back, but not with the little boy. Isn't there someone you could leave him with?"

"No, I'm afraid—"

"Jacob! How is she?"

Jacob turned to find Cynthia Hawkins hurrying through the sliding door of the ER. She was wearing a pair of black yoga pants and a Crimson Tide sweatshirt. Her hair was in a messy ponytail at the back of her head. He'd never seen such a beautiful sight in his life.

"Cynthia! How did you know to come?" He would have called her if he'd thought about it, but his brains seemed to be scrambled like a carton of eggs.

"Your ballet mistress called. Said there'd been an accident, and she thought you might need help with Graham." She knelt, giving Graham a reassuring smile and folding him in her arms. "Come here, sweetie. Want to go play with Reid?"

Wendy was the most efficient woman in Alabama. She must have gotten Cynthia's number from Jacob's emergency file at the office.

He met Cynthia's warm blue eyes. "Gilly's in a great deal of pain, and I need to speak to her right now. Thank you for coming—you don't know how grateful I am. My grandmother is coming to stay with Graham tonight. In fact, she was planning to spend the night. But she won't be here for another couple of hours."

"But—what happened? Did Gilly fall?" Cynthia stood up, keeping a hand on Graham's shoulder.

"She didn't fall. I had her lifted backward over my shoulder, and I think something just twisted or snapped. We'd already done the lift twice today without a problem." He shook his head. "I'm not sure what went wrong."

The nurse cleared her throat. "Now that you've got someone to watch your little boy, maybe you'd like to come on back?"

"Oh—yes. Yes, I would. Cynthia, would you—"

"Of course I will." She took Graham by the hand and smiled at him. "Let's go back to my house, and when Jacob finishes, he can come get you, all right?"

Graham's bottom lip trembled as he looked up at Jacob. "You won't forget about me, will you?"

Jacob crouched and cupped his face, kissing his forehead. "I'll never forget you, son. Be good for Cynthia. I'll come for you in just a little while, after I make sure Miss Gilly is going to be all right."

Graham suddenly gave a little hop and slipped out of his backpack. He unzipped it. "You can give her my book. It makes me feel better when I'm sick."

Jacob took the ragged copy of *Clifford the Big Red Dog* and tucked it under his arm. "That's very kind. I'll make sure she gets it." He offered his knuckles for Graham to bump with his and got to his feet. "I'll call Nonna and tell her where Graham is," he said to Cynthia. "Otherwise she'll worry when she gets to my apartment and nobody's there. Thank you again for being here."

"That's what family's for," she said matter-of-factly and gently tugged Graham toward the door. "Come on, buddy, let's go see the puppies."

"Oh, yeah! The puppies!" Jacob heard him exclaim as he followed the nurse into the triage area.

He found Gilly lying on a bed behind a blue curtain, eyes closed. He thought she might be asleep, but he touched her arm and her lashes fluttered. "Jacob?" she said, licking her lips. "Where's the doctor?"

"He's coming." Jacob showed her the bag in his arms. "Is it all right if I open your wallet to give them your insurance card and ID?"

"Yes, of course." Her voice was a whisper. "Are you okay?"

He stared at her. "Me?"

"I thought you might have had a misstep. Twisted your ankle or something."

"No, nothing like that. I don't know what happened, Gilly." He tried to inject a note of heartiness into his voice, hold the bewilderment at bay. "I'm sure you're going to be fine. It's just one of those funny spasms we have sometimes."

"I'm sure you're right." She closed her eyes again. "I'm sorry I ruined the demonstration."

"You mustn't worry about that," he said, horrified that she would think of the ballet when she was in such pain. "Besides, you were absolutely beautiful."

Her lips curved. "What time is it?"

He looked down at his watch. "A little after four."

"Make the doctor hurry. I've got to get into my makeup and costume."

"You're not dancing tonight!"

"But I have to—I signed the contract. I gave my word." She was panting again. Opening her eyes, she pulled at the neck brace. "Get me out of here."

"Gilly, stop." Dropping the bag, he caught her hands. "You hurt your back. I wish you hadn't, but we have to let the doctor look at you, and you have to rest. Alexandra can do Sugar Plum—not as well as you, of course, but as they say, the show will go on." Gilly was tugging at his hands, tears sliding from the corners of her eyes. "Please, Gilly, lie still. Don't make it worse."

The nurse poked her head around the curtain. "Everything all right back here? Got that ID?"

Gilly subsided, and Jacob gently squeezed her fingers. He looked over his shoulder at the nurse. "I'm coming. What about the doctor?"

"Right behind me."

"Okay," Jacob said. "I'll be right there." Gilly was clinging to his hands, still crying. He had an overwhelming urge to pray over her. "Gilly, I'm going to talk to the nurse for a minute, but I'm right here. I called Laurel, and she'll be here within a couple of hours. We'll get this sorted out, and you'll be back onstage before you know it—just not tonight. Are you listening?" He looked at her anxiously, willing her to relax.

Finally she nodded and sniffed. Her fingers loosened, and she wiped her eyes with the sheet. "Okay. Will you come back in here after you finish ... whatever?"

"I told you, I'm not going far."

"Okay. Thanks, Jacob." She gave him a trembling smile. "Don't worry, I'm not falling apart. I'm not that big a diva."

He brushed the back of his fingers against her cheek, then picked up Gilly's bag and followed the nurse to a tiny anteroom full of medical gadgets, mysterious cabinets, and a messy desk. He sat down on a leather stool and took Gilly's wallet out of the bag. Maybe she wasn't falling apart, but he couldn't shake the feeling that something irrevocable had just happened to her and to him. He knew on a surface level that God was with the two of them, but he could have used some reassurance.

Fourteen

Laurel's face swam in whirligig circles that reminded Gilly of her first grande pirouette. She closed her eyes to keep from throwing up. "Hi, Lolly. How long have you been here?"

"What, baby? Say it again, I can't understand you." Laurel's voice was anxious, motherly.

Gilly was so relieved to have her sister in the same room, she wanted to weep. "Said … Never mind." She was too tired to compose intelligible sentences.

"How are you feeling?"

The sheet scratched her arms, her feet were cold, and she truly *truly* needed a drink of water. "Um. Okay. Go home?"

Laurel laid something blessedly warm across her legs and feet, then brushed her hand across Gilly's head. "Yes, now that you're awake. Want some ice chips?"

That tipped her over the edge. She started to cry. "Please." She gulped. "Sorry."

"Are you hurting? The medicine was supposed to have kicked in."

"It has. I'm not ..." Her thoughts were so tangled. "Oh, Laurel, I'm scared. I've never done anything like—Felt like I broke in—broke in two!" She was blubbering like Rosie when somebody took a toy away from her, but she couldn't seem to stop.

Laurel laid her cheek against Gilly's, impervious to tears and snot and incoherent whining. "Hush, hush, it'll be okay. We'll let a specialist look at you. Please try not to worry."

Gilly might have cried indefinitely, but the ER doctor wandered in with a chart and discharge papers. He was young, buff, and bald, but Gilly couldn't have cared less. She could hardly see him through her swollen eyes.

He peered at her over the top of the chart. "Somebody said you're ready to go home."

Gilly gave a great sniff and looked at Laurel, who jumped in. "She's ready. What can you tell us about her back?"

The doctor's gaze escaped to the chart. "Not much. I don't see anything from the X-ray that indicates a tear, but sometimes that kind of thing won't show up without an MRI. You'll need to make an appointment with an orthopedist Monday." He looked up. "You want me to recommend a specialist? I understand you're from out of town."

"I'm a d-dancer," Gilly said. Her voice felt thick, as if she'd been swallowing yarn. "I need somebody who treats athletes."

"Somebody in Montgomery," Laurel added. "She's coming home with me."

The doctor looked dubious. "I don't recommend a two-hour drive tonight. You need to stay flat as much as possible until you can get to the orthopedist."

Gilly felt her lips tremble. "I guess I can go back to the hotel. But Laurel, you didn't plan to stay the weekend, did you?"

"I'll do whatever I need to," Laurel said staunchly. "I'm not leaving you to deal with this by yourself."

"You can both stay in my apartment." Jacob stood behind the doctor, towering over him. "Or if you need to get back to Montgomery, Laurel, I'll have my grandmother stay over with Gilly. She'd love to help out."

"That's very kind of you," Laurel said, "but I don't think—"

Gilly's squishy emotions suddenly teetered toward Jacob. He looked as tightly wound as a spring in a screen door. Had he been sitting out in the waiting room all this time worrying about her? "Lolly, that might be a good idea. Your girls need you."

Laurel had taken on an astonishing resemblance to their mother. Her dark red eyebrows slammed together. "I'm not leaving you. Cole is perfectly capable of managing without me. On occasion."

Jacob smiled tiredly. "I'm sure he is. And of course you're welcome to stay. I can send Graham with Nonna to Alabaster, and you can have his bedroom." He hesitated. "I was just going to say, I'm familiar with dance orthopedists at UAB Hospital. There are a couple of fellows there with national reputations. And the physical therapists are quite good too. I can recommend one or two."

The doctor was looking harried. "Well, if you all have a plan, I'm going to discharge you, Miss Kincade. When you get home, lie still and take your pain meds, okay? Use the pain as a gauge of how much to do." He efficiently removed the IV drip from Gilly's arm and slid its stand out of the way. "Get dressed, and I'll send someone with a wheelchair." Dr. Buff, Bald, and Beautiful ducked around Jacob and disappeared.

Suddenly aware of her flimsy cotton gown, Gilly tugged the sheet higher under her armpits and frowned at Jacob. "If you're sure we won't be a nuisance, we'll take you up on your offer."

"Good, then." As he backed through the curtain he looked at Laurel. "You remember where I live, right? Nonna's at the apartment—I'll call and have her change the sheets. It will thrill her to be useful." He took a breath as if to say something else to Gilly, then shook his head and disappeared.

Laurel frowned at Gilly. "I'm not sure this is a good idea at all."

"Why?" Gilly suddenly felt like all Seven Dwarves were plying their little pickaxes inside her head. She pinched the bridge of her nose. "There's something wrong with this medicine."

Laurel looked conflicted, as if she didn't know whether to scold, apologize, or holler for the doctor. "Never mind," she said with a sigh. She helped Gilly take off the hospital gown and struggle back into her leotard and tights. It was an excruciating process, and Gilly began to sweat. It was all she could do not to burst into tears again.

Finally, when she lay on the gurney panting but fully dressed, Laurel glanced over her shoulder and put her hands on her hips. "Okay, I'm just going to say it." She leaned close to Gilly's ear. "Gilly, Jacob is clearly in love with you. I don't think you should encourage him by staying at his apartment."

Gilly's mind was suddenly jerked off the agony in her lower back. "What?"

"You heard me. Anybody with eyes in their head can see it. Besides that, he's single, you're single, and it just wouldn't look right."

"Laurel—It's too soon! You're ... mistaken." She wanted to say "crazy looney-tunes nuts-o" but this was Laurel, and one did not impugn her judgment.

Then she remembered that little good-bye scene at the door last night ...

"Gilly, a man does not sit alone in a hospital waiting room for three hours for a woman he cares nothing about."

"He does if the woman's a dancer and he's the artistic director!"

"Sshh! He'll hear you!"

Gilly lowered her voice. "I don't care! Besides, he lives in New York and I live in Alabama. This is a logistical impossibility."

Laurel suddenly grinned. "You are so stoned."

"I am not!"

"R2-D2."

It was an old family joke and it made Gilly giggle. "Come to think of it, he kind of sounds like C-3PO, doesn't he?"

Laurel tilted her head. "No, more like Alec Guinness."

"Uh-uh. Simon Cowell."

"Colin Firth."

"Ooh."

"Are you ladies decent in here?" asked a nurse standing in the opening of the curtain with a wheelchair. "Ready for me to boot you out?"

Laurel jumped guiltily and helped Gilly put on her shoes.

While the nurse helped Gilly into her coat, then assisted her in moving painfully from the bed to the wheelchair, Laurel went to move her car to the ER entrance. The transfer into the front seat of Laurel's Honda was accomplished with a great deal of pain on Gilly's part and a certain amount of breathless swearing from the nurse. Gilly lay back in the flattened seat, swallowing useless groans. "Thank you," she told the nurse through gritted teeth. "Have a Merry Christmas."

"Oh, I will," said Clara Barton cheerfully, duty discharged. "I get off in an hour, and I'm taking my daughter to see *The Nutcracker*."

Gilly had to laugh. "That's lovely. Have fun."

Laurel shut the door on her and went around to the driver's seat. "Are you going to tell me what happened? What did Jacob do to you—or what did you do to yourself?"

Gilly looked at her sister uneasily. "Didn't he tell you?"

"I didn't want to talk to him. I was worried about you. I'm still worried about you."

"I appreciate that." Gilly closed her eyes as they pulled into traffic. She winced as the car's rear wheels jounced slightly against a curb. Good thing they weren't driving all the way to Montgomery right now. Even high on Demerol, she couldn't imagine enduring a plane ride back to New York.

Laurel turned off the radio. "So …"

Gilly sighed. "You remember that biblical-based ballet Jacob told us about, back in October? The dance we did at your house?"

"Yes." Laurel sounded noncommittal. "Tucker's been working on the music."

"Right. Well, Jacob got permission to demonstrate it to his board of trustees. They're considering letting him add it to the spring program."

"But you're doing the mermaid ballet in the spring, right? BNY wouldn't release you to come back here again for any extended time."

"I know. I told Jacob that, and of course he was disappointed, but I offered to do the demo, since he'd already basically taught me the Mary dance. He thought they'd be more likely to approve it if I showed them the solo and danced the pas de deux with him."

"A-huh." Laurel's voice was dry. "I didn't say he was stupid."

Gilly gave her sister a reproachful look. "Anyway, we rehearsed a bit this morning and afternoon, and that went fine."

It had been more than fine. Gilly wished she could scrape the mental image of Jacob's intent brown eyes out of her head. Erase the imprint of his hand on her cheek. She looked up at the ceiling of Laurel's car. "There's baby food on your sun roof."

Laurel grimaced. "I don't doubt it. No wandering off the subject."

"Okay. So there's this girl—woman, I guess you'd say—a dancer in the company who likes Jacob and follows him around. She came in while we were rehearsing. I don't know what she thought—maybe she thinks she was supposed to have the lead—"

"What did she do?" Laurel was in overprotective-mother mode again.

Gilly hadn't meant to mention Alexandra Hyphen-Girl. Certainly hadn't meant to blame the accident on her. "Nothing, she just offered to babysit Graham—"

"Who?"

"Remember? Jacob's nephew? He lost his first tooth today.

Anyway, Jacob basically told Alexandra to get lost. I sort of felt sorry for her, but now I'm wondering if Jacob wasn't a little distracted when—"

"I knew it was his fault!"

"Laurel—"

"It's his responsibility to make sure the lifts are safe." Laurel might be sixteen years older and your basic law geek, but she had been Gilly's confidante since Gilly could talk. She knew most of the ins and outs of the dance world, knew the basic lingo, knew the "rules."

The male partner was responsible.

Gilly had to consider the possibilities. Alexandra had slipped back into the room sometime during the demonstration. Had Jacob glanced over at her, shifted his weight, thrown himself—and thereby Gilly—off balance?

She couldn't say for sure that he hadn't. She didn't want to ask him, because what was he going to say?

But she also wasn't sure she would ever completely trust him again.

As if there weren't enough drama in his life already, Jacob's two-bedroom apartment was now inhabited by an excited six-year-old boy and three women—one of whom was physically incapacitated and high on pain meds, the other two trying to outdo one another in southern hospitality. Besides that, his ballet company was performing without him tonight, and he wasn't sure he was going to make it to the cast party before it ended. Wendy would certainly be able to handle any emergency, but he still felt a little weird about the whole thing.

His immediate concern, however, was making sure Gilly was cared for and that Laurel and Nonna didn't come to blows over the correct and socially accepted way to make up a bed. His grandmother was all for putting on the top sheet wrong-side up, so that, when folded back, the printed design showed. She had seen this on an episode of Martha Stewart back in the nineties, and Jacob had long ago acknowledged the futility of arguing with her. Laurel, a proponent of hospital corners and simple efficiency, clearly thought this was ridiculous. Fortunately, to Jacob's relief, the judge's manners won out over domestic snobbery, and she gracefully ceded the field.

Jacob, meanwhile, had given Graham a bath and packed his pajamas and a toothbrush in his small backpack in preparation for the overnight trip to Alabaster. The two of them were sitting at the kitchen table, Graham eating a peanut butter sandwich and Jacob listening with silent amusement to the feminine negotiations, when Laurel walked in shaking her head.

"If we'd had women like Mrs. Claudia in command of the Allies, the invasion of Normandy would've happened a lot sooner." She opened the freezer compartment of the refrigerator and started scooping ice into an ice pack sent home from the emergency room.

Jacob laughed. "How's our patient?"

"Sound asleep." Laurel zipped the ice pack and shut the freezer door. "We'll be fine here. You should go do your—" She waved her hand—"ballet thing."

Was Gilly's sister being considerate, or did she not want him around? "I'm not especially inclined to celebrate," Jacob said slowly, "but I probably ought to show my face at the cast party."

"Then please, go ahead. Don't worry about us. I'm going to call my parents, fill them in. I'm hoping Gilly won't wake up until morning." Laurel paused in the doorway. "You've been very kind, Jacob, letting us take over your ... letting us stay here."

He glanced at Graham, who was making little pills of his bread crust and stacking them on his plate. "But?"

"But please don't attach any special significance to it." Laurel's expression was guarded, severe.

He picked up the jelly spoon and wiped it off with a napkin. "I don't quite understand," he said carefully, "what it is about me that you all find so abhorrent."

"I'm sorry," Laurel sighed. "I probably sound like a crazy woman. But Gilly's young and has her whole career ahead of her. She's reached a rare level of success. Now she's developed a sort of crush on you, and if you come in like a knight on a white horse when she's this vulnerable, her emotions will run away with her." She glanced at Graham. "There are other considerations as well."

Jacob told himself that he was very tired and shouldn't say anything he'd regret later. Besides, as she'd pointed out, one never knew what Graham would pick up and repeat. "You must believe me when I say I would never do anything to harm your sister. I've made mistakes, as your husband has probably told you. But I've given my life to Christ, and he rules me. Simple as that."

Laurel didn't look satisfied. "I want you to keep your distance—at least for now."

"If one more person in your family tells me to back off—" Jacob stood up, his movements jerky. "Gilly may be the baby to you, but she's a grown woman, and sooner or later you're all going to have to let her make her own decisions and mistakes."

Laurel stared at him for a loaded moment or two. She was a tall woman, clearly used to making an impression. Finally she gave a little huff of annoyance. "Well, then. We agree to disagree. I'll find another place for us to stay tomorrow." She turned on her heel and walked out of the kitchen.

Jacob rubbed his forehead. He had just thrown down a gauntlet in what shouldn't even be a competition. "Come on, Gray, let's find Nonna and—" He looked around and found Graham with his head on the table fast asleep. "Sheesh." He picked up the dishes and put them in the sink, then lifted Graham into his arms. "It has been a long day, hasn't it, lad?" he sighed against his nephew's cheek and carried him into the living room.

Gilly woke up feeling like Goldilocks in a strange bedroom with gray light filtering through white miniblinds and dark curtains. The pillow was hard. Too hard. Her head ached, and pain gouged her lower back every time she tried to stretch her legs. She discovered that if she lay on her side, very still, the pain lessened so she could sort through her thoughts like socks in a laundry basket and find a couple that matched. One, she could hear Laurel talking to Jacob in another room. Two, this was Jacob's apartment, and thus she must have slept in his bed.

Disconcerting enough.

Then she remembered what she'd done to her back.

Fear originated in her solar plexus and radiated along every nerve path in her body until she was vibrating like a cell phone against a wooden table. Which made the pain worse.

Surely this was another one of those wicked muscle spasms every dancer had to deal with sooner or later. She would see the orthopedist, who would recommend a physical therapist, who would give her some adjusted Pilates moves that would strengthen her back until the spasm went away.

Unreasonable fear held her in a vise. Sunday school words drifted down on her in flakes of memory. *Whenever I am afraid, I will trust in You ... For God has not given us a spirit of fear, but of power and of love and of a sound mind.*

Still she shook.

"Laurel?" She sounded pitiful. She bolstered her voice. "Laurel, can you come here?"

Her sister came running. "I was trying to let you sleep. How do you feel?" Laurel leaned over her, the back of her hand against Gilly's forehead.

"I don't have a fever," Gilly said, trying to control the peevishness in her voice. "But my back still hurts."

"Let me get one of your muscle relaxers. I'll be right back."

Laurel disappeared again, and Jacob stepped into the doorway. His face looked taut, like a line drawing in an artist's sketchbook. "Did you sleep?" he asked, sliding his hands into the back pockets of his jeans. "Everyone in the cast is concerned for you, and I prayed for you all night."

She wanted to pull the pillow over her head but couldn't very well throw him out of his own room. "I must have," she mumbled. "I sure don't remember anything."

His dark eyes lit. "That's probably best."

"Oh, no. What did I say?"

"Sometime around two in the morning you were singing the 'Alphabet Song' from *Sesame Street.* Loudly."

"Great. Channeling Big Bird in my sleep."

"Actually I was impressed. Not everybody can correctly pronounce 'Abkadef-Gajeckle-Manop-Kerstoovwix-Iz.'" He leaned against the doorframe, grinning. "Graham loves that one."

Laurel pushed past him, carrying a pill and a glass of water. "Here, sweetie. Take this. We need to keep your pain under control."

Gilly struggled to her elbow and shoved her hair out of her face. She must look like a Cabbage Patch doll. But she frankly didn't care. "Thanks, Lolly." She took the pill and downed it thirstily with the water, then lay back down, panting from a fresh onslaught of knives in her back.

Frowning, Laurel set the glass down on the bedside table. "Dmitri is here to check on you. Do you want to see him?"

She didn't, mainly because she ought to be getting on the plane with him this afternoon. But his feelings would be hurt if she said no. "Sure."

As soon as Jacob stepped aside, Dmitri fairly leaped into the room. "Gilly! I am so very sorry you have injure your little self. The Sugar Plum they pair me with last night weighs half a ton and has legs like a giraffe—no offense intended—" He cast a glance over his shoulder at Jacob. "But I cannot believe you do not feel like dancing with me." He seemed to take Gilly's injury as a personal affront.

Which unaccountably made her feel better. "I don't feel like dancing with anybody," she said dryly. "But if I did, it would be with you. You haven't called Maurice, have you?"

"Are you crazy? I do not volunteer bad news of any sort to Maurice." Dmitri shuddered. "This you will have to do."

"Fine." Gilly relaxed somewhat. She didn't look forward to the chore and planned on putting it off as long as possible. "If he asks, tell him I'll be back in New York by tomorrow."

"Gilly, you're not going back tomorrow." Laurel put her hands on her hips. "You can't lie to him, and you can't expect Dmitri to either, for that matter."

Gilly closed her eyes. "That's not what I ..." Her mental laundry basket was filling with mismatched socks again. "I'm really tired," she mumbled.

She felt Laurel's hand on her forehead. "Okay, then go back to sleep. We'll talk about it later."

"Good-bye, my little fairy," whispered Dmitri in her ear. "I will have your back. Call me when you are feeling better." He kissed her cheek, and she heard him tiptoeing away.

She sighed, thinking she was alone, but when she opened her eyes Jacob was still there, looking at her with something like guilt in his dark eyes. She flushed. "I thought you went away."

"Do you want me to call Maurice and tell him what happened?"

Panic flared again. "No! There's nothing to tell him. I'll see the doctor tomorrow, he'll give me something to ease the pain until I can get home, and I'll ... get better. This is nothing to worry him about."

Jacob shook his head. "All right. Then do you need anything else?"

"I just want to be by myself," she blurted. When he flinched, she added, "To pray. I need to pray."

He hesitated. "I'm going to church this morning, and Dmitri agreed to come with me. May I ask my small group to pray for you?"

"That would be fine," she said to get rid of him. She turned her face into the pillow. "Thanks, Jacob. Have a good time."

He was walking around on two good legs and a strong back and could spring into a jeté or a *balloné battu* if he wanted to. Surely he didn't expect her to be all jolly.

He sighed. "God be with you, Gilly."

"He is," she whispered. But somehow she didn't feel it.

Fifteen

Jacob did not want to think about Gillian Kincade in his apartment, asleep in his bed. Or, rather, in the darkest pit of his brain, where Romans 7:21 dwelled, he really did want to think about it. This could explain why he'd lost his head and invited a gay ballet dancer to come to church with him. The fact that the dancer accepted the invitation continued to worry him all the way into the church parking lot.

The fact that he managed to carry on an intelligent conversation with said dancer, while simultaneously worrying about his own admittedly shaky machismo at said church, was a testament to answered prayer.

Or possibly schizophrenia.

"Tell me," said Dmitri as they pulled onto the interstate, "if you think Gilly's injury is serious." He paused. "You were there."

"I'm not a doctor." Jacob couldn't help feeling defensive.

Dmitri sighed. "Do not misunderstand me, my friend. I have myself been charged with ending a partner's career. It is not a pleasant thing." His voice hardened. "But I am good enough dancer that Maurice does not fire me. I am thinking ... you are out of practice and should no longer make the lifts."

If Jacob had not been thinking the same thing for the past twelve hours, he might have pulled the car over and told Dmitri to walk to the airport. "Perhaps you're right," he said evenly. "But we should hope for the best regarding Gilly's prognosis. As you've noted, we are in a rather physically precarious art. Dancers, like athletes, face injury every day. We deal."

Dmitri sat quietly with his hands clasped for a moment. "Yes, we deal. But Gilly is kind to me when many others treat me as useless fluff. I am very upset when she is upset." He shrugged and looked at Jacob. "I do not know what to do, but I will think of something. You understand me?"

Jacob understood. One more layer in the wall of protection around Gilly Kincade had just gone up. If it hadn't been so frustrating, he would have been amused.

"I don't want her upset either, Dmitri, but we live outside the garden of Eden. Life throws bricks at us sometimes." He smiled when Dmitri's blue eyes narrowed. "But I want you to know I plan to make sure she gets the best medical treatment available. And she has an army of people praying for her. Me included." He took a breath and dove off a spiritual cliff. "Watch and see what God will do."

Dmitri stared at him for a moment. "I watch. Believe me, I watch, my friend."

Jacob wasn't sure what had just happened, but he allowed the conversation to drift to other topics until they arrived at the church's landscaped entrance. Cheerful flags snapped in the winter breeze along the driveway, giving a Six Flags–like welcome.

Dmitri frankly gawked at the looming brick edifice of the church. "So your faith, it is the same as Gilly's? Evangelical Christian?"

"That's right." Jacob pulled into a parking spot in the second tier down from the worship center, and the two of them got out of the car.

"Has she talked to you about it much?" He glanced at Dmitri, who was returning the wave of one of the volunteer attendants.

"A little. I know she goes to church most Sundays, and she invited me once or twice to go with her." Dmitri shrugged, tugging his handsome tweed sports coat into place. "Me, I am too lazy. I like to sleep in."

Jacob smiled. "That's normal. But if your faith means anything to you, church is an important part of your life. I wouldn't miss it myself."

They entered the building, and Jacob caught sight of the Hawkinses waving at him from a table in the café. He almost ignored them in favor of taking Dmitri directly into the worship center. Jacob didn't think his friends would treat Dmitri with anything but respect and kindness, but you never knew. He felt somehow responsible to Gilly, whose concern for her dance partner was sweet and endearing.

But *God* was in control of reaching Dmitri, he reminded himself, not Gilly and certainly not him. Besides, it wasn't as if Dmitri had a homosexual tattoo on his forehead.

Lord, he prayed all the same, *let us not shame you.*

Cynthia stood up to hug Jacob as he approached the table, and Rick offered a hearty handshake, as did Al Wright. Jacob gestured toward Dmitri, waiting with a smile to be introduced. "This is Dmitri Lanskov, one of our guest dancers in *Nutcracker* this weekend. He's with Ballet New York. Dmitri, meet my good friends Cynthia, Rick, and Al."

Dmitri shook hands, clearly trying not to stare at Al's bushy red beard, camouflage cap, and T-shirt that said "Fish tremble at the sound of my name."

Al, in turn, cast a couple of suspicious looks from Dmitri to Jacob and back again. Questions marks were all over his face.

"Where's your sidekick this morning?" asked Rick, pulling up chairs. "Reid always pouts when Graham doesn't show up."

"He went to his Nonna's house last night." Jacob glanced at Dmitri. "We had an accident yesterday in a rehearsal, and my guest ballerina hurt her back. She had to have a place to stay until she could get to the doctor on Monday, so I sent Graham to Alabaster."

"She stayed in your apartment overnight?" Cynthia stared at him, scrappy eyebrows raised.

Jacob backpedaled. "Yes, but her older sister is with her." Now what kind of impression had he made? Dmitri wouldn't understand the big deal about having an overnight female guest.

Al whacked him on the shoulder. "So what does that blonde you had with you a few weeks ago think about that?" He seemed relieved that Jacob had more than one woman in his life.

"I have no idea," Jacob said wearily.

"You have a blonde girlfriend?" Dmitri was frowning, perhaps on Gilly's behalf.

"I have *no* girlfriend," Jacob said, then gave up on making sense of this ridiculous, highly unspiritual conversation. "But I told Gilly I'd ask you all to pray for her. Would you do that?" He looked at each of his friends in turn.

Cynthia's round face softened. "Of course we will. What else could I do to help?"

"I'm not sure." Jacob lifted his shoulders. "Like I said, her sister is here for the weekend, but I suspect Laurel will have to head back to Montgomery soon. This is Supreme Court Chief Justice McGaughan we're talking about. Besides that, she and her husband have two little girls."

"Goodness. That's a pretty influential family." Cynthia glanced at Rick, and some silent communication took place. "Would she need someone to take her to the doctor?"

"Maybe. Thanks, I'll tell Gilly you offered." Jacob looked around when the worship center door opened and congregants of the earlier service flooded into the café, raising the noise level dramatically. He stood. "I'm going to buy Dmitri and myself a donut and coffee before church starts. Anybody else want anything?"

Standing in line at the coffee counter, he watched Dmitri cheerfully answering Cynthia's questions about life in Russia and New

York. Jacob knew he could count on her to head off Al's unintentional tactlessness. He forced himself to relax. This sense of impending disaster had to be all in his head, a particularly subversive attack of the unseen enemy. All things were promised to work for the good of the beloved—wasn't that what the pastor had taught them just a week ago?

All things for good.

He clasped the Bible under his arm a little tighter.

On the way back to the table he ran into Eric and Sandra Sulley. He had not seen them at the cast party—in fact had forgotten all about them in the complications of Gilly's injury. "Good morning." Jacob set the coffee cups down on a nearby table and extended a hand to Eric. Confused to find the doctor's grip less than enthusiastic, Jacob smiled at Sandra. "I didn't see you folks last night. Is everything all right?"

To his surprise, Sandra looked down, blinking back tears. "I'm sorry Brittney behaved so badly, Mr. Ferrar. I hope you'll give her another chance next year."

"Did she not dance last night?" Jacob looked at Eric.

"No, she didn't dance—your witchy ballet mistress wouldn't let her." Eric's face was tight. "I might have known you don't know what's going on in your own company."

The unfairness of the accusation registered along with acknowledgment of its partial truth. "Eric, you know what happened yesterday. I couldn't be two places at once. Wendy always does what she thinks is best for the entire company—and, ultimately, for each individual dancer. Brittney has to learn that temper tantrums won't get her where she wants to go." He was too tired to be diplomatic.

Eric's face reddened, but Sandra put a hand on his arm. "I know you're right, Mr. Ferrar. It's just that Brittney's an only child, and it's difficult to justify denying her what we can afford to give her. And ..." She hesitated. "Keeping her out of all four performances seems harsh. Especially when you replaced her with a younger girl who hasn't even been in the company a year."

"I'm sorry you feel that way." Jacob stood his ground, backing Wendy as he would expect her to back him. "As I told Brittney, life doesn't always seem fair, and God distributes gifts in ways that don't seem to us evenhanded at all." He lifted his Bible. "Think about the parable of the talents. The master gave out different amounts to each of his servants, and he was more interested in what each one did with it than how much they brought back."

"Are you comparing yourself to Jesus?" Eric said incredulously.

"Of course not—" Jacob looked around, realizing Rick and Cynthia were waving him back to the table. "I'm sorry, but Dmitri Lanskov came to church with me this morning, and I need to get back to him." He picked up the coffee cups. "Please tell Brittney not to give up. If she really wants to dance, hard work can sometimes compensate for other shortcomings."

He nodded and made his way back to Dmitri and his friends. There was little he could do about the Sulleys' disappointment except pray they'd get over it. He had more important things to think about now.

Late Monday afternoon Gilly sat flipping through a September 2006 issue of *Good Housekeeping*, regretting the persistent fashion for bared navels. Not that she had much modesty to retain after the examination and series of MRIs she had just suffered through.

Oscar Lobianco, MD, who Jacob claimed was the most respected orthopedic surgeon at Birmingham's teaching hospital, seemed to know what he was doing; truly she had no prejudice against southern doctors as did many of her professional peers. But this was her life, her *instrument* under consideration here. If the girders of a building faltered, collapse was inevitable.

She felt as if the betrayal of her spine had left her rootless, to be blown about like dandelion fluff, and she was doubly resentful of the weakness because she was always so careful. There had been nothing in that cambré back that she hadn't done hundreds of times.

She always warmed up meticulously in order to avoid injury. Besides that, her torso, limbs, and feet were designed by God, perfectly proportioned for balance and form. That was not bragging; it was a documented fact she had been told over and over and for which she was suitably grateful.

I was dancing for you, Lord.

Be anxious for nothing floated through her head as she read the effusive caption of a photo of Jennifer Aniston.

Scripture notwithstanding, she'd be crazy not to worry a little. The pain had not gone away as she'd hoped—assumed—it would. If anything, it was worse. She'd barely been able to tolerate the ride in the car from Jacob's apartment to the doctor's office. Now she propped herself up with sheer force of will, refusing to let Laurel—seated beside her reading an equally ancient issue of *People* magazine—see the extent of her agony. Laurel needed to go home and tend to her babies, and if she thought Gilly needed her, she'd stay here hovering like a lioness.

Gilly refused to contemplate the possibility that surgery might be on the horizon.

Dear God, please not that.

Maybe if she'd been able to go to church yesterday she wouldn't be feeling this discombobulating helplessness. Singing with other believers, listening to the reading of Scripture and a sermon never failed to restore her courage and her joy—whatever might be missing at the moment.

Both courage and joy were sorely absent this afternoon, after that highly unsatisfactory and confusing conversation with Dr. Lobianco. He had listened to her description of what had precipitated the injury—which was exactly nothing in particular—asked her a few more seemingly unrelated questions, and frowned at the emergency room X-rays. Then he'd ordered the MRI and left, presumably to practice his stone-faced medicine on some other lucky person.

Mainly, Gilly just wanted to go home to New York. To get her life back, to thrill to the challenge of creating Maurice's tragic mermaid Ione.

Suddenly she remembered Maurice's warning about Jacob. The thing about him being a womanizer.

Jacob hadn't overtly tried to seduce her in the way Maurice meant, but with deep-set brown eyes and cultured inflection and slight smile had just as surely coaxed her to dance that disastrous demonstration. She hoped his board would vote to let him produce the ballet. Otherwise her sacrifice would be for nothing.

No. *No, no.* There would be no sacrifice. She couldn't think that way.

"Okay, baby?" Laurel put down her magazine.

"I wish people would quit thinking of me as a baby." Laurel pursed her lips, and Gilly felt like the jerk she'd probably sounded like. "I'm sorry, Lolly. I'm just aggravated this is taking all day."

"You've lived in New York too long. You didn't used to be so impatient."

"You'd be impatient, too, if you hurt like this."

"I know, baby—I mean—" Laurel laughed. "I've been a mother for four years. The habit's already ingrained."

"You've always called me that." Gilly looked away.

Fortunately, the nurse appeared in the waiting room doorway. "Miss Kincade? Would you like to come on back?"

The hollow space in her stomach wasn't entirely hunger, though she hadn't eaten since breakfast and it was nearly four in the afternoon. To ease the pressure on her back, Gilly tightened her abdominals, quads, and gluts as she got to her feet. The doctor was going to tell her what to do to fix herself. She would get on a plane for New York and life would return to normal.

Laurel put an arm around her waist, and they shuffled like a pair of eighty-year-olds down the hall behind the nurse.

"Remember the day we went to the Boll Weevil Museum when you were campaigning?" Gilly murmured. "I feel like that statue looking down at her arm in the bottom of the case."

Laurel laughed, jiggling Gilly and making her sorry she'd tried for a joke. "Pretty messed up, wasn't she?"

"Yeah. I'm scared, Laurel."

"I know." Laurel squeezed her gently. "But don't borrow trouble. You'll be fine."

They waited for fifteen more minutes before Dr. Lobianco swung into the exam room, his long Italian face as sober as Laurel's when she had to pronounce judgment on some courtroom loser.

Loser loser loser, Gilly thought as he sat down on his little black stool and flipped on the X-ray light.

"Spondylolysis is a stress fracture of the vertebrae." The doctor tapped a spot on the X-ray. "I thought I saw it here, but the MRI confirmed it. Dancers and gymnasts develop them, most commonly because of excessive hyperextension of the spine." He glanced at Laurel. "It has a hereditary component, but typically doesn't present pain unless there's a sudden trauma or repeated excessive stretching of the lumbar area."

"You mean like a cambré back. Or a grand port de bras." Gilly looked at Laurel, her heart thumping. "Both of which are major elements of the pas de deux in Jacob's ballet."

"Exactly," he said, turning off the light. "I want to put you on bed rest for a few days, then a physical therapy regimen. And a lumbar orthosis—a back brace—for a few weeks, until you're stronger. No dancing, unless you want to cripple yourself permanently. But you can work up to bike riding, swimming, anything that won't stress your lower spine. After three months we'll reevaluate."

"Three months?" Gilly croaked. "I'm going to dance again, am I not?"

The doctor shrugged. "There are no guarantees. Your fracture is pretty severe. But if you take it slow, don't try anything sudden, the tissue usually heals itself."

Gilly found herself speechless.

The doctor rose to offer Laurel a handshake. "I'm honored to have met you, Judge McGaughan. Miss Kincade, I saw you dance Friday night, and I have to tell you, I didn't want to go. But my little girl has been wearing a tutu since she could walk, and my wife insisted we take her. It was almost worth missing the SEC playoffs. I wish you the best. You'll need to stop by the nurse's station to make a follow-up appointment. She'll fill you in on the PTs in our area."

He whisked himself out of the room with a flutter of white coat, leaving Gilly to blubber, "Does that mean my back's broken? What am I supposed to do about *The Little Mermaid*?"

Laurel drew a breath and visibly collected herself. "Let's go talk to the nurse. Sometimes they're more coherent than the doctor."

The nurse was indeed more informative, and had a much better bedside manner to boot. Her face crimped in sympathy as she produced a list of reputable physical therapists in the Birmingham area and offered to call for a set-up appointment.

Gilly stared at the list as if it were written in Swahili. "I'm going back to New York. This won't do me any good."

Laurel took the paper from her. "Gilly, let's talk about that on the way home, okay? I don't want you up there with a bunch of strangers. You don't even have a roommate. What if your back collapses again?"

"Strangers?" Gilly stared at her sister. "I've lived there for four years!"

But the nurse was looking dubious too. "I don't recommend that long plane trip right now. Some of the best PTs in the country practice and teach at our hospital. Maybe you should do a little research before you decide."

One part of Gilly's brain needed somebody to tell her what to do; the other was sick of people making decisions for her. Dance prescribed steps from someone else's artistic vision. Pirouette to the tinkle of the music box.

In any case, well-bred southern women did not argue in front of strangers. She pulled herself together and tweaked the PT list from Laurel's hand. "We'll talk about it later." She gave the nurse a smile, albeit a tight one. "Thank you. I'll make some phone calls." Pushing against the nurse's work station desk, she levered herself to her feet. Her back would not collapse. She was a trained athlete.

She hobbled down the hallway toward the exit without Laurel's support—but paradoxically couldn't help being grateful for her sister's presence.

"I'm sure they have good doctors in New York," Laurel began as soon as they were in the car and headed back to Jacob's apartment.

"Of course they do. Dr. Glaasmacher is the premier dance orthopedist in the country."

"But, Gilly, I've been in that apartment. There's no elevator, and you'd have to make it up and down that flight of stairs every day. When Mom finds out about this, she'll want to come stay with you, just to make sure you don't kill yourself." Laurel sent her a droll look. "Are you sure you want that?"

"I'll—I'll move back in with Victoria."

"Listen, you're not going to be able to dance anyway. Why don't you move in with me?"

"That's very kind of you, Lolly, but the doctors I need are either in New York or ... here." She hated to admit it, but Birmingham was beginning to look like her only choice. She really didn't want to move back in with Victoria and Nicholas's cigarettes and listen to ballet talk twenty-four hours a day when she couldn't dance. "I'll find a ground-floor apartment here, close to UAB. At least you're within driving distance if I get in a jam."

"But who's going to take you back and forth to physical therapy until you're strong enough to drive?"

Gilly squeezed her eyes shut against tears. "I don't know, Laurel! I need time to think before I make any decisions."

Silence throbbed in and around Gilly's head. She felt Laurel's concern, but couldn't make herself absorb it. Couldn't quite push away the terror.

"All right," Laurel said quietly. "Let me know when you're ready to have a discussion."

The implication being that Gilly was childish for wanting to work this out on her own.

When she'd first moved to New York for ballet school at seventeen, her mother had lived with her for a year, flying back and forth to Mobile whenever breaks came in the schedule. It had been hard on her father, who didn't travel well and missed his wife. But they'd sacrificed so that Gilly could have her once-in-a-lifetime chance at the big time.

For a while she'd been utterly dependent on her mother's company, her support, her wisdom. Then gradually she'd looked around and realized most of her peers were on their own; that her own family's close ties were considered abnormal. Mom's constant questioning and advice began to chafe. When she'd been invited to apprentice in Ballet New York's corps de ballet, she'd negotiated for freedom—promised to move in with Victoria, promised to find a church, promised to remember her upbringing. Her mother had reluctantly moved back to Mobile.

And she'd been wildly successful. Nobody could say she'd reneged on any of her promises. Nobody could say the Lord didn't have his hand on her. She'd taken that for granted until ...

Now. Now it seemed God had removed that hand of protection, of outright blessing.

And what was she going to do? Oh, what was she going to do?

Sixteen

Monday afternoon around six, Cynthia called Jacob to say she was on her way over with Graham. Sitting on the couch, he closed his cell phone and stuck it in his pocket, glancing down at Gilly. Because the floor was the only place she could get comfortable, she lay on the carpet on her back, with her knees bent as if she'd been mown down by an army. Her purple yoga pants revealed the fragile lines of her body, and he thought he could have counted each of her ribs through the thin knit top. Worry crawled through his chest.

He could hear Laurel in the bedroom tidying up. She had to return to Montgomery tonight—Cole had called to say Rosie had been crying for twenty-four hours straight and he was afraid she was going to make herself ill—and Gilly would have to go back to the hotel. Even with Graham as a dubious chaperone, she couldn't stay here.

"Would you like something to eat?" He leaned forward, forearms on his thighs. "I could make you a sandwich or a smoothie."

"Thanks, I'm not hungry."

He wanted to argue with her, but something told him that would not be a smart move. "Okay. Let me know if you change your mind." He'd had a long day himself and his stomach rumbled with hunger. A conference with a local costume designer had been conducted over lunch, but he'd not eaten much. He'd been too worried about Gilly. "Do you want to talk about what the doctor said?"

"No." She opened her eyes. "I was thinking about Dmitri. How did it go at church yesterday?"

She was thinking of Dmitri?

"For such a garrulous fellow he's very reticent about anything personal." Jacob smiled. "However, he made it clear he's protective of you. Basically put out a death wish on anyone who breathes on you with ill intent."

Gilly's nose wrinkled. "He's so funny."

"He admires you, Gilly. You have a more powerful influence than you know."

"But I feel like I'm getting nowhere. He's gone back to New York and I'm stuck here—"

"Okay, but he heard God's Word in a powerful way yesterday. I could see him taking it in, looking at the people around him, wondering if it could really be true. You and I have to keep praying. Believe me, some circumstance will eventually bring him face to face with the holes in his heart—if it hasn't already. And guess who he'll turn to."

Gilly sighed. "I know you're right. It's hard to be patient, though."

The doorbell rang, and Jacob went to answer it. As soon as he flipped the lock and opened the door, Graham charged in with Reid Hawkins on his heels.

"Hi, Uncle Jacob!" Graham quickly flung his arms around Jacob's waist, then the two boys tore off to Graham's bedroom.

Cynthia stood on the doorstep hefting a huge casserole dish

covered by foil, a Wal-Mart sack hanging over her arm. She smiled. "Anybody here in the mood for barbecue?"

"You are my dream woman," he said. "Are you sure you're taken?"

Cynthia came inside, wiping her feet on the rug. "Rick seems to think so." She saw Gilly lying on the floor, and her grin faded. "Uh-oh. What's the matter?"

"We're having a terrible, horrible, no-good, very bad day." Jacob took the casserole and headed for the kitchen. "I'll take care of this."

As he set the dish on the stove, he couldn't resist lifting the corner of the foil, sending the tangy aroma of barbecue wafting throughout the small apartment. He could hear Cynthia introducing herself to Gilly, whose response was subdued but polite.

He returned to the living room to find Cynthia sitting on the floor in front of the sofa beside Gilly. He should have asked Cynthia to come over already. She was a genius at sorting out other people's problems.

"I'm so sorry to hear that," Cynthia was saying. "You must be really distressed."

Gilly blinked hard, her nose pinkening. "I'll figure it out. Until I do, I'm going back to the hotel. My sister has to go back to her family and her job, and Jacob has to kick me out." She gave him a trembling smile.

"No way!" Cynthia exclaimed. "You'll come stay with us—we have an extra bedroom, and we're just around the corner from here."

Gilly's mouth fell open. "You can't be serious."

"Why not?"

"Because—because you don't know me from Adam's house cat!" Gilly looked at Jacob.

He shrugged. "Don't look at me. I'm the neutral party here."

"That's a fine solution." Laurel stood in the living room doorway with her overnight bag in her hand. When Gilly looked rebellious,

Laurel sighed. "Gilly, honey, I'd feel so much better about leaving you if I knew you were going to get real food and have a homey place to stay." She nodded at Cynthia. "I'm Laurel McGaughan, Gilly's sister. Thank you for bringing dinner."

"You're most welcome. I'd heard so much about—" She caught Jacob's eyes. "I mean, we've been praying for Gilly. And we'd be honored to have her stay with us." She clapped her hands. "A real ballerina!"

"I'm sure your husband will be totally impressed," Gilly said, a smile curling her lips.

To Jacob it was like the sun coming out after a long, rainy day. "You'll like Rick," he said. "And I have to tell you the real draw, at least according to Graham. In fact, he may stow away in your suitcase."

"Why?" Gilly was grinning now.

Jacob leaned forward. "There are puppies," he whispered. "Two of them."

"Really?" Gilly looked enchanted.

Cynthia nodded. "There were nine, and we managed to give away all but the last two."

"Gilly, you can't have a dog," Laurel said as Gilly struggled to sit up. "You live in an apartment in New York City, for heaven's sake."

"I'm afraid these particular puppies would be even less appropriate," Cynthia said ruefully. "They're golden Labradors. Two months old and they already look like lion cubs. They're eating us out of house and home."

Gilly rolled to her knees, put her hand on her back, and stood up carefully. "Well, if I can't have my big sister while I'm laid up, at least I get to cuddle a puppy." She looked at Cynthia. "Are you sure I won't put you out too much? It'll just be until I can figure out what I'm going to do."

Cynthia bounced to her feet. "We'll be thrilled to have you. I'll take Reid home and freshen up the guest room while y'all have your supper. Jacob can bring you over later." She went to the door of Graham's room. "Reid! Come on, let's go, sweetie!"

"Aw, Mommy!" was the inevitable reply.

In short order, General Hawkins marshaled her one-man troop and marched him out to the car, leaving Laurel to serve up Cynthia's excellent pulled pork barbecue. After quickly downing her own sandwich and making sure Gilly ate at least a couple of bites, Laurel said good-bye and admonished her sister to keep her updated daily on her progress.

Laurel paused in the doorway. "If you need anything—*anything*," she added with a mock-severe frown—"you call, and I'll come running." The frown skewered Jacob. "You have my cell phone number."

Jacob felt like saluting. "Yes. But she'll be fine with Cynthia. And we'll be careful."

"I'm counting on that." Laurel shut the door behind her.

Jacob grimaced. "There couldn't possibly be any criminals left on the loose in Alabama."

Gilly laughed. "You see why I have this gigantic inferiority complex." She painstakingly got to her feet, and Jacob had to forcibly restrain himself from touching her. She'd made it clear she didn't want his help. "I'm going to get my stuff together so I can get out of your hair." Carefully she left the kitchen, leaving Jacob to stare after her.

The apartment was going to seem very empty when she was gone.

Left alone to settle into Cynthia Hawkins' modest guest room, Gilly opened her suitcase, which Jacob had deposited on a small cedar chest at the foot of the bed. She quickly undressed and pulled on her white chenille bathrobe and a pair of athletic socks, then lay down on the puffy lavender comforter.

Used to a performer's gypsy existence, she was not particularly discommoded by moving into a stranger's home. But her back hurt and she was deeply ambivalent about the expression she'd caught in Jacob's eyes tonight when she looked at him over the top of the fluffy head of one of Sunflower's puppies. She knew she ought to disapprove of that calm, lionlike stare, perhaps even run from it, but she couldn't help a sort of feminine *recognition*, a bottomless and almost intuitive knowledge of him. It was the kind of exchange of glances one saw in a Bogart-Bacall or Tracy-Hepburn film. She'd seen Cole look at Laurel that way.

Gilly herself was not at all prepared to deal with that look. Lately, she realized, she wasn't prepared for anything. Maybe that was the point.

When she was younger she'd just assumed she'd meet someone and fall in love. Simple, like her parents—a soul mate with similar goals and values. When her dreams—and some doors God had opened up—took her to New York, the idea of romance took a backseat. Like in the trunk, buried under the jack and spare tire. Dancing won out over friends, family, and even Tucker's lackadaisical courtship.

Now that she took it out and looked at it, she knew she didn't want to remain a solo act for the rest of her life. There had been real potential for something unique and lifelong with Jacob Ferrar. Something almost tangible, that satisfied a longing she didn't even know she had.

Which brought its own fear. She'd *wanted* to help him demonstrate his ballet, because she wanted to please him. Surely a good thing. But the wiser thing might have been to obey the spirit of her contract and let him figure it out on his own.

Everybody knew what happened when you submitted yourself to another person's life and will and ambitions. It could be really really good. Or it could land you in the hospital.

On the other hand, God had seemed to be telling her that helping Jacob was the right thing to do. He would never purposely hurt her, she knew that. The accident was an *accident*. She had a hereditary condition.

Abandoning her tangled and probably pharmaceutically induced thoughts, she flipped open her phone and pressed her mother's speed dial number.

Mom answered on the first ring. "Gilly! How are you, sweetie? Do you want me to come up there? I can have the car loaded in thirty minutes if you need me. You father will just have to eat at the club."

Dad was perfectly capable, when push came to shove, of making scrambled eggs, PBJ, and many other plebian but nourishing forms of sustenance. Gilly laughed. "Thanks, Mom, but I'm doing fine. Jacob has a friend from church who's putting me up in her guest room for the time being."

"Jacob? The ballet director? You're sounding very friendly with him. I have to admit I really liked his grandmother, even though she was a bit on the countrified side. But I'm glad he's taking responsibility for your well-being. It's the least he can do."

"Mother—"

"Oh, you know what I mean." Mom yawned. "Excuse me. I've been working at the Junior League store all day. We made a killing and someone actually bought that hideous lava lamp your great-aunt Dodie gave me for my college graduation."

"They'll probably be back in style in another fifty years or so."

"I would *die* if they came back in style because that would mean old hippies had taken over New York." Gilly could all but hear her mother shudder. "So what did the doctor say, honey? Laurel gave me a very abbreviated explanation on her way home to Montgomery, but we got cut off when her wretched cell phone went through a towerless area. You know I can't bear not knowing what's going on."

"He didn't actually say very much at all. Just called it spondylolysis and handed me over to a physical therapist." *And said I might not dance again,* she added silently. It would never do to tell her mother that. She'd be in the car and on her way north in thirty seconds flat, and Gilly had sworn Laurel to reluctant silence.

"Just don't let them talk you into a chiropractor. Those people are quacks. All right, then, sweetie, I'm going to let you go. You sound tired, and I want you to rest. You've been working too hard this year. I'm positive that trip to Greece sapped your energy and you've never recovered, which is why your back was susceptible. Would you like to say hello to your father?"

Gilly suddenly very much wanted to talk to her father. She wanted to put her head on his shoulder and bawl. "Yes, let me talk to him. I love you, Mom. Good night."

"Love you too, baby. Here he is."

"Gilly?" Her father's deep, slow voice nearly did her in.

"Hi, Daddy. What're you up to tonight?"

"Watching *Hardball.* I still think Laurel should run for national office. She's smarter than all these goof-offs in Washington put together."

Gilly smiled, immediately settled by his rock-steady faith in his daughters. "I think so too. But she's busy raising the next generation."

Her father cleared his throat. Phones made him uncomfortable. "Laurel says you hurt yourself the other day. I want you to take better care of yourself, you hear me?"

"Yes, sir. I'm resting right now."

"Good." He paused. "You still have your hideaway money?"

Smiling, she glanced at her purse lying on the dresser. Inside her wallet there was a hundred-dollar bill tucked between two old photos, one of her parents and one of Gilly and her sisters. The money had been there since the day she graduated from high school. "Yes, sir. I still have it."

"Good. You can always buy a bus ticket to come home."

"Yes, sir. I know." She didn't know anybody who ever rode a public bus anymore, but she kept the hundred to make Dad happy.

"Okay, then let me get back to my show. Your mother and I will be praying for you. Sleep well, Little Bit."

"'Night, Daddy." She closed the phone and lay there listening to the evening sounds of a middle-class American family settling in for the night.

Reid, whose voice seemed to come at two basic volume levels—loud and glass-shattering—was splashing in the bathtub on the other side of Gilly's bedroom wall. Apparently he was waging a battle of D-Day proportions with armies of Marvel superheroes and Happy Meal toys. Cynthia was mopping the kitchen, singing along with her iPod with rather mixed results. Rick—who turned out to be as nice a guy as Jacob claimed—was watching a ball game on TV, in direct competition with the puppies howling on the back porch. The little house was alive with sound and the homey odor of lemon Pine-Sol and love.

Conversely, Gilly felt very alone. She wondered if Laurel had made it home yet and if Rosie was happy now. She wondered what Jacob and Graham were doing.

Before she could get maudlin enough to write in her journal, she noticed the message light flashing on her cell phone. It must have been ringing while she was on the phone with Mom and Dad. She called up her voice mail.

"Hi, Gilly, this is Victoria. Maurice knows about your injury, and he's not happy. You should call Paul first thing in the morning." There was a slight pause. "I hope it's not as bad as Dmitri says. You could lose your place in the new ballet. Oh, and one more thing. Nicholas and I broke up. I hope you're satisfied." The recorded instructions for saving or deleting messages began its electronic lecture.

Gilly slapped the phone closed, her stomach on fire with anger. Dmitri had promised he wouldn't tell Maurice before she could call him—then he'd done it anyway. Oh, why couldn't he keep his mouth shut for one more day?

She jackknifed into a fetal position, then stuffed her fist into her mouth to keep from screaming with agony. Slowly she straightened her body. What should she do? Call Maurice tonight, when he would be either enraged or disappointed or worried or probably a Gallic combination of all three? Or wait until tomorrow when he would either have gained some perspective or gotten even more upset?

Frankly, she wanted to take one of her little magic pills and sink into oblivion. That was what they were for—helping her get past the worst of this initial pain, until she could get back into the routine of regular, healing exercise.

She reached for the little brown plastic vial of pills and twisted off the cap.

If he had never met her, he would have tucked Graham in, watched the news, and gone to bed with a book or his Bible. He sat with the remote control in his hand, the room silent except for the faint sound of Graham singing himself to sleep with his *Sesame Street* CD: "Ab-kadef-Gajeckle ..." The immediate instinct was to call Gilly. *Guess what, you'll never believe this.*

He wanted to tell her everything because she was infinitely interested in little boys and puppies and dancing and being a good friend. But there was no indication that she was particularly interested in one messed-up former dancer. Especially since that out-of-practice former dancer had taken away her most precious possession.

So he closed his eyes and thought about her, wishing he could give it back to her.

How? What could he do to restore her joy? Besides calling on the Healer to take pity? He'd been doing that in a stream of perpetual petition that felt more like begging than prayer. Perhaps that was the problem—he'd been asking like a beggar, not a son. The Bible said to ask in faith according to God's will. But he didn't know what God's will was in this situation. The Bible also said if one lacked wisdom, he should ask. And faith was involved in that kind of asking too.

Did he truly believe in God's goodness? Did he believe that God loved Jacob Ferrar enough to bless him with something so pure and lovely and unearned as the love of a woman like Gilly Kincade? He feared in his heart of hearts that grace was for everyone except for him.

He opened his eyes when his phone rang in the kitchen. Casting the remote onto the coffee table beside Graham's magnetic toys, he ran to grab it. He saw Gilly's name in the ID screen and clutched the phone, broadsided by joy.

"Hi, Jacob. I hope I didn't wake up Graham."

"No, he's asleep, I think. He was singing a moment ago. The 'Alphabet Song,' as a matter of fact." And he, Jacob, was babbling like an adolescent who'd just bumped into the head cheerleader. He looked at the microwave clock and was shocked to find it nearly ten o'clock. He'd been daydreaming for quite a while. "Are you settled in with the Hawkins clan?"

"Yes, they're great." But she sounded subdued, a watercolor print compared to her usual vivid acrylics. "My room is fine. Comfortable." There was a long pause, then she burst out, "Jacob, would you pray for me?"

"Of course I will. Gilly, what's wrong?" Stupid question. He knew what was wrong. But he wanted her to articulate it aloud so that he could remind himself how hopeless was his love for her. He'd wanted her to choose against all odds to leave a brilliant career in New York. To choose him. Jacob was nothing if not a realist. You didn't always get what you wanted.

She sighed. "I'm trying not to succumb to the dark side."

"Really." Suddenly he was amused. And curious. "And you run to me? Now that's ironic. What could possibly be luring the Sugar Plum Fairy out of the land of dreams? You should be sound asleep by now."

"I just got a very disturbing phone call." Her voice was smaller. "From my old roommate."

"Victoria, right?" She'd mentioned the girl once or twice. Sounded like a pill. "What did she say?"

Gilly sighed. "It's kind of a long story. But it started with this Christmas party Dmitri and I went to, the night before we came down here."

He waited, then prompted, "That doesn't sound so terrible."

"It was the usual." She sighed. "Dmitri and I shared a cab home with Victoria's boyfriend."

"You and Dmitri and the boyfriend." He repeated it to make sure he had the story straight. "Okay. I assume this was significant."

"Only because Nicholas is pretty much a selfish jerk. But he'd sat down to chat with me out of the blue, and I wound up feeling a little sorry for him. Dmitri was drunk and Nicholas offered to make sure I got home okay."

Jacob didn't want to picture Gilly swimming around like a goldfish in that glittering sea of sensuality. He made a noncommittal noise to keep her talking.

"Anyway, Nicholas tricked me into telling him something I knew about Victoria. She—she should have told Nicholas herself, but she wouldn't. When he found out, he was so angry—Dmitri made him get out and walk home in the snow." Gilly took a harsh breath. "I could hardly sleep that night and I knew I had to warn Victoria, so I went to her apartment before I left for Birmingham. Of course she blew up like Mount St. Helens."

"Some friend."

"Well, I woke her up, and I didn't have time to be very diplomatic. I had to get to the airport. So I called her that night to follow up, and I'm afraid I made it worse. She keeps making smart cracks about my goody-two-shoes image—"

"You know what that's about, don't you? It means she's feeling guilty. She may even be under conviction. I used to make fun of believers like that."

There was a short silence. "I hadn't thought of that. But ... whatever the reason, I made her angry enough to tell Maurice about my accident, and he's mad at me for not calling him immediately. For ruining his choreography. For disobeying him about dancing the Mary role."

"You've talked to him?"

"I called him as soon as I got Victoria's message. All I wanted to do was take my medicine and go to sleep, but I knew I'd better at least try to—I never expected to actually get hold of him—" Her voice wobbled. "Oh, wow, has he got a temper."

Jacob had been on the receiving end of Maurice Poiroux's incendiary temper himself. "He didn't sack you, did he?"

"No. He yelled for five minutes, then calmed down and told me to come home for decent therapy."

"That arrogant—Did he even ask how you are?"

"Not exactly." He could hear a smile slide into her voice. "Sympathy's not exactly his strong suit."

"I should say not."

She sighed. "I guess he *could* have fired me for breach of contract. I'm lucky all he did was replace me in the mermaid role."

Jacob was silent. In brutal reality, he'd known that would happen. Maurice wasn't going to abandon the ballet just because his choice of lead dancers was injured. After all, when Gilly had backed out on Jacob, he'd been forced to think of another dancer to take the role of Mary.

And if he thought about this much more, guilt was going to eat him alive.

"I suppose," he said reluctantly.

"So. My golden ticket has expired. Exiting Disneyland for the real world."

"Gilly, I'm so sorry—"

"No, listen, Jacob, I didn't call you to make you feel guilty." She sniffed. "If anything, we're both to blame, but whatever—it's not going to change anything. I've got to work my way through this, and I'm serious about asking you to pray with me. I have to believe God is up to something in my life, and nobody understands this thing like you do. If I'm supposed to get over this injury and go back to New York, it's going to take a lot of work on my part and the intervention of prayer. But if not—" She swallowed. "I've got some growing up to do."

He could patronize her and pretend she wasn't right. But he knew from vile experience that sometimes God would strip away glitter in order to reveal true value.

"Right, then. We'll pray right now. But I think you should enlist

Cynthia and Rick too. In fact, we have a small group that meets in their home on Tuesday nights. This week is our last meeting until after the holidays. I'd like us to surround you with prayer, if you'd be comfortable with that."

"Absolutely," she said promptly. "I'd be grateful." She released a breath. "I'm ready."

He hoped he was.

Seventeen

The next morning Jacob took Graham to school for his final day before the holidays, then came home to wander aimlessly around the apartment. He got online to see if his anatomy grade had been posted. He sat at the computer staring at the four and the zero. An A. He'd pulled an A.

You could do this, Ferrar, if you'd go at it full time.

He wondered why he felt little more than relief that he hadn't wasted his money.

Was he really going to quit his job with the ballet and start off on a completely new career track? He'd been putting off registering for another course in the spring. Maybe he could take a course in exercises to protect and heal the spine.

He put his head in his hands. Inevitably his thoughts always circled around to Gilly. If he were a really serious Christian, he would use the time to get out his Bible or read another chapter in

Ragamuffin Gospel. But he kept thinking about her despondency on the phone last night. Must be terribly frustrating for a woman like her, used to getting along with everybody, to have several people upset with her all at once. And then to be flattened by an injury on top of that.

He wished he could take her pain away instantly. But it didn't work that way, at least most of the time. He'd never had a back injury, though there was the ankle ligament he'd bruised when he was dancing in Spain. After three months of hard physical therapy he'd finally recovered and returned to dancing.

Out of curiosity, he woke up the computer and opened his Internet browser. A quick Google search of *spondylolysis* returned a page full of hits, and he started clicking on the links. Most of them told him what he already knew. The fifth lumbar vertebra, closest to the tailbone, was usually the place where stress fractures occurred. With repetitive extension and/or rotation, the small pars interarticularis inside the vertebra, unable to absorb excessive shocks, would develop cracks, sometimes fragment altogether, sometimes hypertrophy—grow to abnormal sizes, causing friction against exposed nerves. Recommended treatment was exactly what Dr. Lobianco had prescribed for Gilly: physical therapy, graduated use of a back brace, biking and swimming.

But on the third page he found a link to an article from a medical journal, posted on the website of . . .

Jacob blinked. *Dr. Wyatt Glaasmacher.*

He began to read. The article reported on the successful treatment two years earlier of a dancer with severe stress fractures of the fifth lumbar vertebra—with laser surgery. Considered invasive and dangerous, the surgery had only been considered when the dancer had not recovered after sixteen months of the more conservative treatment. But it had worked. Within two months she had returned to normal activities, dancing, and exercise.

Jacob sat there studying the photos of the dancer's X-rays, the surgeon's diagrams, the verbal description of the procedure. He could see why there would be risks involved. But surgical techniques had progressed by leaps and bounds in the last two years. Surely this particular technique would be much less dangerous by now.

His heartbeat picked up. Gilly didn't know about this—because if she did, she would've already been on a plane back to New York to talk Dr. Glaasmacher into cutting open her back and making her well instantly. Dr. Lobianco at UAB surely knew about it but must consider it too dangerous. But why wouldn't he at least offer it to Gilly as an option? Maybe he wanted to make sure her body first had a chance to heal on its own.

Jacob sat there until the screen saver kicked in with a series of photos of Graham, then closed his eyes and began to pray. Guiltily he realized he'd been thinking of her injury almost as a blessing in disguise. The longer Gilly stayed, working with the Birmingham physical therapist, the more time he'd have to spend with her, get to know her, woo her.

But, oh God, how selfish.

He wanted the best for her. Whatever that was. Even if it took her away from him.

Gilly had woken up that morning hoping her back would have miraculously healed and she could go home to New York. She didn't know what to do with herself in a day without dance class, without rhythm, without music.

Well, there was music in the Hawkins house, but it was praise-and-worship choruses played on a digitally reduced radio station piped through Cynthia's television. Or it was "Silly Songs with Larry," which she normally had no objection to but under these circumstances—the inability to jig or tap dance or head bang—gave her a migraine. Or it was Rick's steel guitars and mandolins and she-done-him-wrong lyrics. Which she also liked in small bites but not in great gulping twangy nine-course meals. Where were Tchaikovsky, Schumann, Liszt? Gershwin or Bernstein even?

Frankly, she was cranky. Which almost rhymed, but not quite—the story of her current so-called life.

Mid-afternoon Cynthia drove her to her first physical therapy session. Lying in the backseat of the Hawkins family minivan, she tried very hard not to whine. Whiners were pathetic. Whiners should look outside themselves and think of others. Whiners should try to learn whatever lesson God had in mind so they could get on with life. Life was too short to spend it whining.

By the time they arrived at the orthopedic clinic, Gilly had chugged through her stormy repertoire of whining clichés and washed up on the shore of *I don't feel good. I don't like this. Let me out of here.*

An hour later she was lying on a mat, working muscles she didn't even know existed and endeavoring not to burst into language she'd learned on the New York subway.

"I don't like this. Let me out of here," she muttered through her teeth.

The therapist, a young man with blond dreads, a steel stud in the top of his ear, and a nametag that said "Ace," leaned back in his rolling chair and tsked like a middle-aged high school principal. "Gilly-Gilly-Gilly. How am I going to get you well if you resist treatment?"

She looked at him with mild hatred. "I suppose you could do a hundred of these without breaking a sweat."

"As a matter of fact I could."

Her gaze sought less sickeningly cheerful pastures and collided with a pair of eyes so blue she could have tested them for chlorine content and gone swimming. Their owner, huffing sweatily on the Stairmaster next-door, possessed—besides the eyes—a physique designed to slam baseballs over major league fences.

He smiled and winked.

Her face already felt hot as a cherry bomb, so what was one more blush? Doing her best to ignore him, she crossed her hands over her chest and curled up again.

After two more reps, Ace seemed to be satisfied that he had tortured her enough for one day. "Okay, Twinkle Toes, you can go home now." He poked his stylus at something on his laptop screen. "Sleep on your side, not your back, and put pillows between your knees. You can come back tomorrow."

"Oh goody. Can I?" She clasped her hands beneath her chin and batted her eyes.

Ace looked amused. "We have a really good masseuse if you're interested. Ask at the desk and they'll hook you up."

"Okay, thanks." She sighed, suddenly regretting her snippy attitude. "I'll be better tomorrow, I promise. Five more curls."

"Cool." He laid out a palm her for her slap. "You're on. And we'll add some floor swimming."

"Yay." But Gilly smiled at him and picked up the towel she'd left draped across a chair. "See you tomorrow, Ace."

She was almost to the door when a huge shadow blocked the flood of sunshine coming through a bank of plate glass windows. She looked up—and up and up—to meet the pool-blue eyes of the giant from the treadmill. His gray T-shirt and shorts clung to the massive chest and thighs, and his grin told her that he knew he was quite a sight.

Gilly was not in the mood to flirt. Plus she smelled like a gymnasium locker room herself.

She frowned at him and picked up her limping pace. Reaching the desk without further eye contact, she waited impatiently for the college-age receptionist to get off the phone. Cynthia would be here soon, and she needed that massage appointment.

"Is this your first time to work out here?" asked Barry Bonds Junior.

"Yes." She looked at her watch. Hopefully Cynthia hadn't gotten stuck in the carpool line. And hopefully her stalker would give up before she had to resort to violence.

"You'll like it. These guys are good." He paused. "I'm Seth Booker. I play first base for the Barons. If I can get my knee straightened out—and it's looking more hopeful—they're looking at moving me up to the Sox."

Apparently her guess at baseball had been on the money. She'd never heard of the Barons, but even she knew the Sox came in two colors, White or Red.

She sighed, giving up on rudeness. It just wasn't in her nature, even when she was terminally cranky. She tilted her head back to look up at him again. "Congratulations. I hope it works out for you."

"Thanks." He looked disappointed that she hadn't volunteered her name but skimmed her figure, clearly trying to place her sport. "You're too small for volleyball or basketball. Are you a swimmer?"

"Professional bowling," she said with a straight face. When his mouth fell open, she laughed. "I'm a dancer. Back injury."

"Gosh, I'm sorry to hear that. Not that you're a dancer, but that you hurt yourself. What's the prognosis?" He leaned on the counter.

"Lots of hard work and I'll be in shipshape." She hoped. She tried to place his accent. Not really southern, not exactly Midwestern. California, maybe? Then she remembered that curiosity about people had gotten her in trouble already. "Listen, I don't mean to be rude, but I need to talk to this girl before she gets back on the phone. Maybe I'll run into you again sometime."

"Sure. When?" When she blinked at him, he added, "When's your next session?"

"Um ..." She'd have to give him points for persistence. She looked at the receptionist's name tag. "Breanne, my PT says you guys have a masseuse. Can I make an appointment for tomorrow after my therapy session?"

"Sure." The girl scrolled down her computer screen, squinting through her little round glasses. "Okay, here you are. Shondelle has a two o'clock open. Want that one?"

"That would be great."

Her new friend Seth eased behind Breanne's desk and looked over her shoulder. "Gilly Kincade. Nice." He grinned at Gilly, looking proud of his ingenuity.

"Hey!" Breanne hurriedly closed the screen. "You're not supposed to be back here, Seth. Get lost."

So he was a regular. Without a shred of conscience or humility he ruffled Breanne's hair and limped beside Gilly toward the front door. "What club do you dance at?"

"Club? What are you talking about?"

"You know." Seth pantomimed sliding down a pole, then grabbed his knee and winced. "Club?"

Gilly stopped and stared at him. She had simultaneous urges to kick his bum knee and burst out laughing. "I'm a ballet dancer, you cretin!"

"Oh." His face flamed from the neck of his muscle shirt to the roots of his curly hair. "I thought you looked a little, you know, thin."

Then she did laugh—so hard, in fact, that she wrenched her back and had to lean on the wall outside the PT center to catch her breath.

Seth watched her, looking so much like a little boy caught peeking into the girls' bathroom that she almost felt sorry for him. "Wow," he said, when she finally stopped laughing. "Guess I went down in flames with that one, huh?"

"You think?" As Cynthia drove up, Gilly shoved away from the wall. "This has been the most interesting PT session I've ever had. See you later, Seth."

"But—but—I'm really a nice guy. You could at least give me your phone number and let me take you to dinner and apologize."

"You have got to be kidding. Good-bye." The side door of Cynthia's van slid open, and Gilly started to get in.

"Wait! Gilly—"

She turned with one foot on the van's running board. "Even if I had time for going out to dinner, I don't give my phone number to men who hang out in girlie clubs." She softened her voice. "Good luck with that knee, Seth. I wish you the best." She pulled herself into the van, leaving Mr. Baseball standing on the sidewalk covered in chagrin.

"Who was that?" asked Cynthia, pulling out of the parking lot. "He was cute."

"Some jerk who thought I was a pole dancer at a strip club."

Cynthia gawked at her in the rearview mirror. "Is he blind?"

Gilly snorted. "And full of himself." She peered over the seat at the rear bench, where Graham and Reid were playing some kind of little-boy hand game that involved gunshot-like mouth noises. "How was school today, guys?"

Reid looked up. "Good. Miss Allison showed us how to make paper reindeers."

"Awesome." She turned around. Christmas was this Sunday. She could neither make the five-hour drive to Mobile to visit her family nor expect Mary Layne to haul her entire clan up here so soon after the last visit. And even if they came, she had no place to put them all. She was, for all intents and purposes, homeless. Ho ho ho.

Jacob arrived at Casa Hawkins a little late, due to the fact that his first batch of brownies had set off the fire alarm. Both he and Graham smelled like cigars, but nobody had died, and the second batch actually tasted like his grandmother's, so he supposed he should be grateful.

He parked the Jag two houses down from the Hawkins' brick one-story ranch-style home, behind Al and Dorothy Wright's big red Ford F-350 and an SUV. Their group also included a retired couple named Howie and JoDean Lamb. He wondered if Heidi Raintree from his board would be here tonight. Cynthia was in charge of sending reminders to members.

Jacob could hear Sunflower woofing behind the backyard fence as he followed Graham into the carport. So far he'd dodged the bullet of adopting one of the two remaining puppies, but he was afraid he wouldn't be able to hold out forever. Maybe he should post a photo on the bulletin board at the studio and help Cynthia get rid of them.

"What are you smiling at?" Cynthia pushed open the screen door and took the plate of brownies. "Mmm. These smell great."

"Thanks." Jacob surreptitiously sniffed the sleeve of his coat as he entered the kitchen. Maybe the stench had dissipated enough to keep him from getting thrown out. "I was thinking of ways to help you thin the Labrador population around here." He watched Graham cast himself on his knees to accept the sloppy kisses of the puppies, who currently had no name except "Thing One and Thing Two" (Reid), "Poochie-Poo" (Cynthia), or "Hey, Stupid" (Rick).

Cynthia set the brownies on the counter beside a huge spiral-sliced ham and two or three covered dishes. "JoDean made her garlic mashed potatoes. We're gonna die happy."

"That's good." Jacob peered through the space between the kitchen cabinets and the family room, hoping Cynthia wouldn't think he was looking for Gilly.

"She's in the playroom with the kids, letting Reid show her how to make origami reindeer. Why don't you go rescue her?"

He looked over his shoulder to find Cynthia smirking at him. "Sometimes you're too smart for your own good," he said as he stepped around Graham and the puppies.

The family room was crowded with holiday sweaters and Christmas decorations. The eight-foot tree, redolent of fir and loaded with multicolored lights, homemade ornaments, and popcorn garland, took up half the floor space; a fire crackled in the hearth, and four red felt stockings hung from the mantel. Jacob smiled to see that one of them had crooked magic marker letters spelling "Gilly."

He could hear her laughter from the adjoining playroom but stopped to shake hands with Al and Howie. Across the room another group had gathered around a tray of hors d'oeuvres and apple cider. Jacob was glad to see Heidi, lugging a couple of two-liter soft drinks, come through the kitchen door with her girls.

"I hear your Christmas ballet was a pretty hot success, all things considered," said Al, bravely abandoning a heated discussion of SEC football to include Jacob. He glanced at the playroom. "Too bad your little ballerina got hurt. She's a good kid."

"JoDean and I saw her dance in Montgomery," put in Howie. "She's phenomenal."

Jacob looked at him in surprise. The Lambs had a cultured streak—Howie had been in pharmaceuticals and handled his money well—but he didn't know they particularly liked ballet. "I saw that show myself," he said. "The arts festival?"

Howie nodded. "That's the one. JoDean and I were tickled to meet her tonight. She's the real deal."

"She is indeed." Jacob resisted the urge to drift toward the playroom, then gave in. "I'm going to take Heidi's girls in to say hello. They both love ballet."

"You do that, buddy," said Al, attempting an extremely awkward hip-hop arm move.

Jacob just grinned and headed for the kitchen, where Cynthia was welcoming Heidi and her two young daughters.

Twelve-year-old India, seated cross-legged on the floor with Thing One snuggled under her chin, looked up at him with her almond brown eyes shining. "Mr. Ferrar! Look what I have!"

He smiled at her. "Yes, I see. But I have an even better surprise if you'll come here for a second." India was showing great promise as a dancer and had already been cast twice for *Nutcracker* performances.

"A surprise? What kind of surprise?"

"Can I come too?" Seven-year-old Riley handed off Thing Two to Graham.

"Of course. Come on." He held out his hands and helped the two girls to their feet, leaving Graham to solitary canine supervision. India and Riley skipped beside him through the family room into the playroom, where they found Gilly and Reid seated at a card table covered by a red cloth, heads bent over their paper zoo. An Alvin and the Chipmunks Christmas CD was playing on a boom box near the piano.

Gilly looked up, her bright smile taking in Jacob and both girls. "*¡Feliz navidad!*"

"That means 'Merry Christmas'," Reid informed nobody in particular. "Mommy's teaching me Spanish."

"Good for her." Jacob hadn't been to Spain for nearly four years, but sometimes he missed the home of his spiritual infancy with a visceral ache. He put a hand on each of the Raintree girls' shoulders. "Gilly, I want you to meet a couple of my finest young dancers. This one's Riley, and this one's India—who was a *Nutcracker* mouse. Girls, you recognize the Sugar Plum Fairy, don't you?"

She admittedly didn't look very fairy-ish at the moment—more like a gimpy elf. Her red hair was caught up in a ponytail under a conical green felt hat, and she had on jeans and a red sweatshirt with jingle bells sewn on its front in the shape of a Christmas tree.

India gasped and went bug eyed. "Oh, wow! I can't believe this!"

Riley looked slightly less impressed. "Where's your tutu?"

"I don't wear it at home." Gilly gave her an apologetic smile. "Would you like to help us make paper animals?"

"Yes, ma'am!" Riley promptly sat down and grabbed a sheet of paper.

But India stared at Gilly with the heartfelt worship of twelve-year-old girls for "real" ballerinas. "Can I have your autograph?"

"Of course you can. Let me hunt up a pen—"

"I'll go ask my mom!" India tore out of the room before Gilly could get to her feet.

During the exchange between Gilly and the girls, Jacob studied Gilly. She'd put on a little makeup for the occasion, but the corners of her eyes were strained with fatigue. She was holding herself at a funny angle.

"I'm not sure you ought to be sitting up like this." Jacob came round behind her to slide a gentle hand down her back. She had on a brace.

"Hey!" She looked up at him, scowling.

"Gilly, you're wearing yourself out. You should be resting."

She sighed. "I had my first session of physical therapy today. My PT is a sadist."

"Aren't they all?" Jacob grimaced in sympathy. "I did a little research on your type of injury today. What exercises did they have you doing?"

"Hanging ab curls. Floor swimming."

He frowned. "You can't go wrong with basic Pilates, but hanging ab curls are really aggressive for a dancer's injury."

Reid suddenly tugged on Gilly's sleeve. "Miss Gilly, we're going to go play hide-and-seek, okay? Thank you for making animals with me."

Gilly smiled at the boy. "Sure. No problem. You guys have fun." When he and Riley ran off, she met Jacob's eyes. "Guess they're not so interested in grown-up aches and pains." She wrinkled her nose. "I'm a bit tired of the subject myself."

"Then let's go join the party." He put a hand under her elbow to give her a boost to her feet. The bells on her shirt jingled as she stood, and he smiled down at her. "You're a cheerful sort of person, you know that?"

"Are you not cheerful, Jacob?" She stood quite close to him, looking up with those beautiful red-gold eyebrows in their characteristic funny quirk.

He looked away because he wanted to press his lips to the right one, then the left one, then between them. "I've nothing to complain about."

"Well … you've let me unload a lot on you lately. I'm willing to return the favor."

"Are you?" He looked down at her, helplessly, and he could have counted each of the topaz flecks in her green eyes. He swallowed hard.

Her lips parted as ambivalence, attraction, something else he couldn't name chased through her eyes. "Jacob?"

"I'm … I didn't mean this to happen." His lips felt numb.

"It's Christmas, and we're both lonely," she said with a little gasp. But she didn't move away.

He slid his hand from her elbow to her shoulder, to the back of her neck, which tilted against his palm, fragile as a daisy stem. Her breath was so shallow he could almost hear it. "If you don't move, Gilly, I'm going to kiss you."

"That sounds like fun." She closed her eyes and grabbed a handful of his shirt.

So he kissed her, not because it was Christmas and he was lonely, though it was and he was. And not because she was young, beautiful, and gifted, though she most certainly was. He kissed her because he needed her like the desert needed a flood of water, needed the assurance he'd seen in her eyes that he was Jacob, transformed from trickster to wrestler of angels.

His tentativeness had resolved into a strong, lucid torrent of reciprocal passion—Gilly's arms flung around his neck, his hands clasping her waist to lift her, giving him better access to her warm mouth—when a high-pitched little-girl voice carried from the other room: "Hey, Mom, Mr. Ferrar is kissing Miss Gilly in the playroom, so I'm going down to the basement to play hide-and-seek."

Eighteen

Gilly was aware of Jacob's hands under her ribcage, the sting of her lips, the distinct odor of something on fire. Probably her blood vessels.

Then he set her down, carefully, as if she were some porcelain figurine in a curio cabinet. He stuffed his hands in his back pockets and looked away.

To take some of the intensity out of his embarrassment, she leaned forward and sniffed his shirt. "Did you put your head in the oven?"

"What?" He looked at her blankly, then smiled. "Brownies," he said, looking more normal. "The first batch went up in flames."

"Oh." She made herself grin, though she was longing to dive into a closet and have a good cry. "Well, I have to give you props for trying. The only thing I contributed to this party was the paper chain on the tree."

He stared at her, his smile fading. "Are we going to talk about what just happened?"

"Well … we *could*, I guess, but I recommend selective amnesia. It was just …"

She waited for him to fill in the blank. Loneliness. Mistletoe. Pheromones.

But he just looked at her, deeply and beautifully. *Dear God, this is so unfair.*

Finally she sighed and crossed her arms. "I need to think about it some more. I'm not much of a talker, you know."

Then he did laugh, that rare, shocking belly laugh that lit his face and made her want to fling herself at him again. She started to edge backwards around the table.

But he caught her face and kissed her, hard and square on the mouth, then let her go abruptly. "We'd better make an appearance," he said, still laughing, "before we cause major scandal. Come on." He held out his hand, and what could she do but place hers in it and follow him like a sleepwalker?

Everyone consciously did not look at them as they crossed the family room, but she caught Al winking at his wife.

"Cynthia! Do you need any help?" She slipped her hand from Jacob's and scooted into the kitchen, where by now all the women had congregated.

"Everything's ready, and I think we're all here." Cynthia leaned into the family room. "Rick! Will you get everybody together and let's ask the blessing?"

Her husband obligingly put two fingers to his lips and produced a piercing whistle that brought the children running up from the basement and sent the puppies under the breakfast room table. As the adults shuffled into the dining room to join hands around the table, the doorbell rang, adding to the chaos.

Cynthia sighed and looked at Jacob, who happened to be nearest the front door. "Would you see who that is?"

"Sure." He wandered off, leaving Gilly to stare after him, emotions in turmoil. But she felt two small hands grab one each of hers, and she looked down to find Graham on one side and India Raintree on the other. Smiling, she gave both hands a squeeze as the room quieted for the blessing. She glanced at Rick, expecting him to lead the prayer.

But behind him Jacob was standing in the dining room doorway with a very peculiar look on his face. He cleared his throat. "You guys, we have ... another guest. Gilly, look who's here." He stepped aside.

Tucker McGaughan grinned at her. "Hey, Gil. Merry Christmas!"

She managed to make it through the meal without throwing him out on his ear, though it was a strain on her home training. When she finally managed to get him alone—all his famous bashfulness seemed to have evaporated in the light of food, tinsel, and sheer perversity—she shoved him down onto the living room sofa and stood before him arms aggressively akimbo.

"What are you doing here?"

His expression went from smug to confused. "I came to bring you home."

She huffed. "Are you not listening? I can't travel. My back is hurt."

"I brought my mother's Lexus. We'll lay the seat back down and you'll feel like you're in your own bed." His silvery eyes were baby innocent as he took her hand. "Everybody misses you, Gil."

The implication being that *he* missed her. She frowned, suspicious. "Who sent you?"

"Nobody! I sent myself." He tugged her hand. "Come here, Gilly. You're giving me a crick in my neck. When she just frowned at him, he shrugged. "Laurel said you were up here all alone for Christmas, refused to drive even as far as Montgomery. Which is crazy! You can't be that messed up."

She turned around and lifted her shirt to show him the back brace. "I am messed up."

He let the air out of his lungs on a slow hiss. "Boy, Gilly. That sucks."

She faced him again, inexplicably irritated. "Yes. It does. I'm doing my physical therapy to get well, but it's going to take some time, so you can't just waltz in here and whisk me away on your magic Lexus carpet."

His level dark brows drew together as he stood up. "You seem mad at *me*! I didn't do anything." He laid his hands on her shoulders, gently caressing. "I just wanted to help. And I wanted to see you anyway. It's been ..." He looked at the ceiling, calculating. "Two and a half months?"

"Yes, and you've called me exactly once in all that time."

"Well, dang, I've been busy! I'm getting ready for the London tour and I've been writing the rest of the music for this ballet you're supposed to dance in."

"Tucker!" Gilly jerked out from under his hands, jarring her back. She blinked away tears of pain—physical, emotional, she wasn't sure which. "I'm not dancing in any ballet!"

He looked mildly sheepish. "Oh, yeah. I keep forgetting." He shoved his hair out of his face. "Anyway, you've never complained about me not calling before. You know if you need me you can get hold of me."

Gilly stood there breathing hard, unable to answer. Yes, she did know that. And the last couple of times she'd needed somebody she hadn't called Tucker. She hadn't even called her sister. She'd called Jacob Ferrar. Her heart began to thump.

Tucker must have seen something. There was none of the usual *far-out, man* abstraction in his expression. In fact, he looked shockingly acute. "Why didn't you let me know when you got hurt? I had to find out from my mother, who found out from Cole."

Gilly looked at her fingernails, which were, at the moment, bitten to the quick and painted black. "I didn't think of it. I'm sorry, I've been sort of focused on myself the last few days."

There was a short silence. "Are you dumping me?"

She looked up at him, stung. "Is there anything to dump? You don't call me for two months, even when you're supposedly writing music for me? Does that sound like a normal relationship to you?"

He looked hurt. "It's normal for us. We've never been one of these ooey-gooey couples who slurp and slobber all over each other. You know I love you, Gilly. Come on."

"Did it ever occur to you I might like a little slurping and slobbering?" That sounded disgusting, but he'd started it, and she didn't know how to get out of it.

"Wow. We're having a real fight," he said, sounding so bemused that she snorted.

"Actually I've been pretty peeved with you for quite a while, but you never stick around long enough for me to say so."

"Really? What did I do?" He stroked that scruffy little beard and eyed her as if she were some exotic plant he'd never seen before.

"Tucker! Pay attention! This is the whole point!" Could one expire from an overload of exclamation points? "You're gone for months at a time without calling. When you show up, you might or might not kiss me hello. And you are terminally late for everything! We started the arts festival performance fifteen minutes late because you couldn't get your microphone adjusted."

"I'm a perfectionist. You know that. *You're* a perfectionist too, which is why I like you. Well, that and the fact that you generally don't hassle me." He frowned and peered at her through his hair, which had fallen into his eyes again. "Which is sort of questionable at the moment. Do you want me to kiss you?"

If she said she didn't, he would think it odd. But she didn't want anything to ruin the taste of Jacob Ferrar lingering on her mouth. She sighed, stood on her tiptoes, and pecked him on the cheek. "This isn't the time or place." Like she'd been thinking of that thirty minutes ago with Jacob. She took his hand and tugged him toward the family room, where the party had been roaring in the background, oblivious to their conflict. "Come on. Jacob will want to talk to you about the music."

He ambled after her. "I'm not sure I want to let go of this music if you're not performing with it."

She turned—carefully, because of her back, but stiff with tension. "You can't pull out on Jacob. He's counting on you." She gripped both his wrists. "Please, Tucker."

Eyes narrowed to pale slits, he stared at her. "Oh. So that's it."

"I don't know what you—"

"I know I'm not as smart as you, Gilly, but even I can see the graffiti on this particular wall. This is why you're staying here instead of going to Laurel and Cole's for Christmas. This is why you're not going back to New York for physical therapy."

"I told you, I'm staying here because my back hurts too much to travel." She wasn't going to admit anything else, even to herself.

He continued to look at her as seconds ticked by. Finally, he turned his hands to clasp her wrists. "What's happened to you, Gilly? The girl I know wouldn't let a back injury keep her from being with her family on Christmas. The artist I know wouldn't back down from taking on any treatment to get back onstage."

Because he was right, Gilly looked down, ashamed and consequently angry. "You don't know what it's like to be scared."

"Oh, don't I?" Tucker's voice roughened. "Do you remember when I nearly caved in and went back to college because that's what my family wanted me to do? Remember when everybody was telling me show business is too hard and I should just give it up and get a business degree? You said I had a God-given gift that I had a responsibility to share. You said God expects nothing less than all of my heart and soul." He shook her hands. "Look at me, Gilly. Do you remember?"

"I *have* given it all," she said resentfully. "That's why I'm in this fix."

"No. You're in this fix because you let some guy sweet-talk you into thinking about giving up New York."

"I am not!" Gilly stared at him, face flaming. "I would never—"

"Well, that's the next step," he insisted. "You're thinking about thinking about it. And if you're not, you're lying to yourself."

Gilly jerked her hands away and walked into the family room. Tucker was crazy. Lying to herself? About what?

Jacob didn't know when he'd begun to think of himself as a nice guy. But when Tucker McGaughan sauntered into Cynthia's family room with his hand between Gilly's shoulder blades, a host of blue-faced Mel Gibson-inspired warrior instincts roared to the surface.

How could the guy abandon her for months on end and suddenly show up—uninvited, no less—at a church Christmas party and receive a hero's welcome? Jacob couldn't even look at Gilly. He didn't want to see her face blossom with joy. He knew she missed her family. She'd *said* she was lonely. Which was the only reason she'd kissed him.

Still, a chap couldn't hand over the field without a fight. So he took his plate of ham and green beans and homemade rolls into the dining room, where Gilly and Tucker had already joined JoDean and Howie Lamb. This left him sitting like a sidecar on a Volkswagen at one end of the table.

Conversation had stopped. "I suppose you're all wondering why I've called this meeting," he said, trying for a joke.

Tucker seemed to take that as a challenge. "Yeah, I think we should talk about this ballet thing."

Jacob set down his tea glass carefully. "What about it?"

Tucker shoved a hank of long hair out of his face. "We should put it off until Gilly's ready to dance it. I don't have time to mess with it right now, anyway. The band's heading over to the U.K. in a few weeks."

"Tucker, even if I were completely well, I'm—I couldn't dance in

Jacob's ballet." Gilly's voice sounded as if it had shards of glass in it. "My contract with Ballet New York won't allow it."

"You didn't tell me that!"

"I didn't know it until just a few days ago—and you've been unavailable, remember?" Tucker and Gilly stared at one another, familiarity and passion pulsing between them.

Jacob found himself trying to make peace. "Look, it's water under the bridge now. We have to play the cards we've been dealt."

Tucker glowered at him. "Dude, how many clichés can you cram into one sentence?" He looked at Gilly. "So if you weren't planning on doing the ballet, why the heck were you rehearsing it? Laurel said that's how you hurt your back."

"I was trying to help Jacob sell it to his board." Gilly glanced at Jacob. "It's a hereditary condition. The injury could have happened no matter what I was doing."

Jacob reluctantly shook his head. "Not necessarily. I choreographed those difficult moves because I knew you could do them—even though I knew I was pushing toward a lot of strain on your back." He paused, forcing himself to say what could take Gilly away from him. "I told you I've been researching spondylolysis. The doctor probably told you it's common in dancers and gymnasts who perform those backward cambrés regularly."

Gilly shrugged. "Yes. So?"

Jacob paused, took a breath. He'd just shared a soul-rocking kiss with Gilly, and now he was about to wreck whatever small chance he'd had with her. "There's a surgeon in New York who's developed a new laser technique for repairing those tiny stress fractures in the lumbar spine." He made himself say the rest of it. "The recovery time is cut in half—more like four weeks instead of three months. I called him up this morning to ask questions."

She stared at him. "When were you going to tell me this?"

He'd been about to tell her, when he got derailed by kissing her instead. "Tonight. I was just about to—"

Tucker snorted. "Yeah, right."

Jacob ignored him. "But you should know it's fairly risky. It's surgery, after all. The slow route—back brace, physical therapy, swimming, and bicycling—is the tried and true method."

But Gilly was pushing her chair back. "I have to go right now. Book a flight. Get my stuff together."

JoDean laid a hand on Gilly's wrist. "But, honey, it's five days before Christmas. No surgeon's going to schedule elective surgery right now."

"I don't care." Gilly was looking as stubborn as Jacob had ever seen her. "I want to be there the second he's available." She stood up.

Tucker seemed torn between amusement and indignation. "What was all that hooey about your back hurting too much to travel?"

Gilly just looked at him. "Will you take me to the airport?"

Tucker sighed. "Of course I'll take you. *Mi* Lexus *es su* Lexus. But your sister and my big brother are going to kill me. And I still think you're schizo."

Jacob felt a bit conflicted himself. He wanted Gilly to get well. Of course he did. But he was also sending her off out of his reach again. And this time she wasn't coming back.

On the way to the airport, Gilly lay back in the passenger seat of Tucker's mother's car, gritting her teeth—not because the ride was particularly bumpy or painful, but rather to hold her seesawing emotions at bay.

Last night after the meal, the entire group had gathered to pray over her. They'd seated Gilly in a straight-backed chair, the center of a pulsing circle. Gentle women's hands rested on her head and shoulders, with the men surrounding them in layers, hands on other heads and shoulders in a dense web of communion. She'd never known a group of believers like this one. Her upbringing in church had been active and doctrinally sound (as far as she knew), but this sort of metaphysical outpouring had never seemed necessary to her faith. It was at once exhilarating and comforting, humbling and challenging.

God's presence, which, intellectually, she knew never left her, seemed as tangible as oil on the head.

It struck her that the early church might have prayed this way. And it was not nearly as weird as she'd expected.

The murmurs and whispers died away, leaving Rick's voice like a soloist. "Father, we commend our sister to you, asking you to bless her and heal her according to your will. Let us, as the body of Christ, be available to help in physical ways as well as spiritual." He took a breath and released it. "In the name of Jesus we pray ... amen."

Gilly absorbed the soft echo of amens, tender hugs from Cynthia and JoDean, a smile from Jacob. She looked at Heidi, an outsider like her, whose tears streamed down her pale, freckled face. Gilly realized she wouldn't be afraid to bring Dmitri into this group.

But Dmitri was back in New York, dancing in *The Nutcracker*, where Gilly ought to have been. She blinked away her own tears as she hugged Heidi. *Ought to, could have, might be.* Who could decipher the inscrutable way God worked?

Certainly not twenty-one-year-old Gilly Kincade, the broken ballerina.

She'd said good-bye to Jacob under a big sprig of mistletoe, shaking hands as if they were parting after nothing more than a weekend ballet engagement. And Tucker had stood there with his arm slung around her shoulders. *Now* he chose to stick like chewing gum on the bottom of her shoe.

He pulled up at the Delta terminal and got out to help her lever herself out of the car. She was leaning against the wall panting with pain by the time he'd gotten her suitcase out of the trunk and tipped the skycap who offered to take her baggage to the check-in desk.

Tucker stood in front of her looking uncharacteristically worried. "You gonna be okay?" He touched her face.

"I'm fine," she said through her teeth. "Do not, under any circumstances, tell my mother how bad this is, or I might have to hurt you."

Avoiding the gaze of a security officer who was giving him the *move-your-car-buster* evil eye, Tucker shook his head. "With Frances Kincade all bets are off."

"Tucker—"

"All right, all right." He lifted his hands. "Call me when you get to Atlanta. I want to be sure you're not passed out in the jetway."

Gilly sighed. "Thank you for taking care of me, Tucker. I needed you."

He looked at her skeptically. "Remember that, next time you think about letting some ballerina-dude haul you over his shoulder."

"What do you mean?"

"Sir, you're going to have to move your car," interrupted the nice police lady, hooking her thumbs in her neon yellow vest.

Tucker gave her his lopsided grin. "Yes, ma'am. I'm just kissing my girlfriend good-bye." He leaned over and smooched Gilly before she could shove him away, then backed toward the Lexus. "Bye, Gil. Call me."

She watched him drive away, stomped her foot and wished she hadn't, then shuffled slowly into the terminal. As. If.

By the time she landed at LaGuardia, Gilly felt as if she'd been involved in the crash landing of Oceanic Flight 815. Her entire spine, from the top of her head to her tailbone, was on fire. She still had to collect her baggage, survive a cab ride into Manhattan, and figure out how to haul herself and her belongings up a flight of narrow stairs.

Unfortunately, she thought as she hobbled toward the escalator, her big sister had been right. It had been the height of foolishness to tackle this trip by herself.

The sight of Dmitri standing duck footed at the entrance to baggage claim, dressed in jeans and a brown suede jacket with a rabbit fur collar, brought tears to her eyes. "Dmitri! You came!" Figuring somebody needed to know her plans, she'd called last night to tell him she was coming back to New York. He hadn't said anything about meeting her.

He hugged her gingerly. "Of course I came. I thought to myself, 'How is she going to push all that humongous suitcase up the stairs by herself?' And I found out when you arrive, even though you forgot to tell me which flight." He looked pleased with his ingenuity. "Why did you not answer your phone?"

She thought guiltily of Tucker's name flashing on the ID screen as the phone buzzed angrily in Atlanta. She'd turned it off after that. "Um, well, I wasn't thinking," she said vaguely. "But I'm so glad you found me." She hesitated. "You didn't drive, did you?"

"No, and you should thank your God I do not have a license. I am terrible driver." He lunged at the luggage carousel. "This is yours, yes? How do you feel? I am sorry, but you are looking like the white-bread sandwich."

"I feel like a white-bread sandwich. Slow down, would you?"

Headed for the cab stand exit as if he were participating in a fire drill, Dmitri glanced over his shoulder. "Yes, I am very sorry for you. We must get you well."

"I'd like nothing better. I'm calling the doctor tomorrow morning." Thank goodness Dmitri had slowed to a more moderate pace. "How are things with *Nutcracker*? Good crowds?"

He nodded, throwing a hand high to hail a cab. "Over here! Yes, they come, big numbers, and the press gives us many fine articles of happy descriptions. But the fans know you are injured, and Maurice is angry all the time. He wanted the mermaid ballet to be the big spring blastoff, but now—" He opened the back door of a cab that swung to the curb and helped Gilly in. "Now he makes everyone work so hard, even though it is Christmas and we are in *Nutcracker* season."

"Believe me, I'd give anything if this hadn't happened." Gilly leaned against the door, her back in agony. "I'm going to be so out of shape."

Dmitri searched her face, worry in his bright blue eyes. "I am glad you decided to come back to New York. You need a dance doctor, someone who understands our muscles and bones and vertebrae."

Shifting in the seat to try to find relief, Gilly thought about the prayer time at Rick and Cynthia's house. She knew the Physician who had actually *created* her muscles, bones, and vertebrae. He knew the desires of her heart and would heal her in his time. She had to believe that.

The alternative was too bleak to contemplate.

Nineteen

Dr. Glaasmacher definitely needed to get a life, Gilly thought as she pressed the elevator button to take her out of this ruthlessly clean, impersonal medical environment. Concealed fluorescent lighting. Neutral paint. Tasteful but generic artwork. Rows of closed doors leading to hushed waiting rooms. What kind of person continued to see patients in such a place two days before Christmas?

A New York surgeon with demanding, high-dollar patients, that was who.

Gilly didn't consider herself either demanding or particularly high-dollar. But when she'd called and discovered the famous orthopedic surgeon had a cancellation and could see her Friday afternoon, she'd brushed her hair and hobbled down the stairs to hail a taxi. It wasn't easy, holding herself just right and making the long walk from the sidewalk to the elevator. The long flight from Birmingham on Wednesday had left her capable of little more than lying in bed, zoned out on muscle relaxers.

And it was all for nothing. Dr. G, bless his pointed head, wouldn't even consider laser surgery until she'd been through a full regimen of physical therapy. At least two more months. Now she was stuck here in New York for Christmas without family or close friends.

She pushed the elevator button a couple more times and glared at its cheerful yellow light. Disappointment about the surgery had her in an almost physical grip. She could feel her muscles weakening by the second. Inactivity was as foreign to her as drug abuse or cursing or fornication. *Why, God, why now? Why don't you pick on somebody who doesn't like you?*

Right now she couldn't think of a single Bible verse that applied. Yeah, all those summers in Vacation Bible School had done her a lot of good.

Love your neighbor. Obey your mother and father. Don't lie, kill, or steal.

The elevator dinged and opened. Relieved to find it empty, she shuffled in and leaned against the back wall. *I did all that,* she told God, looking up. *Where's my reward?* She saw the video camera in the corner and made a face at it. "You caught me," she muttered. "So sue me."

She came out of the building to find the temperature dropping toward freezing, the sky overcast, and the sidewalk traffic zipping along in both directions. Everybody doing last-minute Christmas shopping. Good thing she'd bought all her family gifts in Greece and left them with her mother. The kids would have their pan pipes and her sisters would enjoy the Cyprian lace she'd bought in Limassol.

Shivering, she decided it was also a good thing she'd bought this coat at Bloomingdale's back in October. She started to stick her mittened hand in the air for a taxi, then changed her mind. A short walk would clear her head. She'd just have to take it slow.

She couldn't help wondering what Jacob was up to. Probably eating his grandma's cooking and playing with Graham. But she wasn't going to call him to find out. Cole had reminded her she didn't used to "chase boys." And she especially wasn't going to run after one who all but admitted he'd knowingly endangered her back. Although that really didn't make much sense if she thought about it too hard. How could he know she had a genetic predisposition to fractured vertebrae?

Unlike some people, he had a very sensitive conscience.

By the time she'd walked a couple of blocks, she was in a full-blown funk. She could call up Dmitri, see what he was doing. Or one of the other girl dancers. She had plenty of friends. But who'd want to be around a depressed person who couldn't go dancing or even sit comfortably in a restaurant or movie theater? All she was good for was lying flat on her injured back.

She couldn't even stand her own company—how could she inflict her miserable self on some other poor unsuspecting soul?

On the other hand, it was still broad daylight, and she had four or five hours to kill before she could go to bed. She looked around. She wasn't too far from Lincoln Center, maybe three or four blocks. What if she put herself to some PT to pass the time?

Good idea, she patted herself on the back. Next question: walk or take a cab? Hmm. The subway would be cheaper than a taxi and take her there in about five minutes.

She headed for the stairs down to the closest subway station. Once she had her ticket, she shuffled through the line, collecting annoyed looks from city dwellers in a hurry, and waited on the platform. The tourists made her smile, especially the kids, and she was in a marginally better mood by the time the train hissed into the dock. Its doors slid open, increasing the roar of conversation and laughter and miscellaneous noise around her as one crowd exited and the other boarded.

She was one of the last to get on, which meant she didn't get a seat. *Rats.* She grabbed a pole as the train took off and immediately thought of Seth Booker's assumption about her occupation. She stifled a giggle, then looked around to make sure she hadn't attracted attention as one of the crazies riding the subway all day because they had no place else to go.

Fortunately, everybody was minding his or her own business—except one of the crazies himself. A weathered-looking, bearded old man in a gray knit cap was sitting on the bench to her left, staring at her with his mouth open.

Gilly hurriedly looked away, but not before noticing he was missing the lower half of one leg and he was crunching on a greasy bag of popcorn that looked like he'd scavenged it from a trash can. After a few seconds she sneaked another look at him. He was still staring at her, so she smiled and let her gaze glance away.

There'd been a time, when she was a young teenager, when she'd actually conceived and put into operation a ministry to the downtown homeless in Mobile. She's called it PBJ—Peanut Butter and Jesus—and talked a bunch of grown-ups in her church into helping her distribute plain sack lunches to street bums every other Saturday. That was such a long time ago, she'd almost forgotten about it. Five years ago? Six?

Seemed like another person entirely had thought that up. The church she visited here in Manhattan sometimes put together mission activities like that, but she rarely had time to participate. She was always rehearsing, going to galas, or performing. Or icing her feet.

She glanced at the old man again, and this time he smiled at her and offered her the popcorn.

Even as she shook her head with a thanks, the admonition about entertaining angels kicked through her brain. *I've done all that*... Her earlier litany of good deeds mocked her. Why on earth did she think she was such a saint as to deserve better than this poor man?

Fortunately, before she could burst into maudlin tears, the train arrived at Lincoln Center. Caught in the mad eddy of exiting passengers, she managed to get off without taking a tumble. She stood on the platform and looked around for the one-legged man who had offered her his popcorn. Apparently he'd stayed on the subway, headed for some further destination. Or maybe headed nowhere.

Like Gilly ultimately was.

Thirty minutes later, Gilly ducked into the physical therapy room and put her coat and bag into one of the lockers just inside the door. She stood there for a minute dabbing at her eyes with a Kleenex. She'd passed Maurice hurrying down the hall; frowning at her ferociously, he'd stopped to fire questions about the prognosis on her back. With what she considered admirable restraint, she'd given him the bad news, listened to his stern admonitions not to lose focus, and escaped into the PT room.

He'd made it sound like she'd committed a cardinal sin by even listening to Jacob Ferrar talk about his ballet.

With a sigh, she turned around and found herself staring at Victoria Farigno's sweaty upside-down face. "Gilly!" Victoria, hanging by the knees from a curl bar, looked astonished to see Gilly. "What are you doing here?"

Gilly limped past her, unstrapping the brace around her middle. "This *is* the PT room, right?"

"Yes, but I thought you were staying in Alabama for Christmas." Victoria flipped off the bar.

Gilly didn't feel like explaining again about the surgery that wasn't going to happen. "I changed my mind. Would you help me with this? I can't quite reach the end of the strap."

Victoria frowned but pulled at the Velcro strap and helped Gilly remove the brace. "How'd you get in this thing?"

"Wasn't easy." Gilly looked around. "Where's Smitty?" The company's physical therapist was generally in the room all afternoon, since the dancers often came in between rehearsals.

"Said he had an errand and he'd be right back." Victoria stood with her hands on her hips, watching Gilly gingerly shuck down to gym shorts and a T-shirt, careful not to jar her back. "You'd better wait till he gets here. I don't want to be responsible for hauling you to the hospital."

"You're all generosity." Gilly eased onto a table and lay on her back. "But you're probably right. I've got a list of stuff the doctor wants me to do, and it needs to be supervised." She glanced at Victoria and waved a hand. "Don't let me hold up your vampire bat practice. Carry on."

Shaking her head, Victoria went back to the curl bar. "I've never known you to be quite so sarcastic, Gilly. It's actually kind of refreshing."

"Like *you* were Susie Sunshine the last time we talked. I got your toxic phone message." There was a long silence while Victoria chinned herself. Gilly sighed. "I'm sorry, Victoria." She tried to think of something innocuous to say and came up blank. Her mind seemed to be filled with gravel. "So, um, how is it without Nicholas around? How're you doing?"

"Just hunky-dory. At least it's quiet. And the toilet seat stays down."

Gilly couldn't help giggling. "See, a rainbow at the end of every storm."

The next silence lasted for nearly a minute, but it was more comfortable. Gilly lay still, listening to Victoria's grunts of exertion, trying to ignore her own pain. It was getting worse. Where was Smitty?

She turned her head toward the door and caught Victoria staring at her. "What?"

Victoria rested her feet on the floor and looked away. After a moment she said, "I thought about what you said."

Gilly pursed her lips. "As I recall, I said a lot. Which?"

"About the abortion. I keep thinking about it, but I don't want to. My mother said she had one when she was in college and it was no big deal." Victoria's voice was quiet, strained. "It's just tissue."

Holy cow, Gilly thought wearily. She had her own issues and was in no spiritual condition to counsel anybody else. "I'm not making any accusations, Vic. You don't want to listen anyway."

Victoria's chin went up. "I'm just saying ... Everybody makes bad choices. You pay the consequences and keep going."

Well, there was a grain of truth to that. Gilly was paying the consequences of dancing Jacob's Mary. But there were bad choices, and then there were bad choices. And then there was all the stuff that was out of your control.

"But what do you do with your pain, Victoria? I don't believe you're quite as blasé as you make it sound. Who do you turn to when the lights are out and everybody's gone? When there's no audience telling you how beautiful and spectacular you are?"

Victoria's already pale face had gone to ivory. She opened her mouth to answer, but just then Smitty's bald-headed little figure bopped through the door.

"Gilly! I was sorry to hear about your accident." He walked around the table she lay on, inspecting her limbs like a butcher in a meat shop. "You bring a prescription with you from the doc?"

She glanced at the lockers. "It's in my bag." She started to roll off the table.

"No, no, just tell me which one. I'll get it." Smitty headed for the lockers.

Gilly directed him to her bag, wishing she'd had just five more uninterrupted minutes with Victoria. The moment was lost. She lay on her back waiting for Smitty to torture her.

God, I've really got a bone to pick with you ...

By Friday afternoon Jacob was in desperate need of physical activity. He called up Al and Rick to get together a pick-up basketball game at the church's gym—a sport he wasn't particularly skilled in but which gave him something to think about besides the almost physical ache of Gilly's absence. He and Graham were planning to meet the Hawkinses at the Zooland Safari that night, then make the drive to Alabaster in the morning. But in the meantime ...

He needed distraction in a big way.

Fortunately, dribbling, shooting at the small, high net, and trying to steal the ball with his hands were so different from soccer, it took all his concentration not to make a fool of himself—for at least two hours. Soaked with sweat but otherwise unfazed, he helped Rick clean up and lock the gym while the two little boys played with the gravel in the parking lot.

"What's the matter with you, man?" Rick stuck the gym key in his pocket and whacked Jacob on the arm as he headed for his truck. "You're not even breathing hard—which is wrong, in and of itself—but I've been talking to you for five minutes and you're off in space." He stopped to put his fingers to his mouth. "Come on, Reid, time to load up. Mom'll have supper ready."

Jerked out of a brown study, Jacob beckoned Graham. "You too, Gray." He ignored Rick's question as they walked toward the vehicle. He wasn't about to say he'd been wishing he could have brought Gilly along with them to the zoo. He'd been thinking about her walking into Cole and Laurel's house with a giraffe under her arm and balloons bobbing from her wrist. Hastily he improvised. "Nothing much. I was just thinking about something weird that happened at the grocery store yesterday."

Well, he *had* thought about it. Briefly, this morning while he was making his oatmeal.

"Weird how?" Rick unlocked the truck and boosted Reid, then Graham onto the high backseat.

Checking to make sure both boys fastened their seatbelts, Jacob got in the front. "Just ... odd. I was picking up a few things and ran into the mother of one of my students. She's normally a very friendly lady, and her kids are great—they're teenagers and always have lead roles in the ballets." He hesitated, thinking about Karen Blankenship's expression when she'd pushed her cart past the cereal aisle, where Jacob had stood trying to keep Graham from opening a box of Cocoa-Puffs.

"But?"

"But she looked right at me and hurried by without saying a word."

Rick glanced at him. "Did you holler at her or anything?"

"No." Jacob shrugged. "Hollering's not really my style."

"No, I guess not." Rick smiled and turned on the radio to a sports station. "Well, you know women. She probably had a hot flash or something."

"Maybe." Jacob was afraid it had something to do with the ballet company. The Sulleys were already angry with him. Maybe they'd been stirring up other parents. Stage-parent drama never ended.

And he was the last man to deny the feminine tendency for a woman to change her mind.

Gilly's decision to leave had left a dull ache in the vicinity of his chest. She'd have no reason to come back to Birmingham, and it was quite possible he'd never see her again.

He'd given up his heart. Recovering it was going to take a very long time.

Twenty

Christmas fell on Sunday, and Harold and Flora had called to invite Gilly to come with them to church. She couldn't bring herself to go. For one thing, it physically hurt to sit in one place that long.

But the real bruise was in her spirit. The past two days had been a misery of pain and loneliness. The stairs were every bit as excruciating to navigate as Laurel had predicted, so she incarcerated herself in the apartment, lying on the floor with the television and her iPod as her only company. She was sinking fast into the Slough of Despond.

Pretend to be joyful in a worship service? No. And since pretending wasn't an option, she refused to inflict her long face on Harold and Flora's kindness.

And the PT clinic was closed for the holiday. Why even get out of bed?

Some time around noon she managed a computer-video conference call with her family, who had all gathered at her parents' house in Mobile—a Victorian mansion that as a little girl Gilly had dubbed the Castle. The sight of Mary Layne's and Laurel's kids going berserk over their new toys, zipping back and forth in the background, or poking a head in to shout, "Hi, Aunt Gilly!" only made her feel more outcast and rejected.

Realizing she'd expelled herself from the gathering didn't help.

When the conference was over, she slammed the laptop shut, put her head down on top of it, and bawled until she threw up. Which wrenched her back and made her cry some more. Thoroughly miserable, she took a muscle relaxer and went to bed. Tomorrow she would go back to see Smitty—at the moment her best and only friend—and get back on the PT wagon. The only way she was going to get well, apparently, was trudging through the valley of pain.

Sometime later she swam out of a restless sleep, surfacing to the sound of a swarm of bees taking over the apartment. She pried her eyelids open and located the clock on the nightstand. Eight o'clock. The room was dim, only a streetlight filtering through the blinds. She looked around. No bees. But the doorbell was buzzing. And buzzing and buzzing.

"Go away." She pulled the pillow over her head.

Buzz. Buzz buzz buzz.

"Good grief, can't a person cry herself to sleep in peace?" Muttering, she rolled off the bed and limped into the living room to scare her visitor away. She knew she looked like leftovers. Plaid flannel pajama bottoms, Ole Miss hoodie, hair in an Olive Oyl topknot. Hah. She pressed the intercom button. "Who is it?"

"Victoria."

Gilly stood there with one bare foot atop the other for a moment before she could summon her voice. "What do you want?"

"Gilly, let me in. It's cold out here."

"Is anybody with you?"

"No. Come on, Gilly."

"Oh, all right." She released the front door lock and waited, leaning against the wall. Momentarily she heard footsteps on the stairs, then a knock on the door. She opened it. "Victoria, it's Christmas. Don't you have someplace else to be?"

Victoria shook her head. "My parents are in Cozumel, and you know what happened with Nicholas." Her eyes narrowed. "Gosh, Gilly, you look like—"

"That's what I feel like too." Gilly put her forehead against the doorjamb. "I'm not really up to company today. So if you don't mind ..."

But Victoria just stood there. "You looked better than this the other day. What's going on?"

"I've been having a few ups and downs." Gilly closed her eyes. "At the moment it's a down."

"Dmitri said you weren't answering your phone, so I thought I'd better come see for myself. Let me stay, and I'll make you some tea."

"Dmitri? Did he send you over here?"

"He didn't *send* me. I asked how you were, and he's worried about you, which made me worry." Victoria pushed past Gilly and shut the door. She took Gilly's arm and led her to the sofa. "Lie down before you fall down."

"I took a muscle relaxer." Gilly's knees buckled, and she folded up on the sofa. "Ow." She shifted to keep the brace from digging into her armpit. Within seconds she was asleep again.

"Here's your tea."

Gilly opened her eyes to find Victoria's face floating above her. "Hey. Where'd you come from?"

"You let me in half an hour ago." Victoria wrinkled her nose as she set a mug on the coffee table. "When's the last time you left the apartment?"

"I dunno. Friday, maybe?"

"Friday? That's when I saw you at the clinic."

Yawning, Gilly pushed herself to a sitting position and reached for the mug of tea. She sipped, and the warmth trickled to her stomach. She met Victoria's eyes. "Why're you here? I thought you're mad at me."

Victoria sat down in Gilly's rocker, hiding her face behind her own mug. "Dmitri told me Nicholas tricked you into telling him about … about … you know. I got to thinking about it, and maybe I've been a little irrational lately." She sighed, her face suddenly careworn. "I guess I sort of brought the situation on myself."

"Sort of?" Gilly laid her swimming head against the back of the sofa. "Victoria, you are one screwed-up chick."

Victoria gasped. "What was in that muscle relaxer? Sodium pentothal?"

"I don't seem to have any control over my mouth today." Gilly grimaced. "I'm feeling pretty sorry for myself—which probably makes me irrational too."

Victoria stared at her. "I don't like seeing you all messed up. You're scaring me."

"Well, you don't like it when I'm preaching either. Make up your mind." Gilly closed her eyes. "I'm sorry, what you see is what you get right now."

"But I need you to be *you.*" Victoria's voice was taut. "I came over here because—because I couldn't stop thinking about what you asked me the other day."

Gilly opened her eyes and struggled to focus. "I asked you …?"

"You asked me who was there to deal with the pain. And the answer is nobody. Nicholas is gone. My parents are on perpetual vacation. There's nobody left when the lights go out but me." Victoria's voice had swung high, caught above her breath, and a storm of tears looked about to break. "You're right—I'm a mess. I pushed you away, when you didn't do anything but care about me."

Gilly felt like she was sitting on a carousel horse with the world around her spinning. Something supernatural was going on here. Even when her faith had been at its lowest ebb, God had apparently been working. She'd hardly thought about Victoria in the last two days. Clearly she deserved no Super-Christian awards.

"Oh, man." She felt her own chin wobble. "I'm sorry, Victoria."

Victoria breathed hard in a visible effort to get her emotions under control. "What for?"

"Let's just say I wasn't as compassionate as I should have been. In fact, until I got a little taste of things not going my way, I might have been just a teeny bit proud. Not intentionally, but you know, it sneaks up on you. Maybe I was thinking I was such a teacher's pet, God owed me his blessing." Gilly was crying again, this time not the racking sobs that had made her so sick after talking to her family, but rivers of remorse that dripped off her chin and cleansed her heart. "So will you p-please forgive me?"

"Gilly, stop." Victoria sat on the edge of the chair, clenching the mug, her face tight with distress. "Of course I will. Please don't cry. I—I need you to be strong."

Gilly heaved a sharp breath and wiped her face on the hem of her sweatshirt. "See, that's it. We're both screwed up. The only difference between you and me is I don't have to stay this way. I'm sitting here in this apartment like it's the end of the world when I have a Defender. I have a Counselor. I have an ever-present best Friend. He's trying to talk to me, but I haven't been listening. I didn't even go to church this morning." She reached into the basket of magazines under the lamp table where she'd crammed her Bible before the trip to Birmingham. She held it up, flipping the pages. "See this? This is the love letter. It's the instruction manual. It's the sword. It's the flashlight in the dark."

Victoria stared at Gilly, her dark eyes narrow. "*You* haven't been listening?" She wildly set down her mug, sloshing tea onto the coffee table, and flung herself onto her knees in front of the sofa. "Gilly, there's a huge difference between you and me. I used to believe it was the teacher's pet thing. No fair you got all the beauty, all the grace, all the perfect little bones and joints and muscles that make up a dancer's physique. When Maurice picked you for the mermaid part I was so jealous I couldn't see straight. And when you hurt your back I was glad."

Gilly flinched.

Before she could speak Victoria grabbed her hands and began again. "I see other things too. I see that you work your tail off, and you don't whine about it like the rest of us. And I've never seen you push anybody else out of the way. I've never seen you lie or make excuses. But when I sit down and give myself a cold, hard look in the mirror, all I can think is ... I'm so—so—" Her voice splintered. "Oh, Gilly, I'm so ash—ashamed. I killed that little baby growing inside me, and it *hurts*, oh, my God, it hurts and I don't know what to do—"

Victoria pressed her face into the sofa and sobbed. Feeling her heart about to break, Gilly laid her cheek against the top of Victoria's head, threw her arms around her, and cried right alongside her.

God, heal my dear brokenhearted friend. Heal her body and soul ...

Sometime later Victoria sat up, hiccupping. "I never cry. This is totally weird." She wiped her face on her sleeve. "Don't you have some tissue somewhere?"

"Bathroom."

Victoria came back with the tissues, blowing her nose, and offered the box to Gilly as she sat down on the sofa. "Do you think he'll forgive the abortion?" Her voice wobbled.

"Nicholas? How would I know?"

"No, God."

Gilly tried to sort out her mushy emotions, numbed brain cells, and electrified spirit. "Wow. Is that on the table?"

"I don't know. I mean, I've never voluntarily talked about God before. All I know is what you've told me and what I've seen you do."

Gilly stared at her, suddenly stark-staring sober. That was the single most terrifying sentence she'd ever heard in her life. "Okay, then, let's get one thing straight first. I have not 'arrived.' This whole 'following Christ' thing is a journey." She put one hand to her sloppy hair and grabbed her sweatshirt with the other. "Clearly I've been struggling too. But you start by doing what you just did—admitting you need God."

"I do, I do." Crumpling her tissue in her hands, Victoria started to cry again.

"Me too." *Me too.*

Reeling with the sudden rush of emotion, Gilly leaned against her friend's shoulder, voicing the words that spilled from her heart. "Oh, God, I'm sorry I've been so unfaithful the last few days. I forgot how much you love me. Thank you for bringing Victoria to take care of me." She took a breath. "She wants to get to know you." She squeezed Victoria's hand. "Go ahead, Vic. Just tell him what you're thinking and feeling."

To her astonishment and confusion, Victoria's response was nothing more than, "Oh, God, oh, God, oh, God ..." and another storm of weeping. As her words became more coherent, Gilly distinguished, "I'm so sorry," and, "I need you," and, finally, "I can't believe you really love me." Gilly could do nothing more than hold her friend and offer her own silent and heartfelt petitions.

At last Victoria released a deep sigh and lay, spent, against Gilly's shoulder. "I never cry," she repeated.

"It's okay," Gilly said. "God bottles up our tears."

"What?" Victoria lifted her head. "Why?"

Gilly smiled. "I'm not sure. We'll have to look it up."

After a quiet moment, Victoria said, "I don't feel much better. That knot in my stomach is still there." Her voice sounded ... afraid.

Gilly sat up, taking Victoria's hands and staring into her face. "Listen to me, Vic." She hesitated, praying for wisdom. "There are some injuries that take a while to heal. You've been through a lot—physically and emotionally—and it's going to take some time to work through all that. We'll find you a good counselor to help. But as far as God is concerned, you get to start over. I mean it. Absolutely clean slate. The Bible says, 'If we confess our sins, he is faithful and just and will forgive us our sins and purify us from all unrighteousness.' I don't hear any qualifiers in there." Gilly glanced at the Bible she'd dropped on the coffee table. "First John 1:9."

"Even an abortion …" Victoria looked doubtful. "But if that's what it says … What do I do next?"

Gilly thought about it. "Now you just trust Jesus and start getting to know him. That's what the Bible and church are for."

Victoria looked distressed. "I don't even have a Bible."

"We'll go shopping for one tomorrow." Gilly cracked a smile. "You like shopping."

"Yeah. And the day after Christmas there'll be sales out the wazoo." They both laughed, a welcome release of emotion, and Victoria sat up. "I just thought of something. Maybe you—Maybe you could move back in with me—at least until your back gets better? I have an elevator, and I can help you with your PT or whatever you need."

This wasn't exactly the answer to prayer Gilly had asked for. She'd wanted her back healed. On the other hand, she'd been praying for Victoria's salvation for several years. "I'd love that, Victoria. If you're sure you don't mind."

"It'll be perfect for both of us." A smile broke across Victoria's face. "We'll get some of the boys to help bring your stuff over tomorrow. Then we'll have a moving-in party—" She stopped, crestfallen. "If you're feeling like it, that is."

Gilly smiled. "We'll see."

Christmas in Alabaster had been extraordinarily quiet. Jacob had stayed up past midnight after Graham went to bed last night, putting together a new bicycle with training wheels. Graham had long outgrown the tricycle Poppa kept in the barn; it was time to face the prospect of running along behind Graham to make sure he didn't fall. Reid was getting a bike for Christmas too, and the two little boys would have a grand time pedaling around in the Hawkins' neighborhood once he and Graham returned after New Year's.

Naturally on Christmas morning the kid got up, literally, with the rooster's crow, pouncing on Jacob's bed at just past six. "Uncle Jacob! Hey, Daddy! Time to get up!"

Resigned to the inevitable, Jacob smeared the sleep out of his eyes and put on a jolly attitude. He managed to hang onto it through Nonna's gigantic pancake breakfast and into the ritual of gift-giving under the Christmas tree, followed by hours of playing with Graham and his new toys.

Late that evening he sat with his grandparents in front of the fire, Graham sound asleep with his head in Jacob's lap. Nonna sat in her rocker quilting, Poppa nodding over a Western in the recliner, and Jacob had the TV remote in his hand, watching an old Christmas movie without much interest. His cell phone rang, startling Poppa awake.

"Sorry, Poppa." He silenced the phone quickly, looking at the caller ID. Heidi Raintree. "I'll take this in the kitchen," he said, sliding out from under Graham and hurrying into the kitchen, where he took a seat at the breakfast table. "Heidi—Merry Christmas."

"Jacob, how are you?" Her voice was tense. "I'm sorry to bother you. I hope I didn't interrupt your family time."

"No, we're just recovering from a day of too much excitement and rich food." He paused. "Is everything okay with you and the girls?"

"Oh yes, we're fine. It's just ... I debated with myself all afternoon about whether or not—Jacob, this is very awkward, but I'm convinced you need to know what's going on."

Jacob let a long moment hang before he said carefully, "What do I need to know? What's the matter?"

She cleared her throat loudly. "I hate this. I'm so angry I could—But they won't listen to me. Jacob, the board is going to meet Thursday night."

"What? Without me? Why?"

"It's something to do with Gilly Kincade not fulfilling her contract. Frank and Eric say we shouldn't pay her since she only danced one performance. Everybody else seems to agree. And they're blaming it on you. That dance you did Saturday when she hurt her back ... Since it wasn't part of the ballet ..." Heidi's voice trailed off miserably.

Jacob sat there with the phone clenched in his hand, incapable of putting the depth of his betrayal in words.

"Jacob? Are you there?"

"I'm here," he finally managed to get out. "I don't know what to say. You say it's Frank and Eric behind this?"

"Yes, but I suspect Alexandra Manchester-Cooper might have something to do with it. She says she saw you and Gilly rehearsing the Mary ballet and that it looked like you were … you know, fooling around."

"Fooling around?" It sounded lewd. Jacob had not even kissed her until the Christmas party at Cynthia's. "She's mad."

"Yes, she's very angry," Heidi said, misunderstanding. "She says you've mismanaged the company's money by spending so much to bring in guest artists when we've got capable dancers within the company. She claims you only brought Gilly down because you've got a thing for her."

"Did Alexandra tell you this? Why didn't she come directly to me?"

"I don't know, Jacob. She'd apparently talked to Eric and Sandra Sulley. Sandra's the one who told me this. She called to make sure I knew India wouldn't be getting any more parts at Brittney's expense once they get rid of you and Wendy." Her voice broke. "Oh, this is just awful. I don't know what to do."

Jacob tried to gather his thoughts. Alexandra was deliberately misrepresenting what she'd seen when she came in on the rehearsal that afternoon. But she had no doubt read his expression well enough to accurately interpret his feelings for Gilly. An angry and hurt Alexandra could cause untold damage.

And Eric Sulley, on a vengeful tear, could destroy him.

"Listen, Heidi, don't worry too much," he said as calmly as he could. "I'll think about it a bit and figure out how to handle it. But I'm glad you called to tell me."

Which was perhaps one of the more ridiculous statements to come out of his mouth today. But it seemed to reassure Heidi. She took an audible breath. "Okay, Jacob. You're smart enough and experienced enough to weather this kind of silliness. I'll be praying for you."

"Right. Thanks." He said good-bye and closed the phone. Sliding down on his spine, he clasped his head with both hands. What would be the proper course of action? What he actually had was hearsay. Neither Eric nor Alexandra had come to him with their grievances — though Jacob had had clear enough indication that both were upset with him. Should he confront either of them first? What was the Christian thing to do?

Unbidden came the image of Karen Blankenship wheeling past him in the grocery store, the guarded expression on her face. Was this why, he wondered?

Good Lord, how far was this whole thing going to go?

Twenty-One

As it turned out, farther than expected. By New Year's, Jacob and Wendy were in a fight for their jobs. He had seen political power struggles in ballet companies before. After all, this was a secular environment, and ethics were relative. Money talked, plain and simple.

The board met on Thursday, as Heidi had warned, and the first order of business was to scrap the idea of Jacob's *Perfume* ballet. It was deemed, no matter how many times Heidi reminded them of the power of the music and the dances they'd seen that Saturday afternoon, too great a financial risk. Drawing a crowd for such an unknown quantity as a religious ballet would be tricky under the best of circumstances, but with the director's judgment in question ...

Nobody except Heidi wanted to go on record as backing such a venture.

As for Alexandra's accusation, it would have been her word

against Jacob's except for the fact that Heidi couldn't deny she'd seen the spark of attraction between him and Gilly. Alexandra also insinuated that Jacob had hit on her more than once, inviting her to church and catching her in dark corners behind stage. Heidi later told Jacob the woman had made him sound like a lecher who ought not have children under his care.

"That's absurd," he said, frozen with outrage. "Eric goes to my church—he knows me."

"Of course it's absurd," she agreed, "but people believe what they want to believe."

He remembered again the incident with Karen Blankenship in the grocery store. How could she believe such things about him? But once the accusations were out there, there was little he could do to reel them back in. His reputation seemed to be blowing away like dust in the wind. Rumors of his wilder days in England and New York began to resurface, adding fire to the smoke.

The ballet school started up again, limping along in spite of several students withdrawing to join a competing company in Birmingham. Wendy continued to direct the day-to-day activities of the school, while Jacob tried to figure out what to do.

On the second Tuesday of January, he took Graham to school and stopped the car in a nearby park with his phone in hand. He had to have some counsel.

He caught Cole McGaughan wrapping up a Republican presidential campaign stump interview. "Hey, brother, it's good to hear from you," Cole said in his friendly way. "How've you been? How was Christmas?"

"Christmas was fine," Jacob said quietly, "but the last couple of weeks have been pretty rough."

"I'm sorry to hear that. What's going on?"

I miss your sister-in-law like crazy, he wanted to say. But technically that was the least of his problems at the moment. "I just need a bit of clearheaded objective wisdom."

"Okay." Cole sounded justifiably mystified. "Then I'm your man."

He laughed. "But my wife might be the one to bring in for the wisdom thing."

"No, it's nothing to do with legalities — at least not at this point." Jacob hadn't considered that angle. His stomach curdled. "At any rate, there's a bit of a tempest in a teapot brewing here, and it involves Gilly. I thought you might want to know."

"Gilly? What about her?"

How to explain this ridiculous situation? Jacob took a deep breath. "My board have taken it upon themselves to try to oust me over Gilly's breach of contract, saying I was irresponsible in having her dance my ballet the day she hurt her back. It's all a bit silly, but they're saying she and I were ... having it on, I suppose you'd say."

"Having it on? You mean ... you and Gilly were ..." There was a long silence. "I thought that was Tucker's creative imagination. He came home for Christmas telling some wild tale about Gilly dumping him for you."

Jacob clutched the phone hard. Gilly had left without telling him anything more than Merry Christmas. "I kissed her at our church Christmas party, but there were people all over the house. We weren't even alone while we rehearsed the demo at the studio — Graham was with us — and that's all we were doing. Dancing." He took a breath and released it. "Cole, I do love Gilly, but there hasn't been time to develop anything like an affair, even if I were still of that bent — which I'm not. And you know she's not." He laid his head back against the seat. "I'm probably not making a bit of sense."

"Laurel and I had to weather our share of misunderstandings before we married. It sounds like that's what this is. Does Gilly know anything?"

"I didn't want to worry her. I truly want what's best for her. I don't blame her for going back to New York, if she's bent on staying in professional ballet. Just because I left for reasons of faith doesn't mean a believer can't make a mark there."

"Okay, I'm just going to play devil's advocate here for a minute, Jacob. If I remember correctly, you left New York because of cut-throat political machinations, overload of sexual innuendo, the temptations of wealthy worldliness. Some of my exact words in the article about you." Cole paused. "Back then I saw your point. You were coming out of all that and needed a break from the temptation."

"Exactly." Jacob nodded, relieved he'd been understood. "Plus a romantic relationship that needed to be broken. I went to Spain to break the cycle. No way I'm going back."

"That makes a sort of sense. But look what you have, right here in the buckle of the Bible Belt. Political machinations, overload of sexual innuendo, and temptations of worldly wealth. Where are you going to run now?"

Jacob closed his eyes. "I didn't say I was going to run."

"No, but you sound a bit critical of Gilly's choice to go back into the lion's den."

"Well, some of that's selfish," Jacob admitted. "I wanted her to choose me."

"I don't think she's had time to choose anything except getting well. We talked to her on Christmas Day, and she seemed pretty down."

"So you think I ought to chuck all this mess and go after her?"

"I think you ought to defend yourself as best you can, hold onto your integrity, and pray for God to give you wisdom and strength. But, yes—if you love Gilly, you'll make some sacrifices for her. I don't know what that means, but the Holy Spirit will tell you."

Jacob sat there, breathing, trying to find his footing. He'd not heard one thing he particularly wanted to hear. But he could feel needles of truth going under his skin, finding his aching spirit. "All right, Cole, I'll think about it. Thank you for your counsel."

"Look, man, this is no easy thing to fix. And you're talking about my little sister here. If you damage her heart, I'm literally coming after you with guns blazing. Got that?"

Jacob couldn't help chuckling. "Got it. I'll keep you informed, brother."

He closed the phone and sat in the weak January sunshine, eyes closed and head back, praying, until one of Birmingham's finest cruised by and suggested he go home. He cranked the Jaguar and drove to the church, where he spent the rest of the afternoon at the altar on his face.

By the time he picked up Graham after school, he knew what he was going to do.

Gilly's phone was ringing inside her bag as she opened the locker. Another grueling PT session completed. Check off one more day before she could go back to Dr. Glaasmacher to talk about the surgery. Nineteen down, forty-one to go. She was headed for a massage as soon as she got rid of whoever this was. Unless it was Laurel. She needed to talk to Laurel.

Not recognizing the number on the ID screen, she nearly didn't answer. She was feeling too grumpy and sore to make conversation with strangers. With a sigh, she flipped open the phone. "Hello?"

"Hi, Gilly, this is Seth Booker."

She had to think for a second. Oh. Mr. Baseball. "Seth!" She dropped her gym bag and leaned against the lockers. "How did you get my number? I didn't give it to you."

"What about me leads you to think I give up that easy?" There was a grin in his voice. "I have a photographic memory, and Breanne at the PT clinic likes me. She said you canceled your appointments because you were going back to New York."

She had to laugh. "You're insane."

"I'm persistent. Which is why I bat .325." He paused. "I was just calling to check on you. I haven't seen you here, and I've been watching for you."

Rolling her eyes, Gilly picked up her bag. "This is getting close to harassment."

He laughed. "I'm going to tell you all about me so you won't think I'm a creep, then I want to hear about you. When did you go to Africa? I went there on a mission trip when I was a freshman in college."

"How did you know I went to Africa?" Frowning, she opened the door and slowly made her way down the hall.

"Your gym bag. Remember? I'm observant."

She looked down at the Africa Mission logo on her bag and sighed. "I have a hard time believing you went on a mission trip."

"Well, I did. Let's just say it was back in my Bible days."

"All my days are Bible days." She said it without much caring if it sounded dorky. She wasn't in the mood for flirting with anybody but Jacob, whom she hadn't heard from in nearly a month. "My trip to Africa was to talk about abstinence in high schools."

He whistled softly. "I might have known," he muttered. "I pick the only gorgeous red-haired virgin in the state of New York to fall in love with."

"You're not in love with anybody but yourself," Gilly said, but grinned.

"Hey! I resemble that remark." He didn't sound particularly offended.

Since she had nothing else to do, she decided to keep talking to him. "So convince me you're not a creep. But you're going to have to work a little harder than 'I went on a mission trip in my Bible days.'"

"My mother would love you." His deep, sleepy voice had probably won him more than a few assignations with pole dancers.

"I'm sure she's a nice lady. Where does she live?"

"San José. She builds computers and runs a wildlife rescue volunteer program. My father's an obstetrician."

"Hmm. I'd pictured you as a beach boy."

"You should see me on a surfboard."

Picturing him in a goofy Adonis pose, fist to forehead, she laughed. "Which Sox do the Barons farm for?"

"White Sox. Chicago." He sounded impressed that she knew what a farm team was.

"My dad's a baseball nut. We went to the BayBears games when I was growing up. They farm for the—"

"Padres," he finished with her. "I almost went to Mobile. Small world!"

"Yeah, it is." Holding the phone to her ear and dragging the gym bag, she felt her back muscles spasming like a Slinky riding down a staircase. She needed to sit down. "Listen, Seth, I appreciate you calling to check on me, but there's really no future in this. I mean, I'm in New York, you're in Birmingham—"

"I know where the airport is. We're in off-season, I can take some time—"

"Seth." She stopped in the middle of the hallway, dropped the bag, and put her hand to her back. "I'm sorry, but there's *really* no reason to keep calling."

"You're involved with somebody else?"

She hesitated. She could mention Tucker McGaughan, whose calls she'd avoided since Christmas and who was now safely in merry old England. That would be a lie. She could mention Jacob Ferrar, but you could hardly say you were involved with someone who sent you back to New York with barely a handshake (never mind the blistering kiss that preceded it) and not a word since.

"I'm not involved with anybody else," she said gently. "I'm just not interested."

There was a long silence, then a muttered rude word. "My mother was right." A lengthy sigh wafted all the way from Birmingham. "Okay. If you say so, I won't bug you again. No matter what it looks like, I'm a gentleman. But save this number and, if you change your mind, call and I'll come running."

Gilly shut the phone and stuffed it in the bottom of her bag, which she zipped viciously. Tears were perilously close to the surface. She closed her eyes and took a couple of deep breaths. She did not want a hunky baseball player. She wanted a hunky ballet director.

What a crazy, completely inappropriate and inconvenient time to discover she was in love with Jacob Ferrar.

When she turned around and looked up again, Maurice Poiroux was standing in the nearby doorway of Studio 1. She clutched the bag to her stomach. "Maurice! I'm sorry, I didn't see you standing there."

He frowned. "The bad time you are having," he observed. "Who is annoying you?"

"Nobody. I'm—Nobody."

"Smitty has you under control?"

"Smitty? Oh, yes, physical therapy." Why was she so rattled? Maurice could not have seen her maudlin thoughts. "Yes, that's going great. I'll be shipshape before you know it." She gave him a bright smile.

He just raised his eyebrows. "Hmph. You look like you need a Prozac."

Jacob had set up the meeting with the board for Friday evening, but he wanted to talk to Alexandra first. In compliance with counsel he'd received from several trusted sources, he made sure, however, that he was not alone with her. That morning he waited until he knew she was instructing a group of homeschooled eight-to-ten-year-olds, arranged for a substitute, and sent for her to come to his office.

She was, of course, spitting mad to be called out of class and came in with her elegant brows forming a shelf of righteous indignation above icy blue eyes. "This is extremely arrogant, Jacob Ferrar," she began, then stopped when she realized Heidi Raintree and JoDean Lamb occupied two of three chairs in front of Jacob's desk. She pinched her lips together. "Excuse me. I thought you wanted to see me, Mr. Ferrar."

"I did," he said calmly, indicating the empty chair. "Please have a seat, Alexandra."

At first he thought she might defy him, but she sniffed and flounced into the chair. "You might want to make this quick," she muttered. "We're working on the last half of the Prokofiev piece for recital."

"I've no doubt you're capable of whipping them into shape," he said dryly. "But I think this won't take long." He glanced at the two women sitting quietly to Alexandra's left. "I'm sure you know Heidi Raintree, who's on our board. And you might remember JoDean Lamb. I believe I introduced you the day you came to church with me."

Alexandra nodded stiffly, barely making eye contact with JoDean. "Yes, I remember. You told me you've had season tickets since you moved here."

"Yes indeed." JoDean smiled at her. "I've enjoyed the performances so much. I was there the night you stepped in to dance Sugar Plum Fairy. Lovely, just lovely."

"Thank you." Alexandra thawed visibly but shot Jacob a resentful look. "Mr. Ferrar, what is this about?"

"This is about your accusations concerning my integrity and personal conduct." He kept his voice as even as possible. "I brought Heidi and JoDean in because I trust their discretion, and I want there to be no misunderstanding about the conversation between you and me today. Besides, since Heidi's on the board, she needs to know what's going on. Is that fair enough?"

She gave him a grinding stare, but in the end all she could do was nod. "What about a representative for me?"

Jacob sighed. "Alexandra, this is not a Supreme Court hearing. I simply wanted to give you the opportunity to air whatever grievances you have against me, with female witnesses in the room to keep things civil. I'll do whatever I can to make amends with you, but there will be no histrionics or name-calling. Are we understood?"

She gripped the arms of the chair. "Oh, yes, we're understood. That's what's always at stake. A power struggle where the man is in charge and nobody's allowed to argue or even disagree."

Heidi held up a hand. "Just a minute. Who exactly is the artistic director in this company?"

Alexandra was stiff with rage. "Jacob. Mr. Ferrar. But that doesn't give him the right to—"

"Yes," Heidi interrupted. "It does give him the right to give orders, as long as they're for the good of the company. I heard nothing in his tone that indicated arrogance or impropriety. I've observed rehearsals with my girls for nearly a year and it's the same with teachers and students. Mr. Ferrar doesn't allow insolence, but he always speaks with firmness and humor and encouragement."

"Heidi," Jacob said, trying not to laugh, "thank you for your endorsement, but I really want to hear what Alexandra has to say. If I need to make changes in my methods, I will." He looked at Alexandra, thinking, *Dear Lord, help me be wise and reasonable. This is so hard.* "All right, so I'm a bit on the peremptory side. What else?"

Her fair face flamed. "That's all, I guess."

He stared at her. "What about the sexual harassment charges?"

"I'm not getting into that with these two church ladies here." She folded her arms and sat back.

He shook his head, stumped. "But if I'm to be charged with something, I need to know what your basis is. These women can be trusted to keep what's said right here."

Her gaze went wildly from Jacob to Heidi to JoDean before landing on the ceiling. He could tell she felt trapped. Well, so be it. She'd been happy enough to trap him.

"Come on, Alexandra," he goaded her gently. "Let's have it with both barrels."

"It makes me sound so … so slutty," she muttered. She glared at him. "I thought you liked me. You watch me all the time—or you used to, until that red-haired girl came from New York. You even took me to church with you. What was that, if it wasn't trying to get with me?"

Jacob heard JoDean gasp, and he gave her a warning gesture. He kept eye contact with Alexandra. Behind the childish rage was genuine hurt. He'd known it would be there, but still, it took him rather by surprise that he could invoke such strong emotion in a woman other than Gilly.

"Alexandra," he said slowly. "I'm very sorry to have embarrassed you. Perhaps at one time I considered going out with you as more than a friend. You're a lovely woman, and I've been a bit lonely." He could assuage her pride somewhat, but he'd have to be careful. "But I quickly realized that we're not really suited well. Besides, I'm your boss. It was completely inappropriate for me to lean in that direction. I didn't end it well, I'll give you that. Events with *Nutcracker* snowballed on me until I was so occupied with digging out of that ..." He paused and gave a little shrug. "I'm going to ask you to forgive me and see if we can start over as friends."

She stared at him, her expression unreadable, for several moments. He could see a muscle working in the fine, angular jawline. "You're just trying to get out of trouble," she said through her teeth.

The cobra rose again. He wanted to shout at her, throw her out of his office, fire her. He looked down at his hands gripping the edge of his desk until he could regain control.

Before he could do so, JoDean was on her feet. "I've heard enough," she said calmly. "You, my dear, are a spoiled brat, and I can't imagine anybody in this company or on the board who would believe anything you have to say against Jacob Ferrar. He's one of the most gentlemanly, Christlike young men I've ever known, and if you're too stupid to realize when you're being offered a chance to save face, then you deserve what you get."

She looked at Heidi. "See if you can talk some sense into her—I'm out of here. I'll see you at church, Jacob. Call me if you need my testimony at any point."

Mouth ajar, Jacob watched her march out with her purse clamped under her arm like a machine gun.

Heidi started to laugh softly. "Bravo." She crossed her legs and looked at Alexandra. "Do you have anything else to say that I might share with the board tonight?"

Alexandra had dissolved in tears. "N-No," she blubbered. "Do you have a tissue?"

Heidi came through and offered the requested item along with a stick of gum.

Jacob pinched the bridge of his nose. He would give anything for a stiff belt of Mountain Dew. "Then I'm going to send you home. You're suspended until the board can meet and decide what to do about your insubordination and false accusations—which, as I think you can see, can be proved to the contrary."

"But I thought—I thought they were meeting to fire *you*!" Alexandra looked thunderstruck.

Perhaps they were. But Jacob saw no reason to show his hand. Besides, the more he thought and prayed about the situation, the less he was afraid. Wendy Kersey had promised to speak in his defense. And he had had a conversation with Karen Blankenship. The reason she'd snubbed him in the grocery store was because she'd heard the rumors and hadn't known what to say to him.

Jacob shrugged. "Alexandra, the truth always comes out."

"The truth is, you humiliated me!" Her mouth trembled.

"But I didn't step out of line, did I—even when you offered sexual come-ons?" He might be making a mistake to press her, but if he could get a confession, Friday's board meeting might go in a completely different direction. He leaned forward a bit, holding Alexandra's eyes. "That's the real reason you're so angry with me. You've been a dancer long enough to know that the only way to rise to the top is with real ability. There aren't any shortcuts."

"I *am* a good dancer!" Her voice rose. "You just wouldn't see it. You kept giving roles to other people. Rebecca Blankenship. Gilly Kincade. And I could be a better ballet mistress than Wendy Kersey."

"But I didn't step out of line with you, did I?"

"No, you freak! I was beginning to think you were homosexual after all!"

Except for Heidi's gasp, Jacob let silence throb for a long moment.

Alexandra clapped a hand over her mouth, tears of chagrin dribbling down her cheeks. "I'm—sorry," she mumbled. "I didn't mean that."

"Oh, I think you did," Jacob said softly. "Do you have anything else to add before you go home?"

"No, I—" She jumped to her feet. "I've got to get out of here." She rushed from the office.

"Good gracious alive," said Heidi.

Jacob sat back, drained. "Ditto."

Twenty-two

Moving back in with Victoria had its complications. True, Nicholas and his cigarettes were no longer an issue, and the elevator was a bonus. But Gilly had been mistress of her own space for so long that folding herself into the daily routines of a psychotically neat social butterfly began to drive her insane. If Victoria happened to be home, every time Gilly set down a glass of water, finished or not, it would disappear in seconds. And the phone rang constantly. Fortunately, since the winter season was in full swing, Victoria was at the studio ten hours a day, taking her cell phone with her.

Which gave Gilly plenty of time to let Smitty, the Grand Master of Torture, have at her in the physical therapy clinic. Nearly every afternoon, she put on her swimsuit and went up to the top floor of Victoria's building where there was a heated pool large enough for swimming laps. Though she was a strong swimmer, she was sadly out of shape; she was nowhere near regaining the endurance she'd had before the accident. And the moment she stepped out of the water and tried to bend from the waist, the pain in her back reminded her she had a long way to go. There was little chance she'd be ready for spring rehearsals in March.

Despite the excruciating slowness of her recovery, by the third week of January she felt up to going back to church. She and Victoria took the subway to the East Manhattan theater and found themselves welcomed with open arms. Gilly introduced Victoria as a new believer, and a date was set for her baptism in the pool at the local Y. Hesitantly sharing her recent travails, Gilly found compassion and support and wondered why she'd held off so long on going back to her Christian family.

On the way back to the apartment, she listened to Victoria's chatter with half an ear and thumbed the pages of her Bible, thinking about the prayer meeting with Jacob's small group in Birmingham. They had prayed for her, but she had yet to be healed.

And her heart was wounded as well. Tucker had called from London two weeks ago to say he'd been to Abbey Road, and he sounded more animated than she'd ever heard him. He hadn't bothered to tell her he loved her—which suited her just fine. No more pretending.

She'd halfway expected, though, to hear from Jacob. His silence stung. Maybe she'd responded too eagerly to his kisses. Maybe she'd been too guarded afterward.

She had no clear idea what she'd done wrong. Maybe it had nothing to do with her mistakes, and Jacob was just the wrong man at the wrong time. She should forget him. He lived in Birmingham anyway and would never leave because of his grandparents and Graham. Her life was here in New York.

"So I did what you said and started telling people," said Victoria.

Gilly blinked and looked at her. "About what?"

"About my decision to give my life to Christ. You haven't been listening to me at all, have you?"

"I'm sorry." Gilly sighed. "Who have you told?"

"I told Ian. He looked at me like I was a freak and changed the subject. But Dmitri was standing there, and he said, 'Good for you. I see the difference.'" Victoria shook her head. "I've seen you live the life for a long time now, Gilly, so I knew it was possible. But it's just bizarre that people can see changes in *me* now."

"It's called producing fruit. If you're an apple tree, you'll grow big fat red apples. If you're a Christian, you'll start to look like Jesus." Gilly couldn't have counted the times she'd heard that platitude, but it suddenly made real, practical sense. She found herself smiling in spite of her melancholy. "So Dmitri noticed. We've got to keep praying for him. He's going to be watching us both."

Victoria sat back, her thin, beautiful face thoughtful. "I know I haven't been a Christian for very long ..." She glanced at Gilly, fingering her purse strap. "But it seems to me if you were healed, a lot of people would pay attention."

"I *will* be healed." Gilly had to believe that. "I'm not giving up. I'm swimming every day and keeping up my therapy—"

"No, I mean something ... supernatural. Do you believe God still does that kind of thing? Or is it just hocus-pocus that people on TV do?" Victoria's expression was serious. She really wanted to know what Gilly thought.

Gilly looked away. It couldn't be a good idea to put God on the spot, to potentially disappoint this brand-new believer. She knew God sometimes chose to give a resounding "no" to prayer requests—and sometimes he said "wait." She'd never seen anybody supernaturally healed, though she'd heard of it happening on mission fields and other places of desperate need. She believed it could happen, theoretically, but did she deserve that kind of miraculous intervention? After all, she was functioning pretty well without it. It wasn't like she was out on the street, scavenging popcorn for meals.

But when her mouth opened, she found herself saying, "Yes, I think he definitely does miracles. I've never seen one, but I sure would like to. Let's ask him and see what he does."

"You mean now?"

Gilly blinked. She'd intended to ask her preacher brother-in-law to pray with her over the phone. She shrugged. "Sure, why not? Technically, we're 'two or more'."

Victoria's lips curved. "Yeah, I can do the math." She paused. "So should I go first, or what?"

Gilly had enjoyed watching Victoria get excited about the Christian journey. It would be fun to see what she'd do with this situation. "Go ahead. I'm the pray-ee here. You be the pray-er."

"Okay." Looking dubious, Victoria closed her eyes. "Dear God, I've never asked for anything this big before, but ... Gilly says it's okay, so ... well, we want our friends to know you, so would you please heal Gilly's back?" She hesitated. "Amen."

Now that the prayer was out there, spoken aloud, Gilly's confidence wobbled. For the trip to church she had worn the back brace under her clothes, though the doctor had said she could reduce her time in it as she felt able. She suddenly wanted to wear it the rest of her life. Terror grew, seized her, nearly as debilitating as when she'd lain shivering with pain in the emergency room. This was what unbelief felt like.

Frantically she grabbed for her faith. Fear was from the adversary.

She took a deep breath. "Thanks, Vic. I'll take off the brace when we get home and see what happens."

Please, God, don't let Victoria down.

By the time they got home, Gilly had convinced herself that she was going to experience a miracle. She couldn't think of a single time in the Gospels when Jesus had come near a person with an illness without touching them in some way. She was no theologian, but it seemed there ought to be some transfer of principle.

So after depositing her purse on the bed in Victoria's extra bedroom, she stripped off her sweater and stood in front of the mirror with her fingers on the Velcro strap of the brace.

"Take it off, dope," she told herself.

Still she hesitated. She felt kind of numb. And scared.

Then she saw Victoria in the mirror, standing in the doorway behind her.

"You want some help?"

Gilly shook her head. "I've gotten to where I can do this in my sleep."

Rip went the Velcro. The brace separated, and Gilly could feel its weight drop off. It hit the floor. She stood perfectly still, afraid to move. There was no pain when she stood erect with her abdomen tucked in.

She rotated her shoulders, slowly windmilled her arms in a swimming motion, watching herself in the mirror. Victoria had put her hands over her mouth.

Finally she got up the nerve to lean forward from the waist.

The now-familiar pain clawed her lower back with a single sharp talon, and she felt her knees buckle with disappointment as she straightened again. "It's still there," she croaked. Her throat was frozen, her shoulders rigid. She couldn't look at Victoria, so she grabbed the edge of the dresser and studied the whites of her fingernails. "Okay, so …"

Victoria ran to slide an arm around her. "Oh, Gilly."

"I'm sorry." She felt Victoria's cheek against the top of her head. The tender gesture brought a rush of tears. She fought them. "So he said no for now. We'll keep praying, and I'll keep working. He's got good in mind for me."

"Okay. If you say so."

"Listen," Gilly said fiercely, looking up to meet Victoria's eyes in the mirror. "The enemy would like nothing more than for me to shut God out and blame him for grounding me." A line from the pastor's message that morning popped into her head. "You know those three guys who brought their paralyzed friend to Jesus? The first thing he did was forgive him for his sins. That's the greatest miracle, Victoria.

That we get to have a relationship with God. The rest is gravy, you know?"

"I don't know how you can say that." Victoria squeezed her shoulders. "I'm a little PO'd on your behalf."

Gilly laughed. "That's because you're a good friend. But there are some things we have to learn the hard way. And I'm learning I'd rather be in God's will and in pain than wandering around on my own in a healthy body."

"If you say so." Victoria didn't look completely convinced, but she bent down to pick up the back brace. "So let's go swimming. I've got to get ready for my baptism."

Jacob was at the computer with the cursor on the Send button of an email when Wendy stuck her head in the door of his office. It was early on the last Friday of January—so early the Jag had been the only car in the parking lot when he drove up thirty minutes ago. He'd composed an email to Gilly the night before and wanted time to go over it one more time before sending it.

Dear Gilly,

I'm sorry I've let it go so long without getting in touch with you. I've thought about you and prayed for you constantly since you left. At first I wanted to give you time to concentrate on getting well without the distraction of my wishes and hopes complicating things. Then my own situation got a little dicey here.

Anyway, it's time I said in so many words how much you mean to me. I'm afraid I've been rather a coward, and I hope you'll forgive me. If you've no objection, I'll give you a call and we can talk.

With all my affection,
Jacob

Affection. There could be nothing objectionable in that, right? And it didn't overcommit himself should she be in the mood to "put up the hand," as Tucker had phrased it.

Still, he hadn't yet had the nerve to actually send it, and he was calling himself all sorts of a fool when he looked up and saw Wendy's raised eyebrows. Relieved at the reprieve, he shut down the email program and beckoned her in. "Good, you're early. I wanted to talk to you before everybody started getting here."

Looking as calm and put-together as always, Wendy sat down and crossed her legs. "Are you not worried someone will think we're having an assignation?"

Jacob smiled. Alexandra's accusations had fizzled after the confrontation last Wednesday. The board meeting two days later had been awkward in the extreme, dealing with financial woes related to community backlash after Gilly's injury. But with the charges of sexual harassment off the table, Jacob found himself perfectly capable of coping with the rest—with the help of his staff and several influential parents who came to his defense.

"If there were anybody who would tempt me, it would be you," he said, shaking his head. "But the building's unlocked and the office door's wide open. Besides, you're too smart for the likes of me."

"Jacob—"

"Listen, I'm going to need your help with something. I've thought of a way to recoup our losses from *The Nutcracker.* I want you to see this."

He slid the DVD lying beside the computer into the disk drive and waited for its icon to appear on the desktop. "I'm going to need twenty of our best dancers willing to work overtime on spec." He met Wendy's curious gaze with a rueful smile. "And I need them to keep their mouths shut."

He'd think about sending the email to Gilly later.

The little triangular park across from the apartment in Tribeca was quiet this Saturday morning. And no wonder. Gilly gingerly sat down on an ice-cold wrought iron bench and decided she must be crazy, sitting out here in subfreezing weather with nobody but a shivering squirrel and a flock of pigeons for company. On the other hand, she could be sweating in agony in the PT room.

She decided to stay a few more minutes.

For the last thirteen days she'd been starting her PT earlier and staying longer. Though it hadn't produced instant healing, praying with Victoria had brought a renewed determination to follow through with her prescribed therapy. She'd felt stronger every day, able to do more reps, aware in an almost extrasensory way of the knitting of her muscles, bones, and vertebrae. Today she'd rolled out of bed without thinking and bent over to pick up the socks she'd left on the floor, to keep Victoria from freaking out.

The twinge in her back had been so minor, she'd jerked upright with a gasp and stood there with her heart pounding.

Thirteen days. There shouldn't have been such rapid progress in thirteen days.

So when Victoria left for the studio, Gilly had taken the subway to her own apartment instead of heading straight for PT. She wanted to check on things. Maybe think about moving back home to get out of Victoria's hair.

And pray. She'd gotten used to a lot of alone time for talking out loud to the Lord. The park, cold as it was, had drawn her. She tugged her knit cap farther down over her ears and stuck her mittened hands into her pockets. "So, Father, what's going on?"

The squirrel looked around, flirted his tail, and took off up a tree.

"This is a pretty ambiguous way to go about this, you know." She looked up at the leaden sky. Looked like it might snow any minute. Maybe she ought to head for the subway. "Instant would've been so much more obvious. But thirteen days." She shook her head. "And no telling how much longer complete recovery will take. It's been, what, seven weeks from the injury? Two to three months was the projected time. Who's gonna believe it was you?"

There was an odd scrabbling noise coming toward her from the street, and for a startled moment she thought God was audibly answering her. Then she heard loud canine panting and a joyful *woof.* Rocky, Ellen's retriever, came tearing past the garbage can on the corner, leash trailing, tongue flapping out of the side of his mouth.

Gilly jumped to her feet. "Rocky! Where's Ellen?" Helplessly she watched the dog race past her, circle the bench, jump on her in an attempt to lick her face. "Down, boy!" She fended him off, laughing. "Do you know where that tongue's been?"

Finally she grabbed him in a hug and fell backward onto the bench. Giving up on her face, the dog began to lick her coat and found a texture he seemed to like. Giggling, Gilly stroked his thick yellow coat and peered down the street, expecting her neighbor to appear any moment. Ellen would be relieved to find her baby under restraint. She was crazy about this dog.

When five minutes went by — Gilly kept checking her watch — with no Ellen in sight, Gilly decided Rocky must have truly absconded. Now what was she going to do? If she tried to walk Rocky home on his leash, he would jerk and tug and do enormous damage to her …

It occurred to her he'd already more or less tackled her, and she'd left her brace at home. She ought to be in pain.

Cautiously she straightened, grabbing Rocky's collar and the end of the leash. "Get down, lover boy." She shoved him to the ground onto all fours. "Let's take you home." She stood up, wrapping the leash around her hand, and felt perfectly steady. Normal. A flood of warmth infused her body from her cap to her boots. "Oh, man. This is going to be really hard to explain."

Twenty-Three

Jacob landed at LaGuardia shortly after eleven on the first Sunday of February and caught a cab into downtown Manhattan. He had several loose ends to tie up while he was in the City, but first he had to find Gilly and explain to her why he'd let nearly two months go by without contacting her.

He'd never sent the email. By the time he'd absorbed Wendy's excitement over their secret project, he knew he couldn't go to Gilly until he'd done everything possible to make things right with the Birmingham company. Even if they ultimately fired him, he didn't want to offer her less than his best.

Besides, he'd still had to deal with the complications of restructuring the company, replacing Alexandra, figuring out a workable rehearsal schedule ... His mind was set to explode from overload.

Still, as he worked, the conversation with Cole all those weeks ago reverberated in his head until he felt like a bell tower at noon.

Finally he was ready to face her, face the past, face the future, and above all face his fear.

So he'd made a few phone calls, booked a flight, asked his grandmother to care for Graham, and thrown enough clothes for a few days in a suitcase. Still, in spite of a stern conversation with himself, his hands sweated as he got out in front of the Downtown Hilton and paid the cabbie. He stood there for a minute, watching foot traffic pass in both directions—mostly tourists, since it was Sunday.

So. Here he was, back where he'd fallen apart. The Big Apple. Which, once bitten into, often sent you into a sort of coma from which many people never woke. He was lucky, blessed, that the Savior had kissed him before the poison destroyed him.

Trying to rid himself of morbid what-ifs, he followed the bellhop to the registration desk, checked in, and went up to his room. He toed off his shoes and sat down on the queen bed, phone in hand, to check on Graham. Nonna answered, chatted with Jacob for a minute, then put Graham on.

"Hey, Daddy! Nonna and me are making cookies."

So much for being indispensable. "Save me one, will you?"

"Yes, sir. Did you talk to Miss Gilly yet? Did you tell her we brought Thing One and Thing Two to Alabaster?"

When explaining to Graham where he was going, Jacob had mentioned that he might see Gilly in New York. "Not yet. I just got here." He couldn't help fishing a bit. "You like Miss Gilly, don't you?"

"I like her *best*! I want you to marry her."

Jacob nearly fell off the bed. "Whoa. Wait, nobody's talking about getting married." Not yet, anyway.

"But why not? I liked it when she tucked me in. She smells like a mommy."

Jacob didn't want to know what a mommy smelled like.

"Reid has a mommy, and it's not fair." Graham's voice got smaller. "She makes him cookies all the time."

"Well, you know, life isn't always fair. Sometimes things happen that make us unhappy, but God is good anyway. He loves us no matter what."

How many times was he going to be required to repeat that? Especially to himself?

"Jesus loves me, this I know," Graham chanted. "For the Bible tells me so."

"That's right." Jacob smiled. "Right now, even Miss Gilly is a little unhappy because she hurt her back and can't dance. But if you ask her, she'll tell you she trusts God to do what's best for her."

"Yeah, but I still want a mommy." Graham sighed. "Can we go to McDonald's for supper?"

"You'll have to ask Nonna. Will you put her back on the phone?"

His grandmother came on the line immediately. "Jacob, don't you come back without that young lady. That's an order."

He laughed. "I'll see what I can do."

After answering her questions about Graham's school schedule, Jacob rang off and lay for a moment with his arm over his eyes, smiling. Deciding he'd delayed long enough, he sat up and propped himself against the headboard. Time to charge in where angels feared to tread.

The phone range twice before she answered, sounding breathless. "Jacob! Where are you?"

"I'm in New York." He hesitated for only a moment. "I thought I'd come round to see you, if you're not busy."

There was a long silence, and he wondered if he'd made a huge mistake. "That would be wonderful. But I'm not at home. I'm at Harold and Flora Cook's apartment. Can you come here?"

"I suppose. I haven't seen Harold in … five years, I think. Have they moved?"

"I don't think so." She gave him the address and laughed. "Oh, I can't wait to see you. Please hurry!"

Jacob's heart took a flying leap. It sounded like she would more than welcome him. Maybe all his worrying had been for nothing. "I'll be there as fast as whatever cabdriver I get will take me."

"All right, then, I'll see you in a bit." She paused. "Hurry, Jacob!"

He laughed and closed the phone, then reached for his shoes and jammed them on. *Oh, Lord, you are surely good. Help me be patient.*

All the way across town Jacob reminded himself that God was on his side. There could be nothing to overcome him. Not that, as he'd told Graham, he was *owed* a happy ending—but he could be victorious in any circumstance that would bring glory to God's name. It was a conundrum he was on the verge of understanding.

The cab pulled up in front of Harold's apartment building on Franklin Place. He paid the cabbie and rang the bell. Gilly's voice came over the intercom. "Jacob? Is that you?"

"C'est moi."

"Yay! Come on up." The lock buzzed.

Jacob took the stairs up to Harold's third-floor apartment and rang the bell. Harold himself answered the door. The old man had hardly aged—same loose-skinned dark face, rimless glasses, and neat clothes. The gray hair might be a bit thinner, the forehead higher, but he still looked like someone who could stand in front of a classroom and give a cogent lecture on Icelandic literature.

Jacob smiled and extended his hand, but Harold pulled him into a surprisingly strong embrace.

"Welcome back, son," Harold said gruffly as he released Jacob. "Didn't think I'd see you again."

"I hadn't planned to come back. I'm only here for a visit." Jacob's gaze drifted over Harold's shoulder to an attractive black woman in a classy ruby-colored dress waiting to be introduced. He smiled. "You must be Flora. We never had the chance to meet."

"So pleased to see you, Jacob," she drawled, shaking hands. "Harold speaks kindly of you."

"Thanks." Jacob couldn't help searching for Gilly. The small living room was empty except for a long-legged brunette seated on the sofa. She had "dancer" written all over her. He looked inquiringly at Harold.

Harold grinned. "This is Victoria Farigno, who's in the BNY corps. Quasimodo, meet Jacob Ferrar."

Jacob nodded absently at the girl, then scanned the room again. Where was she?

Harold chuckled. "Did you think you were imagining things? Gilly's in the dining room. She has a surprise for you."

"A surprise," he repeated. Jacob had never been particularly fond of surprises. They often flew in your face like bats.

"Yes, sit down here beside Victoria," said Flora, taking his arm and tugging him into the living room. "She won't bite."

Jacob sat, looking sideways at the brunette dancer. "Do you know what's going on?"

She smiled. "Maybe." Her eyes were dark brown, deep lidded and exotic, but bright with excitement. She wore a skimpy little black dress with a cardigan over her shoulders, and the long legs were bare in spite of frigid January temperatures. She didn't look like the kind of girl Gilly would hang out with, but what did he know about Gilly's life in New York—except what she'd told him? He began to feel uneasy.

Then he remembered Gilly telling him about a former roommate named Victoria. The one who'd given her such grief after her injury. Could this be the same girl?

He shook his head, completely confused, but before he could ask questions, Gilly herself appeared in a doorway to the right. She wore a black leotard and tights with a filmy little black ballet skirt, and she had on pointe shoes. Her hair was bundled into a messy knot on top of her head.

"Jacob, stand up!" she commanded. Startled, he obeyed without thinking, and before he could blink Gilly had launched herself at him. "Lift, cambré back!"

He caught her as she turned and jumped, and she was bent backward across his shoulder before he remembered her injury. She was going to be in the hospital again. "Gilly," he groaned, in an agony of indecision. Should he lower her or let her slide down on her own?

But she was laughing, legs extended in a beautiful *developé* front. Pliant as a rubber gumball, she reached back, clasping her arms around his chest, and flipped herself backward to the floor like a gymnast. As he turned, she struck an attitude and grinned at him with laughing, brilliant eyes. "Ta-da!"

"What's going on?" He stared at her, dumbfounded.

Harold, Flora, and Victoria were all laughing at his obvious bewilderment. "Told you it was a surprise," said Harold.

"I'm—Gilly, what's happened? Are you—How did you do that? Are you not in pain?" He reached out to lay his hand at her waist. She was panting a little from the exertion, but there was no sign of physical distress in her expression. He hesitantly turned her, with his thumbs examining the delicate vertebrae outlined through her leotard.

She looked over her shoulder at him, eyes shining with happy tears. "We prayed and he said yes. Watch this." Before his astonished eyes she bent over to grasp her ankles. She looked like a hairpin.

"I don't have words." Jacob just looked at her and looked at her. "When did this happen?"

Gilly popped erect, pirouetted, and beamed at him. "Two weeks ago on the subway, on the way home from church, Victoria prayed for me. When I got home, I took off the back brace, and I was still hurting. But I kept doing my PT and, a little bit at a time—but very fast if you think about it—I got better, way ahead of schedule."

"Then you didn't have the surgery?"

She shook her head. "Dr. Glaasmacher wouldn't do it until I'd had at least two months of therapy. So I was all set to have this thing drag on forever—" She glanced at Victoria. "But this is way cooler, huh?"

Jacob caught Victoria's curious gaze. "I thought you two were … you know, on the outs."

Victoria shrugged. "That was before. Everything's different now."

"I'll say." Gilly grinned at Victoria. "I'm going to have my back X-rayed tomorrow, but I'm sure this is permanent." She did a little jig. "I came over here to tell Harold and Flora because I couldn't wait to show somebody—and then you show up too. It's like Christmas, only better!"

Jacob thought of the difficulties waiting for him in Birmingham.

Gilly must have sensed his momentary abstraction. "What are you doing here in New York? I completely forgot to ask."

He shook his head, summoning a smile. "We'll talk later. Right now I want to see an *arabesque percheé*."

She complied, beautifully, smiling.

"Praise the Lord," he breathed as she relaxed again into first position. "I can hardly believe there's no stiffness or residual pain. Honestly, I've never seen anything like this. Are you going back to work tomorrow?"

"I can't *wait*!" Gilly clapped her hands. "Maurice will be so surprised."

"He's not the only one," Victoria said dryly. "There's gonna be some clawing from the cats in the corps who won't be so glad to see you back."

Gilly waved an airy hand. "That I can deal with. Everybody will have to see what God can do. It will be … amazing! Jacob, will you come with me? I want somebody there who can back me up on what happened. You saw the X-rays, right? You saw how bad it was."

He hesitated. "I have some business to take care of in the morning. If you can wait until the afternoon …" He realized Victoria was staring at him, eyes narrowed, a pucker between her fine brows. "Is something wrong?"

She lifted a shoulder. "I'm sorry. You remind me of someone I used to know."

Jacob turned to Harold and Flora, standing arm in arm in the kitchen doorway. “Why don’t we all go for celebratory cheesecake? I’ll treat.”

“Now you’re talkin’ my language.” Harold opened a closet, pulled out a fur-collared coat, and helped Flora into it. “Let’s go before he changes his mind.”

Gilly woke up Monday morning in her own bed, in her own apartment, and lay on her side for a minute or two, quite still. She’d slept like a baby for the first time since she’d abandoned her muscle relaxers. Slowly she straightened her legs. No pain. She rolled to her back. No pain. She sat up. No pain. Glory hallelujah, she really was healed. Completely and wholly. She felt a grin spread across her face.

And Jacob had come for her. Oh, he hadn’t said so, in so many words. And he hadn’t volunteered much about what he’d been up to since Christmas. But he was here. He’d called her first thing, tracked her down at Harold’s place, lifted her over his shoulder, touched her back as if she were something precious. And his face …

Oh, his face when he realized she was completely well.

She’d go through the whole thing again to see that see that smile. Well, almost.

Still grinning, she jumped out of bed, pirouetted her way across the room, and hurried through her shower. Dressed in her favorite sweater and jeans, she packed her dance bag and caught the subway over to the studio. X-rays could come later. She couldn’t wait to show Dianne Woo that she was ready to be back in the rehearsal and performance lineup.

Mondays were nonperformance rehearsal days, set aside to recuperate from the hectic, stressful weekends. The atmosphere was generally more relaxed than the rest of the week. There was no telling where she’d find Dianne, but her office would be a good place to start.

But when Gilly entered the studio’s central hallway, the first person she saw was Dmitri, eating a cup of melon balls with a spoon. His face lit. "Gilly! Good morning!" He leaned down to hug her, gingerly.

Gilly laughed and grabbed him around the waist as hard as she could. "Hugging doesn't hurt anymore."

"What?" Dmitri spun her away from him and looked her up and down. "You are kidding me."

"It's true." She twirled and did a couple of jumping jacks for good measure. "See?

Dmitri looked bewildered. "But the doctor said weeks and weeks of physical therapy. How can this be?"

"This is because God wants to show you his love and his mighty strength. Dmitri, I think he did this for you." Gilly never hid her faith, and she looked for ways to share Jesus' love, but she had a peculiar aversion to being known as an abrasive Bible-thumper. Today, however …

Today she was feeling reckless. She stared up at Dmitri, all but daring him to contradict her.

Sticking his spoon into his cup, he walked around her and poked gently at her back.

She bent over and laid her palms on the floor, then straightened, chin up, hands open. "See?"

His face was chalk white. "But—but—this is not possible! I saw you last Friday in the brace."

"I know! Isn't it great?"

He backed away from her. "I have to go. Rehearsal is in ten minutes. I must finish my breakfast. I have to go."

Gilly stared at the empty hallway with her mouth ajar. Dmitri seemed genuinely frightened. Picking up her dance bag, she headed for Dianne's office. She hoped Dmitri's reaction was not an indication of what she could expect from everyone in the company.

She finally tracked Dianne down in Studio 1, conducting an early workout with a small group of dancers who would be corps de ballet for a *West Side Story* collection. Victoria was here, as were several others who had been in and out of Victoria's apartment while Gilly was staying there. The atmosphere was focused, sweaty, serious. Gilly longed to jump in and dance, but there were a few hoops she'd have to jump through first.

She stood in the doorway for a moment, watching. She frowned. What was Iliana Poiroux doing in this rehearsal? It was primarily designed for young dancers on the cusp of stardom. Iliana was on the verge of moving to mature roles—mothers, evil villainesses, queens.

Finally Dianne glanced at her watch, caught Gilly's eye. Her eyebrows went up. "All right, people. Ten-minute break. Keep moving, stay warm. We're not done. This needs polish." She zoomed toward Gilly, heading off Victoria with a frown. "No time for gossip. Get a bottle of water and get right back."

Victoria made a moue and slinked off to her locker. "I'll talk to you later," she said to Gilly over her shoulder.

Gilly nodded, but focused on Dianne. It was going to take all her powers of concentration to hold her own in the upcoming confrontation. Of the ten ballet masters on staff at BNY, Dianne Woo had perhaps the closest relationship to director-in-chief Maurice Poiroux. She was even friendly with his wife, Iliana, who was brilliant, difficult, and notoriously detached.

Perhaps Dianne could communicate with the prima ballerina because she was herself a hardnosed perfectionist. She tipped her head with imperious command, indicating that Gilly should follow her down the hall to her office. She shut the door behind them and stood arms folded, looking down on Gilly. At five-foot-eleven, she had been a "tall girl" in her day. Now—she was just plain intimidating.

"How's the physical therapy going?"

Gilly swallowed, nervous all over again. "Didn't Victoria tell you? I'm done with PT."

"She came in late this morning. We haven't talked. Let me see the brace."

"I'm not wearing the brace." Gilly lifted her sweater just enough to expose her camisole. "I don't need it because I'm well."

"What do you mean? Dr. Glaasmacher said you'd be in PT for another two to six weeks."

"I know, but there's been a … miracle, I guess you'd call it." Suddenly, remembering Dmitri's reaction, Gilly was nervous about boldly proclaiming an answer to prayer. "I started recovering rapidly about two weeks ago, and I've been dancing since Saturday."

"A stress fracture doesn't go away that quickly." Dianne's dark almond eyes narrowed to slits. "Unless you were misdiagnosed. Maybe that's what happened."

"No, there are the X-rays." Gilly knotted her fingers. Dmitri's fear and Dianne's disbelief. This was going to be more difficult than she'd anticipated.

Dianne stared at her for a moment or two, then took a sharp, hissing breath. "Go to the doctor this morning and come back with an X-ray. If it's clear, you may attend class tomorrow. Then we'll see." She shook her head. "I thought I'd seen it all."

Gilly nodded. She supposed that was the best she could have hoped for. Time would prove that her healing was complete. But she knew in her heart that it was so. She didn't need an X-ray.

Maurice was waiting for Jacob, wine glass in hand, at his customary window table in Vita's. As the maitre d' escorted him over, Jacob lined up defenses that he hoped would not be necessary. Perhaps this was only a friendly meeting with a former employer and artistic mentor.

Jacob reminded himself that he had nothing left to lose. The meeting with Andrew Nelson, chief artistic director of BNY's rival company, had gone well. In silence Nelson had watched the DVD of Wendy and the other Birmingham dancers performing Martha's dance with the villagers. Jacob had filmed it Saturday morning before lessons started, pleased but privately astonished at how enthusiastically the company had taken to the music and choreography.

When the film had come to an end in Nelson's office, Jacob would have assumed he wasn't interested except for the great former danseur's parting question: "Has Maurice Poiroux seen this?"

When Jacob assured him that he was the first to be offered the creative rights to his ballet, Nelson nodded and produced the bad-boy smile with which he'd charmed thousands of movie-goers in the eighties. "Let's keep it between ourselves for the moment, shall we?"

Which he was perfectly willing to do. He would be crazy, in fact, to provoke a confrontation with the man he'd betrayed in his days before Christ came into his life. So he'd been taken completely off guard when he'd answered Maurice's call just an hour ago. "I hear you are in town," Maurice began. "We shall have a chance to catch up. You will meet me for lunch at Vita's like old times."

In old times, Jacob had been a cocky, hotheaded rising star with more testosterone than was good for him. Assignations with the director's wife were one thing, but he had never aspired to lunch with Maurice himself.

Lord, give me grace, he prayed as he shook hands with his old employer. "Maurice, hello. How are you?" As he took his seat he studied the artistic director-in-chief. Age had begun to take charge of the clever, puckish face. Dense webs of wrinkles gathered at the corners of the eyes, and the yellowed smoker's teeth had begun to separate; the hairpiece was more obvious. Jacob checked his own reaction and was relieved to find no satisfaction in Maurice's physical deterioration. The past was, indeed, the past.

"I am well," Maurice replied, tucking his linen napkin back in his lap. He blatantly raked his eyes over Jacob. "You are in prime shape. It is too bad you dance no longer. Do you want to come back?"

Startled, Jacob laughed. "No. Of course not."

"No 'of course' to it. Unless you have injured yourself also." Maurice picked up the menu, but flicked a glance over it at Jacob.

Jacob tensed. "What do you mean?"

Maurice frowned. "I am very aware of the issues of my favorite baby ballerina, little Gilly Kincade. She is not the same since you ruin her."

"I did not ruin her, as you so melodramatically put it. Her back was injured, of course, but it could have happened at any time with any partner." He took a breath to keep his voice from shaking. "Besides, I saw her yesterday. She's made a dramatic recovery and will become one of your major stars."

"I am not talking about her back, you young oaf. It is her heart I am talking. She has lose all her fire for the romance of dancing, and her mind is in outer space like ET or Dr. Spock or some other alien."

Jacob resisted the impulse to smile at Maurice's eclectic comparisons. "I'm sure I have nothing to do with any heart-related issues Gilly might be dealing with." He restrained himself from further arguing. Besides, the waiter had arrived to take their drink orders. "Water with lemon," he requested, shutting the menu. He was not hungry, and he shouldn't have agreed to this meeting.

"More wine, please." Maurice sighed as the waiter slipped away. "Yes, I expect you to say this. Never mind. I come not to talk about Gilly. I come to ask you about your ballet. You have not sold it yet, hmm?"

Jacob let the menu drop. "How do you—"

"Is my business to know what the other company does."

Jacob stared at him. Of course Maurice had always had spies in odd places. He leaned forward, hands flat on the table. "Maurice, cut to the chase and tell me what this is about."

Maurice chuckled. "I see you are still impatient, my friend, after all these years."

"I'm not your friend. What do you want?"

Maurice sighed. "What a hothead. All right, I want to produce your ballet."

Jacob sat back, stunned. "What?"

"You heard me. I want the Christian ballet. There is big money in religious entertainment lately. *Prodigal Son* has been well attended, and time it is to add another one to the repertoire. The role is mature enough for Iliana to do well. She will like it."

"Iliana? You want Iliana to dance Mary?"

"You sound surprised."

The idea was preposterous. "The role is intended for—How do you know anything about it?" He could hardly believe Gilly would have told Maurice about *Perfume.* Or that the great artistic director would even be interested in the dances of an obscure Christian choreographer in Birmingham, Alabama.

"The video I have seen. Pretty jumpy and grainy, yes. But it interests me."

"What video?"

"Dmitri Lanskov brought it to me through the Institute of Choreography." Maurice frowned. "There was a series of short clips made during a rehearsal—in your studio, maybe? You did not know it was filmed?"

Jacob shook his head, thinking back to that disastrous demonstration for the board. The only camera he'd been aware of was Heidi Raintree's, but he'd assumed she was taking still photos for her girls to see Gilly in action. Maybe she'd been filming in video mode instead. Maybe she'd sent the clip to Dmitri. Conjecture was making him dizzy.

The fact remained that Maurice had apparently seen enough of the ballet to interest him. This was miraculous. Jacob began to sweat. And pray.

"Honestly, Maurice, I have no idea where that video clip came from. But if you want to see the real thing, you should see Gilly Kincade dance it live."

Maurice's heavy brows drew together. "I gave her the *Mermaid* role and she puffed it away, ruining her back. Besides, my wife will be retiring after this year, and I want to give her one final solo role to originate. Iliana is great ballerina."

"Of course she is," Jacob said diplomatically. "But Mary is the younger sister, that's the whole point. Iliana would make a better Martha."

"Bah! Boring older sister!" Maurice snapped his fingers. "No. She will dance the lead or you may take the ballet to second-rate company on the other side of the island and let them make a mess of it."

Good Lord, Jacob thought. How much more complicated could this situation get?

The company on the other side of the island was hardly second rate, but Jacob had to concede that Maurice understood and appreciated Jacob's style of dance better than any director in the Western Hemisphere.

He linked his fingers together as calmly as possible and stared at them, avoiding Maurice's ravenlike gaze. Here was the possibility of having his Christ-centered ballet produced on a Lincoln Center stage by one of the two premiere companies in the entire United States. An opportunity he'd not even dared to pray for. He knew what Tucker McGaughan would say to the idea of the Ballet New York orchestra playing his music.

But Gilly would not dance the role he'd written for her. It would be given to Iliana, Jacob's former lover. The thought made him shudder.

And there was Graham to think of. How could Jacob leave his son for months while he helped produce a ballet in New York? How could he deliberately put himself back in the milieu which had nearly cost him his reputation and Christian witness?

Still. The firm offer beckoned like a flag in the distance. He could pay back what BBT had lost in ticket revenue and at least partially redeem his reputation. Should he seize it and trust God to work out the messy ramifications?

"Could I have a day or two to think about it?" he said carefully.

"Think about it?" Maurice barked. "Why for? You are ready to sell to the other company! Yes or no! I must begin now making arrangements for new works." He slapped a hand against the table.

Jacob stared at Maurice for a long moment, resenting this blatant railroading. *Yes or no, Lord? Are you in this? Or is it a temptation from the enemy?*

Twenty-Four

Gilly left Dr. Glaasmacher's office and took the down elevator, feeling as if she'd left gravity somewhere on the ninth floor. She clutched the envelope containing her X-rays tightly against her ribs. Proof. The photos of her lumbar vertebrae showed smooth, clean lines of demarcation. The doctor had been puzzled, of course, but in the end all he could do was smile, agree that some things could not be explained, and wish her well. "I would like to see you in six weeks for a check-up, however." He'd said it with an air of mild anxiety, as if he were longing for a stiff drink.

Smiling, Gilly agreed to make a follow-up appointment and skipped toward the exit.

Now she pushed through the revolving door and headed out into an icy New York afternoon. She couldn't wait to take the X-rays in to show Dianne, but she'd better step carefully, or she'd be back in the doctor's office with something else broken. She'd almost made it to the stairs down into the closest subway station when her cell phone chirped inside her purse. Muttering, she unzipped the purse, fished around for the phone, and managed to get it open before it went to voice mail. "Hello," she said breathlessly, hanging onto the rail as she descended the stairs.

"Gilly?"

Gilly stopped, nearly causing a wreck behind her. People went around, giving her dirty looks, but she didn't care. "Jacob! Guess what—my X-rays are clear! Not that I'm surprised, but isn't it good to have real pictures to show? People are skeptical, which I should have expected ..." She trailed off and waited, thinking she might have lost the connection. "Jacob?"

After an unnatural silence, he said, "Gilly, I need to talk to you. Will you meet me somewhere?"

"Well, of course! I was just headed home. You could come there, and I'll make you a—a sandwich or something. I'm a terrible cook, but—"

"Thanks, but I just ate." He paused again. "Maybe we'd better meet in public. I don't want anyone to think ... Well, you know how people talk."

There was something odd about his tone. Jacob was a very circumspect person, but he wanted to meet in *public*? When she'd hardly seen him since Christmas?

"All right," she said slowly. "Where are you? I was just about to get on the subway."

"How about the espresso bar in Avery Fisher?"

"That's fine." She hesitated. "Is everything all right?"

"Yes, Gilly, everything's fine. I'll see you shortly."

He was gone. She'd planned to call her mother, but Mom would be glad to hear from her anytime, and it sounded like Jacob needed to talk to her right away. Baffled, she continued the descent to the subway.

Jacob waited for Gilly in the icy wind at the huge circular fountain in front of Avery Fisher Hall. Avery Fisher, one of the three buildings making up Lincoln Center, housed the New York Philharmonic as well as several other visiting symphonies. There would be dance and music people all over the place, but at least he could talk to Gilly without the temptation to grab her and kiss her senseless before he unburdened himself.

He'd forgotten to pack his gloves, so he blew on his hands to relieve their chapped tingling. The two years in Alabama had rendered him unused to the frigid New York winter—but at least he'd thought to bring his wool coat and a scarf.

There she was—her red knit cap a beacon bobbing along between the shoulders of a couple of fast-walking, trenchcoat-wearing New Yorkers. He saw when she noticed him, saw her pick up her pace to a skipping run, saw her glowing smile. He savored the smile because it was for him.

It was for what she knew of him.

"Jacob!" She reached him and held out a red mitten.

Noting the yellow envelope clasped under her other arm, he pulled her hand through his elbow. He wanted to kiss her rosy face, but contented himself with drawing her into the warmth of the espresso bar. "You look beautiful," he murmured, unable to keep it to himself. He stopped, looked down at her, and touched her cheek.

She squeaked, laughing. "Your hand's like ice!"

"Sorry." Laughing with her, he found an empty booth halfway down the left wall and sat down across from her. He could have looked at her all day.

"You folks need a menu?" The waiter, probably a wannabe actor, young and impossibly good looking, appeared. He winked at Gilly. "I've seen you before."

"Sugar-free hazelnut latte for me," she said. "Skim, no whipped cream."

"Sure. How about you, sir?"

"Plain coffee," Jacob said absently. "Black."

When the waiter shrugged and departed, Gilly laid the thick envelope on the table and leaned forward. "This is so cool to have you here in my stomping grounds. What have you been up to today?"

"First I want to hear about the doctor's visit." He glanced at the envelope. "I take it you got new X-rays."

"Yes!" She yanked off her mittens and tossed them on top of the envelope, then removed her cap and let the red hair spill free. "Perfectly normal. Dianne will have to believe me now." Her expression lost a bit of its shine. "Dmitri seems almost scared of me."

Jacob looked away. "People don't know what to do with real-life miracles."

"But, Jacob! If God can make my back well, why can't he get through to Dmitri? Surely that's more important."

"I wish I had a good answer for you, Gilly. But you know, free will is involved in this too. God somehow limits himself from coercing people into loving him." Jacob stared at his reddened hands clasped on top of the table. "Love has to be offered freely or it isn't love."

The waiter came with their drinks, rescuing them from a rather awkward silence. A waiting silence, which Jacob didn't know how to bridge.

Gilly blew across the top of the latte mug. She sipped her drink and studied Jacob, eyes fearless. "I want to hear about Graham, but I can tell you have something difficult to tell me. You'd better come out with it before I explode from curiosity. I know you didn't come all this way just to have coffee with me."

He smiled. "I would have, and Graham's fine. But a lot has happened since you left Birmingham. I've done a bit of thinking."

"Uh-oh. That's always dangerous." Gilly wrinkled her nose. "At least, that's what my dad always tells me."

For a long moment he allowed himself to look at her, absorb the generous, eager youth and joy. There was only seven years between them, but at this moment it felt like forty. There was no way she already knew, or she wouldn't be looking at him this way, as if he were Prince Charming and Luke Skywalker all rolled into one.

"I came to New York with the intention of asking you to come back to Birmingham." Her lips parted, but he forestalled her response with an upraised hand. "That was before this wonderful thing happened with your back. It's made me reevaluate everything, but above all, what God seems to expect from me and you." He paused, then made himself say it. "I've never known anyone like you, Gilly, and I love you. But I've come to say good-bye."

She stared at him, eyes huge. "Wait. What?"

"This is very difficult." He pinched his lips together. "Several months ago, I thought I wanted to leave ballet and become a physical therapist. But the instant I met you, and God gave me the *Perfume* ballet, I knew he had more for me to do as a dancer, as an artist. I thought I could choreograph Christian ballets to be performed in my Birmingham studio—you know, one leg in the secular world, one in the world of worship expression. That was a miserable failure."

"What do you mean? Your board loved the *Perfume* ballet! I saw them on their feet."

"They were applauding you as much as the ballet. And then you hurt yourself. They all—well, everybody but Heidi—blame me for asking you to demonstrate that ballet without clearing it through your management here. They're right. That was a serious mistake."

"But, Jacob, it was my decision to dance that day. If anyone's in trouble it should be me."

He shook his head. "It's not just your failure to complete the contract. Alexandra brought charges of personal misconduct regarding our relationship."

"That's absurd!" She looked like an angry kitten. "You know I'll vouch for you."

"It is absurd, but I brought it on myself by not being careful with you. And I'm afraid my rather reckless past came back to haunt me." He laid his hands flat on the table. "I've faced the accusations and defended myself. I seem to be in the clear. But even if I weren't, I wouldn't drag you into it."

"Why did you come to New York, if you're going to treat me

like a child?" She frowned. "Tell me you love me and then push me away?"

"Gilly, I have nothing to offer you. Everything's a mess right now." He saw the wisdom of his decision to do this in a public restaurant, because he wanted nothing more than to dive across the table and kiss her. He gripped his coffee mug in both hands. "My thought was to offer the *Perfume* ballet to Andrew Nelson in order to meet the budget deficits at Birmingham Ballet Theater and go out with my head up. But by the time I got here, Maurice Poiroux had gotten wind of it and preempted the offer."

Gilly's mouth fell open. "Maurice? You mean, we're going to do your *Perfume* ballet here—at BNY?" She grabbed his hands. "That's wonderful!"

"I turned him down."

"What? Are you crazy? Why?"

"Because he wants his wife to originate the role of Mary. And a stipulation would be that I come back here and teach in the Institute of Choreography and Dance Pedagogy."

She held his gaze for a long moment, then slowly released his hands. "I forgot all about Graham. You wouldn't want to move him to the City, take him away from his grandparents."

He sighed. "I've thought about this long and hard. Graham aside, the main issue is that I want the best for you. I can't put you in an impossible situation. If I come back to BNY, there are ... difficulties. Because of the way I feel about you."

Her gaze flashed to him. "You keep saying that, like it's some kind of disease. If you love me, we should make decisions together. You can't hold things back—decide my fate for me, be all noble like a ... like a hero in some Disney movie."

He smiled a little because she reminded him a bit of Ariel in *The Little Mermaid*. "I'm trying to explain." He shook his head, feeling his way through a confusing mass of hope, affection, and plain old insecurity. "I love you, and I don't mean in a teenage-crush kind of way. This is the 'I want to build a life with you' kind of love I wasn't sure existed until I met you. I know I—I've encouraged your family to let you make your own decisions, but I can't help realizing you're very young, and there are things about me you don't know—things there hasn't been time for you to find out."

He stopped, sensed the Holy Spirit prodding him to take courage. He thought about Cole's counsel to make sacrifices. Perhaps this was what he meant—a sacrifice of pride. Perhaps Gilly was right, and he should trust her to deal with his difficulties. She'd certainly handled her own. Still, he felt as if he were diving into a raging ocean storm with no lifeline.

"All right, then, Gilly. If I come back to New York, my past is bound to surface sooner or later. So you'd best hear it from me and help me make my decision with a lot of thought and prayer. Is that fair?"

She nodded, tears spilling over. "Do you have a wife stashed away somewhere?"

"No, of course not."

"You're an escaped criminal? An FBI informant?"

"Gilly!" He laughed.

She sniffed and pulled a tissue from her pocket to blow her nose. "Was it something that happened before you became a Christian?"

"Yes."

"Then it doesn't matter."

"Wouldn't that be nice if it were true?" He sighed and sat up straight. "It does matter, because the ballet world is very small, particularly here in New York. I left five years ago in order to end a—an impure relationship. If I come back, and you and I—we start seeing one another, those relationships will likely affect you and your career. Especially if I move into choreography and artistic direction."

She made a little noise that sounded like *pfsh*. "Do you remember when you first came to Cole and Laurel's house to tell me about the ballet? I asked him about you, and he told me there'd been an affair but wouldn't say with who. It's Iliana, isn't it?"

He stared at her. "How do you know that?"

"Because it's her modus operandi. She's like Potiphar's wife—she seduces every good-looking straight male dancer who shows up. They either cave in and eventually get booted out of the company, or they put up the hand and find a girlfriend quick." Her beautiful, quirky brows pulled together. "I take it you caved."

Shame nearly sent him under the table. "I'm no Joseph, Gilly."

"Oh, for crying out loud. Look at you." She yanked the cup out of his hands, set it aside, and grabbed his wrists. "You're so beautiful you take my breath away, and back then you didn't have any moral restraints to keep you from getting suckered in. Right?"

He looked away. "I suppose," he mumbled, completely unmanned by her backhanded praise.

"I'd be very surprised if you hadn't, you know, taken a sip out of Pharaoh's jeweled cup."

Startled, he looked at her again. She was grinning.

"But wouldn't you ... *mind*? Seeing her every day, knowing ..." He shrugged. "In my experience, women are extremely jealous."

"You have a lot to learn about me, boyo. And I think you don't know yourself very well either. I've seen no indication that you're even remotely tempted to sexual sin anymore. In fact—" A charming wave of red stained her cheeks. "I'd wondered if I might have trouble attracting you physically. But then again—" She stared at him fiercely—"while I'm not *jealous* per se, I am *extremely* competitive and *astonishingly* creative, and I assure you I will make *every* effort to keep your attention where it belongs." She let go of him again, flipped her hair back over her shoulders, and leaned back with a little shimmy of her shoulders. "Do I make myself understood?"

Jacob found himself piqued, repiqued, and capotted. He burst out laughing. "Understood," he gasped, as soon as he was able to catch his breath. "And now we will find someplace very cold to spend the rest of the afternoon so I won't be tempted to take advantage of this *creative* streak of yours." Grinning, he got up, took her by the hand, and tugged her out of the booth. "Ice skating, I think, should be the appropriate venue."

The Rockefeller Center Rink wasn't exactly swarming with crowds on a sleety February Monday afternoon, but Gilly and Jacob had enough company on the ice that she had to pay attention in order to keep from busting her butt. Conversation became a secondary goal. Besides, it was a challenge to hear one another over the music blaring from four 6-foot speakers. So she let Jacob snug her close to his side, her right hand in his, his left clasping hers at her waist, and simply enjoyed looking up at him with their feet shooshing along in relatively smooth rhythm.

She should have guessed he would be an Olympic-quality skater. He had a knack for keeping her on her feet and making her look graceful—a major feat, since, as an Alabama belle, she'd only been skating on rubber wheels before moving to New York.

So many things she had to learn about him. The conversation in the coffee shop had nearly undone her. Frightening to think how close she'd come to losing him to his completely insane insecurity. They still had a lot of stuff to work through. But a God who could do for her what he'd done in the last few weeks could surely accomplish one more tiny good turn.

As if echoing her thoughts, Jacob switched hands and spun her in a smooth pirouette. Smiling, he turned backward and took both her hands, skating in front of her with his eyes on her face.

Maybe she'd been a little overly smug about Iliana. The woman had a powerful influence with Maurice. If she took it into her head to sabotage Gilly or Jacob in the name of revenge, Gilly might as well hang up her pointe shoes.

Lord, please finish working this thing out for us, she sent up as a little side memo. *I don't pretend to have all the answers.*

Gilly found Jacob's insistence on surrounding them with people simultaneously endearing and frustrating. She couldn't tell if he didn't trust himself or her. Perhaps both.

Whatever the case, that evening, instead of a quiet candlelit dinner, he suggested collecting a few friends and taking in a swing dance club. She went along with the idea, mostly because she'd have accompanied him to a buffalo barbecue in Central Park if he'd asked. So she put on one of her flirty knee-length dresses, a pair of leggings and ballet flats, and twisted her hair into a deceptively simple half-ponytail with tendrils curling against her temples.

In the taxi over to pick up Victoria, Gilly caught Jacob staring at the pulse point beneath her ear. He was dressed in fine wool slacks and a tweed coat, with the collar of an electric blue cotton shirt framing his face, and she had to clasp her hands together hard between her knees to keep from flinging her arms around his neck. Remembering her lifelong commitment not to provide undue temptation, she sweetly asked him if it was too late to call Graham.

Blinking, he laughed softly. "Funny, I was just thinking of the last time he mentioned you. He said you smell like a mommy."

Gilly smiled. "What on earth does that mean?"

"The opposite of sweaty socks and wet dog, I would imagine." Jacob gave her an amused look. "I think he's trolling to replace peanut butter sandwiches and salads from our family menu."

"Well, just wait till he smells me after dance class. Barely a step up from wet dog. And peanut butter is gourmet fare in my kitchen." She settled companionably against his shoulder.

To her delight, he took her hand, threading his fingers through hers. But his voice turned serious. "Gilly, I've got to make sure you understand something. If I come to New York, I won't leave Graham behind."

He stomach fluttered. The conversation was teetering perilously close to making plans. Without the essential question having been asked. She understood Jacob's cautious temperament. He wasn't about to commit himself and his little boy without some assurance of safety—at least for Graham.

She squeezed his hand. "Give me your phone."

With a quizzical look, he reached into his coat pocket and handed the phone over.

She opened it, hit the Redial button and found his grandparents' number.

A sweet, elderly voice answered. "Jacob? Is that you?"

"No, ma'am, it's Gilly Kincade. I'm with Jacob, though. Has Graham gone to bed yet?"

"He's just climbing out of the tub, sugar. Let me throw a towel around him and he'll be right here."

Gilly waited, listening to sounds of sloshing and an excited little voice in the background. She met Jacob's gaze and winked.

"Miss Gilly! I had to go back to school today, and I wrote a poem about Thing One and Thing Two! Did Daddy tell you we adopted them just like he's gonna adopt me?"

She caught her breath. "He didn't tell me. Gray, that's uber-cool." She chattered with him several more minutes before Jacob demanded his turn. By that time they were at Victoria's apartment.

"Graham, we have to go now," Jacob said. "Be good for Nonna and go right to sleep, okay?"

Graham's response brought tears to Gilly's eyes. "Okay. Bye, Daddy. I love you."

"I love you, buddy. I'll be home in a few days." The phone disappeared in Jacob's pocket. He paid the cabbie, got out, and opened the door for Gilly.

They stood close together for a moment in front of the apartment building. The temperature had dropped to the thirties, but Gilly could hardly feel the cold. A Jacob-related internal furnace made her want to unbutton her coat and dance down the street. When he reached up and turned the collar of her coat against her cheeks, she nestled against his hand, savoring its chill. He cupped her face, kissed her forehead, and smiled. "Your friends are waiting for us. Come on."

Disappointed, she took his arm and accompanied him into the building. Resisting temptation was one thing, but she would like to have experienced a *little* bit of canoodling. After all, Jacob was a very talented kisser.

When Victoria's apartment door opened, Gilly stared. "Nicholas! What are you doing here?"

"Hey, nice to see you too." He stepped back to let them in, extending a hand to Jacob. "Nicholas Dean. Not sure I should be putting myself on display with you real dance types, but Victoria called, and I didn't have anything else going on."

"Hey, guys!" Victoria's voice came from the back of the apartment. "I'm almost ready. Dmitri's going to meet us at the club."

Gilly gave Jacob a baffled look. "You guys get acquainted. I'll be right back." She scooted into Victoria's bedroom and shut the door. "Hey!" she said in an undertone. "What gives?"

"You mean Nicholas?" Victoria concentrated on her lip gloss. "He's lonesome, and I miss him."

Gilly folded her arms. "You miss having a boyfriend. Nicholas is not good for you!"

Victoria's full, polished mouth turned down. "Am I supposed to shut out all my friends just because I became a Christian? *You* don't!"

"I know, but it's different for me because—because I'm not as vulnerable as you are. Besides, this is not just any old friend. This is—" She lowered her voice and whispered, "Nicholas!"

Victoria clasped her bare arms, rubbing them as if she were cold. "I know." Her voice trembled. "And I care about him a lot. I want him to know the Lord too."

Gilly stared at her friend for a moment, then sighed and put her arms around her. "I understand. But you need to be careful about being alone with him, because he'll pull you down instead of the other way around."

"He told me he's sorry he got so mad about the baby."

"He's probably sorry he can't get in your pants anymore."

"Gilly!"

"Okay, okay." She sighed and released Victoria. "This is fine tonight—Jacob and I will be with you. Just promise me you won't do any more single dates unless it's to church. He's really bad news, Victoria."

Victoria blinked and found a tissue to carefully dab away her tears. "I'm trying, Gilly. This is really hard."

"I know it is."

Victoria glanced at the door into the living room. "Speaking of bad news, I did a little asking around about your wonder boy in there. The older girls remember him. I wondered why he looked so familiar. There are pictures—"

"He told me about it this afternoon."

"He did?" Victoria frowned. "Is he coming back here?"

Gilly shrugged. "I think there's some discussion. But it's too soon to talk about."

"He's in love with you."

"It's too soon to talk about that too." But Gilly smiled.

"Are you girls having a pajama party or are we going dancing?" shouted Nicholas from the other side of the door.

"Coming!" Victoria grabbed her purse.

Gilly followed her into the living room and, as Nicholas helped Victoria into her coat, met Jacob's eyes and shrugged. There was a twist at every turn.

Twenty-Five

Tuesday morning as he approached BNY's Studio 1, Jacob braced himself for the return to his personal Babylon. Maurice had arranged to meet him here with the intention of demonstrating the *Perfume* ballet for some of his principals. Not that the dancers would actually have a say in whether or not the ballet would be produced, but Maurice loved to be the discoverer of raw talent. He loved to exploit that talent, not only for the world of the arts, but to cement his place in dance history.

Under his coat Jacob had on dance clothes—black T-shirt and tights—which did nothing to ease his sense of alienation. He had entered the glass doors, wiped his feet on the gray rug, stood for a moment in the foyer to get his bearings—it was as if he'd never left—and stopped by the office suite to let the receptionist know he was there. After buzzing Maurice, she'd sent Jacob on to the rehearsal studio.

He was early but still found twenty-five or thirty dancers dressed in eclectic dancewear milling about the room. Several of them stood gossiping in a corner.

A clutch of girls near the door glanced at him curiously, then continued their conversation. "Do you know what we're doing this morning?" asked one.

"No, but I heard Maurice is auditioning a new choreographer for the Institute."

"Hope she's better than the last one. She didn't know what she was doing."

Leaning against the nearest wall, Jacob hid a smile. He hoped he knew what he was doing.

He didn't see Gilly. No doubt she hadn't yet been cleared to rehearse. But he knew she'd planned to come in to confer with Dianne Woo, bringing the X-rays with her. Please God she would be reinstated quickly. He began to silently pray.

Some five minutes later, when he was beginning to think he'd been forgotten, Maurice himself strutted past him, followed by his wife. Jacob stayed where he was, content to observe the power couple parting the waters of the dancers, bringing everyone to attention.

Iliana Vetsinova Poiroux was, at forty, still a beautiful woman. She had always reminded Jacob of an ibis, all long limbs, graceful neck, deeply hooded eyes, and exotic mouth. Her long nose, narrow and slightly hooked, would have been ugly on a less regally built woman. As it was, her clothes hung on her with a fashion model's grace of line, and she commanded the attention of every eye in every room.

Gilly's reference to Potiphar's wife was an apt comparison. He still had trouble believing this woman ever considered throwing away a career and a marriage for him—or that he'd fallen for her lure. He'd been truly delivered from danger, though he hadn't seen it at the time.

Reaching the center of the room, Iliana turned to speak to someone and caught Jacob's eye. She immediately reversed her direction.

She reached out both hands as she neared him, her smile transforming her from queenly to extraordinary. "Jacob! I thought never to see you again. How have you been?"

"I'm well." Taking her hands, he glanced at Maurice, the center of a knot of dancers on the other side of the room. Now. Now was the time. He met her large hazel eyes and spoke quickly, quietly. "It's been a long time, Iliana, and I left without asking your forgiveness for my part in what happened."

Up went her eyebrows, and she laughed softly. "Maurice said you are much changed, and I see he is right as usual." She shrugged. "I am not sure there is any forgiveness required. Perhaps you were the more damaged party. After all, I had not to leave." She released his hands, looking him up and down. "But time has been good to you. You are still ... very fine."

He was glad he still wore his coat. Looking away, he said stiffly, "I wasn't sure you'd even remember me. But to be perfectly clear, I wish to forget the past. If I come back here, it will be with the understanding that we will be completely professional."

With slender French-manicured fingers she adjusted the front edge of a lacy red ballet cover-up. "Hmm. I hear the rumors that you are lovers with one of the little soloists. Is that why you come back?"

"I'm here today because I'm negotiating a business arrangement with your husband."

Frowning, she pursed her lips. "And the rest is none of my business, hmm? Well, be careful. We all know how personal relationships can damage the best of professional associations." Smiling, she wandered toward a cluster of young men warming up at a barre near the piano.

He watched her go and slowly, deliberately, unlocked his knees, pushing away from the wall. By the time he reached Maurice, he was in control of the temper that had risen and threatened to strike in the face of Iliana's monumental arrogance. After all, she had apologized after a fashion—or at least come as close as she was likely to.

Still, the thought of that particular woman dancing the role of Mary—the fact that he would be required to work with her closely enough to teach it to her—was enough to curdle his stomach.

Maurice welcomed Jacob, introducing him to the dancers he didn't know. There were two or three who had been around long enough to remember him, guys he'd palled around with in the old days. He kept a slight reserve, unsure how to convey the information that he was no longer the hard-partying, womanizing fellow they remembered.

He needn't have worried. Dmitri Lanskov was part of the group and had clearly forewarned anyone who knew Jacob from before that he was now to be respected not only as a fellow dancer, but as ballet master and choreographer. To his surprise, when Maurice turned the company over to Jacob, the rehearsal went so smoothly that three hours passed before he so much as looked at his watch. He gave a quick synopsis of the story, then played snatches of the music, and was gratified to see the expressions of skepticism shift into piqued interest and, finally, appreciation and concentration. With the exception of working with Gilly, this was his first opportunity to choreograph exclusively on professionals, and he found the process profoundly exhilarating.

Even Iliana observed his movements closely, following him with astuteness and grace, and he was able to explain what he was after with the kind of dance shorthand he'd more or less abandoned on leaving the Spanish ballet. He'd decided to introduce the ballet with a corps scene, rather than a solo or duet, in order to involve as many dancers as possible. By lunch break he saw that he had won them all over to the idea of portraying first-century Jews, some of whom were disciples of the upstart Messiah and some who rejected him.

And he also saw that many of them had a first-time understanding of the charisma of the conflict's central figure, Jesus of Nazareth. They left for lunch, buzzing with conversation about the new ballet.

Soaked in sweat, Jacob stood in the nearly empty studio with Dmitri, Victoria, and Maurice—Iliana had taken him at his word and departed for a massage—and tried to absorb the thing that had just happened. He was coming back to New York. He was going to choreograph and produce his Christian ballet on the stage at Lincoln State Theater accompanied by one of the world's finest orchestras.

Maurice seemed oblivious to Jacob's abstraction and completely ignored Victoria and Dmitri, who waited respectfully for the master-in-chief to depart. "This will be such a different piece for us," Maurice crowed, "and truly a genius I am to steal it out from under Nelson's nose. We will put it in the spring schedule, but we must begin now to work on costumes and sets." He clapped Jacob's shoulder. "I set up meetings for you, on which I must sit because such a green young artist you are, and I help you avoid the big mistakes I make when I am young. We begin tomorrow, yes?"

Jacob exchanged glances with Dmitri, whose blue eyes were alive with laughter. "I'm sorry, Maurice, but I have to return to Birmingham to unknot some kinks that have come up in my company. I can be back in the City by ... perhaps spring rehearsals in March. It'll take at least that long to move myself and my son."

Maurice scowled, unused to being defied. "You will find a weekend when you can come back. We must meet again before I take the company for D.C. tour."

Jacob knew he didn't have much bargaining ground, but nothing ventured, nothing gained. He folded his arms. "If I had a little incentive, I might work it out."

"Incentive? What incentive?"

"Part of my difficulty in Birmingham is related to Gillian Kincade's failure to dance in our second *Nutcracker* performance." He paused significantly. "Many ballet fans in Birmingham make special trips to attend performances when they are in the city. Now that Gillian is well enough to dance again, if I could bring her back for a special gala with my company—something to appease my board—I could perhaps wrap up my stay there with good relations still in place."

"But Gillian is not well enough to dance. She limps around the studio like a broken toy." Maurice waved his hands. "What is this nonsense?"

Then Gilly herself appeared in the doorway and sprang into a series of grande jetés across the studio. "Look! Look! I'm back!"

Giddy with the excitement of her victorious return to the company, Gilly treated Jacob, Victoria, and Dmitri to lunch at Le Pain Quotidien across the street from the theater. She spent the entire hour busily avoiding the realization that Jacob was scheduled to leave on a four thirty flight out of LaGuardia. She hadn't brought up the idea of accompanying him to the airport because she was afraid he'd squash the idea. She was just going to hop in the cab with him, and that was that.

Meanwhile, as they ate organic Greek salad with goat cheese and whole wheat sourdough bread, Dmitri entertained them all with a description of his mother's recent visit to the City. She had come all the way from Russia and spent the first day asleep in his apartment, a victim of terminal jet lag; the next in Chinatown buying plastic-net beaded shoes and knock-off Coach purses; and the third and final day on the observation deck of the Empire State Building, taking pictures of the ends of her new paisley pashmina blowing about her head in a gale-force wind.

As they crossed the street back to the theater, Dmitri wound up his tale by producing a photo, taken with his camera phone, of stout Mrs. Lanskov proudly posed in front of Radio City Music Hall wearing her green foam rubber Statue of Liberty visor, arm in arm with Dmitri and Whoopi Goldberg. She had truly had a stellar time.

Gilly's stomach hurt from laughing. "She's a lovely lady, Dmitri," she said, handing the photo back. "She must be very proud of you."

Dmitri smiled, tucking the phone back into his pocket. "It is better this time. I had not seen her in many years." He glanced at Jacob. "The ballet is not masculine in the village where I come from."

"That doesn't make sense," Victoria said, pulling up her coat collar. Her cheeks were red as apples. "Russia's practically the cradle of ballet."

Dmitri shrugged and held open the door of the theater for them to pass through. "She is orthodox Christian. They reject people like me. This is why I was having such a hard time swallowing what you say about Jesus." He stuffed his hands into his coat pockets.

Gilly stopped short, caught by the hurt in Dmitri's voice. She glanced up at Jacob.

Jacob was frowning, clearly concerned. "Maybe you shouldn't lump us all together, man. Have any one of us said anything to hurt you?"

"Well, no." Dmitri looked down. "Even at your church, they were kind to me. But my sister got married in Kirov, and they didn't want me there. I was going to fly home, and they said don't bother." He glanced at Gilly. "I'd just heard from my sister, the night of the Bruckheimers' Christmas party."

Gilly winced.

Jacob laid a hand on Dmitri's shoulder. "Remember when I told you to watch and see what God would do? Look at Gilly's quick recovery. That's what we call a God thing."

Dmitri looked down at her, his expression softening. "I agree she is a God thing. Maybe I will agree to go to church with you—one more time." He looked at Jacob, a sly expression chasing into a smile. "So ... when you and Gilly get married, are you going to let me come to the wedding?"

Gilly was trying very hard to keep her hands to herself as she waited in line with Jacob to check in. He had very little luggage—one small case, plus his computer backpack, both items he would take as carry-on. In less than ten minutes he would have his boarding pass and be ready to snake through the security line. And then she wouldn't see him again until mid-March.

Of course, she would be very busy, and so would he. They could talk on the phone.

She could remember that he'd said he loved her in an "I want to build a life with you" kind of way and that he hadn't laughed too hard when Dmitri invited himself to their wedding. Still, like Grandma Kincade said, there was many a slip 'twixt cup and lip. Just because he was moving to New York didn't mean things would work out for them to be together in their crazy chosen profession. He could conceivably fall in love with someone who wasn't a dancer, someone who could talk to him about something other than aching joints and bunions.

On the other hand, she thought as she sidled next to him and nearly melted into a puddle when he absently put his arm around her shoulders, *nobody* could love him like she did. Nobody would pray for him as fiercely or protect him from piranha-style prima ballerinas or make him laugh when he was being too serious.

So. She would have to be patient. Pummel and push her body into submission, dance all day, every day, so that she would be too tired to lie awake at night thinking about him. It was a terrible thing, she thought, looking up at him, to be so much in love that one wanted to skip over an entire month.

He looked down at her and gave her one of his Jacob grins. "Hey, cheer up. You'll be coming down to Birmingham before you know it."

"I'm just afraid something is going to happen to mess it up." She sighed. "I didn't used to be such a worrywart."

He kissed her nose. "I think we've switched roles. Suddenly I have this sense that I could conquer the world."

She put her arms around his waist and clung. "Are you really coming back here?"

"I am. Let me tell you why." The line moved forward a notch, and they shuffled forward together. "I used to be convinced that Christian artists—musicians, writers, dancers, actors, painters—ought to do their thing in a vacuum and focus on bolstering the body, the Church. And maybe there are those who are called to do just that. But there's also a need for some of us to shake out into the world, to keep it from going to hell until God's ready to call it quits. It took me a while to see it, but that's what I've been doing in Birmingham, that's what you're doing here in New York. So—Alabama, New York, it doesn't matter where I am, I'm going to take whatever opportunities God gives me to offer my gifts in the widest possible arena." He smiled at her when she looked up at him. "I used to think it wasn't holy to take risks. You've changed my mind."

"Jacob—"

"Not yet." He shook his head. "This is enough for now. Please be patient while I work out the details. Keep praying, have faith in God, and trust me. I'll be back for you."

She gave him the best smile she could summon. It was a little trembly at the edges, but Jacob seemed to be satisfied. He kissed her again and released her to search for his ID.

It was time to let him go.

After a long layover in Atlanta, which he used to set up a series of meetings he did not at all look forward to, Jacob found the Jaguar in the Birmingham airport parking garage and drove home. He walked in the apartment just as Nonna was putting Graham to bed and poked his head into the darkened bedroom.

"Daddy!" Graham shrieked, catapulting out from under the covers. "You're home!"

Jacob found himself nearly strangled by a pair of little arms. He looked over Graham's head and met his grandmother's tired, but twinkling eyes. "Hey, Nonna. Long day?"

She put down *Clifford Plays Fair* and got up to kiss Jacob. "We've had fun, but I admit I'm glad to see you. There's a reason children are given to young people." She put her hands on her hips. "I told you not to come back without—"

"Later." He shook his head as he laid Graham back in the bed and pulled the blanket over him. "School tomorrow, buddy. We'll talk in the morning."

"Will you read me one more story?" Graham blinked up at him sleepily.

"Tell you what. Stay put while I go talk to Nonna a few minutes. If you're still awake after that I'll read one more." He brushed Graham's hair and kissed his forehead.

"Okay." Graham turned onto his side and closed his eyes. "I'll be awake."

By the time Jacob got to the door and turned to look over his shoulder, Graham was breathing slowly and evenly. Out like a light. Smiling, he put his arm around Nonna's plump shoulders and walked with her into the kitchen. "I'm starving. Have you got some soup or something leftover?"

"Coming up." She began to bustle around while he sat down at the table and toed off his shoes.

He sat for a minute, gathering himself, and turned to find his grandmother watching him surreptitiously. He laughed. "Okay, you're dying to know. It didn't go exactly as I expected."

Her face fell. "Oh, Jacob, I'm sorry." She opened the microwave and put in a soup mug, setting it to heat, then took a sleeve of crackers out of the bread box. "What happened?"

"Well, the ballet sold—"

"What? But that's wonderful!" She dropped the crackers and whirled to face him.

"Yes, but not to Andrew Nelson." He laughed at her confused look. "He's the 'other' company—not the one I danced for before. I'd gone to him, thinking to release the ballet and come back home with a check. But before I could seal that deal, Maurice Poiroux heard about it and made me a preemptive offer." He paused. "A much better offer—one that, as they say, I couldn't refuse."

Nonna clasped her hands and laughed. "Jacob! I'm so happy for you."

"Yes, but there's a catch." He rubbed his forehead, avoiding her eyes. His grandparents had bailed him out on so many occasions, it was going to be nearly impossible to extricate himself from the warmth of their love. "I'll never be able to thank you for all you've done for Graham and me," he began, then floundered.

She hurried to the table and sat down across from him. She reached for his hands. "You're moving to New York, aren't you?" There were tears in her eyes.

He nodded. "There's a place for me at the Choreographic Institute. And Gilly's there. It's … Nonna, it's where I need to be. I have to go back and redeem some of what happened there before."

"Well." She squeezed his hands, blinking hard. "At least she's a nice southern girl with good manners and a way with children. Graham's crazy about her." She sighed. "I'm going to miss you both so much. Who's going to eat my cookies?"

"I bet you could find a prison ministry or some deserving group who'd solve that problem." He smiled. "We'll come back often and fly you up for holidays whenever you want. Poppa would enjoy the Manhattan ferry."

"Yeah, and he's always wanted to see the Brooklyn Bridge. I told him he should take me to see *Spamalot* before he's too old to stay up that late."

Jacob laughed. One more hurdle out of the way. Now if he could just survive the next two days.

Twenty-Six

Despite Dr. Glaasmacher's cautions, as well as the skepticism of every one of the ballet masters and mistresses, Gilly threw herself into rehearsals with a vigor that kept her from checking her cell phone for messages every hour on the hour. By Thursday afternoon her feet were literally bleeding from open blisters, but she grimly bandaged them and kept going. Jacob was not going to return to find her pining over him, and she was determined not to remain in the state of professional limbo that had threatened to consume her after her injury.

This was the danger that all dancers feared: being forgotten, old news, yesterday's has-been. Her meteoric arc of success had been interrupted. She had to find a way to launch it again.

Because she showed up on time for class, refused to whine, and pushed herself when her muscles screamed for relief, Maurice relented and cast her as Swanhilda in a revival of *Coppélia*—a first performance in the role for her. Jubilant, she stayed after rehearsals for fittings.

Frankie took one look at her and shook her head in disgust. "You were skinny to start with. Now you're a bag of bones. How'm I supposed to make this thing fit and still leave material for the bigger girls?" Muttering, she whipped a measuring tape around Gilly's waist.

"I'm eating like a horse, Frankie." Gilly squeaked as the tape measure yanked tight. "I'm working extra hard, though, burning calories right and left. I promise I'm not starving."

The costumer regarded her with a jaundiced eye. "You didn't take up smoking, did you?"

"Ew! No!"

"Well, I'm going to leave you some room to grow. Come back tomorrow and try it on, okay?"

Gilly gave her a sassy *Stars and Stripes* salute and released the breath she had been holding. Her ribcage shrank two inches.

Laughing at Frankie's snarling imprecations, she grabbed her coat and ducked out of the costume room. She caught Victoria leaving the building with a couple of other girls. "Hey, do y'all want to get a quick bite before you have to be back tonight?" Gilly hadn't been given a role in tonight's performance of *Symphony in C Major*. In fact, Dianne had instructed her to go home, ice her feet, and stay prone for the rest of the evening.

"'*Y'all*,'" Victoria teased, exchanging glances with Jarrica Black. "She's been talking to one of her sisters again."

Gilly fell into step with the others, and they crossed the street to Europan. It was too cold for the outdoor tables, so they claimed an empty table near the door.

"Hey, Gilly, is it true Jacob Ferrar's coming back to dance here?" Jarrica asked after they'd ordered their food and settled down with a bottle of water and a cup of hot tea each.

"He's not going to dance." Gilly squeezed her tea bag and laid it aside. "He'll be choreographing."

"Oh." Alyson Just squirted lemon into her tea and stirred it. She gave Gilly an arch look. "Phoebe DeGarmo knows him from before. She was telling us some pretty interesting stories the other day."

Gilly glanced at Victoria, who was looking uncomfortable, and smiled. "I bet. He was quite the wild child in his day, I hear."

Heather O'Brien, the youngest member of the group, a brand-new member of the corps, stared at Gilly wide-eyed. "Don't you care? I mean, Phoebe said Mr. Ferrar—I mean Jacob—had a thing for Iliana Poiroux. And that's why he left." She batted her big brown eyes. "Do you think that's true?"

Since Gilly had just taken a big bite of her salad, she just stared at Heather and tried to look unconcerned as she chewed.

Victoria said coolly, "What if it is? People change a lot in five years. Phoebe used to be a size double-A. Now she's a C."

Gilly choked on her lettuce and coughed until Victoria had to bang her on the back. "Oh, my," she wheezed. "Victoria, you'll have to warn me next time." She gulped her water and wiped her streaming eyes. "Look, girls. Jacob's real or imaginary love life, past or present, is something I don't talk about. Like Victoria said—a lot can happen in five years. Jacob and I are doing our best to live for God and do what he says."

"Me too," Victoria added, and Gilly smiled at her.

"Well, I hope Iliana gets the memo," said Alyson, giving Gilly a skeptical look. "But if I were you, I'd put my good-looking boyfriend under lock and key."

Gilly was in the dressing room after final curtain call, halfway in, halfway out of her Swanhilda costume when Jacob's call beeped in. She had already removed her shoes, pads, and bandages and examined the damage to her feet. Two performances tomorrow. She shuddered. Torture.

Then she smiled. There was no place she'd rather be. Well, with one exception, of course.

When she heard the phone tweedling in her dance bag, she yanked the leotard down around her ankles so fast she heard a rip in one of Frankie's seams. Drat. Hobbling, trying to free herself, she lunged for the bag hanging on the back of the chair.

"Hi, Jacob," she said breathlessly.

He laughed. "I was about to leave a message. You're not onstage, are you?"

"Of course not! What kind of looney tune do you think I—Oh, you're kidding." She sat down in the chair and kicked off the costume. "We just got done with *Coppélia*. Stellar performance, if I do say so. Four curtain calls."

"I'd expect no less from my prima ballerina. Just wait 'til they see you dance Mary."

"Jacob—you know Iliana's originating that role."

"Yes, but what they remember is the dancer who breathes life into it. That will one day be you. Depend on it."

She laughed. "Did you call just to blow up my already big head, or do you have some news about the board meeting?"

"I have most excellent news. Dr. Sulley has backed off on his accusations about financial wrongdoing, in light of BNY's offer to sponsor you and Dmitri and Victoria and Ian in a spring midseason gala. It's a very generous offer and will serve as a spectacular fund-raiser for the company."

"Oh, that's awesome! I'm so glad." She stuck out her feet and stared at her bleeding insteps. "Hopefully my poor aching body will be in good enough shape to do it justice by then."

"Yes, and you'd better catch up on your sleep, because I plan to keep you very busy when I come to town in a couple of weeks."

"Oh really?" she said archly. "Just what do you have in mind?"

"Lots of cold-related activities. Ice skating. Making snow angels in Central Park. We'll be very ... creative." He chuckled.

"Jacob ... I love you."

There was a long silence. "I have to go, sweetheart. Sleep well tonight."

Gilly whispered good-bye, closed the phone, and dropped it into her bag. Since the day in the coffee shop, he'd avoided saying the "L" word to her. Sometimes when she thought about it, she worried just a little and argued with God about this unsatisfactory state of affairs. But then Jacob would call her again—sometimes two or three times a day—and the sound of his voice in her ear lulled her into believing everything would be all right.

Surely it would. She bent and grabbed her ankles to prove her back was still well.

Late February

At first Jacob paid no attention to the significant looks that passed between the girl dancers involved in his Monday rehearsals, which took place on the theater stage. He was entirely too wrapped up in conveying his vision for the *Perfume* story and music.

Gilly had met him at the airport Sunday afternoon, apparently unable to stand the thirty-minute wait for him to take a cab across the bridge into Manhattan. He'd kissed her hard, loaded his luggage into the trunk, and held her hand all the way back to the hotel, where he made her wait in the lobby while he changed clothes. They were not going to be in any hotel rooms alone together if he could help it. His ability to maintain some semblance of propriety with her was wearing thinner by the hour, and he'd only been halfway kidding about keeping their dates to cold-weather activities. Thank God for snow.

But then, near lunchtime, he caught a furtive conversation between a couple of razor-thin ballerinas smoking behind a curtain as he demonstrated a series of steps for the entrance of the village maidens in the funeral scene.

"Do you think he's going to do the same thing to Gilly?" whispered one girl. "She's really naive."

"He hardly pays a bit of attention to her," said the second.

"Boy, is she in for a rude awakening when Iliana gets her hooks in him."

Jacob managed not to falter as he turned the dancer he was working with. He had been so completely focused on work that he'd forgotten to worry about the impression he created with this passionate, nosy, gossipy group of women. Gilly was secure in herself; he counted on it. There was no need to hang on her, no need to be possessive.

On the other hand, perhaps it wouldn't hurt to stage a little demonstration. Actions would speak louder than words. Quietly he pulled out his phone.

The rehearsal broke for lunch, and Jacob called the entire cast to center stage for last-minute instructions. "Good work, you lot, thank you." He gave a general nod of approval, then met individual eyes in the group of sweating dancers. "We'll start putting together some of the crowd scenes, so I'll need everybody back here no later than one thirty. Any questions?"

Most of the dancers shrugged or shook their heads.

Jacob nodded. "All right then. See you later. Gilly, wait, I want to talk to you." He saw the two girls who had been behind the curtain glance their way as Gilly moved toward him from the back of the group.

He reached out and took her hand. Lifting it to his lips, he pressed a soft kiss in her palm. "Are you hungry? I've invited Maurice and Iliana to meet us for lunch."

When she smiled, it was all he could do not to snatch her close, sweaty leotard and all.

"What a good idea. I'm starved." She followed him offstage, swinging his hand. When they got out of sight of the rest of the company, she turned and hugged him hard.

Startled, he returned the embrace. "What's that for?"

She grinned up at him, eyes like stars. "For being creative."

Epilogue

Mid-March

"Having that half-naked man looking over my shoulder while I eat makes me nervous." Gilly's mother deliberately turned her back on the enormous Vulcan statue which made Birmingham's downtown park a national tourist attraction.

"At least he's wearing a skirt." Gilly thoughtfully sized up the ferocious hammer-and-spear-clenching god of fire and forge. "If you saw what I saw every day in class, you'd find him pretty ho-hum."

"Gillian Kincade!" Mom looked scandalized.

Laurel laughed. "Mother, you're the one who started her in ballet class at the age of four. What did you think she'd see?"

"I suppose I thought my daughter might grow up with a modicum of gentility." Mom blotted her lips with a checkered paper napkin that failed to hide her little grin.

"Modicum. Now there's a word you don't hear every day." Cole reached for another sandwich out of the overflowing wicker basket Gilly had ordered from a local deli.

Wade winked at her. "And mentioning gentility in the same sentence with Gilly is possibly the worst oxymoron I've ever heard."

Gilly exchanged amused glances with Jacob, lying on his side next to her like a long, lean panther in his favorite black jeans and long-sleeved black T-shirt. The whole clan had come up for last night's Saturday evening gala performance, and since the weather had warmed to the seventies, Jacob and Graham had joined her family for a Sunday afternoon picnic after services at Jacob's church. Gilly was more than a little nervous about how her father and brothers-in-law would treat him, now that their relationship was an established fact. So far so good. The older kids were playing kickball nearby, while baby Rosie toddled about on the bright green grass, looking like a drunken butterfly in her yellow dress. Laurel had to keep hopping up every few minutes to reel her back to home base.

Jacob picked up a handful of grapes and popped them into his mouth. "You'll have to take my word for it that she behaves with a great deal more decorum than a lot of the dancers we deal with day to day." He looked up at her. "You'd be quite proud of her."

"We're all *very* proud of her," said Dad, sitting in a lawn chair bouncing Ella on his lap. He claimed his limbs had gotten too stiff to make sitting on a blanket an option. "The performance last night was ... just great."

Gilly blinked away tears. Maybe her dad didn't have the vocabulary of Cole or Laurel or even her mother, but the sheer love on his face when he looked at her made her want to bawl like a baby. She loved New York, and she loved the thought of having Jacob and Graham to hang out with when she went back, but sometimes she wished she could teleport the rest of her family back and forth at will.

"It was amazing." Mary Layne sighed. "I wish Dmitri and the others could have stayed over for church today."

"I do too." Gilly sighed. "We'll keep talking to them about the

Lord, but sometimes it takes a shock to make people know they need him."

"That was true for me." Jacob smiled at Gilly. "But once I gave myself over, I never regretted it." His eyes, dark and bottomless, burned into hers—right there in front of her family.

She wanted to swoon. Or preferably attack Jacob.

But before she could get her tongue unglued from the roof of her mouth, he looked over his shoulder. "Graham! Come here for a second—it's time."

Graham looked around, dropped the Frisbee he'd been about to throw, and came running. Giggling, he fell to his knees beside the picnic basket and pulled out a long-stemmed red rosebud that had magically appeared between the sack of sandwiches and a package of potato chips. He handed it to Gilly. "This is for you."

"Thank you." Gilly kissed Graham's cheek, then looked at Jacob. "That wasn't there when I unpacked the food."

Jacob just smiled, and her heart began to thud.

"Miss Gilly!" Graham danced from one foot to the other. "Look at the card."

With fingers trembling so hard she nearly dropped the rose, she opened the envelope wired to the stem and pulled out a plain white card. By now she knew Jacob's spiky scrawl. It read, "Gilly, stand up."

Clutching the rose—it snapped in two in her hands—she managed to get to her feet without losing eye contact with Jacob. With his fluid, beautiful body control, he rolled to his knees and looked up at her. His eyes were tender, full of humor and a bit of well-hidden fear.

Fear? Of her?

She drew the rose to her lips and tried to keep breathing.

Then Jacob reached into his back pocket and withdrew a little velvet box. He held it in his hands and looked around at each of her family members, his gaze finally coming to rest again on her face. "I've already talked to your parents about this, and they wish we'd wait a bit longer, but in the end they're willing to trust your judgment, and I can't wait anymore."

He took a breath, bit the inside of his cheek, and smiled. Nervously. "I thought about doing the Rockefeller Rink engagement session, and I thought about renting a jewelry store in the middle of the night like the guy in that goofy Alabama movie, but then I realized you'd much rather be with your family to give us a blessing, so—" He cleared his throat. "Gilly, I love you so much. Would you please marry me?"

"Yes," she blurted.

Then she did attack him. *So shoot me,* she thought. Decorum and gentility were not her gifts.

Fireworks

Elizabeth White

Susannah is out to prove that pyrotechnics genius Quinn Baldwin is responsible for a million-dollar fireworks catastrophe during a Mardi Gras ball.

With her faithful black Lab, Monty, she moves to the charming backwater city of Mobile, Alabama, to uncover the truth. But this world-traveled military brat with a string of letters behind her name finds herself wholly unprepared to navigate the cultural quagmires of the Deep South.

Captivated by the warmth and joy of her new circle of friends, Susannah struggles to keep from falling for a subject who refuses to be anything but a man of integrity, compassion, and lethal southern charm. Fireworks offers a glimpse into the heart of the South and a cynical young woman's first encounter with Christ-like love.

Softcover: 978-0-310-26224-4

Fair Game

Elizabeth White

Jana Cutrere's homecoming to Vancleave, Mississippi, is anything but dull. Before she's even reached town, the beautiful young widow hits a stray cow, loses her son in the woods, rescues an injured fawn, and comes face to face with Grant Gonzales, her first high school crush.

Grant recently returned to town himself amid hushed controversy. His only plan: leave the corporate world behind and open a hunting reserve. Seeing Jana again ignites old memories ... and a painful past. Tensions boil over when he learns exactly why she returned. Jana plans to convince her grandfather to develop a wildlife rescue center—dead center on the prime hunting property he promised to sell to Grant!

With deadlines drawing near for the sale of the property and no decision from her grandfather, can Jana trust God with her and Grant's future, or will explosive emotions and diametrically opposing views tear them apart?

Softcover: 978-0-310-26225-1

Off the Record

Elizabeth White

Judge Laurel Kincade has it all—brains, beauty, and an aristocratic Old South family to back her up. A political rising star, she's ready to announce her candidacy for chief justice of the Alabama Supreme Court.

Journalist Cole McGaughan has ambitions too. Working as a religion writer for the *New York Daily Journal*, he longs to become a political reporter. Then his old friend Matt Hogan, a private investigator, calls with a tip. The lovely young judge may be hiding a secret that could derail her campaign. Would Cole like to be the one to break the story?

Cole sees a clear road to his goal, but there's a problem. Laurel's history is entangled with his own, and he must decide if the story that could make his career is worth the price he'd have to pay. Can Cole and Laurel find forgiveness and turn their hidden past into a hopeful future—and somehow keep it all off the record?

Softcover: 978-0-310-27304-2

Pick up a copy today at your favorite bookstore!

Share Your Thoughts

With the Author: Your comments will be forwarded to the author when you send them to *zauthor@zondervan.com.*

With Zondervan: Submit your review of this book by writing to *zreview@zondervan.com.*

Free Online Resources at

www.zondervan.com

Zondervan AuthorTracker: Be notified whenever your favorite authors publish new books, go on tour, or post an update about what's happening in their lives.

Daily Bible Verses and Devotions: Enrich your life with daily Bible verses or devotions that help you start every morning focused on God.

Free Email Publications: Sign up for newsletters on fiction, Christian living, church ministry, parenting, and more.

Zondervan Bible Search: Find and compare Bible passages in a variety of translations at www.zondervanbiblesearch.com.

Other Benefits: Register yourself to receive online benefits like coupons and special offers, or to participate in research.